Copyright © 2010 by Frances Dyanne Davis
Published by WD Publishing
P.O. Box 1218
Bolingbrook IL. 60440
wdpublishing@aol.com

ISBN: 978-0-9844348-0-0
Manufactured in the United States of America
First Edition

Cover Design by A.M. Wells.

LEST YE BE JUDGED

BY

F.D.DAVIS

OTHER F. D. Davis TITLES:

In The Beginning
In Blood We Trust
The Good Side of Evil (Carnivale Diabolique) Anthology

Titles under Dyanne Davis

The Critic
Another Man's Baby
Many Shades of Gray
Two Sides to Every Story
Forever And A Day
Let's Get It On
Misty Blue
The Wedding Gown
The Color of Trouble

Anthologies:

Continental Divide (Lotus Blossoms Chronicles 11) Anthology
On My Knees (Destination Romance) Anthology

Dedication:

I dedicate this book to THE READERS, who have written to ask about Mr. Omega.

Thank you for your encouragement, love and best wishes. I hope you enjoy, LEST YE BE JUDGED, and consider the ramification of judging. (SMILE)

LEST YE BE JUDGED

BY

F.D.DAVIS

I am he that liveth, and was dead; and, behold, I am alive for evermore

Revelation: 1:11

LEST YE BE JUDGED

Ice formed in Adam's veins and sent a chill through the room. His teeth were set in a firm, vicious line as he closed his eyes in concentration. The roar that wanted to break out and heap destruction on the world was abated by the freeze. He would not give in to the rage that seethed just beneath the surface.

Keeping his eyes closed, Adam raised both hands and stretched them in front of his body, turning to ice everything that came in contact with the energy that was projected through the tips of his fingers. He heard a gasp, a request to stop, but heeded it not. Better that a few sticks of furniture be destroyed or a few inconsequential vampires perish than the entire world. He cared for not one of them at this moment. His concern was for Eve, his wife, the bane of his existence, and the woman he'd forfeited his life for.

With but a thought Adam froze time. He needed a moment to ponder how his life had spiraled so out of control. Naturally his thoughts fell on Eyanna, his wife from more than a thousand years in the past, the wife who'd reincarnated into Eve's body.

Drawing in a deep breath Adam could still see Eyanna. Anger threatened to overcome him as thoughts of exchanging his mortal life, hoping it would save Eyanna assailed him. Adam took in several more bottomless breaths as images flooded him. Him, being turned. Eyanna, being afraid for his soul, afraid of him, throwing herself in the town fire hoping to save him. It hadn't. How could it when for over a thousand years he'd mourned her. And in his mourning he'd become the monster that she'd feared he would.

Only for a time had finding Eve brought joy to his life. Perhaps things could have been different if he'd not known her soul was that of his lost love. Perhaps his conflicting emotions toward Eyanna's leaving him to suffer immortality alone could have prevented him from not showing Eve the physical side of love after he'd turned her.

A deep sigh filled his lungs and burst forward. That deed was not on Eyanna or Eve. It was his and his alone. His stubborn insistence to not bed a vampiric woman was because of Tarasha turning him and nothing more. But that was the reason Eve was now lying in the bed, dying of poisons she'd created. A deep shudder raced down his spine.

A witch.

A vampire witch.

He could almost, 'not' blame her for having fallen in love with Sullivan. But he did. He blamed them both and he'd promised Sullivan that should harm befall Eve there would be retribution.

Now his wife lay waiting for him as he sat beside her bed with the tubing running from his arm to hers, waiting to receive his life affirming blood. He could either save or release her.

With startling clarity Adam opened his eyes and snapped his fingers together softly, restoring time. A grunt of derisiveness fell from his lips making him even more aware of the reason Eve was once again at death's door. His trying to be other than what he was, Adam Omega, 'Vampire,' had led them all to this moment of death and dying. Death would come sooner for some than for others.

No more trying to be, 'Mr. Nice Guy.' What nonsense! He no longer cared what foul names his wife called him. He would do as he'd done for a thousand years. He would right the wrongs that had been done to him. He was in charge. He stretched slowly and lazily, finally opening his eyes, allowing his gaze to take in each player in this macabre drama. Adam shook his head in disgusted remorse. Eve, his wife, was dying from a potion she'd made and coupled with the AB-5 Dr. Meah had invented. It had proven to be a deadly cocktail.

His gaze took in Dr. Meah, a previously loyal friend who'd have to be harshly dealt with. Adam had dozens of scientists working for him and could get dozens more. Dr. Meah's time of service, at least to Eve, had come to an end. It was over, finished.

A gurgling sound caused Adam to focus on Mark, the only human in the room. The mortal was turning a ghastly shade of white as Sullivan's fangs sank deeper and deeper into him. The mortal would be but another casualty in this little war. There was no pity in him for the mortal. Mark should have obeyed Adam's commands. Adam turned his attention to Sullivan, the pale faced, blue-eyed vamp who'd thought he could come in and so easily take his wife. Adam sank his own fangs fiercely into Sullivan's neck. Eve had only been on loan. Now he was calling in that loan.

A hiss of air, a strangled garble, as Mark fought for his last breath. Adam heard the mortal's heart slow, then stop completely. Sullivan's hand fell from around the neck of the corpse and he shuddered as Adam continued to drink from him. Dr. Meah was trembling, his fear snaking through the room and scenting the air with its foulness.

Finally it was done. Dr. Meah had drunk her blood. The poison was gone from Eve; now the healing could begin. The little witch should have left well enough alone.

How long had it been since he'd called her, 'Little Healer?' She should have just accepted her role as mistress of the vampire kingdom, wife to Adam Omega.

There had been no need for Eve to go rooting around trying to become what she'd been in a long dead past. But she had ventured into her past, learning, picking up new skills along the way, thus forcing Adam to acquire those same skills, skills he'd abhorred, skills he'd considered sacrilegious.

A shudder of annoyance braced its way up his spine and he wondered what other things Eve had been working on before succumbing to her own dire handiwork and thought he knew.

He had a surprise for Eve. If his wife chose to be a witch, then he would match her powers. The only difference would be that they would draw their powers from different sources, hers from light, his from darkness.

Adam smiled to himself. The darker arts yielded more power and worked far quicker, much to his delight. He continued gazing at Eve. The huge amber ring Adam wore on his left hand glowed with life. The rich honey hue deepened as did his thoughts. She would not know something that he did not. He would not allow it.

"Adam, stop it. Freezing us and everything in this room is doing no good. It's not going to help Eve." Sullivan growled.

In a deadly slow move Adam turned on the chair, pausing for just a millisecond to gaze at the furnishings and vampires encased in ice. Something primal was fighting to take him over, an urge to kill, maim, and destroy, to end it all. But there was something he had yet to do. Still in slow motion he turned back toward Eve, surprised to see her blanket was a sheet of ice. He stared at her body for a moment, sighed, and then moved a finger over the area around her, turning the ice back into a thin cover, drying it in the process.

Blood danced on the tips of Adam's fangs, Sullivan's blood. As a drop fell away he glared at Sullivan, the cause of all of this, and sank his fangs into his flesh again, this time with unadulterated fury. He didn't drink. His actions now were not for feeding but for inflicting pain. He pierced through vessels, and bones, clamping his jaws together. A silent tremor from Sullivan caused him to relent and he began to retract his fangs from their merciless grip.

Again Adam lifted his eyes to survey the damage. For the first time in a long while he allowed the blood tears to flow from grief, grief at what he'd allowed to transpire. He should have never been moved by Eve's tears, nor her pleas to live a life apart from him, to be allowed to love Sullivan, to live with him. Sullivan's hand knocked Adam's to the side startling him. A bemused expression crossed Adam's face.

"I think you've had enough of my blood," Sullivan said, moving from Adam toward the bed to check on Eve.

Adam gave a low growl as Sullivan attempted to move closer to the bed, closer to Eve. Adam was having none of it. He growled louder as his fangs lengthened and his eyes changed color.

"Don't come any closer." He sent the words with a snap to Sullivan. "I'm taking my wife back. I'm taking her back, right here, right now, and in your bed."

"Can't we make sure Eve has survived before you throw your silly tantrums?" Sullivan asked, ignoring Adam's lowered fangs and the growl. Adam would have to kill him here and now to prevent him from checking on Eve.

"I'm going to kill you, Sullivan."

"Yeah, I know. I've got it. Haven't you tired of threatening me? You've given Eve your blood and if she makes it, I will thank you for that. But you will not have Eve. Nothing has changed, Adam."

Adam chuckled. It was time to take control again. He should never have allowed a woman, his wife, control. He should not have allowed her to sully his love.

"Sullivan, Sullivan, Sullivan," Adam repeated. "How I want you dead. How I wish at this very moment I had the time to make it so." His fist twisted as he applied pressure to Sullivan's heart without even touching him. Then he took in a deep breath and released it and Sullivan. Whatever he decided to do to the vamp he wanted Eve to witness it.

"I'm taking my wife back."

"Just you try it," Sullivan hissed as his own fangs descended. Energy shimmered in waves, casting a silver glow around Sullivan's body. Fear for Eve coupled with his anger at Adam's arrogance in thinking that after two years he could just come back and reclaim the woman he hadn't wanted. The gall of it made Sullivan a bit more forceful than usual. He was breathing hard, trying not to rub his chest. That more than any of the feats Adam had accomplished made Sullivan envious. How he wished that he could tighten his fist and cause Adam's heart to cease beating. If he could cause Adam pain without even touching him, it would be one long, continuous torture session.

"While you try to take Eve from me, where do you think I will be, Adam? And do you think it will be that easy? She loves me as well as you."

"Are we really going to do this dance and pretend that you have a choice in the matter? Don't worry, when I decide to take her, which is right now by the way, you'll be right here. In fact, I insist that you have a ringside seat." Adam stared hard at Sullivan, not blinking, not moving a muscle.

"I gave you one chance to keep her safe. You'll not get another." Adam's voice gentled and the rough edges were swept away as he turned his attention to Eve.

"You should have known better, Sullivan."

Sullivan's pain was palatable. He regretted the things that had happened to Eve but still his regrets made no difference. He could have cost Eve her life. Adam was right, he had known better. Acute shame washed over him.

"Adam..." Sullivan sighed, then called his name again. "Adam, will she be okay? She's so still. She looks to be dead. Her heart is no longer beating." He stared at Adam. "Did it work? Did your blood save Eve?"

"Why don't you link with her and find out," Adam taunted.

Sullivan blanched, his skin losing the little color that it possessed. His blue eyes filled with moisture at having to admit that his link with Eve wasn't strong enough. He'd already tried to reach her. It would have to be Adam to bring her back to this side of life. Adam had made her, only he could go in that deeply. He stared at Adam, not wanting to ask another thing of him, hating that he couldn't give Eve the things she needed. He felt powerless. He couldn't even penetrate her mind enough to know if she were still in there. He'd once again have to rely on her crazy husband.

Sullivan's skin crawled with revulsion and he bit back the snarl that threatened to slide across his face. To get anything from Adam he would have to crawl, make himself humble, and bow before the almighty Adam Omega.

Anger rose and he swallowed that also. He had more important matters to contend with. Eve was the only important thing in his life and he had to know if calling Adam to save her with his blood was going to be worth the look that would surely be in Eve's eyes if she survived.

"Adam, check on her please," Sullivan pleaded, his eyes remaining on Eve.

"You want me to check on my wife for you?" Adam shook his head, chuckling a little as he did so. "Sullivan, you never cease to amaze me."

"Is allowing Eve to linger in that twilight state part of your plan? Do you think your actions will cause me more grief than I already feel? They can't." Sullivan tried for a different tactic. "Surely you're as concerned as I am to know if your blood was strong enough to bring Eve back from the brink of death."

"You think using logic and appealing to my vanity will turn the tide in your favor, cause me to...what?" Adam tilted his head slightly to study Sullivan. He shook his head, causing the locs on his shoulder to move about. With one hand he pushed the long hair from his face and secured it in a purple binding. His movements provided the few seconds he'd needed to distract Sullivan. Killing Sullivan no longer held the urgency it had but scant hours ago. A different plan was forming, one that might prove to be a lot more fun than just killing Sullivan outright as he'd promised. Oh, he'd still kill him, but maybe he'd have some fun with him first, payback. Who knew in the end how long he'd allow Sullivan to continue living?

Adam's gaze followed Sullivan's and both vampires stared at Eve. Then their eyes met and held. It was Adam who broke the connection and turned once again to look at Eve. Maybe it was time his fledgling wife graduated. He'd bring her back to life and when she learned his plans for her she'd wish even more that he hadn't.

"You enjoy having this power over us, don't you?" Sullivan hissed.

A smile graced Adam's lips. He wouldn't deny that he enjoyed the power he had. Being in control of the world was a high. Only one Being that he knew of was higher. And that Being hadn't deemed the affairs of the world important enough to get involved in. Yet. And if the day came that it changed… well then, Adam would deal with it then.

He glared at Sullivan, then softened his gaze as always when he turned to look at his wife, so still, so corpse like as she lay there with his blood flowing through her veins. He turned the ballcock, removed the needle from his vein, waved a finger over the puncture mark, and unencumbered by tubings, moved closer to Eve.

Entering Sullivan's mind Adam scanned his thoughts. The tormented vamp was right about one thing. It was time that he made a mental lock with Eve. He had no doubt that she would pull through. Whether she wanted to was a different matter. Still, it was time, he thought as he ran his finger gently over her face, sighing deeply.

Ignoring Sullivan, Adam rose from the chair and crawled into the bed and pulled Eve into his arms, holding her, planting kisses on her still form. Then he leaned his head back and roared the ancient cry of warriors.

When the last echo died, he brought his head up slowly and stared hard at Sullivan for a long moment. "Like I said, I'm taking my wife back, right here, right now, and in your bed. Holding Eve in his arms, turning her so that she was facing him, he gazed on her, the memory of every moment he'd spent with her filling him. His thoughts from a thousand years in the past caused him to shiver. He pressed his lips to Eve's carotid artery and sank his fangs gently into her, going deep into Eve's psyche and connecting with her thoughts.

"Eve, you know that your time with Sullivan has ended." He waited. When she didn't answer he went deeper, caressing her with his thoughts. "Eve, I know you can hear me. I will not let you die."

"Go away, Adam. I'm having the most beautiful dream and you're spoiling it."

He couldn't prevent the mental chuckle. "So you think you're dreaming?"

"I have to be. I haven't seen you in some time. You don't know what's happened to me and I don't want to be around when you find out. You're going to be upset."

Adam's first thought was to remind her that she'd seen him, talked to him, told him she loved him because she couldn't help herself, but loved Sullivan because she wanted to. Apparently she'd forgotten all of that or maybe she viewed it as a dream. He decided to not press the issue. "Upset?" he asked.

"Okay," Eve whispered softly. "Let me say it. You're going to be truly pissed."

Adam chuckled again. "Then tell me what you've done, wife."

The amber ring on his finger suddenly blazed to life. He could feel an electrical charge and a burn from the gold as it seemed to become welded to his skin. The gift had been a gift from his bride when she was Eyanna and loved him and him alone. He smiled to himself; something in her spirit loved him still.

The ring had not bothered to alert him to Eve's feelings in many months. It was hard to believe that on the brink of death it was he she thought of. But then again, she seemed to have a habit of allowing herself to love him when she was at the brink of death. Adam shook the thought away. Eve would not die, he'd seen to that.

"Eve," Adam whispered again, allowing his words to caress her. "Eve, talk to me, tell me what you've done."

"No, I want to dream."

"Tell me what you've done, Eve, or innocents might pay for that which I imagine."

He waited, knowing that threat more than anything would penetrate Eve's defenses. The thought that Adam Omega, monster that she thought him to be, would harm innocents…. He sighed. She would not be able to allow it. She'd talk.

"In all this time I have not fed in the way you ordered me to do." Eve hesitated. "No one knew, not at first, not Sullivan and not Dr. Meah. As for Mark, he thought I was feeding from him. I implanted memories of the feedings." She sighed. "I couldn't go through with it, Adam, not even with your threats to me."

"What else?" Adam asked, already knowing the entire tale but wanting to force his wife to tell him. This he knew she would resist when she fully recovered. Now in this state she would not lie.

"I used my crystals to try to find a cure, a way to return to being mortal. I…I…coerced Dr. Meah into allowing me to be the trial subject for his new drug, the AB-5. It worked for a time but so many things went wrong. This time I've succeeded in doing what I've always wanted. I will die an almost mortal death. I have a virus of sorts."

"Do you really believe I will allow you to die?"

"No, I suppose you wouldn't."

"What else is there? You said you dreamed. Tell me your dream."

"That I'm mortal and God has forgiven me my sins."

The ring burned more fiercely and Adam felt his heart lurch. He hesitated a moment before answering, then spoke very softly, almost whispering. "I will forgive your sins, Eve."

"I know you think you are my love, but you're not God, Adam."

Adam caressed Eve's face and dropped a kiss on her head. "Then I will take your sins on my shoulders and grant you absolution."

For a long moment there was silence. Then Eve spoke. "Why are you just now entering my dreams, Adam? Why haven't I heard from you before now?"

"You only had to call me, Eve. But you were too busy making nice with Sullivan."

"He loves me, Adam."

"As do I."

"I love him also."

"As much as you love me?"

"I could never love anyone as much as I love you, and you're very well aware of that. But you're also aware that I have no plans to grovel for your affections. With Sullivan there is no groveling, just reciprocated love and respect, Adam. If you'd been able to provide the things I needed you wouldn't have to return now and play the hero and bully, both of which you will surely do." Eve sighed, realizing what she'd just admitted. "This isn't feeling so much like a dream anymore. Is this real, or am I dreaming?"

"It's real." Adam heard Eve's sigh and waited.

"Then I'm dying and you're here to do what… cause Sullivan pain? Make him feel the guilt that he shouldn't?"

"No, I'm here to make sure you don't die…and…" Adam couldn't help but laugh. "You're accurate in your reasoning. I'm here to make sure that Sullivan feels pain. This time he's gone too far. This time I will kill him."

Silence.

"Eve."

When she didn't answer Adam pressed harder, knowing the connection was still there. "You can hear me." he said.

"Of course I can, but I'm trying very hard to blank you out."

Adam chuckled and moved to nuzzle Eve's neck. Taking in a deep breath, he was more than a little surprised. This time it wasn't just a vague fragrance he caught. Eve's entire essence was scented with the fragrance of fresh lemons, as though it were originating from her basic DNA. He ran his tongue along her carotid artery, feeling his blood as it flowed through the veins of his wife.

"It is time, Eve," Adam whispered into her mind, "time for you to return. The poison is gone and your spirit has returned. My blood sustains you now."

"Can he hear us?"

"You speak of Sullivan?" Adam asked. "Not this deeply. Why?"

"Because I want you to think about something. If you just kill either Sullivan or Dr. Meah, what joy will you receive? None. You like the game of cat and mouse too much. I know you. You enjoy threatening Sullivan and even me."

"This time it's no threat."

"I'd like to make you a wager, Adam."

This easy time with Eve before she returned completely to her body was a pleasant diversion. Now they could be civil. Now he could be magnanimous about her foolishness. He could tease her, because now he knew she would survive. His heart lurched again and he swallowed the gratitude for having made it to her in time. At least the fool had not been so unwise as to not reach out to him for help. Sullivan had caused him many problems and from the tone of Eve's voice, he could tell her wager would concern him. Another problem.

"You're forgetting, Eve, that usually when you want to wager I win."

"Hear me out. I'll wager that you will get more joy from allowing both Sullivan and Dr. Meah to live."

"How so?" Curiosity forced Adam to continue listening to yet another insane plan of his wife. But, Eve, being alive and presenting insane plans was a thousand times better than Eve being dead.

"You want to make them both fear what you're going to do, right? Give them, say a month, and tell them you will kill them in a month, or two months. The waiting will drive them crazy with worry. Then when the time is about to run out you can give them an extension."

Adam laughed aloud. "I think the crystal potions you took affected your brain. Do you really think you can manipulate me in this manner?" He laughed again. "It's time for you to wake now, Eve."

Feeling Eve's resistance Adam braced himself, then heard the softly murmured words of an incantation. His obstinate Eve. He'd have to give her credit for trying. He applied a bit more pressure. "Wake up, Eve."

"I don't want to," Eve insisted stubbornly, trying her best to wield her magic. The magic she possessed was something that Adam Omega did not control. "I think I'll remain here a bit longer. I think just the thought that I can control my fate will make you rethink what I've said. You'll begin to worry about me...maybe not about me, but that I can defy you even in my dreams. The great Adam Omega, whose blood is not strong enough to undo what his poor, silly, fledgling of a wife has done."

"It's not going to work."

"What will it hurt, Adam? We all know you're going to kill them. I don't see why you wouldn't want to make them suffer first. That would be more to your liking, I would think. Make them afraid of what you're going to do every moment that they live. Surely you're not afraid that I'll find a way to stop you."

"Of course I'm not afraid and you very well know it." He kissed her gently and felt her probing his mind, trying to access his plans. "Stop that," he reprimanded her as he ran the tip of his tongue over her lips, tasting her, feeling the steady burn of the ring.

"Why are your thoughts blocked from me? Why won't you share your plans with me? There is nothing I can do to stop you, or so you've told me, Adam. Tell me your plans for Sullivan...and for Dr. Meah," Eve pleaded,

"Don't trouble yourself with that. You know who I am. I keep my word. I warned both you and Sullivan what would happen to him if he allowed harm to come to you. He allowed harm to come to you. Now he will die."

"You will have to kill me if you kill Sullivan."

"Maybe I will, but it will be when I tire of you. It will not be today."

"Adam, I am no longer just Eve."

"I know that. I have long sensed the reemergence of Eyanna within you. I feel your power, but it is nothing compared to mine."

He heard a soft chuckle. Could Eve be laughing at him? "Do I amuse you, wife?"

"I believe you're afraid of my magic. I think in this case my magic is stronger."

"Ah, so it's a test of powers that you want, my powers versus your magic? Who do you think would win?"

"It could be fun to find out."

Again Eve spoke words of an incantation and Adam muttered words too softly for Eve to hear and counteract. Forcing the psychic to teach him the dark arts had been well worth the fear he'd instilled and the burly body guards he'd killed. And his brave, silly Eve, so insistent on trying to control him, had not even sensed his magic. Or perhaps she had and thought it was the power of his being a vampire that stopped her. Adam wanted to laugh. He'd missed his wife. It was high time she returned home. He had more than a few surprises for the mistress of the vampire kingdom.

"I'm not afraid of you, Adam."

"Then the poisons must have affected you more than I thought."

"We are necessary to each other. I know that now. I am your Achilles heel as you are mine. You may shout and throw around your lightning bolts, but in the end you will not kill me." Eve laughed. "I feel what you feel, Adam. Tell me, does the amber ring I gave to you not burn you at this very moment?"

"What of it? That does not make your magic stronger than my powers."

"And from where I am it seems logical that I am stronger, that I would win any wager we entered. After all, I have had the ancient powers of nature within me for many, many generations. Mine was a birthright. Yours was but darkness thrust upon you. That you didn't want, I might add. Yes, you've harnessed that power and made it stronger, but it's not embedded into your basic DNA, not like mine, and yours is not as old as mine. As for your ability to control the elements, I can control the elements also, though not to the extent that you can. But I can do things that you cannot. I can command the power in crystals to do my biddings. Can you?"

Curiosity was getting the better of Adam. Would Eve remain this defiant when she was fully awake or would the bravado leave when she left the nether regions of unconsciousness?

"If you're so brave, so powerful, wife, why did you run and hide? Why did you protect yourself with crystals to block yourself from me?" He couldn't stop his smirk at knowing Eve would never again be able to use her crystals against him. He too possessed the knowledge of the stones. Lucky for him that he was one in a handful that the stones talked to.

A rare gift, the psychic had said. *Rare*, he'd thought. *He* was rare. He was Adam Omega. Why would the stones not talk to him? He was the first and the last of his kind. There had been none like him in the past and there would be no more after him. Of course there would always be vampires, but there would never be another him. He was the alpha and the omega. He'd tried to tell Eve that and she'd not understood.

Adam shrugged. Eve's next lessons would not be ones of gentleness. He would have to be ruthless to force her to comply. But comply she would for she must. He would not leave her dependent on others. She must know how to feed. Then when she chose not to, that would be her choice, but still she must learn it and he would not stop until she could do it with skill and efficiency.

Placing kisses at the corners of her mouth, he nipped his finger, drawing a bubble of blood and stuck it into the warmth of her mouth, closing his eyes in ecstasy as her lips closed around the finger and suckled it gently.

"You have not changed, wife. With everything that's happened to you you still defy me. You believe your powers equal to mine. You genuinely believe that to be true?"

"I do."

"Why?" Adam asked softly, running the pad of his finger across her lip.

"Because, Adam, had the situations of our lives been reversed I would have been stronger. If it had been me who had been turned and waited a thousand years to find you, I would not have turned you. But if I had, I would not have abandoned you. You're a coward where I'm concerned. In all your decisions pertaining to me, Adam, you're a coward. Yes, you can kill others without a thought. You can even sit in church picking out the parishioner you will help. You will defend the weak with your last breath but you're too much of a coward to be without me. So you have chosen to control me instead. That makes you a slave to me, Adam, my slave, and that makes you a coward." With those words Eve pushed Adam from her mind with a jolt.

Chapter Two

Adam blinked several times in disbelief. As his vision cleared, his gaze focused on Sullivan, who was watching him warily. For a long moment Adam just stared at the vamp, giving himself time to allow his confusion to clear. Eve had shoved him out of her mind and it hadn't been a little shove. It was powerful, one that befitted the mistress of the vampire kingdom. "*Or a witch,*" a little voice whispered. He couldn't believe it. For longer than he cared to admit he was truly stunned. *The blood,* he thought, his blood had given her this.

"What happened?" Sullivan dropped his cool veneer, rushing to Adam clutching Adam's left arm in his hand. "Tell me, is Eve in there?"

Again Adam stared into the blue eyes of his rival and a small smile came. "Oh, she's in there alright."

"So your blood worked, you've healed her?"

"I think so," Adam nodded, "but there are a few minor adjustments I think I need to make."

"Adjustments? What the hell do you mean, adjustments? Eve is not a car or an appliance. I don't want you messing with her mind."

All playfulness left Adam as he glared hard at Sullivan. "What you want is of no importance. You have no rights here. You remain here out of my graciousness. Eve is my wife, understand, not yours and even if she were....even if she were, she would still belong to me. You have tried my patience once too many times. I do not have the time to bother with you and your wants. Unless you want me to remove you from your own home do not bother me again."

"Damn you, Adam."

"Damn me all you like, just stay the hell out of my way." Adam glared at the other vamp, then at the doctor. Eve was right about one thing:

Others he could kill without a thought. Only lingering emotions of times past, of friendships that once existed had kept Sullivan and the good doctor from being incinerated the moment he'd returned to find his wife at death's door. He gritted his teeth in impatience, then said to Sullivan,

"You have no choice but to wait for me to bring Eve back, so wait!" He raised his hand and slammed Sullivan into a chair. "Stay," he ordered.

"No," Sullivan shouted back as he came up from the chair, "I will not stay. I am not an animal that you can issue orders to and expect me to meekly obey them."

"I could care less if you obey them meekly, though I would prefer it. It would be easier for you that way." Adam smiled as Sullivan's hand came up and shot a bolt of electrical energy at him. Adam did not move, merely smiled at Sullivan and the stunned look on the vamp's face. "Want to try again?" he asked and repositioned himself so Sullivan could take better aim. When this volt also failed to penetrate, Adam stopped smiling. "My turn," he announced in a voice filled with ice. He raised his hand and his eyes narrowed into slits. He released a charge so powerful that the house shook on its foundation as the bolt found its mark in Sullivan's body. The vamp went back so hard he knocked out a good section of the wall.

"Would you like for me to take my second shot now?" Adam asked.

This time Adam raised both hands. He noticed Sullivan did not cower or attempt to cover himself, but instead did as Adam had done and prepared himself for the next volley Adam would send. Only this time Adam didn't discharge the volt. He looked upon Sullivan for a long moment, then held out his hand and helped him up.

"Tell me, Sullivan, three years ago you were not this brave. You would have never thought to take me on one on one. Plot my demise, overthrow me, yes, but hand to hand combat? What happened? What is it that makes you stand up to me now?"

"Eve," Sullivan answered without blinking. "I have something to fight for, someone. I was completely unprepared for the power she'd have over me, the way she'd sneak into my heart and own it and my soul. She does own them, Adam, and I will not so easily give her up. I will not stand by and allow you to make *adjustments* to her mind. I can imagine the adjustments you'd make, the commands for her to stop loving me, to be your obedient little robotic wife."

"Don't be a fool. If that's the way I want things, then that's the way it will be. But I have no wish for a robotic wife. One who simply hates me is more than enough."

Again the vampires locked gazes until Sullivan spoke. "But we all know that in spite of her hatred for the things that you've done, Adam, it's not hatred she has for you."

"But it's your bed she's been warming for the past two years. That does not speak of love to me. And if you know she loves me, you should not have fallen in love with her. That would make you a fool."

Sullivan sighed. "Don't you think if I could have made myself not love her, knowing that she will always love you, that I would have? She loves you and we all know it. But she loves me also and I make her happy. You don't," Sullivan said with bluntness, "And with my last breath I will fight for her."

For what seemed an eternity the room was silent. Adam chuckled as he waggled his finger in front of Sullivan's face. "That little story you just told, why did you feel the need to share it?"

"I wanted to give you fair warning."

"You're warning me…you're warning me? This has got to be a dream. You're warning me? You can't beat me, Sullivan. If I was having my worst day, and you were having your best day, you'd still be unable to defeat me. Now enough talk. Sit there and be quiet."

Before Sullivan could even think to protest Adam had once again slammed him into the chair and this time he could not move. When he went to speak he could make no sound. Adam smirked as Sullivan finally got the picture. "Magic," Adam said, twirling his finger. "It's heady stuff, almost as intriguing as vampiric powers." He laughed again and finally turned away from the glare Sullivan was giving him. Sullivan's glares did not matter.

Now it was time for him to deal with Eve, to reenter her mind. So what if she'd managed to shove him from her mind. No matter, she was still a fledgling.

Cautiously, Adam reentered Eve's mind, intrigued by his wife's newfound powers. She'd actually found a way to make him work to get to where he wanted to be. This time he had to go in even deeper, past all the barriers she'd set to guard her thoughts.

"So you're back," Eve heaved a sigh. "This is getting tiresome."

"No one has ever called me a coward, Eve. I don't believe even you have ever done that. You've always called me a bully."

"I can't remember if I've called you a coward before or not but it doesn't matter. A bully is always a coward. Kiss me, Adam, and let's see how strong you really are."

"Do you think I will become aroused and turn tail and run?" Adam smiled. "I can assure you, dear wife, that nonsense is over with."

"Want to make a bet?" Eve inquired.

"To bet would, as I said earlier, still be foolish on your part." Adam gave a casual shrug of his shoulder. Though Eve couldn't see it he knew she felt it. "I am right and..." He stopped. "What are your plans for me this time, Eve? Your potions didn't work so well on you. So what makes you think you'd have any better luck with them working on me? Your incantations have no power where I'm concerned. Surely you must know that."

"Make love to me right here, right now, in Sullivan's bed with Sullivan standing there ready to slit your throat. Even you can't be in here with me and protect yourself fully from an attack. Sullivan is not the weakling that you think him to be. He will not allow you to harm me, that I'm sure of and yes, Adam, he will even go against you to protect me. But he won't have to, for you will defeat yourself. So, go ahead, Adam, try it and let's see which of us is the most powerful."

"Another challenge?" Adam's hands moved over Eve's body as easily as his thoughts moved through her mind. "Do you think you can resist me? You never have been able to. Let's see if you can now."

He sent white hot heat, sealing it with a kiss of passion. Eve moaned out her pleasure, her arms coming upwards to curl about his neck. He took her lips. Stopping for less time than it took to take his next breath, Adam opened his eyes to glare a warning and point a finger toward Sullivan, freezing him in his seat, then sealing him in ice.

Eve was not fully aware yet. She thought she was in a dream. As her body arched to move to him, her hands ran over his body, pulling at his clothes. Her tongue battled his and her moans of pleasures were ragged and real. Adam tore his lips from hers to taste the blood, his blood. As it flowed into him, a quick spasm of pleasure ran the length of his body and he drank from her.

In an instant Sullivan was up from the chair rushing toward Adam, pushing him from Eve. "You will not touch her, and you will not violate her."

"She is my wife."

"In name only."

"How did you release yourself?"

"Does that matter now?"

"Yes, it matters." Adam shrugged. "I'm going to have to adjust the time and keep you incapacitated for a much longer period. Ready?" Adam asked.

Sullivan was furious. His body trembled with rage and before he could stop himself his hands were around Adam's throat. "Die, die, die, Adam, damn you. Just die." Sullivan growled as his hands pressed even harder against Adam's throat.

"Stop it, Sullivan." Dr. Meah ran into the fray, trying unsuccessfully to pull Sullivan away from Adam. "Think of Eve. Only Adam can return her to us. Let him go."

"No, Adam has no plans to return Eve to us. He's only toying with us and with her."

"Still, Sullivan, she is his wife and…and…don't make me say it. Look at him. Does he look worried? If you wish to see if Eve survived this, I would suggest you let go of Adam," Dr. Meah said softly, looking from Sullivan to Adam. "I'd let go of him now."

Dr. Meah's words penetrated his brain and Sullivan sucked in a much needed breath. The blood fever retreated slightly and Sullivan released his hold on Adam, angered that Adam had not tried to stop him, had put up no defense, and even now stood staring at him as though he were a worthless insect. One day he would wipe the smirk from his face, kick his ass good and proper. But Dr. Meah was right. He'd have to allow Adam to bring Eve back. Then he would take her and run, but not before kicking her husband's ass. That one was a given. He wasn't afraid of Adam, not any longer. And he'd be even more damned than he already was if he stood by and allowed Adam to paw Eve as though he were not in the room.

"You forced her to respond to you," Sullivan snarled, moving away, knowing in his heart Adam had used no force.

"Do you truly believe that? You're not a fool, Sullivan." Adam smiled. "Then again, maybe you are. Remember, I went to the core of her existence, where her feelings are not hidden from me nor masked in fear for what I might do to her…or to you," he said pointedly. "But I don't worry now for a different reason. Eve will not remain with you even if I were to allow it. You killed Mark, betrayed her." A laugh fell from his lips. "She will not forgive your killing the mortal." He shrugged. "You were supposed to be her savior from the likes of me, but you are me, to a certain extent."

Adam ran his hand over Eve, tracing her breasts, moving over her hips, daring Sullivan with a glare. He moved to within an inch of her mound. As he gazed at his wife several unbidden tears found a path down his cheeks. *You would seek death and leave me alone again,* he thought angrily. You need to know how it feels, wife. Several more tears followed the path of the former ones and he shook his head and blew out a breath. Enough of this nonsense. He was about to inflict yet more pain on his wife. It too would be part of her training. He leaned over her and took her earlobe into his mouth, suckling her gently.

"You would do this to her now, Adam, defile her in front of other men? Are you now that depraved? Are you doing this to hurt me, to show me that she loves you still? I already know that and I know that I would not do to her what you're doing to her now. You've taken everything from her, Adam. Must you now take her dignity?"

Adam lifted his eyes, ignoring the blood tears that stained his cheeks. He felt the weight of what he'd done clear to his soul. In fact, it was his soul that was crying out for him to stop. Images of what he'd stood for in his long distant past resurfaced. If it were a matter simply of his sinning, perhaps he could deal with that as he ought. But it wasn't. It was the life of his wife. He'd never be able to let Eve go.

His gaze took in the scene before him as he lifted his head high as though in prayer and tilted his face so that the muscles in his neck corded with tension. Then just as quickly he ended what he was doing and stared into nothingness. He allowed the blood tears to run under his chin, staring as Sullivan faced him, his hate-filled glare lethal. Sullivan was of little consequence. Eventually he would be dead. Adam would kill him as he'd promised.

"Eve," Adam called out, snapping his fingers. "Awake now, Eve." Her eyelids fluttered briefly. She was still fighting him, trying not to return, but it was all for naught for return she must. "How do you feel?" He growled low as Sullivan once again made a move toward the bed. Not this damn time, he thought and sent a message telepathically to Sullivan. "She is my wife and I will check on her condition."

He'd commanded Eve to return and he'd been generous in speaking it aloud so that Sullivan might witness her acquiescence. But Eve hadn't done as he'd ordered. She was going to make him crazy with her defiance. He shook his head and established a mind lock with his wife.

"Eve, I know you're fine. I can feel it in my body. Remember, our bond does not lie."

"What are your plans now, Adam? Will you use this to take control of my life? I don't have many friends and I don't want to lose them. If you harm them, it can never be the same as it once was between us."

"And if I don't?"

"Then I'm sure we can work something out."

"Are you once again offering me your body, or would it be your soul? How far would you go to keep them safe, wife? You've played many roles with me: the whore, the witch and the unfaithful wife. I care for none of them. But I will grant you this: You are brave beyond belief."

"I think I'm the braver of the two of us, Adam. I'm not afraid to make a wager with you and see it through."

"But you lost, my darling. You desired me. You have given me no reason to give either Sullivan or Dr. Meah longer to live. What will I get?"

"The sheer joy of knowing you control them."

"Then return to your body and bargain with me from a position of power."

"What will I find?" Eve asked softly, a slight tremble of fear tingeing her voice.

"Return and find out," Adam challenged. He narrowed his eyes and looked around to see what Eve's first impressions would be. The amber still burned, a good sign, but would it lose its glow when Eve returned?

He'd not tell her more. She needed to return and deal with whatever she found. Of course she wouldn't like it but that was neither here nor there. Mark was dead, that much was obvious. Adam felt no remorse for his death. It would have happened eventually anyway. He stared long and hard at Eve. Besides, who knew when his wife's sentimentality would have gotten the best of her and she'd think of turning Mark just to give him a fighting chance. Adam couldn't have that. He refused to allow even Eve to disobey him totally.

He watched as Eve's eyelids fluttered and she fought to return fully to the here and now. She ripped the needle from her vein and stared for a moment as though disoriented. Then her eyes found his and she frowned, knowing that he was once again the reason for her existence. It was his blood flowing through her, giving her life, giving her strength.

His strength.

In giving Eve so much blood in order to save her life, he'd risked not being at his best. For a few hours Eve would be nearly his match perhaps, but Adam had no intention of letting her know that vital piece of information.

***

Eve didn't want to fight the heaviness that was clinging to her but she couldn't remain in a twilight state with Adam as her only companion. She needed to know what had happened in her absence. Her senses had alerted her to the strength flowing through her veins. She didn't need anyone to tell her any longer that she would not die. How could she? She carried Adam's blood in her veins and apparently enough of it that the poison had been pushed from her system. Still, she felt foggy as she tried to remember the details leading up to this moment.

'*Return now, Eve.*' She heard the sound of Adam's voice and could no longer resist. Her eyes fell on her husband and love fought with hate. He was dressed in purple silk. Eve didn't miss the message Adam was relaying. He was royalty. He'd always thought that, hadn't he? Her eyes roamed over him and she hated to admit that she'd missed him, his beautiful eyes, his slow, easy smile, and his straight even teeth, so white they appeared to gleam. Her eyes traveled over the contours of his face. Every line, every quiver of his lips was etched with power. She took a moment and concentrated on his lips, full, luscious and tantalizing. At that moment he gave her a secret smile before using the tip of his tongue to caress his top lip. Her hands clenched the silk sheets, knotting them more than she'd already done in her twilight state. They were damp, evidence of her writhing showing clearly. She knew it wasn't just a fever that had brought it on. Then again, perhaps it was, a fever named, Adam Omega.

As her eyes moved over his massive chest, Eve became acutely aware of other beings in the room and groaned guiltily, wishing she could pretend Adam didn't affect her. But what was the use? He did. She could only try now to minimize the damage to Sullivan's ego.

"I don't believe you did this to me again, Adam." She shot him a quick look, pleading with her eyes for him not to give away her innermost thoughts and feelings. For an answer he smirked then gave a slight shrug unseen by Sullivan.

Frowning slightly, Eve pushed herself to a sitting position. They were all staring at her as though she'd returned from the dead. *Oh*, she thought, she had. She looked around the room. "Mark," she whispered. "Adam, you found out I hadn't been feeding from Mark and you killed him." She shook her head as she sank back on the pillows. "Now you pick on mortals?" she asked. "Why not?" she answered her own question.

"I did not kill the mortal." Adam shook his head slowly and stared at Eve, his gaze never wavering.

"Then who?" Eve glanced toward Dr. Meah, dismissing him. The doctor would never do it. The words, '*I'm sorry*,' drifted toward her and a knife twisted in her heart. "Sullivan," she whispered, "tell me you didn't."

"I weighed my options and was left with little choice," he answered.

Eve's head snapped up. It was as she'd thought. Adam had been the driving force behind Mark's death. "Your bargain to save me?" she asked. She didn't like where this was heading. "Sullivan…" The hurt clung to her. The one good deed she'd done had been undone in… she looked at the clock. "How long have you been here, Adam?"

"Awhile."

"Long enough to kill, I suppose."

"No, long enough to save your life," Adam retorted.

"Why, Adam? Why did you do this once again? Why did you force Sullivan to kill Mark? And who the hell do you think you are?"

"Who the hell do I think I am? I shall tell you who the hell I am. I'm your husband," Adam answered. "And I need no other reasons for doing the things that I do. I gave you life and only I can take it away. As for forcing Sullivan to do my bidding, I did nothing of the sort. The things that were done in this room were done of free will. I gave my blood to you, Sullivan gave his blood to me and Mark of course provided nourishment for poor Sullivan. Tell me, Eve, how was I to save your life if I didn't have a means to replenish my own blood? As I said all of us were willing participants."

Adam looked toward Dr. Meah, raised a well shaped brow, then shrugged. "Well, on most of our parts anyway. As for the simpering mortal, he wanted to be used to save you. Who were we to deny him the ability to do something useful for once in his meaningless life?"

"It was a life. Mark was trying to protect me." She laughed harshly. "From you, I might add. I know that you harmed him before." Eve swallowed, closing her eyes as she did so.

"How pray tell was that mortal to be your protector?"

"I had finally convinced him to give up being fodder for vampires. I was giving him a chance to have a new life and you took that from him," Eve continued as though Adam had not spoken. Her eyes snapped open. "You didn't have to force Sullivan to Kill Mark. You could have found another way to replenish your blood. We're all aware that it was done to teach me a lesson. I'm tired of your lessons, Adam."

"Sorry to disappoint you, darling, but this time the lesson was not yours to learn." He smiled coldly up at Sullivan. "I will not be judged by any of you. Who do you think you are to judge me? You don't have that right. None of you are any better than I am. None of you know what you will do until you've faced such a situation. Sullivan needed to be faced with that situation in order to know how it felt."

Eve's head swiveled back and forth between Sullivan and Adam. "What do you mean?"

"Don't you know?"

"If I did I would not have asked."

"Eve, it is lucky for you that I love you or I would sever your head from your neck," he raised a finger, "or maybe just cut out your tongue." He smiled. "But for now I will do neither. I am too relieved to see you and believe it or not, pleased to hear your insolent tone. So, I will tolerate it for now because it pleases me."

"Adam, what are your real reasons for my not finding more bodies lying dead on the floor... Why are Dr. Meah and..." She glanced at Sullivan and stopped. "What are you up to?"

"You have many lessons to learn. It was foolishness on my part to think that I could trust you enough to want to live, that you would do the things necessary in order to survive. There has never been a vampire made that did not ingest fresh human blood, whether offered freely or taken by force. Do you think I would have stayed away so long if I'd known the danger you were in? You're a very silly woman, Eve, and for your sake I must do what I foolishly trusted you...," he sneered and spat, "you and your consort to take care of. I will not have you defenseless or dependent. You have lessons to learn and you *will* learn them."

"I did have human blood, just not the way you wanted me to take it. Besides, I told you, I'm sick to death of your lessons."

"That may be," Adam said to Eve, sitting next to her, running his hand down the side of her arm, ignoring her slapping his hand away. He replaced it each time until they stared into each other's gazes and Eve stopped. "I will make sure that your education is left to me. I will be assured that you will know how to feed."

"Your coming back changes nothing. You are not the master of my fate. I am. You cannot order me around."

Eve pushed Adam's hand from her arm, ignoring Sullivan's warning, his mental image of the last time she'd challenged Adam in that manner. "Go ahead and try if you think it will work."

"Didn't I just prove that to you? Your time of playing the vampire whore has come to an end. I did tell you that when I was ready to reclaim you I would. Eve, I'm ready."

"And what if Eve isn't ready to be reclaimed by you, Adam? We both owe you a debt of gratitude but nothing more." Sullivan moved closer to Eve and sat on the opposite side of the bed, taking her hand in his and kissing it, holding on tightly and not releasing his grip until she winced. "Welcome back," Sullivan whispered to her. He turned his gaze at last to Adam, who was watching him with a strange glint of amusement in his eyes. It was time to get this over and done with.

"Well, Adam, you didn't answer the question. What if Eve isn't ready to be reclaimed by you?"

Adam's left arm was propped on the pillow besides Eve. First he allowed his hungry gaze to settle on his wife. Then he kissed her lips lightly before trailing his tongue down the side of her neck. As she shivered, he moved slightly away. With his thumb and forefinger he slowly rubbed at his temple, then worried his chin in an even slower and more deliberate manner. He studied Sullivan through narrowed eyes, amused that the vampire truly thought to take him on.

What strange universe is this? he wondered as he'd wondered in the past. None of this should be happening. He'd been much too lenient with all of them. He brought his gaze from Sullivan to land back on his wife. He ignored the pleading in her eyes not to harm Sullivan, not to kiss her again in front of him. He gave her a hard look, saw the petite flutter at the base of her throat and leaned down and suckled it. Eve's gasp of pleasure filled the air.

"Do you think Eve's not ready to be reclaimed? You were but a brief interlude, Sullivan. Your time is over. Be thankful that you even had it."

None in the room could have missed the deadly intent behind Adam's words. He was unfazed by Sullivan's rage. The calmness with which he spoke belied the true nature of his emotions. Adam was the most dangerous when he seemed calmest.

Rubbing his palms together slowly, interlacing his fingers for several moments, Adam almost appeared unconcerned, sleepy even. He sighed as though bored with them all. "Sullivan, perhaps you should inquire of Eve her intentions."

***

Had she truly thought that Adam would give in to her silent pleas? She wished now as she had many times in the past that she could have them both. Truth stayed on the fringes. For what she truly wished was that Adam wanted her in the same manner that Sullivan did. As her gaze landed on Sullivan, she looked away; fully aware the kiss she'd shared with Adam in her twilight state had not been a dream. It had been real and if she admitted the truth of things, it was Adam's kiss more than anything that made her fight to return to her body. She had been fully conscious when Adam had trailed hot kisses from her lips to her throat. Stopping him hadn't been an option. It never had been when he'd touch her. She'd been drawn under his spell as always, from the moment he'd looked at her with love in his eyes.

In that moment all in the room had ceased to be. Knowing that Sullivan had witnessed it, Eve wished even more that she could find an anti-love potion. She'd never been able to resist Adam's kisses and apparently she never would. She dropped her eyes in embarrassment and took in a breath, sensing the odor of death, mortal death. This she could deal with. Her feelings for Adam she could not.

Instead of saying anything to Sullivan, she directed her comments to Adam. "Why did you do it this way?" she asked again. "Mark didn't have to die."

Eve turned her head and stared at Dr. Meah. She saw the fear in his eyes, read his thoughts. She remembered all that had come before, Adam forcing the vamp to drain the tainted blood from her body. She trembled at the remembered pain of Dr. Meah's fangs piercing her flesh. He now had Eve's tainted blood. Panic rushed through her.

All the people she loved were in this room, embroiled in this nightmare, even Adam. She'd once sought to save him. Now there was no longer any possibility of that. Biting her lips, trying to find a way to address the situation with Sullivan, she took in a deep breath.

Adam was watching her, his look issuing a challenge to her, telling her, she was afraid to confront Sullivan with what he'd done. And the truth of it all was that she was. She didn't want to not be in Sullivan's life, to not be loved by him, to not be held in his arms. A small tremor of fear moved over her. This was not going to be easy but she had to deal with it.

"Sullivan, you made me a promise."

"This wasn't up to Sullivan, Eve. Your life is my gift to you and I will continue to make sure you live until you learn to respect that gift and choose life for yourself."

"I wasn't talking to you," Eve screamed. She could feel the haze of anger clouding her vision. "This is the gift you've given me, Adam? This?"

She glared. "Dr Meah was trying to help me. I wasn't trying to defy you or to die. I just didn't want this. I never wanted to be a vampire and I still don't. You say I don't respect life but you're wrong. It's you who have no respect for life or the desires of others. I have loved you through many things, forgiven you for the unforgivable. But you will not tell me this is a gift, that I don't respect the privilege of being alive. I do. I just wanted to feel like me, mortal, human." She shivered.

"Don't any of you contradict me. I'm well aware that I'm no longer mortal. I know that. Still, for a time my illusion remained intact. Sullivan and Dr. Meah were able to help me with that illusion. And you would kill the two of them for that?" She bent her head, resting her hands on her knees and groaned in agony.

"Adam, you, my love, have taken everything from me. Do you want to make me suffer? My being with Sullivan was never a threat to you and you knew that. Still, you've made it impossible for me to be with him. You were aware that I loved him, that he made me happy. You took that away from me. I don't think I will ever be able to forgive that."

Tears coursed down her cheek and she wiped then away. "I swear, if it's the last thing I do, I will find a way to rid myself of these blasted blood tears. If I have a need to cry I will at least cry real tears."

The knowledge that she couldn't cry real tears made Eve cry even harder. She didn't want to give up the one man in her life who had loved her unconditionally, who'd done nothing but protect her. She'd taken so much from Sullivan and given so little in return, she thought. All the time they'd had together had always been in the shadow of Adam. It was no different now.

It was with a heavy heart that Eve turned to look at Sullivan again. She loved him beyond reason and felt the burden, swift and unrelenting, that she would no longer be able to reside with him. His betrayal hurt worse than Adam's because she'd expected more from Sullivan.

"Sullivan, I didn't expect any better from Adam to have disregard for human life, to kill Mark, just to prove a point. But I did expect better from you." She heaved a breath, looked at the three vampires in the room, closed her eyes, lay back on the bed and wished for death.

"Why him?" Adam asked.

"Because he has honor, because he knows the meaning of love."

"How the hell do you think I knew what was happening? Don't you wonder? I had shut my mind to you."

Eve bolted upright. It couldn't be true. "Sullivan," she said, her voice one long agonized sob as she rose from the bed and made her way to him. "I told you that I wanted to end it. Please tell me Adam's lying, that he just came and you saw a way to help me. Tell me you didn't call him." Sullivan's gaze was on her and it was so filled with pain that she knew the answer.

"I love you," Sullivan said, looking at her and doing his best to ignore Adam. "I didn't want to lose you, Eve. I couldn't imagine living for an eternity without you."

"That's so touching," Adam laughed. "Because only one of you will be living for an eternity. You're no different from me, Sullivan. You with your high and mighty attitude about my rights. Did you have the right to come to me, to go against what Eve wanted? Did you? She wanted to die. Why didn't you let her? Isn't that what you asked me, why didn't I allow my wife to die?" Adam pointed a long, slender finger in Sullivan's direction.

"Judge not. '*Thou hypocrite, first cast out the beam out of thine own eye; and then shalt thou see clearly to cast the mote out of thy brother's eye.' Matthew 7:5.*"

Sullivan turned to face Adam, his fangs bared, a sneer on his face as he spoke. "You think you still have the right to throw scriptures at me?"

"Apparently I do." From the corner of his eye Adam saw the doctor moving away and he squeezed his hand, feeling the beating of the vampire's heart. He narrowed his eyes toward the vampire. "You will stay where you are, Doctor, and see how this all plays out." Adam applied a bit more pressure to the beating heart.

"Sullivan, I did warn you many times, first for sleeping with my wife. But neither of you chose to listen. Now you will have to deal with the consequences of your actions." He shot Eve a look. "Don't say a word," he ordered in a deadly calm voice, "or I will kill him where he stands." He turned again to Sullivan. "I told you if any harm ever came to Eve I'd kill you and I meant it." He glanced toward Eve. "Harm came to her. She almost died." A lump lodged in Adam's throat and he had to force his words around it. "Sullivan, I wasn't kidding."

"I didn't think that you were."

Studying Sullivan, Adam had to give him credit. There was a time the vampire would not have waited around to have his sentence meted out. Adam stretched his arms out and yawned. He truly was feeling a bit tired.

He'd given so much blood to Eve, it had been necessary. Still, he could feel the toll it had taken on his strength. No matter, none in the room was aware of that fact except him.

"Adam, do you mind if I check on Eve?"

For a long moment Adam stared at Dr. Meah. "She is well now, Doctor, no thanks to you." When the doctor cringed, Adam smiled. "The three of you tire me. I want to know everything that has happened in my absence." He turned his back to Sullivan. He could feel the hatred for him coming off the vamp in waves. "Don't even think it," he said, then laughed. "Now as I was saying, fill me in."

Adam deliberately kept his back turned to Sullivan to taunt him. He knew the man was worried about Eve's displeasure with him. Eve's displeasure should not be what was uppermost in Sullivan's mind. Retribution for the harm that had befallen Eve should be what he worried about. Adam would deliver punishment in his own time. He would do nothing before Eve was fully aware of what had transpired? No way. He stretched once more, then turned slowly toward Sullivan. "Start talking," he ordered and snapped his finger. He sank into the overstuffed chair he'd conjured and waved his hand around the room.

"Your tastes in furnishing leave much to be desired. How my wife has tolerated living here is beyond my imagination." Adam stretched, making himself comfortable as he listened to Sullivan's tale of his ineptness in caring for Eve. The more Adam thought about Eve's suggestion to make Sullivan squirm a bit, the more he liked it. He knew Eve had her own reasons, more than likely to whip up some spell that she thought would keep Sullivan safe. *Well, no such luck*, Adam thought and twined his hands together. He laughed out loud and watched as fear became etched on the faces of Sullivan and Dr. Meah. *This was going to be fun.*

Chapter Three

Before Adam could blink an eye Eve was standing in front of Sullivan, her stance definitely protective. He folded his arms across his chest and studied her in amusement. "After allowing me to make love to you in front of his face you now seek to protect Sullivan? How foolish. He'll appreciate this gesture less than an apology for allowing me the kiss," Adam assured her in their private conversation. He'd have to give her credit, though. She didn't flinch. She'd come a long way; he was pleased. Still, this wouldn't do. His blood that was giving her strength and power would not save Sullivan, not this time. "Just take a look at his face," Adam whispered into her mind. "He can't decide with whom he's more furious, me just for existing, or you for loving me."

"Can't you behave just once, Adam?" Eve gave him a scathing look and repositioned herself. She hated to admit that Adam was right but Sullivan's anger was creating an unwelcome frisson.

"You have a problem to take care of, Eve," Adam said. "You've not yet dealt with Sullivan. You keep becoming distracted, scattered. Concentrate, Eve," he instructed and laughed, giving her an air kiss as he took her by the shoulders and gently turned her from him to face Sullivan.

For several moments Eve could only stare at Sullivan. Dealing with him was much harder than dealing with Adam. She and Adam yelled and cursed, sometimes even hit. With Sullivan there was hardly any such drama. That was what was making it so damn hard. She loved him, and in the deepest part of her, she understood his motives, but understanding and being able to live with him were two different things.

Eve shook her head slowly. "Not you, too, Sullivan, not you." She pressed her lips together to keep from saying more, all the time watching as sadness filled his eyes and he reached out for her. She took a step away and saw the immediate pain that came into his eyes at her actions. "Why?" she asked.

Sullivan reached once again toward Eve, then dropped his hands. "I don't expect you to forgive me, Eve. I knew the consequences when I asked Adam to come and save you. I knew what would happen."

"But why Mark? He had nothing to do with this. He wasn't involved in this madness. Why did you take his life?"

"I had no choice."

"You did. He didn't play a part in this."

"He did, Eve."

Sullivan turned from her to glare at Adam. "Mark was my payment. I would have drained a thousands mortals to save you." Anger filled him and he looked away. "I don't expect you to forgive me. I know you hate what I've done. I feel it. But what I did, I would do again."

"You're sounding just like Adam," Eve said in a sad little whisper.

"Maybe I'm more like him than either of us thought. I know now why he turned you. I would have turned you also if it meant you would live."

"Sullivan!" Eve stared at him. "Now I have no one I can trust."

No one she could trust? Adam closed his ears against the painful words. There was one thing about him Eve could always trust and that was that he would love her throughout all eternity. "Eve," Adam called out to her, speaking softly.

"Leave me alone," she roared, her voice fierce, shattering the glass in the house. "I'm talking to Sullivan."

Adam made a move to stand and Eve sent a volt of pure electrical energy toward him. "What the hell," he roared, this time truly annoyed.

"Adam, I'm talking to Sullivan."

"Eve, don't." Sullivan moved to stand between Eve and Adam.

"Don't what?" Eve asked, moving away from Sullivan. "Don't get Adam angry? What will he do? Will he kill someone else? Will you?"

"Eve." Her name slid from Sullivan like a plaintiff moan.

"There you go… 'Eveing' me again. I loved you, Sullivan. I trusted you. You gave me back my life and now you've taken away everything else. I was happy with you and could have lived the rest of this wretched existence with you by my side. How am I going to live this life without you?"

That did it for Adam. His blood or not, he was not going to listen to any more of his wife's pathetic murmurings of love for another man. "Please, Eve, no more, you're boring me." He walked toward them and lasered Mark's body, incinerating it instantly. He gave a slight shrug as he felt cold hatred washing over him. Surprisingly, it wasn't coming from Eve, but from Sullivan. The only emotion he sensed from Eve was anger. He paused, suddenly sensing something else, relief. *At last,* he thought, his wife was happy to be alive whether she admitted it or not. The circle was complete.

He watched as she rounded on Sullivan, putting her arms out to deflect Adam's rage. He grinned at her and shook his head slowly in amazement.

"So you've chosen, Eve."

"Yes, I've chosen."

Adam stared silently as Eve did a slow half turn in Sullivan's direction before glaring backwards, her gaze lethal. She was trembling with anger and indignation but her skin was warming from his blood.

Adam had to smile at the irony. If not for him Eve would be dead twice now. He'd given her life. He loved her with every fiber of his being, had loved her forever and had given her this dark gift that she didn't want. Now she wanted to use his gift to save her lover. If one lived long enough, one saw amazing things and Adam had lived quite long enough. Eve belonged to him. She was his wife, his love, and it was time that she understood that.

"Stop glaring at me, Eve, your disgust will not deter me." He looked toward Dr Meah. "Doctor, I will not kill you immediately" He shrugged and gave Sullivan a smile. "Nor you, Sullivan. I think I will make you both sweat. Eve suggested it and it does have merits."

Adam opened his arms wide and looked at the three as a parent would look at his insolent children. "The three of you bear close watching. You try my patience and it tells me I must remain in close contact with the three of you until I can decide what punishment each of you must receive." He shook a finger as all opened their mouths to protest. "Don't thank me, not yet," he said sarcastically.

"Thank you? Adam, you're crazy." Eve laughed in genuine amusement, wondering what Adam was planning, trying to probe his mind without detection.

"Haven't I told you to stop doing that?" Adam locked gazes with Eve and sat in a chair near her. "You make me tired, my love, you truly do. But playtime is over. I will take you home and I will give you one week to rest. Then you will learn to do as you should have done two years ago. I will no longer trust you to behave like either a vampire or an adult. You will drink if I have to force the fangs from your gums and shove them into a mortal. If I have to I will hold you in place until you've fed." His voice was calm. He sat in his chair and waited for Eve to make the next move.

***

She'd have to bide her time, play this slowly, pretend that nothing was wrong. Adam was probing her mind. And she'd have to remember to keep up a barrier against his probe. She toppled and nearly fell dismissing the three ready to assist her. "No, don't," she moaned. She was the only one in the room who knew her weakness was false. She stared at Adam and saw the weary expression on his face. He didn't trust her but he loved her beyond all reason. She was his weakness, she was totally aware of that. He had gone quiet, an air of anxious apprehension about him. His probe became stronger and she sent him images of her fainting. He blinked, still not sure, and she was aware that his love for her was clouding his judgment just enough for her to do what she wanted to do.

"There is no reason for you to feel faint, Eve," Adam said calmly. "I sense deception on your part."

"No deception, Adam. I just need to take a moment. I'm not used to having so much of your blood in my veins." She smiled sweetly. It has a powerful kick," she said and looked into his eyes. "Thanks, and I really do mean that."

Holding on to the poster of the bed Eve slowly made her way to the head of the bed, trying with all her might not to will the drawer to open, not to demand her crystal to come to her. But this one crystal was a special one she'd prepared many months just for Adam. She had no idea if it would work or not but she knew this much: She had to try. She sat on the bed and sighed heavily in the silent and still room. They were all watching her, that much she knew. Eve leaned her head against the pillow but kept half her body off the bed. She had to time her next move carefully.

"Adam, I do have some thoughts on the lessons that you're insisting that you're going to teach me. I will not feed directly from humans. You lied to me when you told me that you wanted your best scientists to find a means for vampires to live without a need for human blood. But the moment I tried it you became enraged."

"You were never meant to be a lab experiment."

"But who better than I?"

"Anyone. Sullivan could have tried the concoction, the good doctor. I don't care who, just not you."

"It worked, Adam," Eve declared, knowing Adam as well as he knew her, and knowing her statement would get a rise out of him. Just as expected, Adam was up from the chair and pacing across the room, sparks of electricity flying from the tips of his fingers. And he wasn't even trying. Eve shivered, imagining what Adam could do if he were trying. She shivered again. She didn't have to imagine. She'd seen the power Adam wielded. He'd almost destroyed the world. Adam turned from her and quicker than she could have thought she quietly opened the drawer in the small stand next to her bed and palmed the crystal. The moment she held it Adam turned back to her with a knowing smile.

"So, my beautiful, treacherous wife, you feel you're well enough to defy me openly." He smiled. "Did you think it impossible for me to master the parlor tricks you've learned?"

"They are no tricks, Adam, they are my birthright," she said, standing.

"Then perhaps they're mine also for your magic has no effect on me, nor do your crystals." Adam took a stone from his pocket and held it in the palm of his hand. He tossed it to Eve. "Go ahead, try."

"Will you do as I asked and spare Dr. Meah and Sullivan?" Eve said, taking the conversation into Adam's mind to keep it private. She palmed the stone Adam tossed her.

"There is no guarantee that I will. I might and then again I might not." Adam gave her a hard look and narrowed his gaze. "Half the time even I'm unaware of what I might do. So, I'm afraid I can't give you any promises, my love."

"And you're determined to force me to drink directly from humans? I can't change your mind?"

Adam laughed.

Eve laughed but hers was a laugh of supreme conviction. She glanced down at the crystal Adam had given her before tossing it on the bed. She smiled as she stared into the eyes of her husband. Determination fueled her spine as she walked with strength and stood directly before Adam. "One last chance, Adam, don't make me do this."

"Go ahead, baby, take your best shot."

"Remember, you asked for this." She cocked her head a tiny bit to the left. "Remember, I'm just doing as you asked."

Adam Omega, Grand Master Vampire, be gone now from my sight. Let your very essence be sealed in flight. Go now to a time and place before I ever looked upon your face."

Eve smiled and pointed the crystal that was in her palm toward Adam, who was looking at her as though she were crazy. There was not a trace of fear in him, but she'd not expected there to be. What did the great Adam Omega have to fear from his fledgling of a vampire wife, or of the powers of the ages that ran through her bloodline? He didn't fear her and that was to Eve's advantage. "Are you sure, Adam, that you want me to take my best shot?"

"Do it," Adam said calmly, the softness in his tone speaking volumes. He waited patiently.

Then Eve raised her hand and clapped three times. And just like that Adam was gone. Eve waited for a moment to see if her incantation had really worked. She didn't sense Adam. She tried to connect with him in her mind and couldn't. She laughed. It had worked. She'd sent the great vampire back in time.

Sullivan and Dr. Meah were staring at her. For a long moment neither moved. Then Sullivan touched her. "Eve," he called to her. "What did you do? Where's Adam?"

"I don't really know. I sent him back into the past but I can't tell you how far back, not really."

"Since when could you send anyone into the past?"

"Since never," Adam answered as he appeared back in the room. He walked up to Eve, opened her hand and removed the crystal. He arched a brow. "Really, Eve, did you think it was going to be that easy? You should know you can't just put a hex on a vampire. And especially not on me. You wouldn't be able to do it even if I were asleep. I'm protected."

Eve stared at him. "What if you weren't protected? Do you think it would work? Would I be able to send you away?"

"That really doesn't sound like what should be coming from your mouth. I should be hearing about your gratitude and your words of love."

"Didn't I say thank you?" She gave a short laugh. "Thank you, Adam. I'm grateful. I would be more grateful if you'd stop threatening everyone. This was all a mistake. The fault was mine."

At her words Adam's head snapped up and without trying, his eyes became red. He walked away from the woman he loved, circled the room, picking up objects and tossing them to the floor. No rage was involved; it was simply annoyance. His emotions were raw, too raw to engage in a battle of wills with his wife. There was one thing she had wrong. She was not to blame. The fault was his. He took in a deep breath, expelling it slowly.

"The fault was not entirely yours, Eve. Yes, you should have fed as I ordered and no, you should not have mixed chemicals. Still, some of the blame is mine." He moved toward her, allowing the red haze to leave. Adam reached his hand out to touch her, felt her tremble and then felt the burn from the amber ring. He closed his eyes and drew Eve into his arms. As his arms closed around her he breathed in her essence. "I don't know what I would have done if you had died. You gave me quite a scare. I have to admit that," he whispered.

"I know," Eve answered, holding him tightly, closing her eyes to block out the sadness in Sullivan's eyes as he watched them. This moment was not for fighting, but for telling the truth for once. She loved Adam Omega. And she was glad to be alive.

Chapter Four

Minutes passed before Adam released Eve. Even then he kept an arm securely around her waist. He stared at Sullivan, his gaze daring the vamp to make a move. He'd done as he'd promised. He'd taken his wife back.

"A few changes have to be made," Adam said, looking at Sullivan, then Dr. Meah. He saved Eve for last, then gazed for a long moment into her eyes. "I've given all of you too much freedom," he said with a sigh. "As for you, Eve, there will be no more deceptive practices." He tilted her chin upward and held her gaze. "Let me be clear about this. You will learn to feed the proper way." He waved his hand at her protest. "No more. I have to attend to other matters."

In truth, there were other things to deal with. Once he finally took care of Sullivan, he would have to find someone else to take over the vamps' duties, someone as anal about the job as Sullivan was. Adam exhaled noisily. He had too many companies to run by himself. He thought of Suzett, the vamp who'd turned Sullivan. She was very good at organizing things and keeping people in line. He smiled. Maybe he'd offer her a chance to come in and run things on a temporary basis. Adam ran the possibilities through his mind. Killing Sullivan would serve a purpose but would it be his best move? Would it hurt the vampire more to see Eve back in Adam's bed where she belonged? Would it hurt Eve to see the woman who'd turned Sullivan? He laughed. He hadn't forgotten about Eve; she deserved some payback also.

"There are changes I'm going to institute. By the way, Sullivan, you do know you're fired, right?" Adam shook his head. "And Dr. Meah, as for you," he tapped his finger to his chin, "assemble the entire staff. I want to know their interest in taking over your duties."

***

In moments all the top scientists were assembled before Adam. Jerking his thumb at each in turn he listened to them as they answered his questions. Most attempted to relay their loyalty to Dr. Meah by putting in a good word for him.

"None of you seem to want the position." Adam smiled slowly. "Surely there has to be one among you with ambition." When Doctor Lee stepped forward, Adam grinned. *Perfect,* he thought. He listened as the vampire praised himself and belittled Dr. Meah's work in the process.

Adam worried his chin with his thumb and forefinger as he listened to the man. Then he smiled and rose. "I detest disloyalty. Thanks, Dr. Lee, but I don't think I need your services." He suddenly twisted his right hand and closed it into a fist. He squeezed and the vamp fell to the floor. Adam shook his head in disgust as he held the beating heart in his hand, then tossed it to the floor and ignited both the heart and the body. "What?" he said to the inquisitive looks. "He annoyed me. Now who wants the job?" he said to the assembled team.

When no one moved to accept the position, Adam turned to Dr. Meah and smirked. "I suppose you will remain until I have the right person to replace you." He gave a low bow and spoke to the assemblage. "You may leave now. Sullivan, you, Meah and Eve will remain." He touched his finger to Eve's face and caressed it slowly as he slid the opposite arm around her to hold her close. "We will take our leave soon."

Tension was once again building in the room. No one dared speak. Adam kept his fierce glare on them for several minutes, knowing that it was unnerving them. Eve was correct in anticipating what he would do instead of killing Sullivan and Meah straight away.

"Sullivan, you're glaring at me and I think…yes…I do believe I see a bit of fang. Is there something urgent you wish to say to me?" Adam asked, toying with the vamp.

"Adam, why don't we finish this now, just the two of us? I'm sick to death of you. I made a promise that when Eve was well I was going to kick your ass. I think it's about time."

"Sullivan, don't," both Dr. Meah and Eve said in unison.

Sullivan's gaze swept the room and landed on Eve. He slowly lowered his eyes, looking at Adam's arm still around her waist. He saw Adam's fingers pull her even closer and Eve not fighting to move away. His heart lurched. Some things were not in his control.

Adam was waiting for him to make his move. It irritated the hell out of Sullivan that Adam was so damn calm, so cocky, so sure that he couldn't be hurt. For once Adam was not the one pushing for a showdown. And somewhere inside of him, Sullivan was aware he should let it go for now. It would be foolish to annoy Adam even further when he was in a halfway decent mood. But Sullivan was in a foolish mood.

"You know something, Adam. I wish Eve did know how to send you away. But I don't think just to the past would do, maybe to a different planet." He glared at Adam and Adam laughed. "I would like to talk to Eve alone," Sullivan hissed between clenched teeth.

"No," Adam answered.

"You don't control her."

Adam grinned.

"Damn you, Adam."

"I have been damned for many years, but not anymore. As for your wish to kick my ass, it will never happen so why don't we think of something else, something reasonable that you have a chance of achieving." He turned to Eve and grinned. "Any ideas?"

"I've got some ideas but I don't think any of you will like them. But I'd like to ask a favor of both of you," Eve said, allowing her glance to sweep the faces of both vampires. "Give me a moment, a day, to come back from the dead, as it were, and to feel a little better before either of you attempt to destroy the world. Surely your lightning bolts can wait that long."

"I don't trust you, Eve, and I probably never will." Adam glanced at the ring on his finger and watched the glowing stone for a moment longer. "If it were not for this I don't know if I'd even trust your love." He moved from Eve and went to Dr. Meah. "Tell me, Doctor, how do you feel now with the poisoned blood of my wife in your body?" He didn't get an answer. "Don't worry, Doctor, I'm sure your body will purge the blood in a few hours but for now the four of us need to talk. Eve is correct. It's too soon for her to be disturbed and as for punishing the two of you…"

"Punishing us? We're not your children," Sullivan hissed.

"Alright then, how about if I say *killing* the two of you? Would you like that better? Would you like for me to do all that I promised, all that you deserve, right here and right now?"

The unmistakable tension had returned to Adam's voice. He pointed a finger at Sullivan and before the vamp could raise so much as a finger to defend himself he dropped to the floor in pain. "Leave me be,

Sullivan. I'm warning you. You will die soon enough, leave me be." With that he wrapped Eve in his arms and disappeared.

*** *

In stunned silence Dr. Meah waited to see if Adam would return before rushing to help Sullivan. "Why do you antagonize him?" A growl was the only answer as Sullivan clutched his heart.

"This is crazy," Sullivan panted.

"What's crazy is that Adam has left the two of us alive. We still have a chance. Eve is sure to be pleading our case. Can't you just leave well enough alone?"

Shoving everything that he could reach away from him, Sullivan also pushed away Dr. Meah's helping hand. "Do you have any idea how I feel right now? He just waltzed back in here after all this time and took her as though she belongs to him."

"She's his wife."

Sullivan groaned. "She was his wife for the past two years. Where was he? He didn't want her. I did."

"Sullivan, please."

"I'm so sick of both you and Eve calling my name in that pleading tone. I may not be Adam Omega, but I am not without power. I resent the two of you pleading for my life. And I even resent that you'd plead for your own. If he's going to kill us, then I suggest we go out fighting, not like cowards, not like men without power. There are two of us, we can ban together."

"Sullivan, you forget the obvious. For all these hundreds of years none of your plans to defeat Adam have worked. I have no wish to go against Adam. I'm still hoping that he will cool down."

"He's not going to allow you to continue working in the lab."

"No, but he might allow me to continue to live. And you forget that even if you were successful, if you killed Adam you would still lose Eve. Whether you want to hear this or not, he was not holding her prisoner when he took her into his arms. She went willingly. You and I are both aware of her love for him. Look what happened the last time Eve helped you to render Adam harmless."

The doctor stopped and laughed, shaking his head. "Adam harmless? Never. But what did she do when she thought he was in danger?"

This time Doctor Meah refused to back down from Sullivan's anger. He wanted to live. Adam had left them alive. Why rock the boat? "In case your memory is shaky, allow me to remind you. Eve took on a team of vampires, killed four of them and rescued Adam. He was the one she chose to save, Sullivan, him, her husband, and her one great love. He is the one she went away with just a moment ago of her own accord. You were here in this room yet she left with him."

Sullivan raised his hand and Dr. Meah ducked. "Don't kill the messenger for telling the truth. She loves him and it doesn't matter that she understands, or even that she forgives you for what you did. I suspect that right now Adam looks as much like a safe haven to her as you did a few years ago. She doesn't know how to deal with you right now. Yes, she loves you, but you knew how she was going to feel about Mark. I don't blame you for his death. I would have done it myself had Adam demanded it. Just give Eve some time to figure things out. To be honest with you, I thought Adam was going to kill us the moment he saw us. He was so angry. I've never seen such fury in him. You have to be aware of how controlled he is not to have done anything. Who knows what he's planning for us?"

"I understand," Sullivan admitted. "I'm not blind. I may be a fool but I can see clearly. If Eve had not pulled through, we would not be having this conversation. I'm also aware that because she did, Adam was of a mind to be....." Sullivan hissed out a breath between clenched teeth. "Who knows what's on Adam's mind. I only know that what he plans for us he must consider worse than death. Part of me wants to believe that Eve went with Adam to stop the fighting. But I saw the way he looked at her when he spoke to her, and told her how he would have felt had she not made it. And I saw the way she looked at him. In that moment I didn't exist for her. My love was of no consequence. What am I supposed to do? I love her too."

*****

Back in her old home Eve took a good look around. The house was dusty; spider webs hung from the corners. *What a shame,* she thought. Such a beautiful home and for over two years neither she nor Adam had set foot inside the place. Sadness filled her at the neglect of such a beautiful place. She glanced at Adam and their gazes connected. He smiled and waved his hand, restoring the house to its original state. What would a woman give to have that power that Adam used so easily?

"Tell me, Adam. Now that we're back here, what are your plans for me? This doesn't even feel like my home anymore."

"Feelings don't matter. This is your home."

"I don't have any of my things here."

"As you well know, money has never been a problem. You will buy new things," Adam retorted. He gave her a hard look, narrowing his eyes. "Why don't you tell me the real problem? What's really on your mind?"

"What are you going to do to Sullivan?"

When Adam refused to answer her, she worried her top lip with the tip of her tongue and repeated her question. "What are you going to do to Sullivan? I'm alive, Adam, and you can keep it just like that. No one has to die. No one has to suffer. You don't have to do anything to them. You can allow them to live."

"And you and Sullivan? What are you asking me to do about the two of you?"

"It's over."

"He won't just accept that."

"He'll have to."

"Are you saying you no longer love him?" Adam asked, holding Eve's gaze, entering her mind to determine the truth.

"You know better than that, Adam. I can no more stop loving Sullivan than I can stop loving you."

"That makes you fickle."

"Be that as it may," Eve paused and gave him a look that dared him to repudiate her words, "I love you both."

"And you're with me now because of what Sullivan did...because he wanted you to live. You blame him for coming to me, the only being who could save your life. You blame him for choosing your life over Mark's."

"Taking a life is never right, Adam."

"You've taken a life, Eve, if memory serves me correct. You took four lives in order to save me. Please tell me what the difference is in what you did and what Sullivan has done."

"You were in danger."

"And so were you. You know, Eve, I have never understood this and never will. Mortals," he stopped and gave her a mocking smile. "And I can not understand the mistress of the vampire world. Taking a life is wrong until a mortal does it. You did this as a mortal and I'll wager you'll do it at some point as you are now, as the mistress of the vampire world.

And I'll go even further, up the ante if you will, and wager that you will find a way to justify it. For all intents and purposes you might as well still be a mortal. You think like one. You're all such hypocrites."

"And you, Adam, you're not? You don't think that what you do is wrong?"

He gave a shrug. "Let me answer you this way. I admire people who admit to their flaws and to the flaws of others. I admire people who accept others who are imperfect." He laughed and shook his head. "It seems we're back where we started. In the beginning we discussed right and wrong, good and evil. I don't think we'll ever resolve that age old debate. Evil is and always has been in the eye of the beholder, just as goodness is in the eye of the beholder."

"I totally disagree with that. But of course we knew that I would. Just answer me this. What do you see yourself as?"

"Why, Eve, I'm surprised you have to ask. I'm simply Adam. No more no less."

"And Sullivan?"

"Quite a bit less."

Eve couldn't believe she was actually laughing. "You're much too full of yourself. You do know that, don't you?"

"I daresay that is a quality of mine that endears me to you. Believe me, Eve, you've said such few nice things about me that the few times you have I've committed them to memory. But you keep trying to distract me. Because I enjoy watching your lips move as you talk I've allowed it. You must know this: Despite my feelings about Sullivan or what I might eventually do to him, you should not base your decision to end your relationship with him on the morality or immorality of his actions to save you."

"What?"

"Do not judge Sullivan. You do not have that right."

"Are you now Sullivan's champion? You're planning to kill him."

Adam shrugged. "What I plan to do is not your concern. I think perhaps you're wondering how I will view you if you forgave Sullivan for Mark's death."

"Please, you have nothing to do with it."

"I think you're wrong."

"He shouldn't have killed Mark."

"There are many things you shouldn't have done, wife. Shall I name them for you?"

"And will you judge me?"

"I have that right. You do not."

"You pompous ass. I'm not taking back a word I said. Sullivan shouldn't have killed Mark."

"So it is done, Eve. You're judging Sullivan as I said you were. You know you do a lot of that. You are no more qualified to judge him than you are to judge me.

"With my lips have I declared all the judgments of THY mouth." (Psalm 119:13) Whose judgments do you declare?"

"I am not judging Sullivan," Eve denied.

"Oh, but you are, dear wife. Sullivan was only doing what he had to do, what any man who loved his woman would do. He was saving you by any means necessary."

"And you're now siding with Sullivan?" She shook her head. "The end of the world must surely be near."

"Not yet. I'm just showing you that I am not a hypocrite. And you and the rest of the world are. I'm pragmatic."

"Wasn't calling everybody else a hypocrite judging?"

"Touché. See how easy judging is to do? I must regain my control. But you will allow that of late my life and emotions have been a bit frazzled. My wife, almost dead, my enemies surrounding me, challenging me." He pulled her to him and placed little kisses on the corners of her mouth. Then he caressed her lips with his tongue, all the while giving her a smile.

"Tell me something, Eve. When I held you back there I didn't know if you would push away or not. I was ready for that. Why did you not push away? Why did you come with me so meekly?" He smiled again. "Was it all for Sullivan, your worries, your fears?" He heaved a sigh and walked away before Eve could speak.

"You silly male jerk! Of course it wasn't all just to protect Sullivan. I love you," Eve whispered behind his back.

Adam heard her whispered words though he gave her no indication. *I know you love me*, he thought. And that is why Sullivan yet lives. He still needed to figure out what to do with the vamps who'd put his wife's life in danger. And he needed to do what he'd said with Eve. She was going to feed properly and she was going to do it soon.

When Adam returned to where Eve was working on some brew while burning incense, he gagged and asked, "What are you doing?"

"There is nothing here to work with beside the old herbs in the cabinet and some incense. So I'm using what I have here. I'm working on a better spell."

"To use against me?"

"It depends on how you look at it. I think of it more as a spell to protect all of us from you."

"Are you going to try and send me away again?"

"Yes."

There it was. One word: plain and simple. She hadn't yet learned. "Then I have to tell you Eve, I view that as a spell against me."

"See I told you. It's all in the perception. I view it as necessary protection."

"How many times do I have to tell you that you can not put a spell on me?"

"But you implied earlier that I could if you were open, if you allowed it. Correct?"

"Perhaps. But that would be crazy and I do know I'm not crazy. Do I look crazy to you?"

"Not crazy but I know how much you love a challenge. I think I can do it and you think I can't. So why not make a bet and see who wins?"

"You never offer anything for payment."

"What do you want?"

Adam grinned, then leered, allowing his eyes to slowly roam over Eve's body. He touched her with his mind, suckling her and feeling her moan as she leaned into the kitchen counter.

"You have no need to do that," Eve said with a wistful tone.

"Perhaps I don't." He stared at her. "But there is a part of me that would love to make love to you again as a mortal." He peeped in the bowl she was stirring, then locked gazes with her. "I hope your potion works. I truly do. Why don't you send me back to the time before you slept with Sullivan?"

"Sullivan wasn't the problem, you were."

"Then perhaps you should send me back to a time before I turned you. Perhaps we could change things. Perhaps we could begin again." Their gazes locked and held.

"Perhaps," Eve said, "if I can find a way to send you back in time."

"And if you send me away will you bring me back?"

"I'm not sure." Eve laughed for the second time that day. "I don't think either of us will ever be rid of the other. I think we shall be forever tied. I think I would feel your presence no matter where I sent you."

A gleam was in Adam's eyes. He moved toward her. "What if I agree to allow you to send me back, if you can?"

"I thought you said you were protected against any spell I might try to use. How will we get around that?" Eve cocked her head a little and gave him a flirty smile. "What is the source of your protection, Adam?"

"Surely you jest. What have I told you from the moment we met? I am my own protection, Eve. I need nothing else. The power of my mind is sufficient. As long as my will is intact there is nothing you can do to me that I don't want." He couldn't resist gloating.

"And would you allow your will to slip, enabling me to send you back in time?"

"First, I doubt that you can. But if your sacrilegious nonsense really works... As I said, I would enjoy making love to you again before I turned you."

"That still remains our problem doesn't it? That too was your choice, Adam. You didn't have to turn me." She looked sadly at him. "Even after all of that, I still wanted you, Adam. I wanted you to make love to me. It was you who wouldn't."

"So you sought comfort in the arms of my enemy?"

"I didn't plan it."

"I'm aware of that. But the outcome was the same," Adam whispered. A heavy sigh fell from his lips. "At the moment I would even relish making love to you in a time where you didn't freely sleep with my enemy."

This time Adam didn't laugh nor did he smile. He was deadly serious. He could feel the ice slipping back into his body. A bone deep weariness cleaved unto him. If only Eve knew how much control he actually had of his will. It was a strain to remain in this room with her talking freely of her lover and her wish to banish Adam. *We should end this conversation*, Adam thought as he walked toward the massive floor to ceiling windows that covered the entire eastern wall. He looked out on the lake and stared at it until the waves begin to rise. Taking in a deep breath he released it and remembered the last time he'd caused the waves to rise. He'd almost destroyed this home. Taking control of his breathing, he allowed the waves to retreat, and as they did, he once again calmed himself, taking a look at a painting on the wall. He couldn't afford to allow a temper tantrum to ruin the painting. The famous artist was long dead and would therefore be unavailable for Adam to commission another painting from him. He once again turned to face Eve, knowing it wouldn't be much longer before the hurt between them spilled out.

"If I could return you to the past, what would you do, Adam, change history?"

"I'm not sure. I just might. Then again I might not."

"If you found me again as a mortal would you admit to being a vampire?"

"I'm not sure I would."

"I at least had knowledge of what you were when you made love to me. Were you to return to the past and find me again, as a mortal, you would be obliged to tell me what you are."

A smirk turned Adam's lips up at the corners. "I think if you're successful in returning me to the past I would make love to you a moment after meeting you."

"Would you really make love to me as a mortal when I had no idea of what was going on, of what you were, of what I am?"

"That you can count on."

"And what if I resisted?"

He hunched his shoulders. "I doubt that you would. As you said, there is a bond between us that transcends everything else. You belong to me and if you put me in a place where you reside, you will be mine."

"The mortal Eve you can make love to with no problems. But your vampiric wife…. Now that's a different story." Suddenly anger flared in Eve's belly and she took the bowl with her potion and dumped it down the sink. She should have known this would happen. This was always the way things went with Adam, playfulness, lust, then anger.

Adam growled, aware of the same things as Eve. The playfulness was gone. "All of the blame for this debacle we call life is not my doing alone." He gave Eve a scathing glare, one meant to convey his own rising anger. The little witch didn't flinch, not when he growled, dropped fangs and not even when the red obscured his vision. She stood there as though she had not a care in the world. Adam growled again, knowing the truth of the situation. Eve had nothing to fear from him at the moment. With a sigh of long frustration, he continued. "There are many things that have happened between us. You have divided loyalties. Sullivan has been able to accept that but I can not. I have decided that I will make love to you, vampire or not, but not until you know whose bed you truly want to share."

"Spare Sullivan and Dr. Meah."

"As a condition? I don't think so, Eve. That's not how it will work. I took you from Sullivan's home physically. But you must make the decision to come back to me fully."

"You're aware that I have to talk to Sullivan. After all of this time, all that he's meant…all that he means to me, I have to see him. I will not just go from his bed to yours."

"Even if you would, I wouldn't want you." He crooked a finger and brought her to him. Then he trailed his lips across her flesh, taking in deep breaths. "You still have his scent on you."

In spite of knowing Adam was lying, Eve turned her head to the side and sniffed her body. "Liar," she accused.

Adam took in another breath. "Perhaps, but perhaps not. If I deem it so in my mind, then it is so." He stroked Eve's shoulders, moving to her hips with slow, deliberate motions. With the power of his mind he touched her intimately, watching as her eyes glazed over and a soft sound came from her lips. His hands moved of their own accord to stroke her back and the tips of his fingers took each shudder into itself and sent her another in return. Abruptly Adam pulled away mentally and physically. "I miss the mortal, unsullied mortal Eve," he whispered. "I think I would relish a chance to see her again."

"You're really serious, aren't you?" Eve asked, unable to keep the astonishment from her voice. She'd thought Adam was merely teasing.

"Yes."

"And you're going to allow me to try out my spells on you?"

"Hell, I'll help you. I want to go back for a day or two." Adam looked sideways at her. "But I want you to bring me back. Three days' time and I will not do anything that you might regret." He laughed softly. "Leave me there longer than that and I will do whatever I choose." He stuck out a hand. "That's the deal, take it or leave it."

For a half second Adam wondered if Eve would accept his offer. When her hand eased into his, he brought her close, tasting her lips with the tip of his tongue before plunging in and kissing her.

Ending the kiss, Adam cupped her chin. "Don't think I don't know why you want me gone. You're hoping the longer I'm gone from Sullivan that I'll change my mind about his eventual fate."

Eve studied her husband, wishing that things had been different. Had Adam not been so intent on ruling her, turning her and then abandoning her, they would not now be having this conversation. But he had done all of those things. And Sullivan? Sullivan had killed Mark in order for her to live. Eve didn't know what to do with two powerful and overprotective beings who loved her equally. She suddenly realized that Adam was watching her with a curious look on his face. She'd waited too long to answer him.

"Is that hesitation I sense on your part?" Adam asked.

"No, I was just thinking of something else. Don't worry, it's not important at the moment. But in answer to what you said, I'm also aware that you have ulterior motives. Don't think I don't know why you're willing to help me. You're a long way from being innocent, Adam. But I'm going to take your deal in spite of what may happen. Hopefully you'll use a bit of discretion and not do anything that I wouldn't want."

"Trust me, Eve. The things I plan to do, you will want." Adam laughed and produced two glasses, then a bottle of elderflower wine. "This is the drink of many witches," he said, and toasted Eve, curious to see if now given a free rein she'd do what she'd claimed she could. A trip to the past might not be a bad thing, he mused, not when he knew what he would find.

Chapter Five

The energy from the massive crystals resonated to the beat of Eve's heart. Placing her hand over her chest she felt for it, wondering at all the movies she'd seen and books she'd read of mystical beings such as she. All the things she'd heard were not true. Her heart still beat, perhaps a tad slower, but it still beat. She had a reflection, as evidenced by every mirror in her home. Since she'd learned to ingest food and drink, the only real difference was the agonizing, painful craving for blood. It was not something that her body could ignore. She'd tried. And regardless of how it was taken in, the truth was that vampires needed exorbitant amounts of blood.

Sighing, Eve licked her parched lips. She'd been trying to stave off the inevitable. Finally having convinced Adam that she had to talk to Sullivan face to face, he'd relented. She'd even secured a promise that he would not follow her nor would he monitor her conversation. But as she sat in Sullivan's home with him staring at her, feeling as though she'd betrayed him yet again by leaving with Adam she'd been unable to speak of nothing but the most mundane things. She'd wanted to tell him of her plan to send Adam away and of his agreeing to it. Sullivan's eyes were on her as he waited patiently. She knew he was aware of what was coming; perhaps that was why he didn't speak, anything to prolong what was to come.

For a long moment Eve studied Sullivan. Now was not the time for them to speak of her magic. Now was the time to speak of betrayal. He loved her, that much she knew, just as she knew she was loved by Adam.

She closed her eyes, admitting the truth that beat within her breast. She was glad to be alive, to have the sensation of Adam's blood running through her veins. He'd always be a part of her life; she knew that. She swallowed as she opened her eyes and at last went into Sullivan's arms.

"Thank you for loving me," she began, "And thank you for the vacation." Eve shook her head slowly. "I guess if I'm going to be honest I'll also have to thank you for calling Adam." She brought her gaze upwards to meet his. "I want to live," she whispered. "What does that make me?"

A deep shudder of regret traveled through Sullivan's body at Eve's words. The pain in her voice was deepened by the unshed tears. Sullivan had known from the moment he'd chosen to ask Adam to save her life that it would be over for them. He didn't want it to be. Hundreds of years of loneliness had made him yearn for the things Eve had brought into his life. In the back of his mind he'd held on to the hope that he would kick her husband's ass good and proper and take her from him forever.

Foolish dream.

Foolish man.

He was an old fool who would have done well to follow his own advice: No long term commitments.

"Can't you forgive me?" Sullivan asked, trailing a finger through her hair, pressing her closer, dropping kisses on the crown of her head. "Can't you remain with me?" He felt the snort of derision and held her tighter.

"You're going to remain in Adam's home, aren't you?"

"It's my home. I have nowhere else to go for the moment."

"That's a lie and we're both aware of it."

A rustling of feet and Eve glanced behind her. "Dr. Meah, I'll do what I can to protect you. I'm working on a potion, a spell to really send Adam into the past. Don't look so worried," she laughed. "Adam is helping me with the potion. He wants to go back. I think he'll find the mortal Eve more to his liking."

"You're trying to send Adam back into the past? Are you crazy? Don't you realize that Adam with knowledge of the future will definitely change the past? I'm betting he'll add a few more kills to the list. The only one who'll probably make it out of this mess alive will be you, Eve," Dr. Meah said, then shook his head as though to say the entire plan was foolishness.

"Adam only wants to go back a few years." Eve glanced at Sullivan, remembering Adam wanted her before he'd turned her.

"I think it's dangerous to even be trying for such a spell," Dr. Meah spoke again.

"Sorry you feel that way, Doctor, but it's not just for Adam that I'm doing this. If it works perhaps I can send you to a time before you met Adam."

"That would be hundreds of years and frankly, Eve, I don't have much faith in your being able to do any of this. You've already proven that you're foolhardy and reckless. You're not a scientist. You do things willy nilly, not worrying about the consequences. Even now you talk of time travel as though it's child's play. I can see why you annoy Adam. He's right, you're a vampire and you make him look the fool when you play at being a witch."

Tears came to her eyes unexpectedly. She'd never known the doctor to speak so harshly but of course being forced to drink all of her tainted blood could have had an effect on him. "Are you angry with me, Doctor?"

"Yes, Eve, I'm angry with you. You're playing a very dangerous game, one that I already know will have dire consequences for Sullivan and myself. And who knows, maybe the rest of the world. Chose one: vampire or witch. You can't be both."

"That's too bad, because I am both. I am coming into my own. I know that from the beginning of time the power of nature has resided with my family, male and female alike. I am no longer running from that knowledge. I'm embracing it. As for my being a vampire, that was something thrust upon me. I had neither a decision about it nor control over it." Eve lifted her chin. "Besides, I didn't come here to fight. I came to have a private conversation with Sullivan."

"You sought Sullivan out, yet you didn't think you needed to also have a conversation with me. I risked my life for over two years to help you. I lived under constant threats from Sullivan that nothing had better go wrong with any of our experiments. Yes, he knew," Dr. Meah said disgustedly, glaring at Sullivan. "You both had me so busy keeping secrets that it took away from my work. I lived with the constant worry that Adam would find out what I was helping you do and put an end to it and to me. Don't you think I agonized over whether I'd caused your condition, that maybe if I'd found out about your taking the crystal potion and the adverse effect it was having on you I could have saved you. Every moment since it happened I've been plagued by the thoughts, the what ifs… just one day sooner, would it have made a difference? Could I have done one thing differently…?" He stopped and sucked in the rest of his words. Both Eve and Sullivan were staring at him so he dropped his eyes. He'd never wanted Eve to know he loved her. When he lifted his head, her gaze connected with his and he knew his secret was safe no longer.

"I was worried about you, Eve. The least you could have done was let me know that you were well. When Adam spirited you away, it had only been a matter of hours since being revived from near death. I was worried about you from a medical standpoint. That's all it was."

"Dr. Meah, forgive me," Eve said softly, walking toward him and wrapping her arms around him. "You're right. You've been such a good friend to me. I love you for that. You are and always will be my friend. You are one of the few that I love without reservation." She held him tighter. "I truly, truly thank you, my friend." She held on to him until he gently put her away. She noticed the glassy look in his eyes and smiled while giving his hand a squeeze.

"Are you okay, no ill effects? What about Adam? Is he dealing with you harshly?"

There was so much behind his words and she knew without invading his mind all that he'd left unsaid. Eve smiled at Dr. Meah. "I'm okay. To be honest, I think Adam has done nothing because he's unsure if he'll need your help should I collapse." She laughed, caught herself and ceased. "That was in bad taste. I'm sorry. Adam has been so calm, so agreeable." She hesitated at the look that passed between Sullivan and Dr. Meah. "I know what you're thinking, you don't have to tell me. A calm Adam is a very dangerous Adam."

"I think that is the one thing we can all agree on," Sullivan said, finally getting into the conversation.

Shrugging her shoulders, Eve looked at both of the vampires as sadness for the problems she'd brought into their lives nearly destroyed her. "I'm sorry for the mess I've gotten you into," she said to the doctor." She glanced at Sullivan, hoping he'd heed the message in her eyes, that she wouldn't be the one to have to ask the doctor to leave, not after what had just happened. He gave a slight nod, alerting her that he'd received her request.

"Doctor, there are things Eve and I need to say to each other. I also have been worried about her. Do you think you can give us some privacy?"

Eve stared at the doctor, a bit surprised that he'd bristled at Sullivan's request.

"You don't really think wherever you send Adam that he will not return, do you?" Dr. Meah was ignoring Sullivan, concentrating only on Eve, bringing the conversation back to Eve's plans.

Eve held Dr. Meah's gaze. "With Adam one never knows. He may be the most powerful vampire around but he's not a witch and he can't counteract my magical spells without magic." She grinned. "The great Adam having to rely on a trick that his wife can perform? He'd rather die."

"But still…"

"I know, Doctor. Eternity is a long time and eventually Adam will return and we'll deal with it then."

"But what if you only send him a day back in time?"

"That will not be the incantation."

"Eve, you thought it would work the first time you tried. Look what happened. He came back. What is making you so certain now that it will work? As Adam said, I do not believe you can do this and even if you did, none of us, not even you, have any reasons to feel safe. We all know that Adam is like no other vampire ever made. He always finds a way around things. He does the impossible. That's why he's in charge. That's why he's Adam Omega. You could do this thing and the moment we feel safe, at that precise instant Adam could pop back here."

There was reason to be worried. Eve didn't have the answers. No, she'd never tried the spell she was working on. And no, the previous spell had not worked. But that was because as Adam had said she could not "hex" him, as he put it, without his consent. Now, however, she had his permission. She wasn't as much of a novice as the doctor and Sullivan seemed to think. She was aware that wherever she sent Adam he would be pissed the moment he realized she had no way and no plan to return him to the present. But she had to try this. What other choice did she have? It wasn't just for Sullivan and Dr. Meah that she wanted to try this. It was for herself as well. Despite her being his weakness Adam would not hesitate to try and bend her to his will. As long as there were other means, Eve had no intention of drinking from humans. The second Adam became aware of that, plus the fact that she had no intention of bringing him back, there would be hell to pay. That was the only thing she was sure of.

"I don't know if Adam will come back in a moment or a day or when." She shrugged. "I just want him gone. I'm tried of him bullying all of us and I want to do something about it. But this time Adam can only blame me for doing this. Neither of you will be involved. He shouldn't take out his displeasure on you."

A look crossed the doctor's face and he vanished. Eve sat down, taking a good look around at the place she'd called home for many months now. "I'm going to miss being here, Sullivan," she said. "I'm going to miss sleeping in your bed, lying in your arms, making love to you. And I'm going to miss your loving me."

"You don't have to miss those things. I will always love you," Sullivan said, bringing her into his arms and holding her tightly, whispering words of love into her ear, kissing her, touching her. He didn't know how he would continue without her in his life, in his bed. "Please," he pleaded. She placed a finger over his lips.

"Kiss me, Sullivan, and make it a good one."

"You mean?"

"Yes." She turned her neck to his lips and winced slightly as she felt the sharp bite, then moaned as Sullivan's love filled her. It was over.

When he was done Sullivan tenderly kissed the spot his fangs had pierced before sealing the mark. He sighed in sadness as he moved for her to feed from him. He watched the tears sparkle in her eyes and swallowed his disappointment while Eve caressed his carotid artery. She allowed her fangs to lower and bit gently into him, taking his blood, sending him her love. He held on to Eve, not wanting to let her go. The knowledge that she loved him did nothing for the hole in his heart.

"Eve, please," Sullivan moaned as she gave him images, along with her love. For a moment he wondered how he'd feel now if he'd just allowed her to die. Worse. He felt her arms tightening around him. Alive he stood a chance of regaining her respect, her love. It would be a battle, he knew that much. But it was one he intended to fight. Eve had never drunk from a victim, never killed, with the exception of the vampires who would have killed her and Adam, and that was why she couldn't fathom that he'd killed for her. As crazy as it was, the truth of it was that Eve didn't think it was as wrong to kill a vampire as it was to kill a mortal.

"Do you think in the future you might forgive me enough to give it another try?"

"I've learned that one should never say never. You won't believe this, but Adam said I'm judging you and that I'm wrong to do so. He said I had no right to judge you, that you did what you had to do. He actually admires you for it."

"Even though it's not Adam's admiration that I seek, he's right in why I did what I did. You want me to tell you that I regret it." He gave her a sharp look. "That's not going to happen. I'd do it again and again if the choice was your life. That I will not barter with. All of this would be easier if you told me I wasn't wrong about us, that you love me as I love you."

"I do love you, Sullivan. If you think this isn't breaking my heart, please think again. I do not want to go on even another day without you. You have been the only constant in my life, the only good…" She winced. "You will never truly be out of my life, that much I know. I just need a little time. If I'm going to live as many years as you and Adam, then who knows? For now, I can't help but think of Mark. I wanted him to have a life and you knew that." She shrugged. "Adam wouldn't have cared about my feelings. Besides, he didn't like Mark."

"Neither did I."

Eve couldn't help but give him a smile. "I know that. But you loved me and therefore you didn't do anything to harm Mark." She dropped her gaze from his and sighed heavily. "At least until you killed him. Of all the things that have happened and the things I regret, I regret that the most." She folded herself into Sullivan's arms. She'd not said what she had to make him hurt. She'd merely spoken the truth.

"You forgave Adam for turning you but you can't forgive me for finding a way to save you, for wanting us to remain as we were. We were happy, Eve. You love me and I love you."

"Sullivan, it's not that I can't forgive you. It's the knowing that you're not really any different than Adam. I need my old Sullivan. I need someone different from Adam."

"We can be happy again," Sullivan whispered into her ear as he allowed his fangs to sink slowly into her flesh again. The taste of her blood in his mouth made him shiver with wanting her. She didn't answer him. He knew there was nothing more to say.

Chapter Six

The air practically crackled with electrical energy. Adam stared at his wife, mesmerized by her joy. Eve's face was animated and happy, her voice seductive and sweet as she called out to him. For days they'd tried one spell after the other with Adam leaving himself completely open. Hell, he was even assisting her in her endeavors.

Two days of a nonstop shopping binge and Adam's home once again looked more like it belonged to a witch than to a powerful vampire. With only a little coaxing on her part, Adam had retrieved Eve's humongous crystals from Sullivan's home, giving him a cat eating grin during the process. His presence had not been needed to transfer the crystals; he could have simply snapped his fingers and moved them. But what the heck, he wanted to gloat and so he had.

He smiled in amusement as the crystals were once again placed in a circle of protection around his home. He ignored the obvious altars Eve had erected. '*Blasphemy*', he'd told her and he meant it. As he watched her, he remembered their prior conversation about using a pentagram for her protective circle. "Eve," he'd said, "I will not have that symbol in my home. How many times do I have to tell you that?"

She'd come back with, "But it's my home also, Adam. Besides, you know nothing about the symbol. Try and educate yourself first and stop dealing with this as though you're from the Dark Ages. Excuse me, Eve had added. "You really are from the Dark Ages, aren't you?"

Adam frowned. "You're getting to be more and more annoying each day. I don't know if continuously saving your life is worth the bother." That had shut Eve up for less than a nanosecond.

"As I was saying," Eve began, "there is a lot of confusion that surrounds the pentacle and the pentagram. They're simply symbols of faith, much like your cross that you still wear." She flicked at the cross on Adam's chest and ignored his frown.

"Neither of these are symbols of evil, Adam. They actually serve as protection against evil. The difference between the two is slight. A pentacle is a five pointed star, the same as a pentagram. However the pentacle is used for containment of energy whereas the pentagram is used strictly for protection."

"I still don't like it," Adam hissed.

"You're biased."

"I care not for what you call me. I still don't like it. Besides that, if you'd learn to expand your mind and believe the things I tell you, you'd have no need of any such symbols. Your will would be your protection."

"And why then do you wear a cross?"

"Because I'm Adam Omega."

"There's no other reason? Come on, Adam. I know there's more."

"Because others think I can't and more importantly, that I shouldn't, so I do." He laughed. "Is that your reason for the circle, to irritate me?"

"Partly," Eve said. "The other part is because I like it. It's a symbol I've long feared. Now I'm trying to learn to embrace the real meaning instead of the false meaning."

"I still say it's sacrilegious."

Eve nodded as though she were entertaining his words. Then she stared at him and simply said, "Judge not."

Yes, she'd learned how to appease him. It seemed she used those words for whatever objection he might have. He was left with little choice now but to refer to her pentagram symbol as her circle of protection, smile and walk away. He watched her until at last she turned to him, a smile on her lips, which made his own lips quiver with wanting her. He knew he'd kiss her within a matter of moments.

"Adam, I have it. Are you sure you're ready?"

"Do you have the means to return me to this time?"

"Of course."

She was lying, of that he was sure, but no matter, he didn't believe she could send him into the past and even if she did and didn't return him, he'd find his own way back home. He was not without his own devices. He gave his wife a look and a smile, wanting it to work for her. Being a witch seemed to have made her forget about Sullivan for the time being and that was a welcome reprieve. "Go ahead, Eve, show me what you've got." He noticed her slight irritation. "What?" he asked.

"You're speaking to me as though I'm a backward child. You don't think this will work. Well, I do. So, if I were you, I'd take a good look around and say goodbye. Ready?" she asked.

"As ready as I'll ever be. Now get on with it. I have many things to attend to later." He'd barely gotten the words out before Eve smiled and began chanting.

> "By incense, smoke and candle flames
> Away from me I send all bane,
> By cleansing water and power of salt
> Let any harm come to naught."

Adam smiled as Eve lit incense and candles of varying colors, poured water into a bowl and sprinkled salt around her circle. *Another spell that's not going to work*, he thought. He started to interrupt when he noticed her glaring. Sighing, he decided to wait until she'd finished.

> "Send Adam Omega away from me, to a time
> And place before I ever looked upon his face."

Then Eve stopped and smiled. And Adam's blood ran cold. He thought to stop her, but her look was one of pure contrariness. She was daring him. He'd take her dare. There was nothing that she could do to him. He held his ground and listened to the rest of her incantation even though an icy breeze warned him of duplicity in her plans for him.

> "Protect by thunder by oak and thorn.
> Bind Adam from doing harm.
> His power to kill I lock within this charm
> By air, by fire, by land and sea, lead this harm
> Away from me. Let no one on this earthly
> Realm fear the harm from Adam Omega again.
> Bind him now as I command, lead him now
> From my sight. Take Adam into the light."

Bind? What the hell? "Wait, Eve," Adam shouted as he heard the word '*bind*.' "That was not our deal."

Too late, he realized when he felt himself being sucked into a whirlwind. Surprise claimed Adam's thoughts and a smile crossed his lips.

So, Eve was learning. She'd found a way to send him away. When at last the spinning stopped and his equilibrium returned, he looked around trying to get his bearing. This wasn't Sullivan's home nor was it his. Okay, he'd made a deal with the little witch. He'd told her he'd give her three days and he would. Until that time he'd be on his best behavior, visit some old haunts, make a little mischief perhaps. There was no way he believed Eve had sent him back in time. Away, perhaps, but not back in time, but he'd allow her to think it. It would be interesting to see what she would do, if she would run to Sullivan's home the moment he was out of sight. He was of a mind to just pop in on the two of them. *No*, he thought, let her think she really has that kind of power over me. Let her believe. Who knows, one day perhaps she'll be able to do it. He didn't know what the whirlwind was about but he was pretty sure he hadn't time traveled. His part in this little experiment was to see if he could yet trust his wife. She had three days to earn it.

***

For an hour Eve waited for signs that Adam would return. When her waiting turned into a day, she smiled in triumph. The deed was done. Dr. Meah was safe. Sullivan was safe and so was she. Inhaling the breath of freedom, she called out to Sullivan and went to his home.

Surprise wove an intricate pattern across Sullivan's face. "Call Dr. Meah," she said urgently. "I have news for the two of you." She could barely contain herself the excitement was so great. When she was done they both looked at her.

"Are you sure it's not like last time? Are you positive you sent Adam away?" Dr. Meah asked.

Dr. Meah's question Eve could understand, but it was the look of chastisement coming from Sullivan that she found difficult to deal with.

"Eve, you should not have sent Adam away without his powers."

"I didn't take his powers completely," she said, "just his ability to kill."

Disturbed glances passed between Sullivan and the doctor. Their worried gazes frightened her. "I thought the two of you would be pleased. I don't understand why you're not. He's stuck wherever I sent him. He doesn't know how to get back and I don't know how to bring him back even if I wanted to." She laughed until she saw their worries intensifying. Panic began to well up in her. "What is it, what's wrong?"

"A powerful vampire. Strike that. Adam Omega in a time and place without his full powers is not a good thing. He has more enemies besides myself. Real enemies," Sullivan said. "Ones who have no memories of a time of friendship."

"You hate Adam but you're talking as though I shouldn't have done it, as though you're worried for him." Again a look passed between the vampires and a shiver of fear make her wince. "Are you saying I shouldn't have done it?"

"That's exactly what I'm saying," Sullivan answered her somberly. "You shouldn't have done it."

***

With a shake of his head Adam couldn't believe his gullibility. Almost a week had passed and if he were to be completely honest with himself, he'd not much worried about it. He lived his life in what he preferred to think of as 'pre-Eve' fashion. He'd carried on his business, wary of being pulled back through a vacuum when Eve returned him. After six days he'd known that wasn't going to happen. *So where are you, my love?* He called out to Eve and she didn't answer. *Damn that woman,* he thought. Damn him for putting his heart yet again into her hands. He'd given her the terms of the agreement. She was the one who'd broken it, not he. He'd resisted all urgings to go and visit the library to see if perhaps the mortal Eve was there. But it was silliness. Eve could not send him back in time. So he'd stood firm to his word, not even giving in to the temptation to find out exactly what had happened and where Eve had sent him. With a snort Adam realized he didn't know for sure that he hadn't actually traveled back in time. He hadn't bothered to check. Now it was time he did. Again he wondered, *Where are you, Eve? If you really wanted to protect Sullivan you should have sent him away instead. But unlike you, I did keep my word.*

And because he'd kept his word, Sullivan yet lived. It was high time he paid the vampire a visit. He had no doubt that he'd find Eve with him.

Anger at himself and Eve traveled with him as he transported himself to Sullivan's home, intending to do what he should have done the moment the vampire had called him. Forget mercy or the games he'd thought to play. He would just snap Sullivan's neck, sever his head and have it over and done with. He'd dreamt of it so many times, why not do it now?

"Uriel!" Adam blinked "Uriel?" he repeated as the vampire turned toward him.

"Hello, Adam."

"Hello Adam? Why are you here…how are you here? Where's Sullivan?"

"Adam, I didn't know you were coming. Do you think you might give me the respect of requesting admittance?" Sullivan spoke in his quiet way.

Adam strode through the rooms of Sullivan's home looking for Eve. "Where is she?" He turned on Sullivan, grabbing him by the throat. "Where the hell is my wife?"

"Your wife?"

Sullivan tilted his head to peer sharply at Adam. "You have no wife, at least none that I know of and if you did why would I know where she is?"

There was something wrong, more wrong than the fact that Uriel, the little weasel he'd killed more than three years before was still alive and plotting to take over Adam's kingdom. The memory of Uriel biting into his flesh rose sharply, as did the anger at the vampire for hitting Eve. Adam strode forward, glared at Uriel and said, "I've already killed you once but what the hell, I'll find pleasure in doing it again." He raised his hand and leveled it at the vampire, but nothing happened, no energy volts, nothing. He narrowed his eyes to turn Uriel into ash but couldn't make it happen. *What the hell*? Adam growled, stalking over to where Uriel stood, snatching him by the collar and putting his hands around his throat. He would choke the life from him. "Die, you maggot, die," Adam snarled but his fingers refused to crush the windpipe of his enemy. Adam threw the vampire from him, only to have him promptly disappear. He had to think. It had to be something in the spell Eve had used. He growled at his missed opportunity to kill Uriel yet again. The little weasel was gone. No matter, he'd bring him back and then kill him. He glanced in Sullivan's direction. "You're next," he said softly, then laughed.

"What are you talking about? You haven't killed Uriel. What's wrong with you, Adam? Have you truly gone mad?"

"One last chance. Where is Eve?" He brought Sullivan to him and prepared to sink his fangs into the vamp's flesh. "Stop struggling," he said as he bit into him. Something was wrong. Sullivan had no knowledge of Eve. Adam bit down harder, refusing to believe what was happening.

Damn that woman and her crystals. He wondered what she'd done to make him time shift and how far in the past she'd sent him. She'd succeeded, he thought with sudden clarity. *Bravo, Eve*. He'd known he'd been right in learning all that Eve knew. Finally Adam released Sullivan. It was no use trying to force the man to tell him what he did not know. He chuckled and sat in a chair to figure out his next move. Once more he glanced at the vampire who would be him if only he had the nerve. Sullivan had paled even more, his blue eyes wary and filled with alarm.

If he did as he ought to and killed the vampire here and now, he'd not have to worry about him falling in love with his wife. He thought of all the things that had brought him and Eve to their latest moment together. Could he change the future if he fiddled around with the past? Would it work for good or evil and did he care? Adam laughed, not sure yet of his answer.

"Adam, I do not appreciate your barging in here and threatening either Uriel or myself. Neither of us has any idea what the hell you're talking about." Sullivan flicked his fingers, pulled a handkerchief from the air and wiped the crusting blood from his neck. He coughed loudly and sat down as far away from Adam as he could get. Taking his cigarettes from his pocket he lit one as he held it between his fingers and inhaled the smoke from the Turkish tobacco.

"Why don't you just put the damn thing in your mouth and smoke it like a normal person instead of holding it and wishing. Just smoke the damn things?" Adam roared.

"It's a nasty habit," Sullivan replied, "but I love the smell of good Turkish tobacco and I like knowing that unlike some vampires, I can control myself. I don't have to have everything that I think I might want."

This was the Sullivan that he knew and almost enjoyed parrying with. This Sullivan lacked any real courage, but despite that defect he was always trying to find ways to overthrow Adam. This Sullivan hadn't spent two years making love to Eve. This Sullivan wouldn't risk Adam's wrath to save her.

With a smirk Adam shook his head. "Why, Sullivan, I do believe you're speaking of me. Why shouldn't I warn that little weasel that you're going to get him killed? You are, you know." Adam smiled as Sullivan blanched.

"I have no idea what you're referring to."

"You lie," Adam smiled. "And not very well. I have some advice for you should you ever meet a woman named Eve. Run as far away as you can. I can make you a promise. She will be your undoing and the death of you. Do not plot against me with her. You will not succeed."

With those words Adam disappeared into vapor. Now to find out what year it was. It would have been an easy thing to find out from Sullivan, but Adam wasn't ready for the vampire to know things were different. His next stop was the local newsstand. Laughing, he looked at the date, snapping his finger and bringing a calendar to double check. Adam rubbed at the light stubble on his chin. He laughed again as a sense of pride stole over him. Eve's incantation had worked. She'd sent him back to before he'd met her, a little over four years in the past. Too bad she didn't think to send him back to before she was born. Now he knew exactly where to find his wife.

A look upward at the sun told him it was midday. Where else would the mortal Eve be besides at the mundane job she'd held before he'd come into her life. Without preamble Adam appeared at the Fountaindale Library and walked up to the counter, grabbed Eve's hand and watched as she looked into his eyes. He saw the fear as she frowned in confusion. The amber ring was burning like blue blazes.

"Do I know you," Eve asked.

"Yes, I'm Adam Omega, your husband."

Eve pulled her hands from Adam's grasp. "What are you talking about? I'm not married."

He laughed. "You're a lot more than married but that's all that you need to know for now. Tell me something, Eve," he said, taking her hand again and fingering her nametag as though that was the reason he knew her name. "Can't you sense who and what I am?"

"What do you want?"

Adam smiled slowly, lazily caressing her face with the pad of a finger. His gaze held hers. "Isn't it obvious?" He exerted slight control over her and leaned in and kissed her lips. He moaned in ecstasy as the smell of lemons tantalized his senses. Maybe being sent back in time wasn't a bad thing after all. Maybe he'd stay wherever the hell Eve had sent him and enjoy making love to the mortal Eve.

"Eve, I know all there is to know about you. I know of your lifelong dreams, of your belief that evil is chasing you. I know that you're semi-engaged to a little weasel named Eric, who doesn't love you by the way. Then again, you don't love him either, so none of what I'm telling you should be cause for distress. I've come from the future, Eve, not many years, just a few."

He was going too fast in his explanation for her to understand. He shook his head. "Excuse me, you're having trouble keeping up. I forgot you're experiencing things on a different level than I am."

"Sir, whoever you are I want you to leave or I'm calling the police."

"Go ahead and call them, Eve. Do I look afraid?" Her bottom lip trembled and he saw her reaching for a book, a weapon. Same old Eve, he thought. She was always more combative than she should be, plain contrary, he thought. He had no plans to waste time with niceties. No, he was going to tell her who he was and take it from there.

Adam frowned, trying to think of something concrete that might convince Eve quicker than his words. He laughed as he remembered the last parking ticket he'd received on his little vampire mobile as Eve was wont to call the car, simply because he'd chosen to hang a plastic vampire from the rearview mirror. He'd barely noticed the paper at the time, just shoved it into his wallet. Now he beamed at the yellow paper.

"What's today's date?" he asked her, releasing her from the trance, laughing when she hesitated, then told him. He snapped his fingers, producing the parking ticket and handing it over to her. "Look at the date, Eve."

He watched as she did. He was surprised when she didn't seem overly impressed.

"This doesn't prove anything. Now please leave sir. Amy..." She paused, then for some reason stopped.

"Why didn't you call for your friend?"

Eve stared into the man's eyes, feeling faint. She held to the desk. Never in her life had she felt such emotions. The powers emanating from the man before her were real. She felt an attraction to him that defied explanation. And she felt a lust so powerful that she wanted to rip her clothes from her body and strip him naked without regard for the people milling about. There was something strange going on here, a connection to a stranger that felt as natural as breathing. But the nonsense he was spouting couldn't be real. Still, how would he know her secret fears? "Who are you?"

"Didn't I already tell you that? Why don't you ask what you want to ask? Yes, Eve, I can read your mind." Adam chuckled slightly. "And I can read your body. You find yourself attracted to me and can't figure it out. You fear this attraction but you want it or you would have screamed for help by now. By the way, that book you're planning to hit me with... I would advise that you don't do it. I don't like being hit."

"I don't like strangers talking to me in such an intimate manner, as though they know me." She turned to walk away from the desk and moved toward the door leading to the storage area. She blinked when she saw

Adam standing there. She twisted her head to look behind her, where she'd left him standing. "How did you...what are you?" she finally asked.

"I'm a vampire."

"There's no such thing."

"Oh, but there is. There are more things that you have convinced yourself don't exist. But darling I'm here to tell you that they do. Your little world is not all there is, Eve. There are vampires, werewolves, fairies, all manner of shapeshifters and more. And there are witches. Did you know that you're a witch?" he asked. "Well, you are. You have great powers."

Adam entered her mind easily, amazed at the swiftness of her thoughts, the connection of dots she was doing. She knew but didn't want to believe. He'd made an instant decision not to tell her she was also a vampire. What he needed from her now was not her vampiric powers but her ancient powers of magic. Adam moved closer to Eve, too much he realized as her body trembled. She was on the verge of screaming. Take it down a notch, he ordered himself, give her something she can accept for the moment. He walked away from her, back to the counter, and felt the sigh of relief in her body. She was feeling more in control now. *Good*, he wanted her to feel that. "How do you feel about magicians, Eve?"

What...what..."

"Magicians." He paused and narrowed his eyes at her. She hadn't seemed this dimwitted when he'd first met her. "Must I explain something so simple to you? You work in a library, you're not a child. Surely you know what a magician is."

"You arrogant—" Eve brushed past Adam to help some customers. *What a jerk!* An arrogant, know it all jerk who knew more about her than anyone in her life. If it were not for that fact, she would have dismissed him two seconds after meeting him. Forget the attraction, the feeling that she knew him, the instant lust, the craving and the clenching of her muscles at the thought of making love to him. There was something going on, something wrong, and she didn't like it. There was another emotion the man evoked, anger. She wanted to hurt him and hurt him bad. She'd never raised her hands in anger to another human but for some unexplained reason she wanted to hit him with something really heavy, then hit him again.

"Excuse me. I wasn't done talking with you. Do not ever walk away from me again." Adam looked at the man Eve was assisting, staring coldly at him before deciding to speak. "Go! Find another librarian to help you. She's busy." He then turned to Eve and smiled. "Now, as I was saying—"

"Leave me alone, Adam. As you said, I'm busy," Eve interrupted him. She shook her head. "Jerk," she murmured and walked away, leaving Adam standing there staring after her.

Okay, so she wasn't going to be as easy to handle as he'd thought. She should be thanking him for rescuing her from her ordinary job and from the hiding she'd been doing for years in the pews of many churches. Look how little that had accomplished. She'd told him once that she'd ran from evil. He begged to differ. She'd cowered from it in churches on her knees in prayer. Look how little good it had done for her to run from him. He'd found her anyway.

Anger seeped into Adam's pores with the acknowledgement that he needed the knowledge the mortal Eve possessed in order to return to his time and deal with his wife for having the audacity to send him way in the first place. But to tamper with his powers, to take away his ability to kill it would seem, was unconscionable. Then again he'd only tried to kill Uriel. Perhaps he'd have to test the theory with others who needed killing. *And what if she really took away my power to kill?* Adam wondered. No matter he was Adam Omega and he would be fine.

He could feel the purple of his eyes being obliterated by the red and calmed himself. This mortal woman was not his wife really, not yet. He'd need to go easy on her. He sighed. There had to be an easier way to find his way home, one that didn't require Eve's help. Without the least bit of effort he stood in front of Eve, amazed at how well she covered her surprise that she'd left him behind her for a second time and he now stood directly in front of her again. He'd have to give her credit, even though the pulse at the base of her throat jumped with the adrenaline boost and her scattered thoughts revealed she was praying hard.

"Your prayers have been answered, Eve. I'm here to save you." The color drained from her face and he had to touch her to keep her from falling away in a faint. "I'm here to help you remember who you truly are. You're a witch, Eve, a very brave and powerful witch. And you're my wife. I need your help."

"I'm not a witch. I can't help you. I don't believe in witchcraft."

"That's just plain nonsense. You remember. I scanned your mind and the knowledge is there, buried rather deeply, I might add, but I do plan to get the knowledge out of you by any means necessary." He shrugged. "Your being cooperative would shorten it. I don't really have the time or the inclination to linger here longer than necessary."

He reached out a hand and cupped her chin, holding her in place and glaring at any that dared to look in their direction. "I could put you in a trance and force you to do my bidding, but that's so cliché. Besides, the thing of it is you haven't yet learned the information that I need. So you can see your willingness to learn is more expedient. I'll help with that but you have to start studying."

"Studying witchcraft? Are you crazy?"

"Not yet but if I have to keep repeating myself I might very well find myself on the brink of insanity. You're annoying me, Eve, and I find I must take my leave of you. There is just one thing I want you to think about and that's how you plan to help me." He waved a finger in front of her face at the look of disbelief and fear that filled her eyes.

"Don't worry, Eve, you will not go to hell for using your gifts." He vanished, laughing loudly, knowing that he'd scared the hell out of Eve and anyone else that had seen him. By nightfall they would have convinced themselves it was all their imagination.

The world was a different place it seemed, one he liked perhaps a bit better. Almost hysterical laughter caused Adam to cough several times before he got it under control. How evil would it be if he seduced the mortal Eve now and made love to her? Quite, he reasoned, but what fun it would be. He wondered if there would be a way for the vampiric Eve to know he was touching her in the past, before she was turned. That would make it more fun, more of a challenge. Then a thought came to him.

Surely if Eve was in possession of such magic there must be others that had it.

His thoughts went immediately to the psychic who'd helped Eve, the same one who'd been serving him now for many months. Adam reached into his pocket and pulled out the bag of stones he'd gotten from Lora, stones meant to counteract Eve's magic. He was going to have to have another talk with the psychic. She'd failed to inform him that Eve had the ability to control time travel.

Adam sighed deeply. Perhaps the psychic hadn't known. He himself hadn't known. Still, Eve couldn't be the only one with such knowledge. He wondered if there was a way for him to get that information from the mortal Eve without breaking her, without using his powers. He'd have to perhaps erase his previous visit from her mind and start over.

The thought set his teeth on edge. The mortal Eve was proving to be too much work. If he started over with a clean slate and approached her with a bit more caution, she wouldn't be so guarded. The more Adam thought about it, the more he liked it. An innocent Eve, an Eve who wanted to save him, one who didn't know the things he would do to her or what she would become. He could invade her thoughts at will and allow her to open up to him.

As much as he liked putting one over on Eve, annoyance at the situation was pulling at him. Adam inhaled several times before releasing his frustration in a sigh. The same problem would exist no matter what he did. There was no way he could get around it. He had traveled to four years in the past and was dealing with a mortal who had not yet learned to embrace her powers. What good could she really be to him when she'd not yet found the knowledge he required? She'd been running from her abilities as well as from him. With clenched teeth his eyes rolled to the top of his head. It was time to pay Lora another visit.

Damn, he thought. *Why couldn't Eve have zapped me into the future?*

Chapter Seven

Fear rolled off the psychic in waves. If Adam were of a mind to, he could alleviate her fears by telling her he had no intention of harming her, that more than likely he couldn't, even if he wanted to. But he wasn't of a mind to. It never did any good for humans to think he was their friend, that he wouldn't do what he'd threatened. More than likely he wouldn't, but then again who knew. Given enough provocation he might.

Humans provided scant amusement for Adam. He liked frightening them on occasion but that was about the gist of it. He much preferred to do battle with other vampires, the bigger the better. He loved the feel of breaking their bones, seeing spurting blood, of severing their heads from their bodies, relieving them of their hearts and holding the hearts in front of them. As for mortals, they so far had no weapons with which to fight him. So for now they were relatively safe.

The mounting panic he sensed in the psychic was beginning to annoy him. "I do not believe you." Adam sat across from the psychic, his right leg crossed over his left. He flicked an imaginary bit of lint from the bottom of his black, silk trousers and glanced around the room. He noticed the number of crosses that adorned the woman's home, pictures of the Virgin Mary and other such things. He smiled, narrowing his eyes at her and waving a hand. "Has any of this ever worked for you?" he asked.

Terror caused the woman's heart to seize and Adam shook his head slightly and smiled coldly at her. "You will not die, old woman. I will see to that," he murmured softly, lowering his fangs just a bit, enough to frighten her. "You are needed in my plans."

"How can I tell you about your Eve when I do not know of her? I have no sense of the powers she might posses within her spirit."

This was becoming more than annoying; it was bordering on boredom. "How many times do I have to tell you that you will meet her in a couple of years?" He exhaled noisily. For a psychic she was rather dense. Or was there something else keeping her from helping him? Adam wondered. "Psychic, if you wish to live you will be cooperative," he snarled. "You will not attempt to hide anything from me. I can enter your mind at will. You will never be more than a breath away from me. You have me to thank for your life. Your gifts do nothing to guard against me. They didn't help Eve," he said.

"What is it you want me to do?" Lora asked in a voice filled with obvious resignation.

"That's much better. I want you to meet with Eve and I want you to prepare her for me." A chuckle had Adam shaking his head. "Of course I want you to tell her only of my better qualities. Tell her perhaps she's dreamt of me. It will be easy enough to make her believe my visit to her was but a dream." He noticed the way the psychic was staring at him.

"What?" he asked. "Do you think what I'm doing is unfair, evil perhaps?"

"If you use your knowledge of the future, even an hour, let alone four years, to change time or some event it could have dire consequences in the future."

"How would you know that? You have no idea how to travel either backwards or forward in time. You don't even believe it can be done. So, how do you know what will happen if events are rearranged here in this time?"

"I don't, Mr. Omega. I just got the oddest sensation, like a warning that what you are about to attempt could be dangerous. You could do something here that could rewrite history."

Adam thought about that for a moment and grinned. The idea of rewriting history appealed to him greatly. Perhaps he'd go back in time and kill that bitch, Tarasha, before she'd turned him. He felt Lora staring at him and stopped his thoughts. *One problem at a time,* he chided himself.

"Mr. Omega, I'm sorry to be so insistent but everything that's in me, is telling me to warn you of the dangers. You will need to be very careful."

"Being careful and worrying about '*what ifs*' is for mere mortals to lose sleep over. That's not my concern. Believe me, I plan to do a lot of things differently in this time period."

"You're looking to make this woman fall in love with you?"

"My wife. Eve is my wife and she already loves me."

"But not here…not in this reality."

"Lora, I'm being patient with you for one reason and one reason only. I have decided it is best not to force Eve. I want you to pave the way and make it smooth." What good would it do to tell the woman that his way had only made Eve get her hackles up? Who knew what he'd have to do to force her to bend to his will? Did the woman not think he knew that doing certain things could have an impact on the future? The one thing he didn't want when he returned home was a broken Eve. He rather liked his wife with the fire she possessed. He had no desire to quench that fire. It was the only reason he was willing to give his wife more time, to show a bit more patience. Well, as much as he could in any case. But to have this mortal continue to question him was unacceptable. He growled low in annoyance, hoping to stifle her endless warnings, but when he saw her heave out a frightened breath and open her mouth to speak, he knew he'd had no such luck.

"But…but if you force someone to love you sooner than they might have, you run the risk of them not loving you on their own."

"Let me worry about those things," Adam grinned. "Just do what I've ordered you to do. Teach me and you shall be rewarded. Don't teach me and well…" He shrugged. "Who knows what will happen?" He laughed and folded the psychic into his arms and whisked her away to the library where Eve worked.

Of course Adam had no real plans to harm the psychic but her mind was very strong. She needed to feel fear in order to cooperate. In truth he'd gain nothing more than a mortal enemy if he pushed her much harder. Right now she feared him more than hated him and Adam intended to keep it that way.

"Go," he ordered Lora. He folded himself into mist as Lora walked toward Eve, asking for her help in locating books regarding the psychic realm. Phase one complete. Adam smiled and whispered, 'Very good,' into Lora's ear. So what if Eve began her study a tad bit sooner. What would it hurt? He was pretty sure it wouldn't cause any great ripple in time if he made a suggestion here and there. His groin lurched and he smiled, admitting that he had more on his mind than a harmless suggestion. Who was he kidding?

Watching Lora, reading her mind as she talked with Eve, Adam was acutely aware that the psychic wondered why a powerful vampire would want to know the secrets of magic when under normal circumstances it wouldn't have any effect on vampires. His life had never been one of normal circumstances and more than likely never would.

He couldn't help but smirk as a thought came to him. So how does a Grand Master Vampire become a warlock of great powers? It was simple. He wanted it and it was all a matter of training. Something that would take a mortal aiming for this achievement many years to accomplish was of little consequence for him. For him it was instant knowledge. From the moment Adam had become aware of Eve's own burgeoning powers and her studies, he'd endeavored to do the same. She would not be allowed to know something he did not. And since ordering her didn't work, he'd had little choice but to learn, the same as she had.

He'd devoured all the information he could from every source, books, witches, warlocks, and he soaked it all in like a sponge. The only bit of information he'd been unable to find was information about time travel. Since leaving Eve, he'd gone to every single source he could think of and probed their minds about time travel. When that didn't work, he'd simply erased from their minds the question and his visit. None seemed to have the knowledge that he wanted so badly.

Adam growled, knocking over a shelf filled with books, ignoring patrons as they wondered how the shelf had fallen. He'd remained invisible not out of fear of being seen but because it served no purpose to be seen by the mortal Eve at this point. It seemed since the day he'd found Eve she had been the primary focal point of his existence. He should have paddled her behind long ago and made her behave in a proper manner.

No, he thought. *I should not have turned her. I should not have turned away from her once I had. I should have made love to her as I wanted. I should not have allowed her to love another.* He groaned. Some of the blame lay with him and he didn't like it.

So be it. He would remain here in the past, for the moment. It seemed he had little choice in the matter. But eventually he would find his way back to his present and he would deal with his wayward wife. While he admired her abilities, her disobedience was disheartening. What would she do if she were in trouble now that she was truly unable to reach him? He was laying odds that she had no idea where he'd landed or how in hell to bring him back.

Adam frowned. Of course he knew she'd not bring him back even if she could. Eve was as always betraying him to protect the lives of others. He wondered what she would do when those lives no longer needed her protection. He mused over what a just and fair punishment for her crimes might be. There had to be something other than death by his hands that would rattle his wife's cage. By the time he returned it would be with that knowledge.

***

This was going to be so much fun, Adam thought to himself as he walked through the doors of the library where Eve worked, and wandered around looking for her. When he found her, he stopped in front of her and smiled. He couldn't help but notice the quick jump of her pulse at the base of her throat. There was fear in her eyes and something else. Recognition. Good. Adam snapped his fingers and handed over the bouquet of flowers that he produced out of thin air just for her.

"How did you do that? You're a magician," Eve smiled.

"Of sorts," Adam admitted.

"How nice. Are you here to register for the occult program we're having?"

Adam studied Eve for a long moment, reading her mind, knowing she was trying to remember where she'd seen him. He ran his tongue over his lips, knowing what his tongue would be doing with Eve before long. He stared at her, then smiled again, putting his hand out to touch her, running it down the side of her face, using the tiniest bit of power to keep her rooted in place. He'd never used his powers on her before other than when she'd dared him. Now he would. She'd not played fair and neither would he. With a snort of amusement Adam realized it had not occurred to Eve to fiddle with all of his powers. Still, the idea that she'd stripped him of his power to kill was going to make things interesting. He'd have to find a way to reverse that as soon as possible.

"Eve, do you believe in the unexplainable?" he asked. "The truly wicked, the power and pleasure to be gained from those things?" He laughed when she didn't answer. "I'm sorry, perhaps I should introduce myself. You will have to indulge me and not turn in disbelief from what I'm about to tell you. Can you do that?"

"I thought you were here to register for the program. I'm not the one taking care of that." Eve pointed toward the desk. "Just go up there and someone will be able to help you."

"Only you can help me, Eve. It is you I came to see. You see, I've come from the future." He laughed. "I'm not talking far into the future, just a few years, but in that time period we know each other."

Eve walked away. "Excuse me, sir, I have to help some other patrons."

Adam couldn't help himself. That wasn't altogether true. Of course he could avoid what he was about to do, but he didn't choose to.

He'd already visited the mortal Eve in her dreams. She should be able to connect the dots rather quickly. She was just behaving as she always did. She was stubborn. "I'm your husband," Adam said, and turned her around gently by the shoulders to face him. She laughed and turned away.

"Did you not hear what I said, Eve?"

"Yes, I heard you."

She was treating him as one treated the insane, humoring him as she slowly moved away, wondering what would make a good weapon. This woman since the day he'd met her had always wanted a weapon to use against him. When other women only thought how to get themselves into his bed, this one thought of ways to keep from making love to him. If she didn't take him a little more seriously, and quickly, he would be forced to do something more drastic than being nice. "Aren't you even a little curious about who I am?" Adam asked, annoyed that Eve was ignoring him.

"You've already told me. You said you were my husband."

"And so I did." He held her gaze. "Do you think I'm crazy?"

"I should." She trembled. "But for some reason I don't think you are." Eve shook her head. "Or rather I don't think you're crazy when you talk of being my husband but..."

"But still you wonder about my mental health. Don't. I speak the truth. My name is Adam Omega and I'm a vampire, Eve. I'm the thing you were taught to avoid, to run from at all cost. I'm the one '*Being*' you fear the most. But I'm also the one '*Being*' you've pledged to love." He touched his hand to her left breast, felt the shiver as it slid through her, heard her catch her breath and heard it quicken even more as he stared at her.. "I am lodged in there, in your heart and I'm here to release that knowledge."

"If that's true why don't I know it? Listen, I have a boyfriend."

Here we go again, Adam thought. *Déjà vu*. He laughed. I know all about your so- called boyfriend and the operative word is *boy*. I'm a man, Eve. Eric, that simpering wimp, doesn't want you. He doesn't want any woman." Adam gave a careless shrug and smiled at her. "But you already know that, don't you?"

An instant before she screamed he'd known she was going to and snapped his fingers, putting all in the library under. He sealed the doors as well as the phones. Not a moment too soon for her loud and obnoxious scream ripped through the air. Adam shuddered briefly at the sound.

"Help me, help, somebody. Please help me," Eve screamed.

"I am the only one able to help you, Eve, and I stand willing and able. Just please stop that racket," Adam pleaded.

Eve ran through the library, trying unsuccessfully to shake anyone awake. She reached for the phone and dialed. Getting nothing, she glanced at Adam and raced for the door. She should have known it would be locked. This had to be a dream, a very bad dream. Make that a nightmare. She screamed as loud as she could. She had to get away. Eve looked behind her, thinking Adam would be there but he wasn't. He was seated at a table, a magazine open before him. And he was ignoring her.

What a racket! Adam had forgotten the caterwauling that Eve had tried the first time he met her. This time he had no intention of allowing any of the horrid sounds to drive him away. This was too important. He'd told his wife before she'd sent him back in time that he'd come back on his own or force her to return him. This he would do. As the volume of her screams increased, Adam opened his hand and snapped his fingers, producing ear plugs in one hand and a bottle of water in the other. He leafed through magazine after magazine, wondering how long she'd carry on in that feverish manner. Hours later he was still wondering. She was wearing him out. All the immobile mortals were beginning to become a problem. Sooner or later someone would come looking for them. He'd kept the entire library shut down for much too long trying to wait Eve out. Damn, she was stubborn.

"Eve," Adam bellowed disgustedly, hating that he'd had to resort to yelling just to be heard. "If you promise to cut out all of the noise I will release them and leave for now. Can you promise me that you will behave?"

Her lips were trembling and faint moistness was gathering in her eyes, making them large and luminous. Why had he ever thought she'd be easier to control? She was afraid but still wouldn't give him the promise. Stubborn, foolish woman. Adam released his hold a tiny bit. He had no plans to take it slow but he also had no plans to waste time. He was not staying in the past any longer than he had to. But before he left he would make love to his wife while she was still mortal. He'd made up his mind. "Forget Eric, you're mine, Eve," he said and vanished.

***

That didn't just happen. I'm dreaming. There are no such things as vampires. People cannot vanish into thin air and I don't feel this all consuming love for someone who doesn't exist. It's finally happened. I've gone insane. Eve clutched her hand to her heart and moaned, shaking her head and pulling herself together as Amy, her coworker, came toward her. She knew it wouldn't do any good to ask Amy if she'd seen the handsome man with purple eyes she'd been talking to, but she did it anyway. "Amy, did you see the man I was talking to?"

"What man?" Amy answered. "I didn't see anyone."

"God help me," Eve prayed silently.

***

Adam strolled into St. Michael, stopping at the font of holy water and blessing it. Then he dipped his finger in it and made the sign of the cross on his forehead. He stretched his arms out and closed his eyes, waiting for...there it was. Eve's blood called to him. He looked around the huge sanctuary, annoyed for a moment, then disappeared only to reappear at Eve's side.

"Move over, Eric," Adam ordered. Eric stared at Adam, then Eve, but didn't move.

"Move now or I will move you. And I will not be gentle." Adam ordered setting his teeth in a firm lock. His voice came out strong, sure, and lethal

"I...I....excuse me," Eric said weakly as he slid away from Eve.

For a moment Eve stared at Eric then turned her attention to Adam. "You're not real. You're not real. This isn't happening to me. I'm in church and this isn't happening." She reached her hand toward Eric. "Eric, let's leave," Eve pleaded.

"You will remain seated, Eric, do you understand? Be a good boy and maybe I'll keep your secret." Adam watched as Eric blanched, moving his mouth without sound. But he did as Adam ordered and remained seated.

"Who are you? What are you?" Eve stammered.

"I am Adam Omega, your husband, and I am a vampire." Adam touched his finger to Eve's forehead. "But haven't we gone though all of that? I told this to you when I saw you at the library."

"If you're for real, if there are such a thing as vampires, that makes you evil. You're..."

"The spawn of Satan?" Adam asked with a chuckle.

"Yes," Eve replied, shaking.

"I never swore allegiance to Satan. Never. If you want to call me the spawn of anything, call me the spawn of God. You'd be more accurate. But to put your mind at ease," he smiled and shrugged, "or maybe not, I am the spawn of none and I resent your saying or thinking it. I am giving you an advance course in what our relationship is. I don't have the time that I took with you before. There will be little courting, if any. In a few days' time at most you will share my bed. Tonight you can have time to reacquaint yourself with me."

"Eve, what's going on here? Who is this and what is he talking about? Have you been cheating on me?" Eric demanded.

Adam laughed out loud, ignoring the shushing of the parishioners. "Eve cheating on you? Come on, Eric, get real. Besides, didn't I order you to sit there and be quiet?"

"You can't talk to me like that. Eve and I are practically engaged," Eric whispered in a voice filled with fear.

"I can and I will talk to you that way, Eric. I just did. You are not marrying Eve so get that through your skull. In fact, as of this moment you are no longer dating her. Do you understand?" Adam's words were said with a definite coldness. When he noticed two ushers heading toward them, he froze the entire congregation with the exception of Eve and Eric.

"Things will be done differently this time around, Eve. Now both of you sit back and enjoy the service." With that Adam brought the sanctuary out from under, picked up a bible and laughed softly as he opened it to the scripture Father Keller had mentioned. He couldn't help laughing as he listened to the fiercely pounding staccato of Eve and Eric's hearts. They were both terrified and it pleased him.

With one arm Adam pulled Eve to him. He leaned into her, inhaling her scent and wanting to drink from her. He allowed his fangs to descend just a bit, enough to puncture Eve, touching her when she jumped. "I will not hurt you," he promised. "I want to make love to you, Eve," Adam whispered into her ear. "I want to touch you in all of your hidden places, to suckle you and make you come over and over again." She attempted to leave and he put a hand over hers. "Leave and I will say these words to the entire congregation." Again he put the congregation under and smiled at Eve, sliding his hand under her skirt, fingering her. Ignoring her fear, he turned her to face him and brought her to him, kissing her hard, lowering his fangs a wee bit more, allowing her to feel them. His hold on her was strong. Still, he nearly had to pry her legs farter apart. Her heart was beating rapidly but she was responding to his kiss, moaning and writhing in pleasure.

Wack!

Adam fell back, surprised. Clutching his head, he blinked to clear his vision. *So she wasn't writhing in pleasure.* He moved a bit away from her to observe her. She was clutching a hymnal, obviously what she'd hit him with.

"Whoever you are, whatever you are and whatever you did to everyone, undo it now or so help me I'll beat you until there's not a bible or hymnal left in this place."

Adam rubbed the side of his temple. It appeared Eve caused him pain no matter the time period. He could have sworn she was a lot meeker when he'd first met her. Maybe not, he thought, maybe he'd just gone too far too fast. "Okay, I'll release them."

"And don't you ever touch me like that again without permission."

"Then give it."

"Go to hell, Adam."

"This feels so extremely familiar." He smiled slightly at her. "Been there, done that." She glared at him and he glared right back. He was not making it any easier on her than he already had, not this time around. He'd wasted too much time being nice the last time he'd met her, in the future, in the past. Who knew. It was becoming a bit confusing. Still look where being nice had gotten him with Eve. Back in the past. No, Eve would be controlled with a firm hand this time. He couldn't believe her insolence as she rose to leave.

"You leave and they remain as they are." She sat and he purred into her ear, licking the side of her face. Drawing away when she clutched the hymnal tighter, he laughed. Adam waved a finger and brought the congregation from under again. Then he grinned at Eve, again showing a bit of fang. "Your attention should be on the service, Eve." Adam laughed softly and began singing with choir.

His voice rang out loud and clear. Ripples of memories of times long past attempted to clutch at him. They were pleasant memories so he allowed a few. This was a thousand times better than being in the Vatican. Here Adam joined in the service, singing, reading the scriptures with reverence and rejoicing in the fear he'd instilled in Eve and Eric.

It was the ending of the service that brought Adam out of his reverie. The rustle of bodies making their way toward the back of the church to leave and those making their way to the front to say a word to his friend, Father Keller amused Adam. "Come along you two," he ordered Eve and Eric as he made his way toward the front.

***

Eve hesitated, wondering if she should make a run for it. But she'd look like ten kinds of fools running from the devil while in the church. Still, her warning bells were sounding rather loudly. Something known yet unknown was commanding her to run. It was a warning, she knew that much, a dire warning. She looked at Eric, then at Adam's back. "He's a magician," she whispered to Eric. "I don't know him. He just showed up at the library a couple of days ago. He keeps coming back. I think he's crazy…he's stalking me."

Seeing Adam Omega again, having Eric see him, as well as the usher who'd attempted to head their way to quiet him told Eve his previous visits to her were not her imagination. Only the first time had seemed to be more like a dream. The dream had pulled fears Eve had never voiced. It had to be more than a coincident. She wanted to scream, to run but Father Keller was coming toward them and Eve could already tell he disapproved of her relationship with his adopted son. Adam turned suddenly and stared at her.

"You're right, I am stalking you. Now come here as I told you to do."

"I am not a dog. You can't give me orders."

"I don't have time for this. You will do as I say."

"Do you really think you can control me? If so, think again." Eve was past disgusted with Eric that he wasn't trying to protect her. He'd not uttered a word, hadn't even pulled out his cell to call the police. Okay, so their relationship was a sham but it was a sham she was more than willing to go along with if it kept her from evil. She stared back at Adam. Apparently the ship had sailed for that. But how? she wondered. This was a church. The devil couldn't enter the church.

"The devil sits in your churches every day, Eve. The devil sings in your choir, read the scriptures, prays for you, preaches to you, and gossip about every member of your congregation." Adam shook his head sadly. "Didn't you know that? Now come."

Eve turned and made for the door but stopped when the sudden invasion of fingers between her thighs caught her unaware and made her moan out loud. She felt lips suckling her breast and a tongue icy hot trailing kisses over her flesh. Embarrassment colored her face as wetness cascaded down her legs. This couldn't be happening. She turned back and there he stood, smug and assured. She wondered how he was doing it.

"You will come to me now or I will sling you over my shoulders and carry you out. I want to tell Father Keller about us." That said, Adam walked toward the minister, knowing Eve would follow.

"Father, as always it's nice to see you. I wanted to tell you how much I enjoyed your message this morning. I found it...interesting," Adam said, holding his hand out to the man.

"Thank you, Adam. I see you've finally met my son Eric and his young lady. All the years you've been coming here I'm surprised you didn't meet before now."

"I've seen him. " Adam turned to give Eric a secret smile. "He always appeared to want to remain in the background before, among his male friends."

For a moment longer Adam held Eric's gaze and continued smoothly, as though he'd not watched the fear come into Eric's eyes, or the slight confusion that the minister showed. Adam thought it amusing that his good friend had insisted on being called Father though his church was non-denominational. *Whatever*, he thought. If it served the man's vanity, so what.

At last Adam released Eric from his gaze and returned his attention to his friend. "I'm sorry to disappoint you but Eve is not Eric's young lady...well, not anymore," Adam replied coolly. "Eve belongs to me and I do not share." He turned to smile sweetly at Eve. "Speak the truth, Eve. To whom do you belong?"

"Father, I don't know this man. I met him only recently."

"That was not the question, Eve." Adam tilted his chin and stared straight into her eyes, connecting with her on a cellular level. "To whom do you belong, Eve?" She was fighting him, trembling, biting her lips. Hmm, she was strong and he'd not counted on that. *Very well*, Adam thought. *More drastic measures are called for*. He didn't have time for her stubbornness.

"Eric, you may go now. It is not your fault that things didn't work out for you with Eve. She was never intended for you. She belongs to me. I'm sure your father can tell you that. As soon as we're done here, Eve and I will be going to lunch to discuss our future. Father, I trust you will help your son get over any disappointment he may have." Adam turned to look at Eric once more, then looked back at Eric's father. "Father," he paused then smiled. "Would you like to speak to Eric now?"

The minister opened his mouth several times, unable to speak. He blinked rapidly. As he looked at Adam, his mouth quivering just the tinniest bit and his eyes fearful, he played with his hands. After coughing several times he patted Eric's shoulder and Adam nodded his approval

"Yes, Eric, sometimes people are soulmates. Apparently Mr. Omega has found his and has no doubts about it." He turned toward Eve and tried not to glare. "Mr. Omega is the largest contributor to the church. How lucky it is for you that he has claimed you."

"Claimed me! Claimed me? Do I look like lost luggage? You're acting like him, like I don't get a say in this, Father. Perhaps you don't know everything about your friend that you should. The man says he's a vampire. That means he's evil and you want me to go with him. Does he have you under a spell or are you crazy?"

Father Keller was trying his best to quiet Eve. Adam merely grinned, continuing to observe the people trying to talk to the priest, the women who were vying for Adam's attention. "Go away," Adam said. With those words they all scattered.

"Eve, Adam is not evil. There are no such creatures as vampires. You've been reading too much nonsense. Just be logical. If anything you said were true, Mr. Omega would not be able to sit in a house of worship. He could not hold that bible there." The minister pointed to the bible in Adam's hand. And he could not wear a crucifix."

Confusion was pushing in on Eve. This conversation seemed vaguely familiar. "This is a dream, isn't it? And I'm going to wake up? Someone pinch me. Pinch me, Eric, pinch me hard. I need to wake up."

Eric moved to do as Eve requested and Adam snarled. "You will not touch her. Did you not hear me say she belongs to me? I will pinch her." And he did. Hard. When she yelped in pain he laughed. "Hard enough?"

"What do you want," Eve asked.

"Am I not speaking in a language that you understand? What language do you speak? Tell me and I will speak in your native tongue. I speak and understand all tongues. I want to understand yours," he said coyly.

"What do you want?" Eve repeated.

"I want you. Didn't I say that?"

"Eve, Mr. Omega is a very generous man, a billionaire."

"And I should sell myself for how much, Father? Just because he's rich doesn't give him a right to boss me around, or for you to tell me to go off with him."

Eve ran toward the back of the church and after ten steps she came to an abrupt stop, unable to move. Once again she felt his hands on her body. To say she was terrified was an understatement. But she wasn't running any longer. She'd made up her mind. She was tired of running. All her life she'd run from an unknown darkness, something much larger than herself that was seeking her out. Some evil… Adam surely qualified if what he said was true. She tried to reason it out. If Adam was a billionaire and she had lunch with him, perhaps he'd find her company so boring that he'd lose interest. It would be just like a man to want what he couldn't have. Maybe she'd make a play for him. She looked up at the stained glass windows that she dearly loved. *But not here, not in church.* She wouldn't be the little bunny running anymore. She'd present herself to him as a money grubbing, dumb gold digger. That should make him run and run quickly.

"Release me, Mr. Omega," Eve whispered low, "and we can have lunch."

"That's better," Adam said softly. "And, Eve, get that nonsense out of your head about making me run."

So Adam was a little more than a magician. He could produce flowers from thin air, seem to disappear and was able to put an entire congregation under some hypnotic spell. But she knew that had to be a trick. The one thing she knew that wasn't a trick was his ability to touch her from far away. She shivered. Now apparently he could read her mind. She was curious if still afraid. She'd always heard that the best way to know one's enemy was to keep him close and for now, at least for lunch, she would keep Adam very close.

Chapter Eight

It had all been too easy. Her boyfriend/ almost fiancé had been ordered to give her up and just like that he'd complied, not even pretending to put up a fight. And the minister... She 'd known he wasn't overly fond of her but to say some crap about Adam being a billionaire and that she should be grateful he'd chosen her... Eric and his father could both go shimmy up a tree. She was a big girl. She'd handle this so-called vampire her damn self. Eve tried with everything that was in her not to react as she slid onto the plush leather seat of Adam's car.

Claustrophobia began to set in, something she'd never had, and a tremor of terror skittered down her spine. She could barely breathe. Then her eyes met his and what had been hard became impossible. She stared into his purple gaze and became hopelessly mesmerized. Tingles of pleasure danced over her flesh as Adam made a show of buckling her in, lying that the belt was damaged. All the while his fingers were touching her flesh, burning her, making her want him without reason. This was all crazy; he had done something to her.

Eve swallowed, trying her best not to relay her physical reaction to being touched by Adam. She hated the thought of him reading her mind. If she could, she'd do something to stop such an invasion of privacy. He had no right to know how much his nearness was affecting her. She looked at him and he blinked as though he'd been caught.

"Stop reading my mind."

"Say please."

"Please stop reading my mind," Eve rasped between clenched teeth, "or you may not like what you find there."

Adam chuckled. The mortal Eve was still the same stubborn, ornery woman that he'd left in their not too distant future. He watched as her hands came out and touched the vampire that dangled from his rearview mirror. Her head was tilted and she looked absolutely delicious. The carotid artery on the left side of her neck was stretched taut from the way her body was positioned. He stared at it, needing to taste her so badly in that moment that he no longer gave a damn about teaching her a lesson.

"Are you for real with this?" Eve asked, trying to be polite but unable to stop the sarcasm from coming through.

"I am."

"I don't believe you. If the teeth aren't fakes, then any disreputable dentist could have put them in for you. You're just an eccentric man with too much time on his hands and too much money."

"So, you don't believe me. You don't believe vampires exist?"

"Hell no!"

"Then allow me to show you, Eve." With that Adam leaned over and sank his fangs into Eve's flesh, drinking the sweet nectar that tasted strangely a bit like honeysuckle. He sighed as he drank from her while restraining her hand in his steel embrace.

"Stop it, you're hurting me...please stop, Adam."

He shuddered once, then again. Damn, why did she have to say please and why did she have to have tears in her voice? He sighed and licked the wound he'd created, planting soft kisses there, remembering a time when she'd refused to say please or to beg him for mercy. He'd made a promise then that he'd never physically hurt her again. He remembered that promise even if Eve had no knowledge of it.

He brought his mouth from her neck, allowing her to see the drops of her blood that dotted his lips and lingered on his fangs. "Kiss me, Eve, so you may know this is no joke."

At first she looked as if she might refuse. Then surprisingly, she moved toward him, opened her mouth and arched her head back. Adam wanted to laugh at the picture she was presenting, the sacrificial lamb. She was curious and brave; wanting to know the truth made her even braver. She was his Eve. Retracting his fangs, he moved his lips over hers and captured her tongue, kissing her with all the passion that a thousand-year-old vampire had to give. She was shuddering, gasping for air, pushing at his chest.

"I believe," Eve murmured. "I believe. You're not human, you can't possibly be. No human male could kiss like that."

"What about my drinking your blood?"

Her hand went to her neck and she wiped away at the now dried blood. "That was real, wasn't it?" Then real fear entered her eyes. "Did you just turn me into a vampire?"

"No, my darling, I didn't."

"Are you going to?"

How did he answer her that?

"Adam?"

"I'll do my best not to," he said honestly. He had no plans to turn Eve while he was here. He hoped to be back in his own time long before she tried to take her life. He gave her a look. "As long as you remain healthy your life will be yours to do with as you please. I would only interfere if you chose to shorten your life."

"I have no plans to end it."

"As long as you keep it that way you will never become a vampire, that I can promise you." His heart pounded and he ignored the knowledge he possessed about her future. What did it cost him to offer her reassurance when she needed it so badly?

***

Adam was almost pleased. Things were moving along at a rather brisk pace. He was spending time with Eve. She was not totally accepting and she was much too curious for her own good. He'd reminded her that curiosity killed the cat and could very well kill her. He'd seen fear in her eyes for a moment but it had not lingered. Had it not been for the reason he was in the past, he would have been glad to spend more time with the mortal Eve, take it a bit slower perhaps, but there was no possibility of that. He had to return to his time and make sure his wife was punished for her misdeeds.

Progress was being made on other fronts as well. It had more than a little to do with his improved mood. With the list of names Lora had given him, Adam had made connections with many whom he'd not known before. Practitioners of the dark arts were more than willing to help him, though they would remember nothing of their time with him. It pleased his purpose and theirs.

Always a quick study, he'd soaked up the knowledge like a sponge and within a matter of hours was much better than those who sought to teach him. Still, the primary key to his returning to his own time was eluding him. But for wanting to return to confront his wife, the time away wasn't altogether unpleasant. He could linger a while longer her with this

Eve. She wasn't as pliable as he'd thought she would be, but she was more inquisitive, not quite as afraid. He barely thought of Lora's warning to him about his actions having an effect on the future. He'd put a quick end to any thoughts Eve harbored about that sniveling Eric. She should have never wasted her time. There was one and only one Being for her, and that was him. He'd not spend forever here. And he'd not waste a moment of it doing as he'd done the first time. He was making love to Eve whether she consented or not. He almost laughed at what he knew Eve would call it. That was just too bad.

"Mr. Omega?"

Adam's head snapped upwards. He'd almost forgotten where he was. "Yes, Lora, have you been able to locate anyone who can time travel? When the old woman bowed her head, Adam growled, knowing she hadn't.

"What do I have to do to get this information?" Adam fumed. "Surely if Eve could do it someone else can. Hell, she hasn't known about any of her powers until recently."

"Powers, Mr. Omega? I thought your wife was…is a vampire."

"She is." Another growl formed in Adam's throat as he remembered Eyanna. "She's also a…." He couldn't say the words. "She dabbles in the arts."

Curiosity shined brightly from Lora's eyes. "Mr. Omega, is your wife…is she…a witch, sir?"

"She fancies herself as such."

"She managed to send you here, did she not?"

Adam stopped his pacing to turn and glare at the psychic.

"You never said just how your coming here into this time was done. What did your wife do?"

At last, Adam thought, something that was making the woman take a genuine interest, something other than fear of what he'd do to her. "She used an incantation," Adam admitted tiredly.

"I know of no incantation that would be strong enough to perform such a feat."

At this Adam laughed. The woman clearly did not know Eve. He ran the memories back through his mind, making each into a picture that he could examine. As he pulled the memories out one by one in life-size holographs, showing her, he heard Lora gasp and shook his head. What he was doing was mere play. He studied the smug look on Eve's face as she said her words, the smile that played around her soft, kissable lips. His gaze lingered there but his memories were of him making love to her. He would do that again very soon.

"Mr. Omega, look at her hand. What is she holding? What is she pointing at you?"

Adam's gaze dropped to Eve's hand. He'd almost forgotten. His brow wrinkled in concentration. "It's one of her thousands of crystals."

"What kind? Can you sharpen the image?"

Adam turned slowly, his arm outstretched. "This is not a great enough feat for you, now you require more details?" Adam attempted to bring the image into better focus but couldn't. He was annoyed at not being able to do it and annoyed that Lora had asked. It was obvious when his mind had recorded the visual his thoughts had been more on kissing Eve than worrying about any threat she posed. "That's as sharp as it's going to get," he announced.

"But her face, her lips most especially are very clear." Lora frowned.

"Because I was not worried about what Eve had in her hands." *I was thinking how sweet her kisses were*, he thought to himself. My mistake. "What can be done now?"

"I can no longer help you, Mr. Omega."

Lora moved slowly backwards and Adam glared at her. "Stop it this instant," he hissed. "I will not harm you. You have done as I asked and you still may prove useful. What, if any, are your suggestion?"

He saw immediate gratitude and rolled his eyes. Perhaps he really was a bully. No matter, he was not now in a bullying mode; he needed to return to his proper time. Sullivan and the good Doctor Meah had yet to be dealt with. He was at a slight disadvantage dealing with the mortal Eve when she had absolutely no knowledge of who and what she was. It hadn't stopped her being obstinate, but it had stopped him. He couldn't very well dish out punishment to the mortal Eve for what his vampiric wife had done. If only this Eve were a little bit more timid, but she wasn't. That hadn't changed.

"Lora, what's next?"

"You need a witch, Mr. Omega, a very powerful and old witch. I'm a psychic, not a witch. Your Eve used witchcraft to send you here. It will take witchcraft to return you."

A vampire resorting to such nonsense, Adam thought, hissing his displeasure. Once again he rolled his eyes. "So be it. Give me the name of an old and powerful witch."

"I... I... don't have the names of any. But if you can give me a couple of days I'll have what you need."

"Lora, when I'm done I will wipe all memory of your helping me from you." He saw relief flood her face, heard the swift intake of a breath, and the old woman trembled.

"What, you don't want to remember me?" he laughed.

"Mr. Omega, please be careful. I would think messing with time would have to have some effect on the future."

"And this affects my life how?" Adam's voice was calm and polite but the words were sarcastic, as he'd meant them to be. Now if Eve had sent him back in time to before he became who he now was and without his knowledge that creatures of darkness did indeed exist, then he would have a problem.

"Two days, Lora. I want the information and you will be rid of me." She almost smiled and Adam almost let her. "But, Lora, we will meet again in the future when Eve comes to you." Her face paled and Adam vanished. It wasn't good to allow mortals to think they were in control at any time. He'd learned that lesson the hard way.

***

Who would have believed a week ago that her life would be so consumed by what she'd heretofore thought of as insane nonsense? Now Eve was frantically trying to find a way to survive her nightmare. There was no one that Eve wanted to bring into this mess with her. She'd thought briefly of inviting her friends to lunch and telling them, but intuitively knew it was the wrong move. They wouldn't believe her and she'd lose her friends. Besides, dealing with Adam Omega was a full time job. He followed her everywhere, a well dressed, unbelievably gorgeous, hunky stalker who spoke in an elegant manner and shot her hormones through the roof with lust. But a stalker nonetheless. So far she'd managed to stay a half step ahead of him but listening now to his silly proclamations, she wondered how long she'd continue to have the upper hand.

"The time has finally come, Eve. Tonight's the night that I truly make you mine. Again."

For all that he professed to be, Eve found Adam Omega annoying and cocky. True, when he kissed her she was transported to another time and place and her heart lurched. And when she watched him walk...God....um um um. She'd never seen a man walk with such deliberate power, his steps causing a rippling effect throughout his entire body. He moved like a dancer or a panther. She smiled to herself, thinking she had his moves down perfectly. Adam Omega moved like a dancing panther, all sin and sexuality and elegance rolled into one delicious male body. He could make her wet with nothing more than a glance but she was not his puppet.

There was something about Adam that she could feel tugging at her brain, something that she thought she should know but she couldn't get it to come out. It was as though she were a student and a not so bright one. Then there was the strange voice that kept whispering to her. She couldn't make out the words but it sounded like her own voice. For some reason it sounded like a warning but she wasn't sure. She was only sure that the voice became louder and more frantic when she was with Adam.

He was testing her. She was very aware of that fact and didn't like it. If he'd even so much as tried to seduce her, maybe she wouldn't mind so much. But this, his throwing his weight around, expecting her to just give in, well... As far as their making love, it was going to happen and she knew that as well as she knew her name was Eve Moses. A tingle ran down her spine and she shivered shaking her head to dislodge the thought.

Eve Omega, mistress of the vampire kingdom. She blinked. Where had that thought come from? Adam was smirking at her. Of course. He'd planted it. He was shaking his head 'no,' almost laughing as though he'd read her thoughts and now knew she was praying he'd sent it.

A tiny moan caused Eve to fall backward before she caught herself and stood facing Adam, squaring off with him, determined not to be bullied. The thought that one short week ago her life had been ordinary and dull had her wishing for the dullness, wishing this was nothing more than a dream. If this was a dream, it was the first one she'd ever had where she'd completed several twenty-four hours cycles. This was going on far too long to be a dream. A slight whoosh of air and Eve's sweater was gone. Then her pants were ripped from her body. She stood staring at Adam in her underwear. He grinned and she stood before him nude. Fear should be the only thing she was feeling but it wasn't. She wanted Adam with an urgent intensity. She watched fascinated as his clothes skimmed from his beautiful muscular frame. His chest appeared solid, as though carved from granite. Her fingers itched to touch it so she moved a step backward before she gave in. Then her gaze fell on his massive erection and she wanted to fall on her knees and take him into her mouth.

Something was wrong, something was very wrong. "Stop, Adam," she said, turning from him and trying to clear her head.

Think, Eve, think, she admonished herself. God, the man was beautiful. Never had she seen a man built like Adam. His body was chiseled way past perfection… and the way his eyes blazed at her… The purple was lit by lust and passion. It nearly stopped her heart. At first she'd thought he wore contacts but knew now he didn't. What mortal had eyes so beautiful? She trembled. Adam wasn't mortal. He was a damn vampire. He was evil and he'd drunk her blood. One arm came up to cover her breasts while the other covered her entrance.

Why am I standing here naked ready to jump into bed with a stranger, a vampire? Yet I want him so badly I feel I will go insane if I can't have him inside me. This is not normal, she reasoned out. *Something is more than off.*

Adam's breath blew against the side of Eve's face and his tongue came out and trailed a path of lust along her earlobes. Then he fell on her and began licking her body, turning her and licking her back, her hips, her thighs. He was licking her everywhere. And everywhere his tongue touched she burned. "No, Adam," Eve managed to croak out through the emotions that were swirling throughout her body, making it difficult to think, let alone talk.

"There will be no 'No's, Eve, not a single one. There will be you and me and yes."

There will be no…who in blue blazes did he think he was? So he was a vampire? So what? She still got a vote in this thing. She thought about all the vampire legends she'd heard about, all evidently false or at least false in the case of one Mr. Adam Omega. He appeared to make his own rules. He came into the church, wore a crucifix, held the bible, sang hymnals and ate. He'd eaten and ordered his food to be prepared with extra garlic though even now his breath wasn't reeking of it. Eve forced herself to concentrate.

"Stop, Adam, no."

His hands moved between her thighs and his breath fluttered over her breasts but he didn't stop. He wasn't taking no for an answer. His fingers were probing her, making her shudder where she stood, taking away any sense of reasoning.

"Adam, no, slow down. Let me think. Something's not right. I think…I think… you've put me under a spell."

That was it! Eve attempted to push away but felt her body falling forward as Adam's fingers made their way deeper inside her body. She wanted this and wanted him, but she'd said no. He should stop. She should stop. She closed her hands and concentrated, willing some innate power to give her the strength to do what she should. Her hand went down to remove Adam's finger from his thorough loving of her and she made contact with his hardness. A gasp came unbidden at her first contact. Heat radiated from Adam that made it impossible to not at least touch him. Almost as though she were in a trance, her fingers moved to hold him. She couldn't help it; she was thrilled to feel the shiver of delight that claimed Adam. The effect she was having on him emboldened her. In disbelief Eve's fingers moved over his length and she squeezed, aware that she was sending a double message, aware that something drastic would have to occur to prevent either of them from continuing. Her body burned with wanting Adam but it was an unnatural, ravenous burning.

God, give me strength. Please, I need to stop, she pleaded

"No, Adam. I said no," she screamed and removed her fingers from the grip they had on his hardness. Then in the next breath she removed her own body from being impaled by Adam's finger. Adam was looking at her in annoyed surprise.

"Did you not hear me, Eve? I said there will be no 'No's.'"

"Are you crazy?"

"Do I look like I'm crazy?"

"As a matter of fact you do, and you sound crazy."

"Look at you, you're panting for me. You want me, Eve, try and deny that fact."

"I'm not denying it. I want you."

"Then what's the problem?"

"That. Why do I want you so badly? Why is it that I can barely control my lust? I've never been like this, never. I don't trust you. I think you've done something to me, hypnotized me into wanting you."

"Do you really think I would have to go to such lengths?"

"It's not that I think you would have to go to such lengths. But I think you would go to such lengths to ensure you get what you want. You don't care about me or my feelings, only about yours. Your intention is to make love to me whether I want you to or not."

"You said you wanted to."

"I know I said I wanted to but I also said no."

"And I said that didn't matter."

"Right there, Adam. Do you see what I mean? You think you can order me and have me make love with you." Before she could finish her thought his hand shot out and tweaked her nipples. The smirk on his face irritated her, his words even more.

"You still want to."

Okay, vampire or no, he was pissing her off big time. Of course she still wanted to. That was part of the problem. She wanted to know what this undeniable attraction was to the man standing in front of her. Eve narrowed her eyes. She feared him, yes, but on some deeper level she sensed she loved him, had loved him for a long time but that was impossible. Wasn't it?

"I want to know why I'm attracted to you."

Adam raised a brow. "Isn't it obvious?"

"You're gorgeous, I give you that." When he smirked Eve couldn't resist adding. "But so are a lot of men." She watched as his smile slid down. *Good*, she thought.

"You know, Eve, it's rather ridiculous for us to be here having this conversation in the nude with me in the condition I'm in," he said, pausing to look down at his massive erection. "And you in the condition you're in," he said, smirking.

"Then put my clothes and yours back on."

"No."

"I thought you said we weren't allowed to use the word no."

"The rules are for you to follow."

"Okay, that's it. No more. Touch me again without my permission and you will wish that you hadn't."

"Excuse me," Adam said, striking a pose. "Exactly what do you think you can do to me? You're my wife. I've already given you several days to get used to the idea that I would be making love to you tonight. What more do you need?"

Was this guy for real? Eve wondered. What cave had he crawled out of? "First off, we're not a couple." She shook her head. "It takes two people to engage in the act of making love. You're talking about making love to me as if my only function is to be there. That's not how it goes, Adam."

"Since when?"

"Since forever."

"Now it's you who's not for real. That is not my nature. I do not ask. I take what I want. I want you." Adam stopped for a moment and gave Eve a long, hard look, assessing her. "I love you, so I've given you the courtesy of informing you of what we will do."

"Geeze, thanks." She glanced down, amazed that Adam was still as hard as the proverbial rock. Would nothing deflate him or his engorged ego? She reached for a sheet from the bed and wrapped it around her body. "Like I said, you will not touch me again without my permission or you will wish you hadn't." At that precise moment the sheet was snatched away. Eve was ready for him. While he was smiling she snatched the lamp that until then had been sitting on the bedside table and lowered it with all the force she possessed.

Adam touched a hand to his forehead and stared at Eve, wondering what was different from his plan this time around. She hit him with a lamp before when they'd first met and he'd tried to have a little taste of her. This was getting redundant. He shook his finger in front of her face. "You should not have done that," he said.

"What are you going to do now, bite me without my permission, make love to me when I say no?"

"I should leave you to that wretched Eric." He saw the light of hope flare in Eve's eyes and continued. "But I will not. You belong to me." He waved his hand in a dismissive fashion. "Don't protest, Eve, there is no use in it. But I have a question for you. How would you like it if I slammed a lamp over your head?"

No answer and he'd not expected one. "You wouldn't like it. I want you to think before striking me again. If you don't want it done to you, then don't do it to me. I can make you a promise same as you made to me. If you ever again raise your hand in anger to strike me, you will learn firsthand how it feels to be struck."

"Same goes for me, Adam, think before you touch me."

A chuckle fell from his lips. "You see, I do not care if you touch me in certain places." His gaze moved downward to his erection. "In fact I relish your touch when it's not given to cause me pain. So your words have little meaning." He rubbed his hand over his head. "That hurt. I don't enjoy being hit and you've done it twice now. This time was more foolish on your part. You should never hit an unclothed man. That shows lack of judgment on your part."

Eve's raised brow was his answer.

"What if we compromise? We'll talk," Adam offered.

"Good."

"And cuddle," Adam offered.

"Talk yes, cuddle no."

Shaking his head slowly, Adam moved forward until he could feel Eve's breath warming his cheek. "Why do I have to tell you again about that word?"

Breathing was becoming a bit more difficult. Ragged, hoarse, lust filled sounds came from Adam. He felt her body shivering pressed against his and he inhaled. A formidable foe had not been what he'd expected, and definitely not one so beautiful. He gazed in her eyes, searching for remembrance, knowing something had to be there. He just needed to bring it out.

For a microsecond it was not as much fun trying to seduce the mortal Eve in order to teach his wife a lesson. Her eyes opened wide and despite her words he saw desire. The lesson no longer mattered. Mortal or mistress of the vampire world, she was still his. He wanted her and he intended to have her.

Will you drain her? For a fleeting instant the thought worried him. *No more*, he thought. *Eve may not have future knowledge but I do*. He would not drain his wife nor would he turn her, at least not now. There was no need. His wife waited for him just a few years in the future. Until he returned to her he would feast on the mortal version.

"Talk and cuddle. Come," Adam said, lifting a finger, waving it and turning down the sheets. He lifted Eve into his arms and placed her in the bed, following after her. "Tell me your objections, my love," he whispered into her ear. "Then tell me how much you want me, how much you love me. Tell me you don't remember me, Eve."

"I do but only vaguely, like a dream that I can't quite commit to memory. Am I really your wife?"

"Yes."

"But how, Adam?"

He shrugged. "Are you sure you're ready to know?"

"What do I have to lose?"

"Your sanity."

Adam was serious. He thought about it for a moment before deciding the truth wasn't in his best interest so he would lie. "There is another vampire, Sullivan. He's an enemy of ours. He found a way to send you back in time to make you forget me. I didn't believe you'd ever forget me or our love."

"Did he send you also?"

"No, my love. I searched until I found someone to help me. I came back here in this time for you. I love you and want to take you back. There's one slight problem. I don't know how to get back. I need you to find a way to send us both home."

"But…I have no idea how to do what you say. I'm not altogether sure that you're what you say. Until a week ago I had a normal life… now…. This is crazy, Adam."

"I know it seems impossible but it's true. If I don't return home soon I will cease to exist. I will die."

Adam blinked rapidly to hide the urge to smile. He'd played the right card. This Eve was just as emotionally flawed as the other. He held her as she made odd gestures, shaking her head, biting her lips as though trying to figure out a puzzle.

"That can't be right. I don't remember any break in my own timeline. I can trace my memories from my childhood until this moment." Her head snapped up. "You're lying."

"You don't believe I've been sent back in time?"

"You, I'm not sure about. But I know that I haven't."

Damn, Adam thought. Why did she have to be so logical, wanting to analyze every little thing? Why couldn't she just listen to him and believe him? Well, he'd tried. "Eve, you will stop questioning me about whether you were sent back in time. You will not remember your entire life, there will be gaps. It will hurt to try to piece it together." He smiled, trying his best to make it a smile of sadness.

"It hurts more than you will ever know that you don't remember me or our wonderful life together. Since you remember every moment of this lifetime, tell me." Adam moved away from her and slung his legs over the side of the bed. "I should have known when I found you wanting another man that something was terribly wrong. Go ahead, Eve, tell me. Tell me how you were able to betray me."

"I…I…" Eve could feel the beginning of fear creeping up on her once again. Her memories were jumbled. They were nothing more than dusty threads that she couldn't quite catch. She kept trying and only slivers of images would appear. "I can't remember," she admitted at last. "That still doesn't mean I know how to send you home."

"Us, Eve, send us home. You have to trust in me. Give me your complete trust. Will you do that?" Adam asked. He would have her trust with or without her cooperation. For now he'd give her a chance to do it the easy way but he wouldn't wait much longer. He'd run out of patience.

"I'll try. That's all I can give you at the moment."

Stubborn, too stubborn for her own good. A smile tugged at the corners of his lips and he decided to take the offered olive branch. "That's all that I ask at the moment."

"How do you think I can help you though? I still don't know how."

Swinging his legs back into the bed he pulled Eve into his arms. "Do not be frightened of what you are, my love, for it will be what will help us in the end. You, my love, come from generations of witches. Thousands of years of power are in your lineage. You can summon that power and make it yours. Matter of fact, in the future you have harnessed that knowledge. You're a force to be reckoned with, I promise you." He felt the pride in her and smiled as he kissed the top of her head. How easy it was for mortals to sin without even realizing it.

Pride was a sin.

"Are you sure?" Eve asked

"Trust in me," Adam answered.

For a moment there was silence between them. Both concentrated, one trying to read the other, the other trying to hide what he didn't want known.

Adam let out a breath and used the minutest of persuasion. "You can help me. You had great powers and were becoming a match for Sullivan. You were studying books on witchcraft and told me you would have a way to combat anything that Sullivan might do to us. We talked about time travel. You were going to search for a way to send Sullivan back in time because you were determined that he would not interfere in our lives."

A zing of electrical energy zapped Adam on his left hand, enough that he shook his hand and looked down, wondering why the ring had done that. Could it be the mountain of lies? No matter, he'd use whatever was at his disposal, he thought, looking at the ring and hoping that what he was planning would work. He showed her the amber ring. "You once gave this to me long ago. I can make you remember, Eve, if you'd let me."

"I don't want you biting me."

"I won't hurt you. I promise that this will be the easiest way for me to give you the memories." He looked down, trying to hide the smile that wanted to come. "This is your choice. If you want to know about me, about us, then this is the way to do it."

Eve didn't know if she completely trusted Adam, but there was something about the amber ring that sat on his finger. What if he was telling the truth? Could he really be a vampire and she a witch? If Adam were really and truly a vampire then it would stand to reason that more of them existed, that another vampire, Sullivan, had taken her away from Adam and was denying them their life together? That would explain the instant attraction, the unnatural lust she had for Adam. But to have him bite her? She shivered as Adam drew her near. They were still without clothes, lying in a soft bed and he was touching her.

"Our children miss their mother."

"Children? We have children?" Eve moaned and touched her hand to her belly. "Why can't I remember that? I want to remember it. If it's true, Adam, help me please," she pleaded. "Do whatever you must to make me remember."

Adam held her gaze. "Are you certain of this? Is this your choice, Eve?"

When he heard her whispered 'yes,' he gently pushed her head to the side, lowered his fangs and bit her neck tenderly. For a moment the thought of the wrong he was about to commit pierced his core. It gave him pause, and then the memory of his wife sharing Sullivan's bed for the last two years was enough to make him do it. He would implant memories that did not exist, of children, and he would give her snippets of the happy times they'd shared.

And he'd show her Sullivan with his eyes bulging and the havoc he'd wreaked as he'd battled with him. Sure, the outcome would be a bit different. The destruction he'd caused he'd attribute to Sullivan. Adam prevented the chuckle which wanted to come out. His *'own'* Eve, mistress of all that he had, would be in for a bit of a surprise. He'd connect with her now in this time in her mortal state and he'd do it on a cellular level. He'd make her feel it four years in the future. That he was sure of.

Adam drank from Eve. As the sweet nectar hit the back of his throat he forgot about anything but the pleasure he was receiving. Evil had a name and at times it could be his. But at this moment his intentions weren't merely to teach Eve a lesson. He did love her beyond all reason and suckling her, tasting her innocence, was like nectar from the gods. Who wouldn't do the same in his position? He'd challenge any to say they wouldn't. Who could judge him when none knew what they would do until the time came. Look at Sullivan, how easily he'd betrayed Eve to keep her alive. Love did strange things to any being.

Chapter Nine

What the...? Eve slapped a hand at her neck and almost swooned. If she didn't know better she would think someone was drinking from her. A moan slid from her throat and her knees went weak. Her eyes closed in ecstasy. Damn him, she thought. Who but Adam Omega, her husband, was strong enough to make her want him from wherever she'd sent him. She didn't know if she'd sent him back a day, a week, a month, or ten years into the past but wherever he was, it was apparent he'd found her. That put her at a distinct disadvantage. When lips covered her right breast and suckled, Eve nearly lost it.

"What's wrong, Eve?"

Her frantic gaze sought Sullivan. She saw him watching her with a worried expression on his face. Dr. Meah ran to her and reached out to touch her.

"No," Eve said, smacking his hand away and ignoring the curious frown Sullivan had on his face. "I don't want either of you touching me. Go away," she said. When neither moved she glared. "Then I'll leave," she said, disappearing and wondering where she'd end up, grateful when she ended up in her own home. She was almost getting the hang of transporting herself from place to place, but still on occasion it didn't work. This was one time she didn't want to end up in Sullivan's bed.

Beside herself with worry, Eve ran for her book of spells. There had to be something in there, anything, to stop the feelings. Lust so powerful that it could not be called by any other name forced her to her knees and she held on to the door of a cabinet, moaning in pleasure. "Adam, stop," she pleaded with her mouth, but her body, her traitorous body, was begging him to continue. She shuddered hard and fell to the floor as she felt Adam's erection slam into her. Damn, not like this, she thought, willing herself to stand, to reach for one of her books. She had to find a way to stop this nonsense, this torture, this sweet, sweet, sweet torture.

Tears were coursing down her cheeks she wanted to curse herself for the thoughts and feelings she was having but the things Adam was doing to her body were rendering her powerless. She couldn't think one single cohesive thought. She was all feelings and they were pulling her under with wanton pleasure. *Ride it out*, her mind whispered, *just ride it out*.

Riding it out was made impossible by the things Adam was doing to her. She had but one choice left. Enjoy it. Running for her bed she dove in, pulling the mounds of comforters over her body. If Sullivan followed her, at least she could pretend it was a relapse instead of the massive invasion of her body that she was feeling. There appeared nothing for her to do but close her mind to Sullivan to prevent him knowing of the feelings Adam was provoking. It had been way too long since Adam had touched her in this manner. Despite her joy in loving Sullivan, it was Adam and only Adam who had coaxed such wanton delight from her. And it felt so good—though her guilt over enjoying what Adam was doing made her wish he'd hurry and stop.

Almost.

More than likely Sullivan would forgive her for enjoying Adam's lovemaking but he would be hurt nonetheless. It didn't matter that she'd broken things off with him; she still loved him and didn't want him hurt. Then again, she loved Adam, and she'd always been a sucker for his touch. Now was no different. She felt his touch in her center and closed her legs tight, writhing with the unseen hand, knowing she would remain in bed until Adam was done with her. She pitied her younger mortal self in whatever time zone Adam had landed in. God help her if she was without knowledge of Adam's power. She wondered if there was a way she could help her mortal self, somehow send herself a message. As pleasure raced through her, the message was forgotten. All she wanted was more.

"Damn you, Adam."

***

Damn you. He heard it, the sound loud enough to make Adam stop what he was doing for a nanosecond. His wife was well aware that he'd found her and was making love to her. The thought warmed his undead heart. There wasn't a damn thing she could do about it. Evil? Yes. Deliciously evil and he loved it. Maybe he'd spend a bit more time in the past than he'd planned, enough to teach his errant wife a very good lesson. Adam Omega would not be defeated, not even by witchcraft. Silly woman to have thought so.

But right now it was time to deal with the mortal Eve, this innocent version whom he'd fed half truths and… he shrugged inwardly, lies. Oh well, so be it. He felt his body readying as he thrust repeatedly into Eve's sweet wetness. Mercy but she felt good. He held on for a moment longer until he felt the beginning of her release and then his own. He held her in his arms as she climaxed, taking her shudders deep within, running his fingers lightly over the curve of her hips, sending delightful aftershocks to finish up the volcanic explosions. When she stared into his eyes and held his gaze, he held hers in return. When she said, 'Wow,' he smiled.

"Eve, my love, do you see all that I've been through looking for you?"

"I do but why didn't you tell me all of this before instead of ordering me about?"

"That was my mistake. Forgive me, my love. I should have told you of our enemy. Sullivan nearly destroyed our lives. I had no desire to bring him up to you initially. I only wanted to reclaim you. I've missed you so much."

Eve was trembling with rage. She'd felt this evil that had wanted to consume her for years. Now it had a name. *Sullivan.* She hoped Adam could forgive her for thinking it was he. Sullivan had taken so much from them. She could feel a simmering anger that was slowly turning to hatred toward the unseen vampire.

"He caused all of those floods and hurricanes, the tsunami, the earthquakes?"

"Yes," Adam answered solemnly.

"But why, Adam?"

"Out of his hatred for us, Eve. Sullivan is evil and must be stopped. He's a mad power hungry being. I've tried for many years to intervene when he goes on rampages, killing mortals without regard, turning them into what we are, vampires, Eve. Sullivan is making more vampires." A weary sigh escaped just as he'd planned. *I would have made a damn fine actor.* Adam gave a brittle chuckle and took in a breath of air, holding it for a few seconds before releasing it.

"Now perhaps you know just how important it is to return to our own time. Sullivan must be stopped, Eve. I was the only one with even a little bit of control. The voice of his conscience, you might say, and that is why he hates me. You, he hates for two reasons: You love me and you're mortal. Sullivan has a deep hatred of mortals. Without us there who knows what will happen to the world. You have to help me save not just us but the world, Eve. You need to find the stone to return us both to our time."

"But I don't know anything about stones, Adam."

Adam sighed. Too much too soon. For now he'd drop the matter of the stones. Eve was holding onto him, needing him, and he was going to give her exactly what she needed. He would worry about returning to his time period later.

Mr. Omega, be careful what you do here. It could impact the future.

Adam chuckled softly as he remembered Lora's words. What did he care? That was just his intention. At this moment if Sullivan crossed Eve's path she'd kill him on sight. Now that would be what he called poetic justice. He pulled one luscious nipple into his mouth as his fingers probed, exploring her nether regions. When neither of them could take it any longer he entered her again and reclaimed her, taking her orgasm, riding it out and continuing until the crescendo built within her time and time again. For hours he made love to Eve without ceasing until her sated voice pleaded with him, 'No more.' It was then and only then that Adam allowed himself his primal release. The others had been merely physical. Now it would be a complete joining. He burrowed into Eve's warmth, riding her hard, taking his own pleasure and drinking from her as he came. She was his completely.

***

Shudders of pleasure raked over Eve's body for several hours. When she felt the last of them she knew instinctually that her human self was incapable of taking more. But she was a vampire and she wanted more. She snorted, trying to breathe normally. Eve tried to send her thoughts to Adam not to stop but gave up after an hour. It was then and only then that she allowed herself to truly think about what had occurred. If Adam Omega was in the same time zone with her at that moment she'd kill him.

It angered her that he'd made love to her mortal self so freely. None of the things that had transpired in the past two years would have ever happened if he'd been as willing to make love to her. *The arrogant, insensitive jerk.* How in the world could anyone make a person into something they hated and expect nothing to change?

At last Eve was able to move. She stretched her limbs, feeling deliciously sore and sated. *Damn you, Adam,* she thought again as she rose from the bed at last and headed for the shower, turning the water to scalding in order to wipe away her own depraved thoughts. She would have to find a way to get a message to the mortal Eve. Damn, she thought, but how? She had no idea where she'd sent Adam and no idea how to get him back or how to get a message to herself. Perhaps she should have left well enough alone. But that would mean that both Sullivan and Dr. Meah would be dead.

She bit her lips, glad that she was not connected with Sullivan at the moment. He hated that she thought Adam would kill him. He'd hate even more knowing that Eve knew it would happen. It wasn't just some random thought. Adam was Adam. And Sullivan was not. As much as Eve loved Sullivan for his bravery, it would take a lot more than that to defeat her husband.

Chapter Ten

For once it seemed his travels had taken him to a place he called home. Though a place he didn't spend near enough time in, Adam loved the time that he did get to visit his villa on Santorini Island in Greece. He made his home in what he thought was the most beautiful of the five islands. He'd built his villa high on a cliff on the northern tip. Its stunning view of the Caldera and the Aegean Sea refilled the well within him. Of course the volcano eruptions that had once spewed lava was now little more than a water filled crater.

Since the early days Adam had sought comfort in Greece. Something in his soul rejoiced whenever he returned, as though he'd had a part in the building of the ancient monuments. Without exception it was his most favorite place in the world, Vatican City coming a close second. Stretching out on the beach Adam shifted, smiling as he basked in the sun. This was also one of the places where he used to shout from the mountains that he was not afraid of the sun. Not long after he was made, he'd challenged the sun in these very islands. He'd burned a little initially, but that had been all. He'd lain on the dazzling beaches and swum in the crystal clear waters whose shimmering colors and unparalleled sunsets he'd bragged about to other vampires. That probably more than anything else was the point where the hatred had begun between him and the vampire masses. They'd called him rash and a braggart, unconventional. And perhaps he had been all of those things, but it was those very traits that had enabled Adam not only to survive the early years of being a vampire but to thrive and become who he was now. Adam Omega, *Grand Master Vampire*. He chuckled briefly at the moniker Eve had given him and returned to his reminiscing.

He'd tried to get others to do as he'd done and first only one had
been brave enough to follow his lead, Evan. He had been his one true
friend for longer than Adam could remember exactly. He knew it was
more than eight hundred years. The two of them had tasted all that Greece
had to offer, sampling the women, the food and the blood all made richer
by the ever warm rays of the sun. In their younger days they'd explored
the cave houses and the quaint alleyways. They'd traveled the whole of
Greece and when they were able, they'd each claimed an island and made
it their home.

Now as Adam sat on the beach eating baklava and drinking a glass
of Visanto, he gave a contented sigh. For now all was right in his world.
Taking a glance around at the splendor, he was missing only one thing.
He'd have to bring Eve here to this place, the Eve he'd married, his own
little healer and the vampiric little witch she'd become. Though he'd
feasted on the still mortal Eve, it was his own sweet vampiric Eve that he
wished to share this glorious sunset with. Snapping his finger for a refill,
he glanced at one of his many employees. This one home he kept well
staffed regardless of how long he was away from it. It was special to him.
Sipping the wine, he gave an appreciative nod, knowing that in essence
he'd decided to allow his wife to remain a thorn in his side. How else
could he bring her here to this retreat? He laughed. He very well couldn't
if she were dead.

It was time to set out and find the ancient witch. Adam was more
than aware of that fact. If he ever intended to get home and he did, he had
to get about the business of finding someone who might be able to help.
But it was with a heavy heart that he left his villa for he knew not when he
would return.

Finding the location of the witch had not proven difficult, though
for mortals it would have been. Planes did not travel to the island on a
regular schedule and during the winter months not at all. Another reason
to be glad he was a vampire. His traveling didn't depend on any airline.

Out of politeness Adam walked up the rugged rock-strewn trail
following the path to the witch's home. She'd been alerted by Lora that he
was coming. He could have just materialized inside her home but had
decided to be polite. Witches could be rather tiresome about any being
entering their home without first receiving an invitation. Since he required
the old crone's help, he'd decided to play nice. An hour after meeting Yas
and explaining who he was and his reason for being there, he regretted his
decision. The woman was more annoying than either Eve. Obstinate was
a better word for it.

Adam groaned as he once again tried to explain to the woman the difference in his ability to turn to mist, to just appear wherever in the world he might want to go, and to travel backwards or forward in time.

"Woman!" He allowed the exasperation he was feeling to come through in his voice. "If I were able to travel either backwards or forward in time I would not need you, would I?" He thought his question a rather reasonable one, but apparently Yas did not.

"Vampire, have you not bent time to your will?" she asked.

Adam's teeth were on edge. He allowed a bit of fang to show and the old witch waved a hand at him and smiled in amusement. Imagine a mortal not fearing him, even a witch. She should have reason to fear. But this old woman whom Lora had sent him to intrigued him. She had a lot of power, that much was obvious. She claimed a long ancestry line, not nearly as long as Eve's, but several hundred years. Adam was hoping that would be enough.

"Vampire, has the cat got your tongue?"

"Old woman, my name is Adam Omega. I've reminded you of that several times."

"And I've reminded you my name is not old woman. It's Yas." She shrugged. "Either way, Vampire, you didn't answer the question."

Adam shook his head for a moment. Mortals were becoming increasingly tiresome. Perhaps it was time he revoked his orders not to kill them unless absolutely necessary. Perhaps annoyance could be deemed absolutely necessary. He chuckled slightly. "Yas, in answer to your question, yes, I've bent time. It's child play for me to stop time."

"Then you are ahead of me, Vampire. I have never mastered that."

Adam sighed.

"Do not trouble yourself, Vampire," Yas spoke, ignoring Adam Omega's glare. "I think if anyone can learn the secret of transporting to another dimension or another time you should be able to. You transport yourself where you want when you want. Why can't you just blink and return?"

"Again, if I could blink and return then I wouldn't need you, would I?"

Annoyance had reached an entirely new level. Mortals were going to make him rethink a lot of things concerning himself. If he were truly evil he'd stop the old woman's chatter right now, put her under and force her to give him the information that he required. But he was waiting, albeit impatiently. Adam heaved, exhaling a breath before rolling his eyes to the top of his head and then narrowing his gaze. "Can you help me?" he asked. He saw a mostly toothless smile. Something about the woman forced him to smile in return.

"I am not familiar with time travel," Yas said slowly, keeping her eyes on Adam.

"Then why the hell am I here? Why did I bother to come to Greece for this game playing? I do not have time for this," Adam roared, no longer patient as he stormed about the room, the urge to blow something up rising to the forefront. But he quieted his spirit. This was not the way to handle things. These measly possessions were not his and he'd restrain himself, not destroy them. Forcing himself to calm down and retract his fangs, Adam folded his hands over his massive chest and peered from his lofty position at Yas.

"Let's try this again, for I do not believe Lora to be a fool. She knows better than to toy with me." He gave the woman a look. "Perhaps it's your advancing years that does not give you that same fear." When the woman merely smiled at him, Adam shook his head, knowing his trying to strike fear into the old woman wouldn't work. There were actually certain lines even he wouldn't cross and bullying the elderly was one of them. He'd pressed the point, threatened and still it had not worked. Short of actually carrying out his threats Adam was out of ideas on how to get the old woman to tell him what she knew. He thought of his wife. She'd called him a bully a dozen times. If she could see him now, she'd undoubtedly call him a wuss. Adam rolled his eyes upward and once again shook off the feeling that he was being toyed with. He'd tried reasoning, now he'd try honesty.

"Yas, I truly need your help. If there's anything that you can do to help me I shall forever remain indebted to you. There has to be a reason why Lora gave me your name."

"There is, Vampire. You will need my knowledge when you do return to your time in order to best your wife."

"Best my wife?" A laugh deep and heartfelt came from Adam. "Do you not know who I am? I am Adam Omega. There is none in the world more powerful than I"

A cackle greeted him. The woman continued laughing until tears rolled down her cheeks. Her tears of mirth brought Adam to her side. He kneeled down and touched his finger to the liquid. He thought of his Eve and her sadness when she shed the blood tears. He ran a finger over the old woman's face. "Do you know any spells to create tears…real tears?"

"Yes." Yas studied Adam before another peal of laugher shook her, making her body vibrate with it.

"Why are you laughing at me?"

"Because of the fix you've managed to get yourself in. It tickles me that someone with your powers would have need of mine. Oh yes, I know very well of the power that you have. I sensed your power before you were even near, but having you in my home, listening to you," she stopped and laughed some more. "For all that you are, there is one stronger than you. She is the reason you're in this fix. Your wife, Mr. Vampire, is stronger than you it would seem. She has used trickery, witchcraft and undoubtedly your love for her to control you. One day it will come to a decision you must make. Either you will be forced to kill her or she will kill you."

Adam stared at the woman, listening but not speaking.

"I think you would hesitate to kill your wife, Vampire, but I don't think she will hesitate to kill you."

"Yas, for the love of....tell me why you insist on calling me Vampire? Why can't you call me Adam?"

"I could call you Adam but I call you Vampire for several reasons. First, you are a vampire; second, you don't like it. Third, Vampire," she paused, "for all of your huffing and puffing you have a soft heart. You do not wish to harm mortals." She shrugged her shoulders. "I have annoyed you beyond belief and your need to destroy something is coming off you in waves, yet you've held that feeling in. You are not as evil as you want others to believe."

"Are you sure about that?" Adam snarled. He waited while Yas shook her head at him as though he were a naughty child.

"Why is it that you don't think I'm evil, that I won't hurt you, or even kill you?" He raised a brow. "Perhaps I would drink my fill of you, then kill you."

"But you won't, Vampire. Your soul is not evil."

"Yas, I believe you are deranged. Are you serious? You truly don't think I'm evil?" Adam couldn't help but ask.

"I know that you've done many evil things, but I do not think you're evil."

"Wouldn't it stand to reason that if one does evil things then one is evil?"

"Not in my book. I learned long ago never to throw the baby out with the bath water."

In disbelief Adam narrowed his eyes. He was enjoying the conversation with this particular mortal. She was operating from a different place than most mortals he dealt with. She was speaking without anger, greed, fear, lust, or love. Generally his conversations with mortals and vampires alike revolved around some emotions. He chuckled and thought of Eve. She was generally angry when dealing with him and as for Father Keller, it was his greed that kept the man quiet, his wish for Adam to pour more money into the church and into his own private coffer. Of course he knew what Adam was but he denied it even to himself in order to one day stand before God and declare that he knew it not. Adam laughed, ignoring Yas's look. If Father Keller thought that alone would save him from the pits of hell he was sadly mistaken.

"Vampire, it would seem that your mind wanders. You are no longer thinking of our conversation."

"Forgive me. I was thinking of my wife. Can you please tell me what such a quaint saying, 'not-throwing-the-baby-out-with-the-bath-water,' has to do with this conversation?"

"That should be rather plain. I do not know what made you do the evil that you've done. But I do know that the being standing in front of me is not evil."

"Perhaps I put a spell on you. Perhaps I've shrouded my evil essence."

"You came to me because I have knowledge and power. I'm sure you're aware that I would have spotted any enchantment you attempted to use. No, Mr. Omega, you're not evil. And since I do not think you're evil I will teach you what you need to know to have complete dominion over your wife."

"And that wouldn't be evil."

Yas smiled and Adam did likewise.

"I like you," Adam said. "You're a rare mortal."

Yas regarded Adam with compassion. "I know the reason you want to have tears. It's a gift you'd like to give to your wife to make amends for the wrong that you have done to her. It will not be enough but it will be a start. That gift I can and will give you. But to return to your time... I think you already know the answer to that one. The one who brought you here will be the one to return you home."

Adam groaned. Eve, his reluctant Eve.

"Yas, my mortal wife does not know the answers that I seek. I have probed her mind, pushed her to the brink. She does not know."

"But she does. Your wife comes from a line far superior to mine. I've visited your wife. When Lora told me of your request I paid her a visit."

Her eyes twinkled and she laughed. "I have mastered bi-location. I can send my energy to another place. Once or twice I was able to send my image. For your wife, only my energy was required. Her powers are dormant but she's aware of them. She doesn't want to be gifted, shunned for her gifts as many in her line during earlier times were. But she knows. You will have to get her to accelerate that."

Laughing once more, Yas gave Adam a sly grin. "I assume you've already accelerated your plans with her."

"Lora was worried that my interfering while in this time would affect future things, but you aren't. No, you're reveling in the mischief making. Tell me why you aren't afraid of the damages that I might cause?"

"Why should I be? I'm old. I don't have many years left."

"I've figured it out, old woman." Adam took Yas's hand and brought it to his lips, kissed it gently, then released it. "Pardon me, Yas, for that slip. You possess a bit of mischief yourself and if you were to judge me you'd have to judge yourself." He stroked her cheek in concentration. "Very interesting. I like that philosophy...I heartily approve. Judge not lest ye be judged."

"Can I speak plainly to you?"

For the first time Adam noted the tentative tone of Yas's voice. He smiled at her. "Am I to believe that you haven't been speaking your mind up to now?" He heard her chuckle, saw the sparkle in her eyes and nodded. "Go ahead, Yas, speak plainly."

"There are some things that I know. I do not have to pry to know these things. I'm often given a glimpse of something that I have no need to know." She paused. "You probably will not like what I'm going to say."

"And will that stop you?"

"In this case it will. I know that beneath the kind and gentlemanly way you've treated me there is power and there is violence you're capable of. It's not that I fear you or your power," she shrugged, "but I'm also not crazy. I'm aware that you are a very dangerous man. There have not been many times in my life when I've treaded lightly but this is one. As I said before, I do not believe you to be evil and I do not think you will do anything to harm me purposefully. But I sense an explosive temper. I don't doubt that others could pay for my crime. I don't want that. I want to extract a promise from you."

"A promise? Yas, I'm sick to death of giving promises. One thing I've always prided myself on was keeping my promises and yet I've held my hand and not done the violent things I promised myself. Keeping my promises is part of who I am." Adam stared at the old woman, narrowing his vision, knowing that she already knew that. *What the hell?*

"What promise is it that you require?"

"That no one will suffer for what I will say to you."

"I give you my word. Speak."

"It's about your promises. It would not make you less than the powerful being you are to break one if you really are not of a mind to carry it out."

A smile played around Adam's lips. *Sullivan.* How had Yas known? She had not probed his mind, of that he was sure. He thought of both Sullivan and Dr. Meah and his threats, no, his promise to make them pay for hurting Eve. Adam groaned and closed his eyes. Dr Meah was a loyal employee to whom he'd done enough already... but still...some things were expected of him. He himself expected certain things. Allowing a frustrated sigh to come out he looked at Yas. "You have a solution, I suppose."

"Slight of hand, Mr. Omega. Everything is not always as it seems. You're as intelligent as you are powerful. There are, however, a few tricks I've mastered that I am willing to teach you, things which may give you another avenue should you want it."

Another avenue for dealing with Sullivan and Dr. Meah? Adam thought it over. "I can't say whether I will use what you teach me but I will consider it. I am a lover of knowledge and knowing there are other options should I wish to avail myself of them will be....it might prove fun." Adam laughed and produced an armful of roses. He studied the old woman before him, then handed them over.

"I could prove a valuable ally for you, Vampire," Yas cackled. "But I'd need my memory intact. I could put a spell on your wife or on you." She paused and gave Adam a sly look. "I could make her love you forever. I could make her obedient."

"I could make her obedient if that was what I truly wished, but it is not. As for you putting a spell on Eve to make her love me or vice versa, you can not use spells on a vampire."

"Your wife did."

"That was quite different. Old woman, I keep a barrier of protection around me at all times. I would not be so open to you and even if I slipped I would spot your spell and come looking for you."

"That I know. But I'd need my memory of what I'd done to you in order to reverse it."

"Do not try it, Yas. It would not be wise. Just like there is a tracer to anything done by a vampire there is also a tracer attached to the works of magic. No matter how complicated or how convoluted the trail, it would eventually lead back to the person who wielded it and that person would have to face the consequences."

"It would be a gift. Besides, you said it wouldn't work so why would you concern yourself with me and my spells? It would be a good thing to leave me whole."

To this Adam laughed heartily and shook his head. "You, my dear Yas, are a treasure but as I said, what things I do to you will be for your own protection. Perhaps I should have said it's very difficult to cast a spell on a vampire. Your powers are no match for mine, no witch's powers are, not even Eve's. It would be unwise and, dare I say, a costly and deadly mistake for any witch to attempt to hex any vampire. Even the lesser vamps would be able to tell and they would demand retribution. You'd not want to ever chance that. Heed my words, old woman. This is not a game. Beware of what you do. Trust me. You would not want me to come looking for you because you'd done something to Eve. Besides that, I believe I told you I do not desire her love at the hand of a spell."

"I will not argue that point but I would love to meet with you again when you've found your way back home. I'm as aware as Lora that when you're done with us you will wipe our memories clean."

"It's for your own protection," Adam offered again.

"See what I mean, Vampire, you have a soft heart. What if I asked a small favor? Would you grant it?"

The woman didn't have to ask the question. Adam knew her mind. She wanted to remember him. Perhaps he could arrange it, make it seem a dream. But he would give no promises. He hunkered down besides the old woman and held her hand in his. He could feel the buzz of power strumming through her. He held on a moment longer, getting her blueprint, her DNA as it were. He had no doubt that the witch would indeed try her hand at some silly love spell.

"I would not tell any about you," Yas pleaded. "I value this meeting. I have never met a true vampire and had never thought that I would. I can feel that a change has come to the world. You are the instrument of change and I merely want to be a part of that movement that I feel can't be stopped.

"Help me," he said, "and we shall see. One thing I can guarantee is that the rest of your days will be filled with whatever you desire. You shall want for nothing."

"I want for nothing now."

"Let's start the lessons," Adam laughed. This mortal he liked.

"Take my hand then," Yas spoke in a slow voice, "and listen to my words. I have to ask for your permission to work with you and you have to grant it. That is the ethical way."

Adam shook his head. "Don't try anything funny, I know all languages."

"Do you now?"

"Yes, and as a matter of fact I speak in tongues so you can not slip anything past me." He smiled. "Old woman, you're not very good at hiding your intent." He touched her wrinkled face. "No love spells."

"It has been agreed," Yas answered, "no love spells." Then in the next breath she began to chant in a sing-song voice in old Gaelic fashion.

"What the hell was that you just said?" Adam asked angrily.

"I thought you knew all, Mr. Omega.".

"I know that it's Gaelic and I know that you'd better not do it again."

"Or what, Vampire? I know your weakness. You have a soft heart. Besides that, you like me." She began the chant again.

"Stop that, Yas."

"Why? You don't even know what I said."

"Do not say it again."

Yas smiled and repeated the chant a third time. When she was done she stared at Adam. "Did I put a spell on you? Do you sense magic at work?" To her surprise Adam laughed.

"I feel nothing nor do I sense the working of magic but I am not stupid. I know that your chant was a spell of sorts, not permission to work with me. As for the language you spoke, I know why I do not understand the tongue. You made it up. You made up your own language. How original. Just be warned, if you can play games so can I. Now I will not tell you whether or not I will allow you to keep your memory. I am Adam Omega, Yas. I make the deals."

"Perhaps you do. Or perhaps it is I who won this round." This time Yas didn't say the words of the chant. The vampire standing in front of her was extremely intelligent and as he'd said very adept at picking up languages even ones made up by a powerful witch. No, this time Yas thought the words of the chant. Then she smiled.

"Together, together,together;
Healed are the rifts between them.
Warm is the light that springs across
The gulf that is no more.
Happiness steals upon the scene,
For love is the word and love is the light.
Differences forgotten; unthinking words erased.
Love is the salve that heals all hurts."

Adam kissed the withered skin, turning it young for a moment, handing Yas a mirror to see her reflection. She laughed and their gazes locked. "No more tricks, Yas, and I may just give you what your heart desires."

Yas turned from side to side admiring the beauty she'd been some fifty years in the past. She smiled in appreciation.

"If you gave me what my heart desires, Vampire, that would be you." She gave him a long look and nodded. "Oh yes, that would be you on red satin sheets."

"Behave and let's begin. There is much work to do and the time is short."

"Very well," Yas sighed as Adam took away the mirror and her youth. "If you insist, then you must have basic knowledge. You're going to need sacred tools and an altar."

For one long unbelievable moment Adam was speechless. He thought of Eve and all the paraphernalia she owned. He took inventory of Yas's home. She indeed had an altar. *Sacrilegious,* he thought, the same as he'd thought of Eve's ways. "I will not draw a circle. I will not have an altar, none of that."

"But....Mr. Omega."

"Now you call me Mr. Omega. No, Yas, I will not do as you ask. No sacred circle, no tools of any kind. I will work with the power of my mind and my mind only. I will learn your spells and your incantation. But if I can't speak it, I won't do it."

"You're going to be a lot of trouble, Vampire."

"I will reward you for the trouble, don't worry. I was sent to you because you're powerful. I did not come all the way to Greece to find a kitchen witch. I know that you're not. I also know you have no need of such ritual tools, that it's mostly show or force of habit. I also have no need of such tools."

"At a minimum you should have a protective circle," Yas insisted.

Adam was shaking his head vigorously. "That can be done through visualization. As for the rest, I'm sure you can figure out a way around it." Adam laughed as he caught Yas's low mumbled words.

"If you weren't so...so.." Yas turned and looked at Adam. "If I were only thirty years younger," she stuck out her tongue and made a lewd move, "make that twenty years younger, I'd be sampling you for all of this work you're having me do."

"Yas." Adam coughed, stunned by her words.

"What? I'm old, not dead. Nor am I blind. You are one fine specimen. There is something about you that makes me tingle like a lusty young woman. You are so beyond sexy that you don't want to know my thoughts. The way you walk, so measured, each step full of power. Your hands—" Yas closed her eyes. "You brought back memories that I thought were long dead. You wonder why I will help you. The answer is simple. It's my thank you to you for giving me a glimpse into what it must be like to be a woman in your bed."

"Yas," Adam whispered softly, his voice filled with an apology.

"Don't worry, Vampire. I realize I'm much too old for you."

"Not really, Yas. Considering my age you're jail bait, very beautiful jailbait."

"You call this withered flesh beautiful?"

"All women are beautiful regardless of their age. And all women can still feel the release of passion. Adam touched the pad of his finger to the old woman's head and held her as she moaned and fell against him. When she could stand she looked at him gratitude in her eyes.

"For what you have just given me, Mr. Omega, I pledge the remainder of my life to you."

"I thank you, Yas. But I know where you're going with this. I still must take the memories of this visit away from you when I leave."

"Even the incredible gift you just gave me? Can't you leave me with the memory of that?"

This was one gift he could and would leave the witch with. "Yes, Yas, that memory is yours. As you said, it was a gift." He gave her a slow, seductive smile just to see her eyes light up. Then he wagged his finger at her. "You're an incorrigible witch. It's time we began working in earnest."

As always Adam's thoughts returned to Eve. There were many reasons he needed to learn from Yas and all of the reasons were attached to Eve. Vampire, witch, or Little Healer, his wife would not be allowed to keep secrets. And that was the gist of it.

***

He'd not thought he'd have another day in his home but working with Yas had totally tired him out and he'd returned to the villa to rest. He slept for more than fifteen hours. The sleep of the dead refreshed him so much that he decided to spend a little more time in Greece. A walk along the outskirts of Oia served its purpose. Adam was in a decent mood. Taking in a deep breath, he inhaled the salt scent of the sea. He glanced upward, observing the village from below. The view of the blue and white painted churches was breathtaking with the deep blue water as the backdrop. Adam loved the churches here almost as much as he did the Vatican. If truth be told, he loved churches, the more ancient, the more history, the more he loved them.

Walking toward the village, he smiled at the memories that emerged. If he couldn't bring Eve here at the moment there was one that he could. Evan. He opened a line of communication to his friend. It had been some time since the two of them had traversed the Grecian delights good food, good people, some of the best blood in the world and always the vampire party if one knew where to look. Adam knew where to look.

Within moments Evan was at his side, giving Adam a look as though to say, why are you disturbing me? Adam laughed and laughed some more. "I have a story to tell you that you will not believe."

"I believe all that you say," Evan replied, staring at Adam.

"All?"

"All."

"Would you believe me if I told you that I've traveled back in time?" As he'd known he would, Evan was staring at him, not speaking but waiting. "Seriously, Evan."

"One more of your many feats? You've now mastered time travel? I'm not amazed, not really. It was only a matter of time. And if not Adam Omega, then who?"

"Eve Omega." Adam gave a slow and easy smile, watching Evan's eyes light with interest.

"Come again."

"Eve Omega, my wife, the mistress of my kingdom."

To this Evan really did laugh. "Since when did you get a wife? I've been your friend for over eight hundred years and I've heard you speak of but one wife and that was Eyanna. I've never heard of an Eve."

"You actually have but it will be in a year or so after I meet her for the first time. Okay, I know that sounds confusing, considering that I've already met her in this time period, but the first time... Am I boring you? I know this story is jumbled and confusing but I'm trying to tell you the way this all happened."

Evan was fidgeting, looking annoyed at having been bothered. Anger rose quickly in Adam. "Go now, Evan, I've tired of you."

"You're angry because I don't know what the hell you're talking about? What about me, Adam? I was making love to my wife."

"This is more important," Adam answered and tapped Evan's head with his finger. "If you wish to know what I'm trying to tell you, then you will not behave so impatiently. You are the only one that I want to know this. I need you to affirm this when I return to my time. I didn't send myself here. I was sent here against my will."

Okay, so against his will was a bit of a stretch. He shrugged and continued his tale. "I'm trying to find my way back."

The amusement in his friend's eyes at his predicament followed by the snorts of laugher that he'd tried unsuccessfully to hide caused Adam to pause once more in the telling. "Are you quite finished?" he asked at last, rolling his eyes and blowing on the tips of his fingers, a subtle warning to Evan not to push too far. A warning which Evan decided to heed.

"Okay, Adam, I'm going to need some proof now. You say in a year or so you will meet your great love, your Eyanna who will be named Eve Moses and you will marry her yet again? You say she will be able to send you back in time. Let's say I buy that. Can you tell me how she accomplishes that feat?"

"She's a witch."

"A witch? But witches have no power over us."

"Tell that to Eve."

"You, bested by a woman." Evan bent to pick up several stones from the path and toss them out into the sea. He was chuckling, trying not to, but the effort was making him laugh all the harder.

This time Adam flicked his fingers lightly, setting ablaze small bushes and a couple of trees. "This has ceased to be amusing," he warned.

"Please, you know you find humor in your situation or you would not have come to me. You know I'm the only one who shares your droll sense of humor, the only one to dare laugh at the great Adam Omega, and to his face no less."

"Why do you think that is?"

"Think? There is no thinking involved. We're both aware that you would be lost without me. You need me to talk you out of some of your more dangerous feats. And you need me to bring you back to what you truly are."

Adam raised a brow and sneered. "And that would be?"

Rising to the bait as he always did, Evan didn't hesitate to answer Adam. "That would be a man so torn by his past beliefs that he seeks to destroy all that he ever believed in. A man whom most in the outside world would look upon as a vile, evil creature. A man most conflicted, wanting to believe again in anything, a man who's truly lost."

"You make me sound like some kind of invalid," Adam hissed.

"Not at all. I make you sound real, flawed. There is nothing wrong with being flawed, Adam. And even if there were it wouldn't matter. You, my friend, are flawed."

"And what of you, Evan? What are your flaws?"

At this Evan laughed. "I'd say my greatest flaw is that you are my best friend, that I love you above all others. You are closer to me than blood. No woman has ever meant as much to me, no child, none but you."

"If anyone should hear you speak in such a manner they would get more from your words than your meaning. It's sounds as though we've been more than friends, more than brothers. Have we and I've forgotten about it?"

"See what I mean?" Evan smiled. "You can only joke like this with me. Should anyone ever say anything that would call your manhood into play, they would instantly be dead. But with me, you can joke about it." Evan lifted his head and stared deliberately into Adam's eyes. "And that is because you love me as I love you."

"While that might be true, unlike you, Evan, there is a woman that I love more."

"It would be this Eve?"

"It is."

"In that case I must meet her. Have I met her in the future?"

"No."

"Any reason for that?"

"She lives in America and there was no reason." Adam twisted his mouth to the side in concentration before giving his friend a look.

"There seems to be a reason now," Evan insisted.

"Why, Evan, I think….don't you know there are consequence for meandering around in time and changing things? Who knows what will happen when you meet with Eve." Adam gave a derisive smirk, knowing curiosity had captured his friend. "I will tell you where she works and you may visit her, talk to her, but only for a minute or two, no more. She will not be allowed to remember me from this time so it stands to reason that she can't meet you longer than a passing moment. I have no choice but to erase her memory before I return to my own time."

"Knowing all of this, that my meeting her could change things even slightly, that you're going to erase her memory, you'd still allow me to visit with her even for a moment? Adam, a moment in time could greatly change things."

"I know and hopefully things will change in my favor. I want you to remember this meeting because I will be returning home shortly."

"If you have the means, why not now?"

"Because there are a few vampires I wish to associate with, Melvina for one." Adam chuckled at the groan Evan gave. "Something happened with Melvina a while ago." He stopped, shook his head and continued. "Something will happen within a couple of years. I'm thinking that changing the outcome may do something to soften her up so things will be a bit different the next time I meet her in the future." Adam noted the way Evan was using his teeth and tongue to play over his lips, an old and odd habit he had when trying to persuade Adam that something he was doing would create problems. All Adam had to do was wait him out. A few seconds later when Evan began to speak, Adam smiled to himself.

"What you propose is dangerous and besides that, you have no way to know how it will all play out. You could make nice with Melvina and in the near future she could want you more than ever. Perhaps you should leave well enough alone."

"Evan, Evan, Evan. When have you ever known me to leave well enough alone? You so need me in your life. You are so dull left to your own devices. I will not leave Melvina alone and I will not stop tampering with time. Why you ask? Because I'm curious. I want to see what will happen if I change things. I'm bored alright. The world could do with a bit of shaking up." Touching Evan's arm, Adam moved him in the direction of a jewelry story. "I want to buy a gift for my wife."

"Which one, the one here with you now or the one in your future?"

Thinking about it for a moment Adam looked again toward the sea as though he'd find the answer in the water. "Perhaps I'll buy a gift for each of them. Now, enough talk. It's been a long time since we've been here together. I want to lunch at the Restaurant 1800. I'm in the mood for baklava with sweet olives and pistachios." When Evan smiled, Adam knew he had him by the taste buds. "Or perhaps we could have roasted fillet of red mullet wrapped in grape leaves and served with their spectacular tapenade sauce."

"Or chocolate mousse with nuts and caramel syrup," Evan answered, getting in the mood. "Or grilled lamb chops."

"Honey parfe with pollen and sweet dough," Adam came back.

"And a glass of Visanto," Adam and Evan said in unison. Adam knew then no more convincing was necessary.

"But, Adam, Restaurant 1800 is strictly by reservations only. We don't have one."

Both vampires laughed, again turning to mist and heading for the restaurant to share a meal.

Chapter Eleven

Smoke filled the room, nearly obliterating the fact that the couples dancing and milling about were all vampires. Adam gazed around the room assessing the danger level. High, just the way he liked it. Absently rubbing his hands together, he smiled when he spotted the look on Evan's face. "What?" he asked.

"I should have known that a delicious meal at the 1800 was only a prelude to your real intention for calling me. I can feel the vibrations and I know you can as well. There's going to be trouble. They already know you're here."

A grin graced Adam's face. "Isn't this the greatest?"

"By greatest you mean not being able to go into a simple club, listen to some music, and have a drink, then I would say, no, it's not the greatest."

"No, I meant that when you're wound up and need to let off some steam and not just go on a random killing spree, you can always go where you're not wanted and relieve the tension with those more your equal."

At that Evan could only stare.

"Seriously," Adam continued unfazed, "this is as close to therapy as I'll ever get. I always know when I'm in the danger zone and I find a way to relieve the stress before it gets too great."

Adam sighed and closed his eyes. His words had always been true. Until he'd met Eve he'd had firm control of his anger. Because of her he'd nearly destroyed the world. Another long sigh that sounded a bit more like a growl came out, and with it the tension in his body amped higher. He needed someone to get in his face and he needed it now. He dropped his fangs slowly and growled, issuing a challenge

"Adam, just once can't we please just behave?"

"I did not ask that you interfere."

"But you know that I will."

"That is your choice, Evan. If you don't feel the need, then don't do it. Go home or go elsewhere. I make no apologies for what is about to happen."

Before the words were out of Adam's mouth, three longtime enemies sidled up to him. Fools. Before, he'd always allowed them to live, a little worse for wear but still alive. Tonight there would be no such grace. Adam turned his head slowly to the side, his eyes hooded. "Do not interfere, Evan. I need this and they are barely enough to take the edge off."

Turning his attention back to the vampires before him, Adam asked calmly with a shrug of his massive shoulders, "Have you said your goodbyes?" Then he laughed and leaped forward. He wanted the physical touch. He needed to feel bones break beneath his hands, sever a heart, rip out a lung. When none of those things happened, confusion clouded his brain. The three vamps should be dead by now. Kicking the crap out of them was not what he'd intended as his foot rose to deliver a forceful kick. As one came near, Adam spun, tilted forward and dropped the vamp to the floor, giving him a blow to the head as he fell. When the last of the three had been dealt with, Adam kneeled down beside them and growled, "Tonight you find me in a generous mood. If you wish to remain alive, leave now."

Standing in the middle of the room, he growled long and loud and gave a nod. "Is there anyone else?" he asked in annoyance. His reputation preceded him. None were willing to take the challenge. He flicked at his left shoulder and frowned, then sat and snapped his finger for the bartender. After his drink was served only then did he turn toward Evan.

"Thanks for not getting involved." Evan was staring back at him, a strange expression on his face. "Why are you looking at me like that?" Adam asked in annoyance.

"Adam, what happened?"

"What do you mean, what happened? I just kicked the crap out of three vampires. I told you I needed the rush."

"What you told me and what happened here tonight are two entirely different things. I know you well. Those three should be dead. You wanted them dead. Adam," Evan said. "I entered your mind. You were confused about why they weren't dead. Tell me what's going on."

"Do you at least not have the sense to seal this conversation?" Adam asked, sealing the conversation himself before turning again to

Evan. "I wasn't sure before but now I am. When Eve sent me back she used a spell to partially bind my powers."

"A witch cannot bind your powers, Adam."

"This witch can. I gave her permission." Adam groaned and closed his eyes.

"You fool! You actually gave a woman power over you. Are you crazy? You could have been—"

"What, killed? Not likely, Evan. We both know that's not going to happen."

"This woman you profess to love left you helpless," Evan snapped. "Why in hell would you want a woman like that? Why would you love her so deeply? I don't care if you believe she is your lost Eyanna. I'll have to tell you, Adam, neither version is a bargain. They've both worked to your detriment."

"Eve did not leave me helpless. She took away my ability to kill. Who's to say why we love so strongly? Surely I've given you many reasons through the centuries to stop loving me. Yet you haven't. You've remained steadfast in your loyalty and your love. You have remained my one true friend and my only family. So how can you ask me how I can love my wife? I love her because I do. She is my world, Evan. My heart and my soul belong to her. I'm not a fool, I know the pain this woman has caused me both as a mortal and as a..." Adam had not meant to say so much. He'd had no plans to tell Evan he'd turned Eve. He remembered Evan's reaction in the future to the news that he'd turned Eve.

"What do you mean, Adam, mortal... or?'

"Mortal or witch was what I was going to say, Evan. It matters not. I love her."

"If it weren't so damn serious this would be funny," Evan hissed in pure disgust. "Adam, you have far too many enemies to remain this way. You must get back to your time and demand that Eve take off the spell."

"Do you really think I want her to know it worked to that extent? That would give her leverage over me. I have someone who can take it off."

"Good, let's go."

In a flash Evan sprang from his chair and pulled the concealed sword from his body, swinging it with all his might, connecting and severing the head of a vampire who stood a good two feet from their table. As the body of the vamp crashed to the floor, the room went silent. Blood dripped from the blade and Evan turned slowly to address them all.

"Just because Adam is not in a killing mood tonight does not mean that I'm not. We came to have a drink, not to fight. Bother us again and this will be your fate." He walked toward the felled vampire and cleansed his bloody blade on the dead vamp's clothing before putting his sword away. He glanced at Adam, who merely hunched his shoulders and leveled his gaze at the vampire on the floor, turning the body then the head into ash.

Adam stood, walked to the ashes and ran the toe of his black boot in the ashes, scattering them about the room. He smiled at the crowd, shook his head and then as cool as a summer breeze he returned to his seat and waited for Evan to sit.

This time it was Evan who sealed their conversation. "Adam." That was the only word he spoke.

"I knew he was there, Evan, I would have handled it." Adam clenched his teeth and turned away, the lie scalding his tongue. His mind had not been on the vamps in the room but on Eve and what a fool he'd been to allow her to cast a spell over him. Still he should have heard or even sensed the vamp. There wasn't a damn thing wrong with his power to sense danger. He'd have to keep his focus on his surroundings. Such inattentiveness could get him injured and was definitely not good for his reputation. It infuriated him that he'd been unaware of the vampire's approach or deadly intent. His awareness that Evan knew the lie for what it was bothered him even more.

"Just because you've turned from me does not mean I will not pursue this matter. It's far too important for me to give in to your childish snit. Why bother lying to me when I know you as well as I know myself? The truth of the matter is that he didn't need handling, Adam, he needed killing. And I think you're aware of that fact. You're wasting time sitting here, where you're not wanted, instead of going to this witch and having her reverse the spell."

"I will go but in my own good time. I will not have any here thinking they were the reason for my leaving." The laughter came out before Adam could stop it. His friend, his stand-in confessor, his brother, was angry with him and worried. For the first time in days Evan's concern was the only thing in Adam's world that felt close to being normal. "Do not worry, Evan, I have every intention of returning to Yas."

"I'll go with you," Evan offered.

"I'll go alone."

"This time you will not. I'll not leave you alone without all of your defenses intact. What a stupid woman you're married to." As Adam growled and reached for him Evan moved away. "What are you going to do, kill me for disparaging her name? Oh, wait a moment. You can't because you allowed Eve to bind your powers." Then he laughed. "This woman I have to meet."

***

Materializing inside Yas's home Adam ignored the look of fear in the old woman's eyes. Now he wished he'd left her with some of her memories intact. "Yas, do not trouble yourself, you have nothing to fear from me. We've met before. Listen, this will take much too long to explain,' he said, reaching for her. "I will not hurt you, I promise." And before she could blink he anesthetized the area and bit into her, giving her back the memories he'd taken from her. When the deed was done he released her.

"Vampire," Yas said, patting his face. "You're back," she glanced at Evan, "and you brought a friend. What can I do for you this time?"

"Can you remove a spell?" Evan asked, ignoring Adam's glaring at him.

"Of course I can," Yas replied. "Why, Mr. Omega? Did your wife curse you?" Yas cackled. "Vampire, you need some magic of your own." She reached around her neck and brought away an amulet shaped like an arrowhead. "This is an instrument of healing," she explained. "The turquoise will heal the spirit, the amber will heal your body and the carnelian will heal your mind." She studied Adam, her eyes open wide as her hand moved toward his left hand and she attempted to touch the amber ring he wore. "This ring excretes untold powers of the ages. Your wife gave this to you?" she asked pointedly.

His glance followed hers and Adam snatched his hand away before she could touch the ring. He ignored her question and her gift. "I don't need healing. I need you to take away a spell."

"You would refuse my gift?" Yas asked.

The hurt came through loud and clear in the old woman's voice, making Adam wince from the force of his harsh words. "Thank you, Yas." Adam fingered the amulet for a moment. "Now tell me how to properly cleanse it from your essence. This amulet is permeated with your magical power." He arched a brow toward her. "From the look on your face I gather that's the point. You think I need the extra protection." He started to put the amulet around his neck and paused as Evan entered his mind.

"Adam, do you really think it's wise to put the witch's amulet on, especially now in your condition?"

"My condition? I'm not ill, Evan. The amulet will not harm me." He quirked a brow toward his friend. "Nor will it help me."

"Then why wear it?"

Glancing quickly in Yas's direction, Adam kept the conversation in their minds away from Yas. "It's a gift from a friend and it will make her happy."

"What type of spell did Eve put on you anyway, Mr. Vampire?"

Adam groaned inwardly, trying to find a way around what had to be eventually answered. He didn't want the mortal to know he couldn't kill. It was akin to being seen in one's underwear. Sparks of electrical energy shot wildly around the room as Adam tried his best not to look in Evan's direction. As he'd known, his friend had a smirk. There was but one way for him to deal with the old witch and that was honestly. He'd have to admit his weakness for the moment. With his teeth tightly clenched he took in a huge breath filling his lungs, expanding his chest. The decision was made. As much as he wished he didn't he needed the witch's help. A witch had gotten him into this mess and it would take a witch to help him out of it. *Damn!*

"I'm not altogether sure," Adam began. "Eve was just supposed to be trying to send me into the past, which she accomplished, but at the end of her incantation she said something about binding my powers, preventing me from doing harm. "I need to do harm, Yas, do you understand? Sometimes there are those who need killing. I have to be able to do that."

Yas narrowed her eyes and looked at Adam as though she could see through him. "And your friend, is he your enforcer? Is he to make sure I do as you ask, that if I do not he will harm me?" She turned to Evan. "I don't sense the same kind of heart in you that I sense in this one." She pointed to Adam.

"Yas," Adam warned, "would you please stop spouting nonsense? I didn't return to you for that purpose."

Dealing with mortals was the most frustrating thing of his existence. With Evan thinking he was his conscience, it was all the vampire would need to hear, that a mortal thought he had a soft heart.

"Just get on with it, Yas."

"It's not that simple, not this time." Yas moved about the room. "This time I demand payment."

Both Evan and Adam arched a brow in her direction. "And what would your payment be?" Adam asked.

"Leave my memories intact."

"I can't do that, Yas."

"Then I can't reverse the spell."

Growling, Adam lowered his fangs and allowed the red haze to fill him. "He reached for Yas and held her. "You will do what I say," he ordered.

"Or what, you will kill me?" She laughed, then swatted his hands. "Now stop holding me so tightly. I'm an old woman."

Adam closed his eyes and sighed in frustration. "Yas, please." He looked toward Evan who was laughing quietly.

"It would be dangerous for me to leave you with the knowledge of what has taken place. I can not agree to that." Yas was ignoring him. For over an hour Adam pleaded with her and for over an hour she refused to answer. She just continued with whatever she was working on, throwing bits of powder and herbs into a cauldron and stirring.

"I can give you new memories of me," Adam offered.

"Will I know that you're a vampire?"

"Is that a condition?"

As he stalked about the small rooms, Adam was trying to figure out a way to keep a promise to the old woman without doing anything to put her in danger. *Options,* he thought. *Sleight of hand.* He finally turned and faced Yas with a broad smile.

"If you wish to remember that I am a vampire, then yes, that can be arranged. But the memories will be different. That we can not bargain on. Do we have a deal, Yas? What are you doing," he asked as he saw that she kept her back to him and continued throwing things into her cauldron. "Are you going to help me?"

"I was always going to help you," Yas said and grinned at him before turning slightly to include Evan.

It was a good thing for this ancient mortal that he liked her. "Then begin, Yas." Adam said impatiently. "I have a score to settle."

Adam watched enthralled as Yas placed a large black candle in another cauldron and filled the cauldron to the rim with water.

"Now, breathe deeply," Yas instructed. "Meditate, visualize the power flowing and growing with the candle's flame. Yes, I'm talking of the power that was used against you," she answered the unasked question. "You will do this until the flame sputters and makes contact with the water. Then you will visualize the spell's power exploding into dust, becoming impotent."

For a long moment witch and vampire stared at each other until Yas gave her cackle and turned to Evan. "Come along, Evan," Yas said, taking Evan by the arm. "This will be Mr. Omega's job to do alone. He does not need our presence."

Sometime later Adam joined them with a smile on his face. He watched as Evan rose cautiously.

"Did it work?" Evan asked.

"Let's see," Adam whispered as his hand shot out and he circled Evan's throat, nearly crushing it in the process. "It worked," he answered, "and the next time you enter my thoughts uninvited I will…" He laughed. "What I do will not be pleasant. Now let's go."

"Didn't you forget something?" Evan pointed toward Yas as he rubbed his throat.

"Oh yes, thank you, Evan. Yas," Adam smiled at her. "Are you ready?"

"Yes, Vampire, I am."

Adam gently bit into Yas, filling her mind with dreams and beautiful memories of things that had never happened, erasing all traces of the things that had, erasing Evan from her memory as well. No need to bring his friend any undue problems in the future. When the deed was done he put Yas to sleep a moment before he and Evan turned into mist and disappeared.

***

Strains of a long forgotten love song drifted from the door of the club as Adam and Evan entered, both dressed from head to toe in black, both wearing long black dusters that caught the slight breeze they'd created. And both walking deliberately in slow motion for the effect. Heads turned as they entered, they glanced at each other and smiled.

It might have been Adam who initially attracted the female vamps but it would be Evan who made love to them. He had no such qualms against making love with vampiric women who were up to the vigorous task.

"You wanted to try and smooth things out with Melvina. Now's your chance. She's heading over here," Evan whispered.

"The smoothing out is for the future," Adam reminded and smiled broadly as Melvina approached. She was nearly drooling. Adam wondered if he would have noticed that if he didn't have prior knowledge that Melvina had somewhere along the line fallen in love with him. *What had he done?* he wondered.

"Melvina," he greeted her, his voice smooth as velvet caressing her skin as he spoke, noticing goose bumps appearing on her flesh, the little shiver of anticipation. *Ahh*, he thought, so that was what he'd done. He'd perfected that manner of speaking so long ago that it was a natural part of him, as natural as breathing. He thought of Yas, an old woman way past her prime, but one who'd desired him. All these years he'd been making love to the women with the power of his voice and he'd not thought once about it.

He smiled and took Melvina's hand in his. Kissing her palm he smiled at her. He had hundreds of years of making up to do for loving women with his voice, his touch and not going farther. Tonight with Melvina he would go as far as he ever went with vampiric women. Tonight he would drink from her. Too bad she couldn't reciprocate but that was the one line he wouldn't cross. Only Eve had drunk from him with his permission. That was the way it would remain.

Many hours later both Adam and Evan were sated. Evan had enjoyed a harem of their women, and Adam three mortals. Adam's eyelids were heavy, the lids were nearly shuttered with sleep yet he was enjoying the company of his friend. He studied Evan from his nearly closed eyes until Evan glared at him in annoyance, unable to read Adam's mind to know the reason for the intense scrutiny. "How can you be gone so many hours from your wife? She's mortal and mortal women are much more clingy and territorial. Doesn't she question where you've been?"

"She would if I didn't send her constant images that I'm there with her."

"Ahhh," Adam laughed. "I see the secret to a successful marriage to a mortal."

"I wonder if I were you what words would I say to you? A scripture perhaps, Evan smirked. "I think I have it. Judge not, Adam."

"I wasn't. I was merely making an observation. That's too much work for my taste."

"As much work as making love to mortals then wiping their memories clean? It's sort of the same thing, Adam."

"Touché."

"You know, Adam, you wouldn't have to go to such lengths if you'd let go of your memories of being made. That's the only thing that keeps you from fully being with our women. They're our equals. Why don't you let go of the memory? It's past time."

"How can I let go of that memory, Evan? If I did I would have to let go of memories of Eyanna, of my wife. I can never do that."

"But you said you found her again, that she's Eve reincarnated. So why can't you let the memory go?"

The amber decided to pick that moment to glow. "This is the reason. This is the wedding gift my bride gave to me and it was this that alerted me to Eve's true essence. It assures me of Eve's love, and even her life. I'm afraid if I gave up that part of Eyanna I would lose a part of Eve. I can't take that chance."

"But you could change that memory of being turned. You could allow it to fade. I could help you, Adam. I could relieve you of that burden. You could make love to any vampiric woman you choose." Evan was silent for a few seconds. "You could make love to your wife. Think about it, Adam, the offer is there."

"You know me, Evan. I have to do things for myself. I have to conquer my own mind on this, not just have a memory erased. I'm not a child and I'm not mortal. I'm Adam Omega."

"Yes, I know," Evan laughed. "You're the super vampire extraordinaire." He held his glass up to Adam and they clinked and drank. Then Evan looked at his friend. "Should you ever need what I offer all you have to do is ask."

For an answer Adam merely smiled and switched the subject. "I love the way you handled your sword."

"When was the last time you touched yours?"

Shame stole over Adam at having to admit that his own swordplay was a bit rusty. "It's been awhile," Adam admitted, "though watching you in action I think I will reacquaint myself with it. I'd forgotten how much fun using the blade can be."

"When you find a way to return to your wife will you still pick up your blade or will you forget it and our visit as easily as you wiped away that old witch's memory?"

"I'll make you a promise. I will begin regular practice with my sword the moment I return to my true time."

"All that you say is so incredibly unbelievable."

"But you believe me?"

"I have no choice. I will always do as you ask. When have you ever needed me and I was not there?'

"Never." Adam sighed. Why else do you think I came to you. What I ask you to do now is of the utmost importance. I want you to remember our time together, Evan, because as soon as I return I want you to meet Eve in all of her glory, my beautiful and deadly vampiric, witchy wife. I want you to know the reason for my loss of mind."

"You will keep your promise to relearn your sword?"

"Yes, that is a promise I will keep my friend. We will touch blades together as we've done so many times in the past."

Refilling both of their glasses, Adam allowed himself a moment of sadness. "Drink up, my friend. I'll leave you soon to check on the mortal Eve's progress. She's not learning as quickly as I'd anticipated."

"What? You thought because you wanted her to cram four years of knowledge and studying into a few days that she would, that she even could? Adam, you set an impossible task and I think you're aware of it."

"I'm not a man of patience. While I'm stuck here, who knows what the mistress of the vampire world is doing. She's quite a handful."

"And you love her."

"I love her madly," Adam answered, smiling broadly, bringing his glass once more to clink against Evan's. "Loving my wife has always been my undoing."

Chapter Twelve

If one could drown in exasperation, then Adam was drowning. He hated to admit it even to himself, but part of the reason he'd lingered so long in Greece was his increasing annoyance with the Eve of this time. She constantly doubted him, giving him looks that he couldn't decipher. Sometimes she outright refused to do the things he ordered her to do. He had to have the patience of a saint to indulge her in her shenanigans. It would have been so much easier to force her to do that which he required. From time to time she had him wondering if perhaps Lora was right. Maybe he had inadvertently done something to alter events. He wasn't sure but he felt that Eve was a good deal more obstinate than she'd been the first time he'd met her. This one gave his vampiric Eve a run for the money.

In disbelief Adam stared at her now as she stood in the exact same store she would stand in in just a couple of years. In that time it had appeared she'd known exactly what stone to chose. This woman in the store with him now was trying his nerves, vexing his spirit. She appeared to be without any talents or knowledge. He hated to depend on her for his returning home. She wasn't doing a very capable job as far as he could tell. He gritted his teeth to keep from yelling at her. The one thing sure to close her down was his tone of voice. The mortal cared little that he was a vampire, that he was powerful, that he could kill her with but a thought. She cared not because she knew he loved her. *Love*, thought Adam, it was a nuisance at times.

"Eve, buy the entire store if you must. Surely something here calls to you."

Adam spread his arms wide. He was dismayed at the slowness with which Eve was adjusting to the fact that she had powers. Were it not for the fact that he was making love to her several times a day, he would not be able to tamp down his impatience. Granted, he'd had to use his powers to persuade her to take the needed time from her job. Assisting mortals to find books was not important to him, especially in the face of what he was dealing with. This was not where he belonged. Who knew what his wife and Sullivan were cooking up? As much as he enjoyed sharing the mortal version of his Eve's bed, he wanted, no, he needed to return home. A growl slipped from his throat as he held up several crystals for closer inspection.

"Adam, I'm trying." Eve spun around at the sound of disgust that was in Adam's voice.

"I'm sorry, I know you are," Adam said walking up to her. He sighed deeply. Despite his wish not to continue using his powers on Eve, he was left with little choice. She was not tapping into the ancient powers. He'd have to give her a reason to push harder. Encircling her in his arms, he sent her mental images of the fictional children they'd left behind, then images of Sullivan plotting harm against those fictional children. He held Eve in his arms and was aware the instant her anger at Sullivan reached its peak. She was a mother, she would do everything in her power to save her children. He trailed a finger over her cheek. "We can leave now if you're stressed." Adam's voice was soft, melodious, just as he'd intended. He trailed a finger up and down her arms, feeling the quaking emotions that lay beneath the surface. Now wasn't the time to push but to allow Eve to do that which he wanted. "Don't worry, Eve, I'm sure I'll think of something."

"No."

Eve moved from the comfort of Adam's embrace. This vampire, this Sullivan, had to be stopped. He was planning to harm her children. *Were her children still babies? If they were, how was that possible since she'd lived this life for so long? She'd have to ask that of Adam but for now she had to try her best to do as he asked and find a way for them to return to their children regardless of their ages.* Her voice caught on a sob. She couldn't let harm come to her children. She reached for Adam's hand, grateful for him and for his love, grateful that he'd come for her. Now they were both stuck here unless she could find a way to send them home. She would do it if it were the last thing she did. Sullivan would not be allowed to destroy her family.

She moved to the center of the store and closed her eyes, then opened her arms wide. "I need quartz," she said slowly. She turned toward Adam and opened her eyes. "Why are you smirking?" she asked.

"Not smirking, just pleased. I knew you'd remember. Is there any particular quartz you need?" Adam asked, moving away from her, reprimanding himself for his enthusiasm. If this was to go smoothly…if he was to get Eve to remember her spell and the stone she'd used, he'd have to control his emotions. He walked toward a shelf that held clear quart reached for a piece and held it out toward Eve, waiting for her nod of approval.

"No, larger," Eve spoke up coming alongside him. "They have many larger stones in the back." She closed her eyes for a moment. "The stones are being held for a healer. I want those."

"They are not for sale," the clerk quickly replied as his eyes skimmed over both Adam and Eve. Then he stood there staring at them.

"They are now!" Adam growled low turning swiftly on the man, dropping his fangs and allowing the red to obliterate the purple of his eyes. "I will pay you double, but we will take the stones."

"Adam," Eve cautioned.

He counted to ten before turning toward her. "Do not tell me how to negotiate," he warned. "I am not in a mood to be chastised." He turned back to the clerk. "Eve," he said slowly, watching as the clerk trembled, feeling the shiver that claimed Eve and the ripple of doubt that ran through her mind. He sent warmth and love to crowd out the uncertainty and continued with his purchase. "I will not harm him," he whispered.

When they were done he could feel the ripple in time. It would be years before Eve would begin her quest for knowledge. He'd tend to it before he left. He'd erase Eve's memory. Well, maybe not completely. He hadn't decided how much knowledge he'd leave her with, but he would erase enough.

***

So many huge quartz crystals dotted the room that Adam could swear that Eve had to have the stone she needed. At his insistence she'd bought dozens of books on crystals. When she found the means to return him, maybe he'd leave her with those and just take away the memory of why she had them. He smiled to himself. Then again, maybe he should leave her working on something to rid them both of Sullivan. That thought made Adam laugh out loud. Maybe that was the way he'd go. His folly sobered him. That would not be the way he would take care of his problem with Sullivan. No, when Sullivan met his end it must be at Adam's hand.

His Eve's earlier suggestion that Adam allow them to stew now had its merit.

That thought made Adam turn toward Eve. He saw only confusion in her eyes. This Eve, this mortal, did not have the knowledge of her not too distant future. At this moment, in her mortal state, his wife would undoubtedly fight hell itself to find him. Four short years in the future she'd do nothing but laugh at his predicament.

"Adam." Eve started toward him. "What's wrong?"

"Nothing my love," he whispered, deciding to calm her fears by making love to her. Knowing that his future Eve could feel him making love to the mortal Eve made his loving of her all the sweeter. He laughed and reached for Eve, falling on her, suckling her breast as his hand slid between her thighs.

I wonder how you're explaining the moaning, Eve, he thought and went at loving the mortal Eve in earnest.

***

"Where are you getting all of this energy, Adam? Even your stamina shouldn't be this great. Give it a rest," Eve screamed out to the cosmos, knowing Adam could hear her as he made love to the mortal version she'd once been. She was going to lose her mind if Adam didn't stop. She'd acted too hastily. She should have known that Adam Omega would find a way around what she'd done. She had to admit finding and wooing her mortal self was the perfect revenge. She couldn't be around Sullivan or Dr. Meah because she had no idea when Adam would begin making love to her. She felt every single stroke, every caress, every probe and there'd not been a single thing she could do to prevent it.

Shame colored her features. Prevent it? What a lie. She'd begun welcoming Adam's touch, shivering in anticipation. What kind of slut did that make her? "Damn", Eve said aloud and struck out at the lamp that was on the counter, breaking it into a million pieces. Adam Omega was a problem no matter where he was or what he was doing. She needed to figure out a way to get him back where he belonged.

A moan slipped from her mouth and her head rolled back as she felt Adam's fangs biting into her, making her swoon with lust. She tried to assuage her guilt by reminding herself that he was her husband. She loved him and always had. She ran for the bed and climbed into it, pressing the pillow between her legs, hoping it would prevent her from feeling Adam's fingers invading her body. "Stop, Adam," she whispered into the cosmos. "This isn't fair."

Then it hit her. Of course it wasn't fair. Adam was doing this to keep her from Sullivan, not trusting that her breaking up with him over killing Mark would be enough. More than likely it wouldn't have been. She still loved Sullivan and she truly understood his dilemma in trying to save her. In fact she was glad of it. But she didn't need another Adam to take her over. No sooner had she thought that than Eve screamed out in ecstasy as Adam took the plunge and drove her over the edge.

"*Adam, Adam,*" she moaned, "*why can't you come home and do that?*"

***

"Adam, I think I have it." Eve's voice was excited as she held the stones out for Adam to examine.

"Are you sure," Adam asked, trying to keep his level of excitement down. They'd been through this many times and each time he'd taken the stones from Eve and attempted to return to his own time, erasing the memory of finding the stone from her, only to have it not work and the work have to continue.

"Yes, Adam, I think this is it," Eve continued. "This one will take us back and this is probably the stone Sullivan used to bring you here. See, look here in the book." She extended it to him. "I think I understand the process. Now I just need an incantation."

"Can't it be something simple?" Adam asked. His question earned him a smile.

"I suppose you're right. It can be simple."

"What if something happens and we get separated? Will I be able to use the stone without your incantation?"

A shrug, then a look of doubt crossed Eve's face. "I'm not sure."

"Let me have the stones," Adam commanded softly, holding out his hand and closing his palm as the stones were laid inside. "Sorry, my love," he said calmly as he smiled and brushed his lips across hers. That was all the time he needed to put Eve under and erase her memory of the two stones she'd just given him. He watched as she blinked and decided she needed sleep, a deep sleep. As her head dropped forward, he smiled and cradled her body against her chest. "Rest easy, Eve," he whispered. "I must go home."

The stones burned in his palm, a blessing perhaps. Adam's own studies had long since revealed he had an affinity to the stones, just as Eve did. Not everyone could coax the power from the stones. Hopefully this would work; he'd already spent close to a month here. It had been fun but he needed to know what was happening. He glanced back at his innocent, sleeping wife and smiled. She wasn't as easy to command as he'd thought but she was a lot more moldable than his vampiric wife who knew full well her own powers. She was the one who deserved to be punished for her actions, not the mortal woman he was leaving.

Here goes, Adam thought as he pocketed the stone that could return him to the past, should he have a desire to return. He laughed. Why not keep two Eves, one of whom he could make love to at will. He'd have to give it some thought. It was as he'd always said; good could come from all things.

Rubbing his chin, he paced back and forth trying to think of words that would take him back to the point in time where he wished to be. He'd thought to go back before Eve sent him into the past but he didn't want that. He wanted her to have full knowledge of having done it so that she'd be aware that she'd be punished for it.

"Timeless travel be easy now. Twenty nine days I have lingered here. Do my bidding with righteous fear. Take me forward from whence I came with the twenty-nine days' passage of time that I've gained."

Adam sealed his palm around the crystal, closed his eyes and pictured himself back in his time. He felt a breeze, slight but there. The same thing had happened when he'd been transported. He dared to open his eyes and laughed out loud. He was home. If nothing else would have told him that, the smirking Eve presiding over her potions would have. He stood as he was for a moment staring at her.

"So you made your way back, I see." Eve said moving away.

"How long did you plan to leave me there?" Adam asked. "You should have sent me farther back."

"I know that now. There would have been no need to send you anywhere if you could ever be reasonable. There is no need to kill Sullivan or Dr. Meah. Sullivan and I are no longer together."

"That's not the point. I promised and you know I never break a promise." He tilted Eve's chin and stared into her eyes. "I'd forgotten how much fun you used to be."

"When you weren't threatening me or using me as your personal buffet, oh yeah, Adam." Eve thunked herself on the head. "We had great fun."

"We've had great fun for over three weeks recently."

"You raped me!" Eve blurted.

"So you did feel me! Good. Was it as good for you as it was for me?" He came closer.

With a shove of her hand Eve pushed Adam from her. "I was going to bring you back."

"Why?"

"Because I didn't like the feeling of being violated by you."

"You didn't like it?"

A moan slid from her lips as she felt Adam suckling her breast, his hand sliding between her thighs, his fingers entering her wetness, though he was nowhere near her. She glanced backwards at her husband not surprised to see a satisfied grin on his face. "Adam, stop," she pleaded in a whimper.

Adam wore a satisfied grin. "Do you really want me to stop or do you want me to continue until you've found your release?"

"I want you to stop, Adam."

"Very well, I will."

For a long moment their gazes remained locked as they read the other's thoughts. Then Adam spoke. "I didn't tell her goodbye. I have to return and tell her that."

"You found a way to return?"

"Of course."

"You're not going to tell her goodbye you're going to erase her memory."

"I took care of her memory. There are other things I want to do."

"Make love to her?"

"Yes."

"No, you can't. I forbid you to touch me."

"You can't forbid me and even if you could, that Eve wants my touch. I'll see you shortly."

"Adam."

Adam stopped and waited. "Yes, Eve," he finally said when it became apparent that she wasn't going to speak.

"Are you aware that here in our present you've never once told me when you were leaving. You'd just take off for months at a time."

"Are you jealous?"

"More like curious."

"More like jealous. It's not as though I'm cheating on you, Eve." Adam shrugged his shoulder and grinned. "It's you I've been making love to."

"If you had not turned me, it could have been me all the time."

"If you had not tried to take your life, turning you would not have been necessary."

"So as always we're back to this, your thinking my being a vampire is my fault."

"Yes."

Adam walked slowly toward Eve. "But my not making love to you is my fault." He saw the slight shiver that touched her as he came closer. He held her face in his hands. "You are loved by me beyond measure. And I am aware, my love, that I am loved also by you. Did you know that I carry your heart with me? I carry it in my heart. Are you aware that several times a day for the past two years I had to talk myself out of killing you as you lay with Sullivan?"

"That's not love, Adam."

"Believe me, Eve, it is. Love restrained my hand."

"Not guilt?"

"No, darling, never guilt. Only my love for you kept you alive. *Gra anois agus go deo.*"

"What language is that and what does it mean?"

"It's Gaelic and it means love, now and forever. It is that love for you that will bring me back to you." He smiled at her as he reached out with the pad of one finger to caress her lips. "It would be so much easier to return to where you sent me and make love to you repeatedly, but having to erase our memories and plant new ones isn't quite the same. It's you, but then again it's not." He watched as a smile graced his wife's lips.

"So how was I?"

"You were magnificent."

"Stop it, Adam." Eve laughed, moving away as he pressed closer. "I don't mean that. I meant was I so easy to control?"

"I wish. No, my darling, obnoxious little wife, even without knowing your powers, you were a handful."

For a long moment Adam stared at Eve. There was much between them, things that had yet to be resolved. They'd each hurt he other beyond belief. But this moment in time was not for remembering the recriminations. It was for remembering just how much Adam loved Eve. How much he loved the taste and scent of her. The longer their gaze remained locked it was inevitable that they kiss. Tilting Eve's chin slightly

Adam's lips closed over Eve's and he kissed her, pulling her to him. Hard and fast he plundered her mouth, taking from her and giving in return. Her arms wrapped around him and the scent of her blood called to him. He took it, drinking from her, feeling her almost swoon, knowing what it was taking for her to hold herself back from doing the same. She thought he would reject her. He lifted his head high enough to whisper, "Drink, Eve." When he felt her fangs pierce his skin he shuddered and held her close. He was not going to push her way, not this time. When she was done he stared into her eyes. "You are mine, Eve, and I do not share. This time of foolishness is over. Your commitment to Sullivan should be over as well."

"It's not that easy, Adam. He's been my friend and my lov —"

"I'm giving you fair warning, Eve. Don't say it."

"Fine. I'm not out to have a fight with you. But you have to know this isn't easy for me. Sullivan has been here for me when you haven't. He's never once left me, Adam. He's made me feel adored, cherished and safe. He's respected me and my wishes."

"He didn't respect your wish not to call me. He didn't respect your wish not to kill a mortal to save you."

"And you don't think I see your hand in that?"

"Maybe so, but Sullivan had a choice. Tell me something. Why do you find it so easy to judge? You are not the judge of me, nor are you the judge of Sullivan, Eve. You are not sinless, not even in this matter. I dare say it's your fault that all of this happened and before you give me that damn look, it started a thousand years ago. As Eyanna you betrayed me and my love. And as Eve, you betrayed me every chance you got. You took it upon yourself to sleep with my enemy, then begged me to be understanding, knowing that it was going against everything that was in me to allow it, to allow either of you to live. From the moment I met you, you have made me behave in a manner I do not like. You are not a stupid woman, yet you are a conniving, lying witch who plays the whore when it suits you. Your anger at this moment means nothing to me for my words are the truth."

Adam stopped the barrage of words. He'd not meant to say what he had but even so he was not taking back a single word.

"Do you really think that? You're insane. You've bullied me, left me near dead, taken every friend I had in my mortal life away from me. Made demands that I couldn't comply with. You call me a whore because it helps your warped perspective of the things that have occurred. It gives you a sense of right if you can lay what you've done to me at my doorstep.

But you can't. You're hurt me beyond belief, Adam, not just now, but from the moment I met you. You've caused me hardly anything but pain."

"And you have broken my heart. The heart of a thousand-year-old vampire is not an easy thing to break but you have done that, Eve, and you had no regrets. You think I care that Sullivan is hurt? Let me assure you I do not. You have been given more than you should have received and yet you ask for even more. I think I did myself a disservice by admitting that you were my Achilles heel. I want you to make no mistake, Eve, Achilles heel or not, love or not, there is a certain limit that I will not allow even you to go beyond. If you cross that line, there will be no more 'Eve, mistress of the vampire kingdom.'

"If there is no more Eve there will be no more Adam because you will wither and die."

"I lived a thousand years before I found you. I will live a thousand years after. You do not hold that kind of power over me."

"I think I do."

"There, right there. That is the fundamental difference between us. You think… I know. Trust me, my darling, I love you madly, but when all is said and done I remain Adam Omega and I am not ruled by my love or my lust. If I were so easily controlled by my emotions you would have been dead the day you plotted with Sullivan against me."

Pausing to study her, Adam made an indistinguishable sound in his throat. Shaking his finger in her face, he breathed in several times to calm himself. "But we were not originally talking about me. We were speaking of Sullivan and the time you were with him by my grace."

"Your grace or not, I was with him for two years. He's loved me, made me happy and I've loved him."

"Loved?"

"I still love him, Adam."

"And me?"

"I love you more." Eve's head fell forward. "That's no secret. I've never lied about this to either of you, or to myself."

"You can not have us both."

"I'm aware of that but…."

"But?"

"I don't trust you. I trust Sullivan and I don't want him out of my life."

"It would seem that choice is not yours to make. I will give Sullivan one week to leave for good or I will do what I must."

"Adam, you know he's not going to go for that. He loves me and he's not going to leave me nor will he act the coward in front of me."

"Then he'll leave me little choice, will he?" Now I must go."

"After being here with me, after kissing me as though you meant it." She stooped licked her lips and looked away. After taking my blood and allowing me to take yours, you're still going to make love to her aren't you?"

"Yes, and all the time I will be thinking of you." Adam stared at his wife for a long moment sensing the sadness in her. He sighed deciding to give her the gifts he'd bought for her now rather than when he returned. She was his weakness and he didn't want to see her sad.

"I almost forgot. I brought you something from my little adventure." Adam reached into the pocket of his duster and pulled out several pieces of extravagant jewelry. The baubles received scant attention and a mild, thank you. He smiled and handed her over several chunks of honey amber. The smile was a bit warmer. Some of her sadness lifted and so did his. "I have one more gift for you," Adam said in a slow, seductive voice. "I'm sure this one will bring more of a smile to your face."

"You didn't have to bring me gifts, Adam. There's only one thing I want."

A long and weary silence filled the air between them. "I think you'll want this as well." Adam pulled the gift from his pocket. As he held it in his palm, he watched Eve. He saw the moment her heartbeat stilled, then sped up. Her eyes opened wide and she gasped in surprise.

"Adam, it's an Athema!"

"I know. Every witch should have one... even a vampire witch." He waited while Eve took the blade from him, examining it, running the blade over her delicate skin.

"The blade is dull but it's only meant to be used as a ceremonial blade, not for actual cutting."

"But, Adam, you find this...all things of this nature sacrilegious. How could you? Why did you buy it for me?"

"Because, you, my love, do not find them sacrilegious." It was then he was rewarded with the light that shone from Eve's eyes. He felt surrounded by her love and went to her. Holding her head between his hands he slowly massaged the side of her head, touching his forehead to hers. "You are most precious to me and I love you without reservation. I meant it when I kissed you. I always have." His lips settled over hers. Pulling her closer, he gave her several kisses. When her arms wrapped around him, he grinned and whispered the incantation in his mind that would return him to the past. As he spoke the words so that only he could hear he gave Eve a long kiss.

When they broke for air Eve smiled as she watched Adam palm a crystal, knowing he'd thought rather than spoken his incantation, knowing it was because she would have heard it. He didn't trust her and she didn't trust him. As her fingers touched the mist where Adam had previously stood, she shook her head a bit. She glanced first at the jewels, then clutched the Athame to her knowing what it meant that her husband had given it to her. She had to admit, she did like his style.

***

He'd not lied about having other things to do when he returned to the past. He visited all that he'd seen before to make sure their memories remained erased. It was two days before Adam sought out the mortal Eve. He'd deliberately lingered, ignoring that she'd be worried about his abrupt disappearance, perhaps even angry.

Adam stood outside the public library where the mortal Eve still worked and where he knew she would be. It was time to erase the memories of those at the library who'd seen him. And it was time to let go of this innocent mortal Eve and return to his wife. His flesh quivered at the thought of not making love once more to his innocent mortal Eve. This Eve loved only him. There was no Sullivan to compete with. For a moment he wondered why he wanted to return home. With a sigh he pushed the heavy glass door open.

I will return because I'm Adam Omega and I don't run.

Walking into the room Adam twirled his finger and pointed in all directions to freeze all those in the library. He moved to Eve and snapped his fingers to bring her out of the trance.

"Adam, where did you go? I fell asleep. And when I woke you were gone." Tears filled Eve's eyes. "I've been worried about you."

"I know," Adam whispered then sighed heavily.

Eve blinked as she looked around at the patrons and employees not moving, but instead were standing as if they were stone statues. "What happened? Adam, what did you do?"

"Nothing much." Adam waved his hand dismissively. "I want to tell you goodbye."

"Goodbye? What do you mean? Where are you going? Are you going to leave me here to face Sullivan alone?"

There was panic in her eyes, fear for her safety then a strange glow. Anger, Adam noted.

"Then go you worthless piece of shit. I will not beg you to stay."

Adam shook his head slightly as he reached out a hand to caress her cheek, only to have her slap it away. "I wonder how far back in the past I would have to go to find you meek and mild." He chuckled. "But I don't think I'd like it any other way." Still, he didn't think he wanted two Eves hating him. One was more than enough. And so he'd lie to her, give her hope, love. What would one more lie hurt?

"You misunderstand, my love. I had a vision our children are in danger and I have heard of someone who can help us, a woman who lives in Greece. I'm going there to see if she can. I wanted to tell you goodbye before I just took off."

"Adam, I'm sorry... I thought..."

"I know very well what you thought. Why would you ever think I'd want to leave you?" He pulled her into his arms, savoring the moment, feeling her soft sweet curves fill his arms. Breathing in the essence of her, he etched the scent of lemons on his heart. He allowed the smell to embed itself into his lungs. His hand trembled as he touched her. The urge to take her back to the apartment and make love to her once more was overwhelming. But he was hearing the voice of another Eve, his vampiric wife, the true mistress of the vampire world. *"If you had not turned me it could have been me the entire time."*

A shudder of remorse rolled through him and he restrained himself from the lust. Damn. If only he could replace the conniving, lying, backstabbing, two-timing whore of a wife with this mortal version. But he would be living a lie, accepting defeat and that was unacceptable.

"But I love you more." Adam heard Eve's words loud and clear. She was trying to make him not make love to her mortal self. Even though it was her, she was threatened by it, jealous, perhaps feeling a bit betrayed. Adam pulled back. He understood those feelings well. He growled and crushed this mortal, innocent Eve to him, kissed her with all the pent up passion and love and wiped her mind clean of him. Then he put her under and walked out of the building. When he was out he turned, looked back and waved his hand again, knowing that within a couple of seconds all in the building would return to their lives unaware of a slight loss in time. He thought of Yas, the ancient witch. *"Yes, Yas, I bend time when it suits me."*

Now it was time to visit all that he'd allowed to see him and take away their memory of him. He wondered if he should leave Sullivan and

Uriel to wonder about his rant and laughed. Maybe he would but Lora and Yas had to be taken care of.

***

Now for the most important task of all, returning home and dealing with his recalcitrant wife. He'd erred in thinking that simply showing her how to feed would work; he'd erred even more by giving her a mortal to feed from. He should have known. Had she properly fed, none of the things that had happened to her would have. Perhaps in time she could try her little experiment but not now. Now she needed to become strong, to replenish herself, and that wasn't going to happen with some artificial blood the doctor cooked up in the lab. Nor was it going to happen by the use of Eve's stones or her magic. She needed fresh blood and she needed it straight from the human tap. He would see to it that she took it. After her first drinks she would feel the compelling, undeniable thirst and he could stop worrying about her. She would begin behaving as a proper vampire, as mistress over all.

And you will feel even more distanced from her? Adam whirled around. A conscience? Could it be? Who knew? Eve had caused all manner of strange things to happen to him. He wouldn't be a bit surprised if she'd managed to provoke a twinge of conscience in him. He shivered at the thought.

"I'm back," Adam announced. He watched Eve warily, not forgetting Yas's warning but not really concerned about it either. What could his wife do to him? The thought brought a laugh. After his recent adventure maybe he wouldn't be so cavalier in his opinions of what she could and would not do. She was capable of almost anything. Why wouldn't she be? She was his. He'd made her and damn it to hell she was a woman. A very lethal combination.

"So we have one week, master?"

"Did you think to insult me by calling me that? I rather like it." Adam laughed as he moved slowly toward her.

"I knew you would. Seriously, what are your plans and do I get a vote?"

"You voted. Your party nominee lost. I won. We do things my way. First lesson, Eve," he said, moving even closer to her, taking her in a steel embrace, "is to make sure you're properly fed. There will be no more near death experiences for you. Do you understand that? I will not worry every time I'm gone for a few hours that you've done your fool self harm."

Eve struggled to rid herself of him but it was no use. Her powers did not equal his and her magic was having no effect. She raised her hand and slapped him and he slapped her back.

"Do that again and I will take you over my knee like a child. Now stop it. You will feed tonight and that will be the end of it." Enfolding Eve in his arms, he spirited her away. Coming to a club he picked out a man and put him under. Then he turned toward Eve. "Now," he ordered, "Feed."

"No, I will not and there is nothing you can do to make me."

With a shake of his head he sighed in disappointment. "Will you never learn to stop baiting me? I can make you, Eve, and I will make you." He saw the fear mount in her eyes, felt her body stiffen in his arms as he put her under, not much but enough that she would move in the manner he saw fit. She would do this and she would do it now and do it right.

"Anesthetize the area, Eve," he ordered, pressing on her harder. She was putting up a good fight, he'd grant her that, but when this night was over Adam would know that his wife was not defenseless. Blood filled his eyes at the thought of her vulnerability. She should never have been at risk. Sullivan had been entrusted to care for her; he'd failed and he'd pay for that. Now he had to deal with protecting Eve whether she wanted it or not. "Drink, Eve," he commanded and watched her turn pleading eyes toward him. "Drink," he ordered, applying a bit more mental pressure.

When Eve's fangs pierced the mortal's flesh and her mouth lowered to drink, Adam watched her carefully. She was full of trickery. When she was done she lifted her head, her hate-filled gaze promising revenge. That didn't worry Adam. He could take care of himself; he just needed to make sure that his wife could. Two damn years. Unbelievable, simply unbelievable.

"Seal the area, Eve," he said softly, thinking she wouldn't obey but this she did without hesitation, touching the man gently, wiping her face with the back of her hand at a stray tear that fell.

"He's not your pet or your lover, Eve. He's food and that's all. Now come." He enfolded her again, trying to ignore the pungent scent of lemons. He had a job to do.

Mortal after mortal the same procedure was done until Eve was feeding with precision-like accuracy, knowing when to take a little and when to take more. There was just one more thing he needed to make sure she could do, and that was to find her own victims and put them under and take what she needed. She had to do this without the threat of him bending her to his will.

"I have a gift for you, Eve."

"A dead body?"

"I have a way for you to end those blood tears you hate." He waited, saw the hope flare in her, then the recognition that this gift wouldn't be given freely. She closed her eyes and moaned.

"What do I have to do?" Eve asked.

"Live."

"But I am living."

"In the past I trusted you to behave as you should, Eve. You didn't do that. I want you safe. Can't you understand that?"

"I can understand that you want me cowed."

"Not cowed, Eve, never cowed. I want you safe but what I offer you now is a peace offering, my way of making amends."

A harsh laugh fell from Eve's lips and she spread her arms out wide. "Do you really believe that it will make amends for all you've made me do tonight?"

"Yes."

"Then like I said before, you need help."

"Do you want to not cry those blood tears anymore?" He waited, saw the struggle going on in her, and knew beyond anything else Eve wanted to alleviate them.

"If you weren't always making me cry…"

"That's neither here nor there. Do you want the gift?"

"Where did you get it?"

"A gift from a friend."

"And your friend…is she dead now?"

At this Adam laughed. Eve thought him a bully, a killer, evil. He gave her a gentle smile. Lucky for her Yas had not thought him evil and had given him the one gift his wife would value above all else. But she was right, the gift wasn't free. He had to know she could and would feed if need be. Eve had to be able to protect herself if he were not around. She had to remain strong. It took fresh infusions of blood from time to time for optimum performance. Nothing was as good as fresh blood, and it couldn't get any fresher than going to the source.

"Well, Adam, what do I have to do to get this gift?" Eve asked.

"Seven."

"What are you talking about seven?"

"Seven is the number of completion. I want your lessons complete, so it will be seven."

"You're talking in riddles now, Adam. Speak plainly." When he said nothing, Eve narrowed her eyes and went into his mind, stumbling back in horror at what she saw there. "Oh no...Adam, no, I can't..."

"You don't have to. I won't force you, Eve. It's strictly up to you."

"But I'm full. I have no need of blood."

He shrugged. "As you wish."

"Can I think about it?"

"Until tomorrow."

Adam's face was stone. He would give it to her anyway eventually, but getting her to do this would be better. Once she'd done it, hate him or not, it would be sealed. She would be the mistress she rightly was and her tears would no longer run red.

"Adam, please."

He smiled. She thought to woo him with a soft voice and pleading brown eyes. It wouldn't work. He loved her far too much to ever leave her vulnerable again. Adam handed Eve a small amber bottle. "If you drink this, you will sample the gift you'll receive when you finish the task. You need to feed without my forcing you. Seven, Eve."

Adam uncapped a small amber bottle and gave it to Eve. "Drink my love and tomorrow we'll talk." Without another word, he disappeared.

***

Pacing the floor for hours hadn't helped Eve one little bit to find an answer to her dilemma. Adam had offered the most powerful inducement of all. She'd long faced some facts: She wasn't mortal and for the time being it didn't seem that she had a way to change that. She absolutely hated the tears, maybe more than anything that had happened to her thus far. What would she give to rid herself of them? What line would she cross?

Judge not.

A terrible sigh filled the room and Eve wrapped her arms around her body. She wasn't stupid. Adam was trying to teach her a lesson. But she'd seen the look in his eyes, however brief, the sorrow for the faintest of moments for what he'd done to her.

For all the hours of pacing she'd done, nothing was different. She was so angry with Adam that she could throttle him. Never mind that she'd known it was coming. Never mind that after the fourth feeding she wasn't as disgusted with herself. Never mind that after the tenth she knew exactly what Adam meant by the adrenaline rush. And never mind that somewhere in his twisted soul was his need to protect her. She knew all of that; she'd be a liar if she claimed otherwise.

Eve sighed again and sat down to think. She'd felt the pain in Adam. The thought that he might lose her wore heavy on him. She was his weakness and like it or not, he was hers. She swallowed the thought to doubt that the brown bottle would do what he'd said. Adam prided himself on not lying, though he was adept at bending the truth when it suited him. The truth of what he'd said was something she could determine so easily.

A single shudder began on her left pinky toe and traveled to her crown charka making her a bit woozy.

Adam Omega was now more than vampire. And Eve Omega was now more than the mistress of his kingdom. She had erred when she doubted that Adam would try to learn the secrets of magic. But he had, the very thing he'd called sacrilegious. And for what? One reason and one reason only controlled his actions: to have dominion over her. He couldn't let her have one damn thing that was her own. She should be worried, she thought as she picked up the amber bottle, uncapped it and tilted it to her lips. She knew for sure that it didn't contain poison. Adam didn't want her dead; he wanted her alive. That much was obvious. She allowed the liquid to trickle down her throat. Closing her eyes she swallowed.

For one long agonizing moment Eve imagined she knew a little of what Adam had endured for so long. She had run away from danger as fast as she could. Even now some small part of her was still calling out in prayer, knowing that no voice would answer. She would still be a vampire. What good were her prayers? She wasn't like Adam, able to have the right quote for every occasion but the situation she was faced with now called forth a scripture from long ago. *What does it profit a man to gain the world and lose his soul? Matthew 16:26*

That was the choice she was now faced with. It was a hard choice, especially since she no longer had any hope that God would come to her rescue. As crazy as it seemed, it was Adam who was bringing her some measure of relief from her predicament.

Conflicting thoughts continued to rage within her. There was Adam, her tormentor, the reason for her pain. Then there was Adam, her savior, the bearer of an unbelievable gift. But was she ready to accept the consequences of her actions in order to accept Adam's gift? She didn't have to fake the tears. Every single time she thought of her life they came. Sure enough the hot tears fell and ran lighter. She touched her finger to them and cried out in joy. Clear. She couldn't believe it. Oh God, she couldn't believe it.

Running for a mirror Eve stared at herself in disbelief. She was crying and the tears were clear. She couldn't stop this doomed cursed existence, but those damnable blood tears were gone.

"Thank you, God," she whispered. "Oh, God, thank you."

"But I am the one that gave you the gift, Eve."

Adam. She should have known. No matter. "Thank you, Adam, and I do mean it from the bottom of my heart. Thank you."

He materialized beside her. "So you're pleased?"

"What do you think?"

"And the seven?"

Eve had almost forgotten. Almost, but not quite. She stared up at Adam, holding his gaze. "Would you really take away my ability to end those damn blood tears?"

"Would I take away my having to worry about you every moment you're from me? Would I worry that someone somewhere will attack you and you will be too weak to defend yourself because you've only been taking in artificial substitutes or blood frozen from the blood bank. That maybe if you'd had something a bit fresher you'd be a match for whoever is out there? I wish I could tell you that this gift is without a price, but that I can't do my love. This has to be sort of a quid pro go. I give you something and you give me something in return." Adam sighed hating what he was putting Eve through but it could be no other way. "I will give you the formula and you will give me the assurance that you can feed on your own."

"But...I...I...I did, Adam."

"No, darling that was with my being there and using force to get you to feed."

"Why is all of this so important to you?" Eve whispered.

"I want you safe. You are a part of me, Eve. And like it or not there are some that hate you simply because of that. I have tried many times to warn you of the dangers. "

"You made me. I have your blood in me. I can feel the strength I have." Eve stared for a long moment at her husband. "I would think that anyone tangling with me would know that and feel my power and leave me the hell alone." She continued to hold Adam's stare. "You forget that for more than two years I commanded respect from your employees. You weren't there with me physically, but your blood gave me a certain power." She tilted her head. "I was feared because I had your blood, Adam. And I didn't have to feed."

"True, you are of me, but you are not me. You are not ruthless, cold or calculating."

"You said I was conniving. Calculating is the same thing."

For a moment Adam stared at Eve. Wrong or not he didn't like it pointed out. He shrugged and continued, "You can not be merciless."

"And neither can you, Adam," Eve whispered, moving into his arms. "You make everything so difficult. Instead of giving me flowers to show your love, you ask for my soul. Why does everything with you have to be so hard?"

Her head tilted back and she stared into his eyes. His love washed over her like spring rain, erasing the hurt, the pain between them. But it was only an illusion. They were joined through eternity in battle. This was just a momentary truce. There would be other battles to fight.

"How does this work? You withhold the potion from me until I've done the seven?"

"Essentially."

"Then what?"

"After you've finished the circle of completion I will give you the means with which to make the potion yourself. You will no longer be at my mercy." He caressed her cheek. "I'll still wait until tomorrow for your answer. I'll see you later." Eve clutched his hand in hers and looked into his eyes. She spoke but one word and that one word was enough.

"Yes."

Chapter Thirteen

"Suzett, it's been a long time," Adam smirked. "Much too long, my friend." He opened a bottle of "Cristal" and poured it into flutes. He held one out to Suzett and laughed. "Excuse me, I almost forgot," he said, snapping a finger and bringing a warm bottle of blood. He poured. "You really should try something new, my dear." He stretched his legs before him, having not stood as the vamp entered the room. He gazed at her, shaking his head in amazement that each time he saw her she looked different. Now her head was completely bald and she had piercings covering a good portion of her body. The silver gleamed against her ebony skin.

"Why have you sent for me, Adam?" Suzett asked, accepting the blood he offered. "You've never once sent for me in all the hundreds of years we've known each other. Even when I saw you a few years ago it was nothing more than a nod I received from you. Maybe a hello. I don't remember. I'd say if anything you've had very little use for me."

"Until now," Adam replied softly.

"Why now? Why not before?"

"You lack class and sophistication." Adam shrugged. "It's nothing personal."

"I'm very glad it's nothing personal."

A smile lit Adam's features. "That's what I like about you. You're a vampire and you know it. None of this silliness acting as though you're mortal having your feelings hurt by mere words."

The vamp tilted her head and stared at Adam for a long moment. "Why would I allow your words to hurt me when if you wanted you could do so much more to me? Listen, I can't kill you. You won't bed me and frankly, I see no point in being your enemy."

"Does that mean I can count you as an ally?"

"Are you in need of collaborators, Adam?"

"Not so as you'd notice but a pair of eyes in another part of the world is always a good thing."

"Well, I'll be damned. The great Adam Omega coming to a female vampire with a request."

This time it was Adam who observed her. "Call it a request if that is what you wish, but trust me, Suzett, it is not." He smiled slightly, sipping his champagne until he felt the full effect of his message taking hold. Why pretend that what he'd said wasn't an order. It was and he had every intention that it be carried out.

"What is it that you want, Adam?" Suzett asked as she moved a distance away from him. "I hear that you've done what you've forbidden the rest of us to do. You turned your wife." She paused for a moment, remembering all the hundreds of vampire females who'd unsuccessfully attempted to bed Adam throughout the centuries. None had succeeded. Yes, he'd allowed them to pleasure him but he'd never reciprocated, at least not in the way that was common for them, not in the way the women wanted. Many had come to think of it as an honor to do that much for Adam, considering he so rarely had anything to do with the females of the species. "Have you gotten over your little aversion?" she asked hopefully.

"For one, Suzett, only one." Adam noted the smirk Suzett tried unsuccessfully to hide. It meant that she'd heard, as probably had every other vampire the world over. The great Adam Omega had at last found his weakness and like Samson a woman was his undoing. Only in Adam's case it was a vampiric woman. Why play games? Adam narrowed his eyes. "It would be much better to have me as a friend, Suzett. Don't you agree?" he asked softly yet with a sharp edge to each word. He waited a moment until she'd apologized and then he continued.

"I have a job for you. I want you to pay Sullivan a visit."

At last Suzett smiled. "Sullivan?" She blinked. "It's been so long…hundreds of years since I've so much as thought of him. But yes, I remember him well. I turned him you know." Her voice became small and a tinge of anger coated her words. "That was long before your decree went out and you started killing those I'd made."

Adam shrugged. "It was necessary. Judge not what I do, Suzett. I do think it's time for you to pay Sullivan a visit."

"Are you trying to make your wife jealous?"

"First off, let us be clear on things. It is none of your business why I called you or why I demand that you visit Sullivan. But to humor you I will answer the question. Your ability to make my wife jealous would be highly unlikely. No offense, but I do not think you're capable of doing that. Eve is not in competition with you for Sullivan's affections.

"What about yours, Adam?"

"You're not my type and never were. Even if you weren't a vamp, I would not be interested in you," Adam said in a matter of fact manner. He saw no point in denying the truth.

"Ouch," Suzett winced. "I can see why Melvina is so pissed off at you. Were you this honest with her?"

"Just do the job I want you to do and ask me no more questions. I could care less if either of you is pissed at me. It would serve you well for me not to become pissed at you. Just so you know, it matters not to me if you time your visit when Sullivan is alone or with my wife. Just do it.

I am not asking you to find out if Sullivan has feelings for you still. I just want you to pay him a little visit. There is information I will require later from you. As you just mentioned it's been many years since you've seen him. As his maker it might be interesting to see if you retain vamparic contact."

Vampires. Women. Damn, Adam thought. Combine the two and you had definite problems. He should not be giving the vamp any idea of what he wanted. That he was doing so annoyed him, but he had his reasons for calling Suzett. There were things Eve was doing that Adam needed to know about. He'd made a deal to give Eve three days to say her goodbyes. So far she'd not tried to return to Sullivan's home and he'd not entered Adam's domain, so Adam had to wonder where this goodbye scene was taking place.

***

Fury filled the very air that Sullivan breathed. Calling himself ten kinds of fools did little to appease his mood. He was too old for such nonsense; he should have known better than to fall in love. As if that wasn't bad enough, why did he have to fall in love with a woman that belonged to Adam Omega, the vamp's wife from a thousand years in the past. Adam Omega's sole reason for becoming a vampire had been to protect his wife. Having found her reincarnated as Eve hadn't diminished the need but escalated it. Sullivan had known all of this. Hell, every vampire the world over knew of Adam's love for his wife. Still, it had happened. Sullivan had done the unthinkable. He'd fallen in love with Eve and there was no going back.

A bolt of energy surged from the tips of his fingers as he slapped at an imaginary speck. The inability to control his emotions was more than a sore spot with him. He was not Adam Omega. He wasn't a spoiled, brash, arrogant asshole. But that was exactly the way he was behaving.

This isn't doing a damn bit of good, he thought, then laughed. Maybe it wasn't Adam's fault that he always acted in such a crazy manner. Perhaps it all had something to do with the woman they both loved. True, Adam has always behaved in an unseemly manner, but not Sullivan. Sullivan had never felt this rage, this helplessness, not with Suzett, not with Joanna. Only with Eve Omega, a woman he should have known not to love, a woman who would forever be in love with her husband. The thing of it was, he'd known that and even if he hadn't she'd told him. He couldn't blame her for that one; she had never lied to him about her feelings. But damn it all, she'd loved him too.

Loved.

The use of the past tense did what Sullivan's rage could not. It stopped him cold. That was what was at the root of the problem: the thought that Eve no longer loved him. He'd told himself he would be prepared for the day her love would be taken from him. But he wasn't. It was a lie.

Sullivan did that which he hated. He sighed, a huge sigh of sadness. The hopelessness of the situation insisted on it. That was much safer than what he wanted to do, which was to sweep into Adam's home and reclaim Eve. Another sigh slipped out. What if Eve wouldn't go? What if Adam killed her if she did?

An inch of fang lowered and the taste of blood was on his tongue. Adam's blood. Never had Sullivan wished more for a way to defeat Adam than he did now. While he didn't doubt Adam's love for Eve, he also was aware that Adam would and could just as easily kill her if he chose to do so. The thought of him doing just that was what kept Sullivan from forcing himself into a home where he was not wanted. Well, that and the fact that Eve didn't want to have anything to do with him past urging him to run like a coward from her husband. That he would not do.

For a moment Sullivan stopped his pacing. Eve was known for protecting others. Could that possibly be the reason he'd not seen her for the past month? Hope flared at the thought and died just as quickly.

Maybe at the moment she was protecting him from Adam but what about before Adam returned from his tryst into the past? The more he pondered, the more disgusted he became with himself. If it were not such a reckless act, he'd do as Adam and destroy half the world. But what would that solve? Would it erase the look on Eve's face when she saw Mark's lifeless body? Would he no longer feel the pain she'd felt at that moment, the betrayal? He'd never forget it, hadn't for one cursed second.

Taking in a deep breath, Sullivan wavered once again on the brink of anger. This time it was directed solely toward Eve. How could she have lived with him for two years and so easily let him go? He'd been with her longer than Adam in this lifetime. Her allegiance should have been with him. He was the one who had been there for her, not Adam. He was the one who'd worshiped her body. Again, not Adam. Adam had run away because he couldn't stand to see what he'd created. He'd made Eve into a vampire and couldn't take it, wouldn't make love to her, yet threatened to kill them both when Sullivan did. The damn fool. Sullivan had tried to warn him that Eve would not live an eternity without love in her life.

At last he had something to smile about. The one thing Adam could never take away was the love he'd shared with Eve. She'd loved him once, and he'd loved her. In fact, he loved her so much that he truly had no wish to live if she were not in his life.

A sharp laugh came from Sullivan. He might just get that wish since Adam had issued a new edict that he was going to kill both him and Dr. Meah in one week. That might very well happen but Sullivan was not running from the preposterous loon.

Anger flared again. For weeks Eve had dismissed him, refusing to see him, to connect with him and then out of the blue she'd opened her mind to his, called him with her mind and pleaded with him to run, even cried. Her desire for him to run left a bitter taste in his mouth. He'd failed her, failed to protect her, to command her to behave as a proper vampire, to take a victim and feed. But she'd had enough of taking commands from men and that had never been what their relationship was about. He was for her, a safe haven. He'd known that going in. Sullivan was what her husband was not. Reasonable.

What an irony. Since losing Eve he was turning more and more unreasonable. He would not run. He would stand his ground and he would fight Adam Omega to the death. That was not his worry. His mind was the thing that worried him. He had never been so scattered, so bent by the winds of a woman's affection, and he couldn't reconcile how easily Eve had thrown him to the side for his one crime against her. He'd done the one thing that assured that. He'd killed a mortal. But he'd killed Mark to save Eve's life and hell yes, he'd do it again. If the need arose, he'd kill a thousand mortals to save her, just as he'd attempt to kill the one vampire that stood in their way.

There had to be a way to kill Adam. And if there were, Sullivan would take great pleasure in doing so. But so far Sullivan had found no way. The thought of not being around to protect Eve, to love her, make love to her… He shivered with want and need as the memories of their lovemaking cascaded over him. What he wouldn't give to feel her curl against his body, to enter her and reach completion. He groaned with the ache of wanting her, knowing no other could fulfill him as she did. That alone was worth fighting for the right to love her.

This time Sullivan didn't attempt to tame the energy that filled his body and raced to destroy. He aimed at a few inanimate objects, shattering the things to dust. He kicked at the ashes, letting off steam, then brought the shattered objects back to their original shape.

If only it were that easy to restore his broken heart. What an old fool he was. Had he thought he was Adam, that he could do things that Eve didn't like and she'd forgive him as she'd forgiven her husband? The things he'd done wrong in their relationship had been because of his love for her. Twice he'd failed her and she'd banished him and taken away her love. Two indiscretions: calling Adam and Killing Mark. Didn't he deserve to be forgiven, to get another chance? Were her second chances and forgiveness reserved only for Adam Omega? What happened to strike three and you're out? He should have one more strike.

Sullivan began his endless pacing again. This was not doing any good, nor was his mantra that vampires were not monogamous. He should just find a nice female vamp and lose himself in her, forget that he'd ever met Eve.

An ache deep and abiding filled Sullivan, something ancient. He felt the way he did when he visited the graves of long dead family, empty, lost, alone. He didn't relish that feeling. For over two years Eve had filled his world with light and love. Closing his eyes he roared out her name, demanding her to answer, getting nothing, no response, no door open to him.

The need to think of something other than the loss of Eve's love permeated every cell in his body. He resorted to anger. At least then he didn't feel as helpless. He felt the fire that burned in his belly. There it was, his reason. Once more he allowed his mind to focus on Eve's warning. How dare she just contact him to drop a bombshell?

"Seven days is all he's giving you. Take it and go, Sullivan. I don't want you to die. Please leave. Let him cool down for a few years, give him time to forget. Go, Sullivan."

And just like that she'd cut communication. Several days had passed since her warning and Eve had not dropped her shield against him.

Sullivan sighed heavily. He'd known what he going to be in for. He tried to convince himself that nothing mattered but Eve. That she was alive should be enough. It wasn't. He swallowed. He wanted to talk to her once more, hold her if that were possible. In a few days he'd have to do battle with her crazy husband and the chances were it would be his last. Didn't Eve even care a little? How could she so easily forget him?

A groan slid from his lips as he felt the presence of a vampire in his home. He turned slowly, knowing who it was.

"Why are you here?" he asked, making no move toward Suzett. His gaze flicked over her, over her perfectly shaped bald head. The last time he'd seen her she was sporting hair past her behind. Her onyx skin gleamed; her eyes, always too large for her small angular face, were open and curious. He'd not seen her in at least four hundred years. He wondered why she was there. He'd never even felt her probing his mind.

An air of warning touched Sullivan. He'd not seen Suzett, had not even uttered her name until he'd told Eve how he'd come to be a vampire. Something was amiss. *Eve*, he thought and blinked. He moved with sudden swiftness toward Suzett. If she were here to harm Eve, as much as he'd once loved her, he'd kill her without a thought. He'd pledged his life to keep Eve safe and he'd die honoring that promise. He swallowed and remembered his upcoming battle with Adam. He'd have to take care of Suzett quickly.

"Aren't you glad to see me?" Suzett purred.

That sound had once given Sullivan instant erections. He'd loved her throaty growl and her husky purring, but the spell had long been broken. He no longer desired her.

"It seems rather odd that you're here. It's been what…over four hundred years? I've never in all that time thought for a moment that you were thinking of me, not one fleeting thought. Did you?" he asked, "and please, no lies, just the truth."

"Frankly no, I didn't."

"Then why now?"

"Eve Omega."

"Ahh, I see."

"No, you don't see."

"Then suppose you tell me. Sit," he offered, then sat beside her snapping his fingers and handing her a glass of her beverage of choice.

"O negative?" Suzett asked.

"Does it matter?"

"It does taste a bit sweeter than the others."

At that Sullivan smiled. There was some truth in that. "I remembered, Suzett. It's O negative. Now back to the matter at hand. What is it you want with Eve?"

"I hear she's your consort and wife to Adam Omega." She wagged her finger in front of his face very gently. "That's just plain asking to have your ass handed to you on a platter. Adam Omega is going to kill you. Did you think he wouldn't? All that I've heard, Sullivan, it's hard for me to believe. You were never this reckless man. Why now do you suddenly have a death wish?"

A small chuckle rattled in Sullivan's throat but didn't come out. A smile pulled at his lips but was never fully formed. "I do not have a death wish, quite the opposite. I have found the one being in the entire universe who completes me."

"And you would die for her?"

"I will not cower before her crazy husband."

"Why do you call Adam crazy? He's not."

"He almost destroyed half the world. I'd call his actions a little much, and I'd call him crazy for doing it. He turned Eve, went against all the rules he'd made for the rest of us. How many of your vampiric children did he kill, Suzett?"

Sullivan's eyes narrowed into slits and he reached for her hand, holding it tightly and probing her mind. "So, you've now sided with my enemy. Adam sent you here. Why?"

Confusion was clouding his brain. This was not what he wanted. He needed to be sharp.

"I need to know your mission."

"To be honest with you, Sullivan, I don't know. Adam wanted me to pay you a visit."

"To make Eve jealous?" Sullivan asked curiously.

A loud snort filled the room. "Please, that arrogant bastard told me the likes of me would be no competition for his dear wife, that she'd not even give me a second thought. What do you think?"

Before Sullivan could answer she'd stripped and was fondling him, holding his penis in a death grip.

"Stop, Suzett!"

"Ohhh, that sounds so weak, kinda like Michael Douglas in that movie *Disclosure* when he was asked what he did when the woman took him in her mouth and made love to him, and he said, "I said stop.""

Suzett laughed and lowered her head, taking Sullivan into her mouth. She was surprised when Sullivan pushed her away.

"It's been so long," she moaned, "and you know how good I am. Come on, let me give you just a little blow job. It can't hurt anything."

"No. I don't want it and it can hurt everything."

"You mean Eve? I made you. I had you jonesing for me so bad you would have given up your mother to have me give you just one lick, and now you're telling me no. What the hell is going on? What the hell has this Eve got?"

Wrong move, Sullivan realized as he tucked himself back into his clothes.

"Are you trying to tell me that Adam Omega's wife is better in the sack than I am? I don't believe it. She's been a vampire for just a couple of years and you think she's better? Maybe you've forgotten just how good I truly am." She snapped her fingers, disrobing Sullivan in the process.

"It's not about the sex, get that through your head," Sullivan said angrily. "I love Eve. That dampens my libido for you, not your abilities. Yes, I remember how good you were." He saw her bristle. "I know how good you are. But I don't want you." Damn, another mistake. He shrugged. "I haven't wanted any woman since Eve." With a wave of his hand Sullivan redressed himself, casting a disgusted look in Suzett's direction.

"Your ass is going to die because of this little twat and you don't want me."

Sullivan shrugged. "And by the way, Eve is not a twat, or a bitch, or any other derogatory name you want to fling around. You'll call her Eve in my presence or you'll leave. Don't try me, Suzett," Sullivan warned. "I'm in no mood to play."

"So where is this Eve you're so bent on protecting?"

Sullivan glared, refusing to answer. Surely Suzett knew the situation.

"Oh, that's right, you betrayed her, saved her life, killed a mortal and instead of thanking you, what did she do? She turned you over to Adam. And in a few days you die for that. For what Sullivan? She doesn't want you. Leave with me tonight. Adam is not so desperate as to travel the world looking for you. I'm almost sure he wanted me here to give you a way out. Let me be your way out. We can be together for a time, maybe a year or two. You're far more interesting than you once were. The old

Sullivan would have never in his wildest imagination thought of taking a woman from Adam."

Her chin lifted. "Did you do this because of Joanna? She was a vampire groupie, a whore. All of us knew this, all but you. I do believe I even tried to warn you once or twice. Suzett shrugged. "Then again, maybe not. I don't remember, but I do remember hearing about it and how crazed you became because the little tramp died in Adam's bed. I did think of you then and wanted to offer you a bit of comfort, to urge you to let it go. Maybe this Eve Omega is just payback for Adam draining that mortal twat. Your actions are suspect. Are you sure it's love you have for this Eve? Maybe you no longer know who or what you want.

"Believe me, Suzett, my love for Eve has nothing to do with Joanna. Besides, as hard as this may seem for you to believe, I no longer blame Adam for Joanna's death."

"Impossible."

"Not impossible. I know the truth about what happened and I have accepted it." He smiled as he thought of Eve and then swallowed. "I love Eve because I don't know how not to love her."

"Let me help you, Sullivan. Let me make you feel pleasure beyond belief. I can even give you pain if that is what you wish. Come away with me. You're the last of my makings. I do not wish for you to die."

Annoyance pulled at Sullivan. He was sick and tired of everyone thinking he could not defeat Adam. Hell, he couldn't, but Adam would not get away unscathed. Their past battles had proven that. More than anything, it bothered Sullivan that Eve had not bothered to come to him. He looked at Suzett, trying to figure out her true plan, and knew instantly it was best Eve didn't come, that she kept pretending she could live without him in her life. He allowed his eyes to close briefly. *She was pretending*. She had to be.

"I want to meet this Eve. Call her to me."

At that Sullivan laughed. "Are you crazy?"

"I can make you bend to my will."

Sullivan laughed even harder. "Try it." He shook his head as he felt the energy from Suzett reach out and twine around him. He waited until she was done, then with a snap of his finger caused the energy to dissipate. Disgust claimed him at the look of surprise on her face. "What is wrong with everyone? I'm a damn vampire, an eight- hundred-year-old-vampire. Did you think I'd learned nothing in all my years of existence? You have no power over me, Suzett."

Damn, Sullivan sighed as he felt Eve's presence. He'd wanted her to come to him for over a month and this was the moment she chose. He whirled around, angry that she'd waited. "Sullivan," she called to him, her voice soft, hesitant and hurt. That alone stopped the anger. He went to her and tilted her chin with his finger.

"There is no need to worry, my love. I am not Adam. I desire only you. I love only you. This is Suzett," he said. "For some reason she came to see me. I find it odd that I haven't seen her in over four hundred years but suddenly she's here and wanting me to run away with her, wanting me to resume our old relationship."

Sullivan gave Eve a smile and ran his hand down the side of her face. "I've missed you." She clasped his hand in hers but didn't speak.

"Suzett, this is Eve."

Instant hostility filled the room as Suzett snarled and made her way toward Eve. Sullivan moved between them. "No," he ordered Suzett. "You are close enough. You will speak to her from where you stand."

"Very well," Suzett replied testily. "Eve Omega, you have messed with what's mine. I do not like it. Why did you bring this upon Sullivan? Surely you had to know Adam Omega doesn't share. You belong to him. Are you totally stupid?"

"Watch it, Suzett," Sullivan warned.

Eve glanced briefly at Sullivan before casting her gaze on Suzett. "I belong to no one. I am not a chattel. I'm a woman."

"That's the problem. You're a vampire who can't admit she's no longer mortal." Suzett gave Sullivan a look of disgust. "Both Adam and Sullivan are enthralled with you. Personally, I don't see the fascination. I understand the rumors are you have lived without feeding. That can't be possible. But I've heard other rumors…" Suzett squinted to examine Eve. "Are you a witch? Have you bewitched Sullivan?" She narrowed her eyes, her voice turning more menacing. "Is that the reason Sullivan no longer desires me? Vampires are not known to be monogamous. We don't worry about being faithful. Eternity is too long for those worries. So what spell have you put on him?"

"I do not need to put a spell on a man nor do I need to attempt to use my will against him." Eve stepped from behind Sullivan. "Nor do I need Sullivan to protect me from the likes of you."

Eve felt the gentle touch of Sullivan's hand on her arm and pushed it away. Before she could think, Suzett had grabbed her and pulled her to her. She was hurting her but Eve refused to wince. She put out her hands and pushed the vamp from her, surprised to see her sailing backwards. She didn't think she'd pushed that hard. She stared at the other woman, knowing she'd just made an enemy. She didn't care.

"I am getting sick to death of being ordered around by vampires. My world should not even have you in it." Eve paused and glanced at Sullivan. "Nor you. or me," she added, dropping her voice. "You should have asked me if I love Sullivan. That should have been your concern."

"What difference does that make? Your love is going to get him killed and I don't want him dead. If something happens to him I'll—"

Once again Sullivan came to stand between the two women. He was ready for anything. There was no way he'd allow Suzett to put her hands on Eve again, though he was damn proud of the way Eve had defended herself. "Watch it, Suzett. This will be my last warning to you concerning Eve. What you were about to say I'd advise you not to say it. You will do nothing to harm Eve."

"You would go against the one who made you?"

An indifferent shrug and a weary shake of his head were Sullivan's first reactions. "I love her, Suzett. None of this is her fault. Besides, you would have to contend with Adam if harm came to Eve. We both know you don't want to deal with him."

"You two are talking about me as though I'm not in the room. Sullivan, there is no need for you to worry about me. I do not need either you or Adam to take care of me. Regardless of what you might think, I'm not weak, Suzett."

"No, you're not and I will not underestimate you again. But, darling, you don't know what vampire strength is. Mess with me, push me again, and you will find out," Suzett sneered, baring her fangs.

Eve was determined to stand her ground. "I didn't come here to have a cat fight. I came to talk to Sullivan. You touched me first and you got what you deserved." Glancing at Sullivan Eve asked, "Would you like for me to leave?"

Like for her to leave? Hell no, Sullivan thought, looking at her. He'd been wishing for the past month that she'd come to him. "No, Eve," he said, "I do not want you to leave. Suzett, it was nice seeing you. Tell Adam thanks, but no thanks."

"You're putting me out for her, choosing her over me? Think hard, Sullivan. This might be the last choice you get to make. You already have Adam for an enemy. You do not wish to make one of me also." She tilted her head and glared at Eve. "Perhaps since you're here toying with what belongs to me, I'll go and toy with what belongs to you."

For several seconds after Suzett left Eve stood as she was, just looking at Sullivan. Then she said, "So that's your great love, huh?"

Laughter rang out and Sullivan pulled her into his arms. "She's not the love of my life and never was. You are. Suzett was my sexual explosion." He held Eve tight when she would have moved away. "How are you?" he asked, looking at her. "There is something different about you." When Eve turned her head he turned it back. His heart lurched. He knew what it was. "Did you?"

Tears ran unabated down her cheeks. "Yes," she admitted, still ashamed of her actions.

"Oh, my poor, poor, Eve, my poor baby." He dipped a finger in the clear tears and stared at her in amazement. "How?"

"I'm going to hell, Sullivan."

"Then, my love, I will be there right by your side for I have done the same thing, only many times more." He opened her mouth, ran his thumb across her teeth, felt the sharpness. "How do you feel?"

"A mixture of things. I know that if the need arises I can feed without killing. I can also feed without damning another soul to this existence. I know the difference in the fresh blood of mortals." She pulled in a deep breath. "And I know the shame of having done it."

"Then why did you?" He growled, a long and agonizing sound, before clutching Eve to him and kissing her everywhere that his lips could reach. "Forgive me. I'm so sorry for having said that. Why the hell did I ask you that? It sounds as though I'm accusing you of something and I'm not. I know the reason you did it, the same reason that I killed Mark, that crazy ass husband of yours, the great Adam Omega."

"Adam was right, Sullivan. I'm a vampire. I can't turn back. I needed to know how to do the things that will best protect me."

Her words stunned him into silence and he released her and walked away.

"Sullivan, please don't…I've been racked with guilt. That's one of the reasons I didn't come to you sooner. But think about it. You know I needed to know. Would you leave me defenseless? What if I need blood and I can't get to a blood bank, or to the stash you have here, or have none of Dr. Meah's pills?" When he didn't answer she continued. "I made a deal with Adam. He will allow me to take control of the experiments to find the right formula. I can keep working on finding a way for vampires one day not to need humans in order to survive. That day is nearly here, Sullivan. We just need some fine tuning."

"You're frowning, Eve. I know that you're not telling me all of it. So, what's the problem?"

"He's not going to allow Dr. Meah to work with me. I've pleaded with him to spare him…to spare…" Eve's heart seized as she looked at Sullivan. "Adam won't tell me his plans for him."

"But you think he's going to kill us both in a few days. Is that it, Eve? Is that why you came to me, to spend this night as a death watch? I've told you many times, hell, you've seen it. I'm not without powers." He stopped ranting and stood there. "After all that we've meant to each other I should not have to tell you this. I have lived with the knowledge that you do not love me enough to sever yourself from Adam."

He held up a finger to stop her protest. "I knew what I was getting into with you going in. I am not running from Adam. Leave, Eve," he ordered. When she refused to go he roared, "Leave me."

Eve stood fast, tears streaming down her face and wishing it were different. "I can't leave you."

"If you don't have a little faith in me you shouldn't be here." Sullivan took several steps back and turned away from her. How he wanted her. With everything that was in him he wanted her. He was too old for this nonsense. He wouldn't beg her for anything, not to believe in him, not to forgive, not to hold him. He groaned inwardly. He needed to hold her at that moment more than he needed to take his next breath. Then he felt her arms slide around him. He inhaled as she laid her head against his back and pressed her body close to his. He couldn't give in to her yet but he relished her touch.

"Sullivan, I have no wish to see you and Adam in another battle." Eve held him tightly. "It's not that I don't think you can hold your own against Adam. I've just seen too much violence. I want neither of you harmed. What good will it serve? Adam is much too bullheaded to listen to reason."

"That's the point of your visit, isn't it? Adam is too stubborn, so once again you want me to be the one to give in, to run so you don't feel you have my blood on your hands." He turned to face her, in his haste knocking her hands from him. Staring into her eyes, he brought her against his body. "I will not run, Eve, not now, not ever."

Then he kissed her. It was a possessive kiss filled with more than wanting or love or even something so mundane as possession. His kiss was meant to convey to her just how much he loved her, that she belonged to him, not to Adam. "Eve, I will not give you up to him. This I swear. Adam is a vampire same as I am. He is not a god and he can be defeated.

I am not running. I am not leaving you to his mercy. And I am not going to die. Trust me in that, Eve. Tell me you trust me, that you believe me."

"I do believe you, Sullivan," Eve whispered, wanting to believe him in that moment more than she'd ever wanted anything. She did not want Sullivan dead. Nor did she want Adam dead, not at the moment anyway. She had a few days yet to come up with something.

"Now can you forgive me for killing Mark, now that you've tasted *the* blood?"

What could she say? He was right. Her sins were quickly piling up. She could swear she could hear Adam laughing at her. *Judge not, Eve*, she heard in her head. *Judge not.*

Chapter Fourteen

Annoyance had reached a new level Adam admitted to himself. Twirling the amber liquid in the snifter, it took him a moment to drink. He stared instead at Suzett. She'd dared to question him yet again. It was now official. Adam could definitely trace the time line of this insurgence, the mini uprising, if you will. He was calling it his Post-Eve period. Vampires of much lesser status and power had thought to challenge his edicts by making more vampires. They'd thought somehow that he wouldn't know or that since he'd made one himself, the ban had been lifted.

A deep snort of disgust escaped him. The ban would never be lifted. In fact for the past three days he'd done nothing but pursue the newly made and kill them and their makers. There'd been little joy in that, nothing more than a job had been accomplished. Still, it had to be done. Now here he sat in one of his favorite restaurants unable to enjoy his drink or his meal because of the vampire sitting across from him. He held her gaze in silence until the proper amount of fear showed. When he felt her edge of panic he spoke.

"You did as I asked?" When Suzett remained mute Adam growled, "Answer me. What is wrong with you?"

"There is nothing that I can say that will not incur your wrath, Adam. I already gave you my report."

"Then give it again," Adam snapped. "Give it until I'm satisfied."

"I'm sorry, Adam. I did not mean to question you. That was not my intent. I was just confused. It's your energy." Suzett blinked. "Yes, I did all that you asked. I went to Sullivan. You told me you didn't care if your wife was with Sullivan. I didn't ask her to come, she just showed up."

Suzett bowed her head. Anger was radiating off Adam in waves and had created a band of energy around his body extending out at least a foot. She trembled in fear, having never seen anything like it. Right now she was hoping he couldn't tell that she'd had a minor shoving match with his wife. She tried to calm herself, to behave in a normal fashion, to ask Adam the questions she normally would if she were not so afraid. Finally her nerves were calmed and she asked, "Adam, are you done with me? Can I leave now?"

"Why are you looking at me with such fear, Suzett? What have I done to instill that in you? I have not harmed you nor have I threatened to do so."

"Can you not see what's in front of you? Look," Suzett whispered and pointed.

Turning his gaze from Suzett Adam peered at the band of energy in amazement. *Damn it all*, he thought. And here he'd thought he was in control of his emotions. This would not do. He'd not known he was giving off that kind of energy. As he turned his head slowly to observe the mortals in the establishment, he became aware of their fear, their stares. He growled low several times. *Eve, what are you doing to me?* He closed his eyes and concentrated, commanding his essence to retreat, thinking once more that this would not do. It annoyed him that another vampire had witnessed his loss of control. When his energy returned to him, he shook his head and moved his hand in slow motion from the right to the left, relieving the mortals of their worries. He'd have to be more careful.

"You were not aware of what was happening, were you, Adam?"

Adam growled, refusing to answer.

"I've never seen a vamp do that, never. No wonder you're so feared." Suzett rushed her words. "You are different from the rest of us, aren't you? I know of the many attempts on your life through the centuries and not a scratch, nary a one." Her eyes narrowed and she studied Adam closely. "What is your secret, Adam? For I know beyond a shadow of a doubt that there is more to you than being a vampire. I've now witnessed it with my own eyes."

"I see that your fears have left you, Suzett, and that the cat no longer has your tongue. I do believe I liked it better when you were cowering in fear instead of being a nosey female and pestering me with questions."

"I'm still afraid. Maybe that's the reason that I'm questioning you, out of fear. I just have a couple of more questions, please," she pleaded.

"You care about your wife being with Sullivan. That's what did it, isn't it? You're going to kill Sullivan because of it, aren't you, Adam?"

"Did I not warn you about questioning me? I do not answer your questions. You answer mine." He gave her a hard glare. "Will you be able to feel it when Sullivan is no more?" He watched as a look crossed Suzett's face.

"Generally we can feel it when anyone of us dies and especially those we've made. But for the past hundred years or so more and more of us are feeling it less and less."

Adam gave a snort and looked at her, then he smiled. "You may leave me now, Suzett. You have served your purpose." When she remained he pointed a finger at her and sent her on her way. Whether she could feel Sullivan's demise or not Adam would find out very soon.

All the pieces were in place. He'd considered his options and now it was time to end the dance. Everyone had waited too long. It had become tedious at best. He could no longer allow such reckless disregard for his authority. With that thought in mind Adam opened a channel and bellowed for all the parties involved. Then he materialized inside Sullivan's home.

***

"It's about time," Sullivan said as Adam entered his home uninvited, as usual. You've called this little meeting, Adam, so I'm assuming you want us to grovel before you. We will not do it, either of us. Sullivan stared across the room, including Dr. Meah in his statement but found the doctor wasn't meeting his eyes. "No matter, I will not grovel." His gaze connected to Eve's and he walked to her. "I have loved you like no other and I always will."

"Adam," Eve called, the one word conveying all that she wanted. When Adam turned toward her, his eyes were cold, no warmth, no love, only bitterness and determination.

"I'm not going to let you hurt them." Eve moved, positioning her body in front of Sullivan and the doctor. "I don't care what you think they've done. You will not harm them." She began an incantation and seconds later a bubble of energy encased them.

"Childs' play, Eve," Adam responded and laughed, aiming a finger at the energy bubble, dissipating it into nothingness. He saw the surprise in Eve's eyes. "What, darling? Did you think there would be any trick that you could learn that I could not? Now be a good little witch and move aside. I have work to do."

"He's right. I want you to move," Sullivan said, touching Eve tenderly before aiming his next words toward Adam. "At least I see this time you have concern for your wife. Do try to keep your aims at me, will you?"

"You know, Sullivan, you talk too damn much," Adam said, using his finger to move Eve aside while aiming a volley of pure energy at Sullivan. No matter what he decided to do, in the end he would cause the vampire some major pain. When Sullivan attempted to do the same as Adam had done, his volley hit a barricade Adam had erected around his body and boomeranged back to him.

Adam laughed in amusement. "I could do this all day but I don't have the time nor the patience. You could have left, Sullivan."

"Go to hell, Adam."

"You first," Adam countered, sending another volley but stopping in the nick of time when Eve once again ran in front of Sullivan to shield him from harm.

"Stop this nonsense, Adam. Stop it or I swear I will hate you for eternity. I will never forgive you for this." She closed her eyes and aimed her hands at Adam, shooting out energy only to have hers do as Sullivan's had done and bounce off the barricade and return to her.

"Temper, temper, darling." Adam wagged his finger at Eve. "Can't you see this is useless? You will not win. Did you also forget who I am? I am not you, nor am I Sullivan. You are no match for me, either of you. Why don't you combine your powers and try it."

"I know you, Adam. You don't want me dead. And I don't plan to remove myself from Sullivan's side. You'll have to kill me to get to him." Eve was insistent, stretching out her arms to block both of the vamps from Adam's threat, making sure he would have to hit her with his powers to get to either of them. She was banking that he wouldn't do it.

Pointing a finger at Eve, Adam smiled. "I really don't have to kill you, darling. All I have to do is this." He pointed a finger at Eve and zapped her away, then waited until she returned. "I can do this all day, my love, all day and all night...throughout eternity. Give up."

"You bastard. Who the hell do you think you are? Eve," Sullivan snapped, turning his attention to her. "Stop it right now. I do not want you fighting my battles. Do you understand me? You're a two-year-old fledgling. I'm an eight-hundred-year-old vampire. You may be married to Adam but you're my woman and I protect you."

Fury cascaded down Sullivan's spine. Adam was not using all of his powers as though he had nothing to fear. The knowledge of that

irritated the hell out of Sullivan. It was past time for him to do what he'd
wanted for so many years. He'd kick his ass. But how was he going to
accomplish that? He almost laughed. Maybe he should make the
suggestion that they fight as men, no powers involved. If that were the
case he'd stand a better chance. But it was not the case. His gaze fell on
Eve and he did what he most wanted at the moment. He grabbed her and
bent her backwards, kissing her with all the passion and love he had in
him, knowing it would be the last time he tasted her. Then he swerved
around and pushed Eve's body from him, ready to take whatever Adam
had to give.

"I love you, Eve," Sullivan whispered as he glanced toward her. I
want you to live. I didn't go through having you hate me to lose you."

Adam glanced at the two of them. He could toy with them or he
could be merciful and end it now. "You don't have to worry, Sullivan, Eve
will live. That much I promise you. You forget, I love her also."

"Love," Sullivan sneered. "You have no concept of what love
entails.

"Maybe I don't but as the years pass I'm sure Eve will teach me."
With that Adam opened both hands, palms out, and aimed two different
beams. His right hand pushed Eve away, slamming her backwards onto
the bed; his other flattened Sullivan.

For a tenth of a second Adam paused, hearing Eve scream out
Sullivan's name, hearing Sullivan answer that he loved her. He barely
moved in order to dodge Sullivan's electrical barrage. He paid no heed to
the destroyed furnishings that had received the charges instead of him.
Adam no longer hesitated. The decision was made. He concentrated all his
power in one steady beam in Sullivan's direction and a moment later
Sullivan was cinder dust on the floor. Adam then turned toward Dr. Meah
and opened a mind lock. "Make it good doctor," he said.

"Dr. Meah, it's now your turn. Adam spoke sternly and loudly
ensuring that Eve heard.

"Oh no. Adam, please show mercy," Dr. Meah pleaded.

The words were corny, sounding a bit rehearsed. Adam sent a glare
to the doctor and again executed a mind lock. "Don't overdo it. Are you
ready?" he asked making sure no one else, namely Eve, had entered the
man's mind.

"I'm ready. Are you sure this will work?"

"It will work. We have to do this quickly and you can not flinch."

"What of Sullivan? Did you really—"

"Do not pry or I might change my mind. Sullivan is my concern as are you. The option I chose for him is not for you to know. Now let's try this again and don't oversell it. Put up a bit of a fight. An energy block should do nicely." He saw the almost smile that crossed the vamps' face and warned, "Don't get cocky, just follow directions." With that Adam severed the mind lock and stood in front of Eve, blocking off the barrage of energy volts she was tossing at him. She was so distraught her aim was off. She wasn't seeing him and those damn blood tears were back. It was obvious she hadn't taken her daily dose of the potion. But why? For a moment he started to confess but decided against it, locking gazes with Dr. Meah and giving him the signal.

"You can't just kill me, Adam. I'm a vampire."

Dr. Meah's voice was raised in anger and electrical sparks emanated from the tips of his fingers. *Weak,* Adam thought, but they would have to do. Now to time it just right. Sleight of hand, he thought and blinked several times, reaching out his hand to comfort Eve, knowing she'd turn from him. Now was the moment he'd been waiting for, the cover.

Adam shook his head. "Too late, Doctor, too late. You should have never given my wife your poison, not without my permission." Adam squeezed his hand tightly, then slipped it briefly inside the pocket of his silk trousers. Reaching for the prepared potion he brought his hand out and in one quick motion he dropped the tiny object and allowed it to bounce against the concrete floor. With one finger he ignited the bundle, glanced at Eve and watched as the doctor died. Then he used his eyes to incinerate him also, nothing to save, no vampire to come back.

Now it was he and Eve alone, as it should be. Now she would be forced to behave. That would be her only punishment, her survival without the man she'd betrayed him with. She'd just have to learn. He stood and waited, timing her movements to her glare, to her hatred. Their eyes locked and Adam vanished. It was done. He'd eliminated the other men in Eve's life and he'd earned her hatred in the process.

Adam took in a deep breath of air, cleansing his lungs of the evil he'd done. Deceit could be as devastating as the real thing. For a moment he felt regret and immediately banished it from his mind. He'd warned Sullivan and he'd warned Eve. He'd warned all of them. What kind of leader would he be if he didn't follow through on what he said? What kind of leader would he be if those beneath him no longer feared him?

And what kind of life would he have when the woman he'd wanted for so many centuries no longer loved him? He'd felt it, that severing of her love, not just disdain or hatred but the ending of her loving him. A shiver claimed Adam and he wondered why he'd done it. Of course he could have shown more mercy, not allowed Eve's heart and her spirit to be broken with lies and deception. But he hadn't. What of his heart? How could his wife so easily love another? With his consent or without it, Sullivan should have never been in her life, her bed, her heart.

A grimace of disgust for where his thoughts had traveled gave Adam pause. The things he'd done had not all been done out of jealousy. It was true that his wife's survival had at all times been uppermost in his mind. Eve was a vampire and she needed to learn that lesson. Two damn years and she'd not fed properly. It was time she did. He didn't regret having forced her into knowing the proper way to feed. That was the only way she would survive this hellish existence.

Yes, she might hate him.

But she would live.

He thought of Yas and her way out. Better to put all thoughts of the ancient witch from his mind. Her teachings would remain secret until he felt it was time to reveal them. He put a firm lock in place, hiding away forever the knowledge of Yas from Eve's probing. All of this had been done for her. She must not find out the truth.

Chapter Fifteen

Power threaded its way through Eve's veins. She could feel the build up in each cell. Eve opened her mouth and screamed out to the heavens. "Why?" she screamed. "Why? I didn't ask for this." She fell to her knees, allowing the blood tears to flow. There had to be a way to end it, to destroy that which couldn't be destroyed.

How long had it been?" she wondered. Since knowing Adam she'd fluctuated between hating and loving him. But now, this thing he'd done... This finished it between them. She would find a way to end this. The world didn't deserve the horror of her kind. Eve felt a shudder rip through her.

Her kind.

Her kind used to be human, not any longer. Now she was neither all vampire nor all witch. She was neither dead nor alive and she needed to be one or the other. If she was not damned already she would be when she was done.

For a long moment she stood in the room waiting for something to happen, for Sullivan to come back, for Dr. Meah. She even prayed that some miracle would be performed and that Mark would be returned, whole, healthy, mortal.

Weeping uncontrollably, she knew if Sullivan hadn't survived, then neither had Mark. Sullivan had been an eight-hundred-year-old vampire. He'd warned her about crossing Adam, constantly telling her she was a fledgling. Yet he was dead and she was alive. Was it mercy or torture? She'd been happy for a brief time in Sullivan's arms. Now there was nothing for her to look forward to except eternal nothingness. She shook her head, unable to fathom the idea of a forever existence of pain, loving no one and being love by none. She thought of Adam. In his insane way he loved her but that could no longer be enough. For a nanosecond Eve froze, no moment no thought, she stood as though dead and when the moment ended one thought stood out in her mind. She heaved a weary sigh as the truth of her thoughts hit home.

Either Adam would kill her, or she would kill him. That was the way it had to end. No other way was acceptable. She wanted both herself and Adam both banished from the face of the earth. She had to plan. If nothing else, when she was done she'd force Adam to take action to end the nightmare he'd made of her life. He must have known that once she'd fed in the way he'd wanted she'd continue to feed the craving.

Eve swiped her fingers in the blood tears and wiped them on the side of her clothing. The price had been much too high to rid herself of them. Bringing her fingers upwards she winced at the sight of the blood that covered her fingertips. She still hated those damn blood tears. She'd already paid the price she might as well continue using the formula. She was already damned; now she just needed to be dead, really and truly forever. Adam couldn't revive her once she truly died.

***

Three days later Eve knew what she was going to do. The fog of her mind had rolled away as though some unseen force had wiped the slate clean and had given her a chance to start all over again. Three days she'd sat entombed with death, looking at the ashes of Sullivan and Dr. Meah, remembering those of Mark. Now it was time to do what she could to save mankind from vampires. For what she planned to do the price of her soul would be required, that much she knew, and she was ready to give it. She would in every way become what Adam had intended her to be. Not only would she be his wife, she would be the vampire match for him. And she would 'out evil' him if that was what it took. She had a strong feeling that would be what it took.

A cold emptiness claimed Eve as she plotted and planned, pulling her out of her body. She soared high above the clouds making a wish and when she returned to her body she was more the mistress of the vampire kingdom that Adam had desired, more that, than the old Eve. She would do what must be done.

Eve turned slowly around the room, wondering if this was truly the end of the happiness she'd known so briefly. She thought of Adam returning from the past where'd he'd made love to her mortal body so magnificently that he'd made her feel it as well. When he'd returned she'd had hopes that all could be forgotten. And it could have been if Adam had forgotten his damnable code, if he'd not insisted that he needed her to behave. She was not his child. But now she would behave. She would behave in a way that would rival him

Thoughts of Sullivan filled her with grief. She thought of the doctor, then Mark and then her mind focused on Adam. He didn't have to do what he'd done, but then again that was Adam. Adam, master of the universe, the same master who'd said he was trying to find a way for vampires and mortals to co-exist, the same one who'd decreed that she had to feed, to have fresh blood. No more AB-5. No more artificial blood for her. What a damn contradiction. A shiver raced through her body, one that she knew well. Adam was probing her mind. "Go ahead, you bastard, she said. "Try and stop me. I am your wife, your creation. I have your blood in my veins and like you, I cannot be stopped."

**

An intense inspection told Eve the many weeks it took to have the huge black Hummer reinforced was worth it. For what she planned to do the vehicle had to be nearly indestructible. Now it was. She'd used her new powers testing it. "Adam, ready or not, here I come," she said and drove off.

Reaching her destination, for a tenth of a second Eve hesitated. The vampires inside the building had done nothing to harm her. But as the weariness of the word *vampire* eased across her fevered brain, she accelerated the vehicle and aimed the Hummer at the heavy glass doors. When the glass failed to shatter, she halted and got out of the vehicle. Closing her eyes, she concentrated. She was Adam's mate, his equal, she had his power. She had to believe this now or be trapped by Adam forever. That she didn't intend. She would save humanity; then she would save herself.

Eve concentrated until a power surge filled her body, then her brain, and she screamed out. Clear tears spilled down her cheeks. She was aware her eyes were that hated red, that naught of the brown remained or would return until she'd done what she came to do.

Another scream ripped from her throat. This time the sound was animalistic and her eyes became lethal lasers, blowing the heavy protective glass apart. She walked into the building as sunlight trailed her scoring vampires where they stood. In that moment instead of cursing

Adam she was glad she had his powers, that she was impervious to the rays of the sun.

As she continued walking through the building amidst the screams of vampires she refused to acknowledge their pain. Many looked toward her in shocked dismay. She ignored them and continued on her mission erecting a protective energy shield to surround her body. Vampires did not belong in the world. Humans would not be their restaurant of choice, not if she could help it.

For a long moment Eve's vision clouded and she began aiming, striking without being able to see, using her inner senses to feel where the danger was. Much more experienced older vampires rushed to capture her. Eve ignored them, remaining encased inside her protective energy field as she continued her work. It was as though the entire building were falling down around their heads. They screeched and ran, begging her to stop. No, she would not stop. They were an abomination. She was an abomination and she fully intended to rid the world of all of them.

"Please, Eve, please stop. No one here did you any harm. We've all befriended you."

She paused for a moment, recognizing the voice. She wouldn't, she couldn't have compassion. Compassion was what had gotten her in this mess in the first place. The compassion she'd felt for Adam, then the love, then this life he'd forced on her and the deaths that lay at her feet. Sullivan, Mark and Dr. Meah would be alive if they'd not tried to help her. No, someone had to stop this, make it right, make the world safe again. Someone had to open the closet and get rid of the monster.

"I'm coming for you when I'm done here," Eve said as she stood in the middle of the room and watched vampires incinerate and burn, dropping into ash before her. "I'm coming for you, Adam. Soon," she murmured, and continued through each room of the huge complex, going to the lab and destroying it. Adam had never intended there to be a way for vampires to exist without feeding on humans. He was a liar and she was going to destroy this part of his lie.

"Adam," she screamed loud and long. "I hate you. Do you hear me? I hate you."

***

"I hear you, Eve."

A flicker of sadness passed through Adam's soul. Like matches that had been extinguished he felt each vampire's death, a swift ending, at least that was merciful. On the other hand what Eve had done the payment would neither be swift or merciful. He knew that first hand. A life for a life. He'd thought in the beginning that it all equaled out. He'd meant to save his wife, himself, and their world from creatures of the night and look what it had gotten him, a thousand years of torment, of living hell. His immortal soul groaned with the weight of what he'd done. He hadn't been able to convince his wife to feed properly without coercion. But he had made her into a killer without even trying.

"Well done, Adam," he chided himself, "Your creation. Your wife. Your mess." Pain radiated through his limbs and a sense of loss permeated his spirit. For a brief moment Adam wanted nothing more than to obliterate everything in his sight. He coalesced his cells into matter and transported his body to his favorite haunting place. Rome, the Vatican.

Mortals stood in the circle of St. Peter's Square. And once again Adam wondered why something that was a circle was called a square. Why not St. Peter's Circle? He laughed, ignoring the low murmur of his friend calling out to him, trying as he always did to prevent Adam from going into the Vatican. It was a useless task. And this time Adam would not walk into the building as he usually did, under the guise of a mortal man. He wasn't mortal. He was a vampire and the world had better get used to that fact. He was not a vampire seeking redemption. He growled low in his throat, warning Evan off. Adam was in no mood to play right now. It had been hundreds of years since he'd felt blood on his hands as much as he did now. He opened his mind wider, searching for Eve, finding her, almost wishing he hadn't. The weight of her hatred for him cursed something in him but it was the look in her eyes that slayed him as he'd watched her love for him drain away.

For Eve Adam had done things he'd never done in his entire existence as a vampire. His love for her had made him weak. And a weak vampire was definitely not a feared vampire. And if Adam wasn't feared he was dead. His many sins would assure him of that. Look what had happened but a few scant years in the past. Eve had plotted with her dead lover to bind him. He'd made a promise to Eve and he'd made one to Sullivan. He'd warned them both that he would end Sullivan's life if Eve's life was ever put in danger by the vampire's hand.

"And there was no other reason?"

"None," Adam answered his internal thoughts, his voice roaring over the vastness of the room, creating a backdraft so visible that the

mortal women clutched their skirts about their legs and held their purses to their bosoms while the men looked around in alarm, pretending to have a bravery they could never attain. Adam stood in the middle of the room and roared again. He wanted someone to know; hell, he wanted them all to know, to feel his pain. He deserved that they mourn with him, that they lose their…he ended the thought. He didn't care about their faith.

Marble tiles popped up as he made his way to a fount, dipped his hands in and washed them. "Hail Mary, full of grace the Lord is with thee." He stopped as liquid slid down his face. *Drat those blood tears*. He dipped another hand into the water and washed his face, coloring the water red. And he wondered what the hell he was doing. A groan escaped him causing Adam to rear back his head and roar some more, allowing his pain to fill the great room, feeding on the fear of the visitors, hearing the cracking of several of the gold-gilded statues.

And they thought what he did was sacrilegious. *Thou shall have no other gods before me, no graven images,* What the hell did they think these things were?

His arms open wide, Adam bellowed, "What have I done? I didn't ask for this. I never asked for this. All I wanted was to serve and then to love. What was my sin? He aimed his eyes laser sharp and sure at several more statues and amidst the screams of '*Earthquake*' from the worshippers, he felt more tears slide down his cheeks as he walked back toward the exit. There was no need to wash again in the holy water. Then he thought of Evan waiting for him and knew he did have a reason. Adam didn't need the vampire analyzing him again, thinking that he was seeking absolution, that he terrorized the worshippers in order to provoke the wrath of God. Nothing more could be done to Adam; everything had been stripped from him long ago. There was no longer any hope for anything better.

Ever.

Adam shuddered in disgust as his memories washed over him. He'd prayed many times in the past for many things. He'd prayed for Eyanna, that the church not abandon her or him. He'd prayed that the plague of the vampires be lifted from their lands. And he'd prayed for his wife's safety. When he'd received no answer, he'd prayed that his decision to join with the vile creatures was the right thing to do, that it would save his precious wife and when she'd still died, he'd prayed for God to bring her back. Now after several hundred years of praying, he was perfectly aware that his existence was cursed. There would be no answers to his prayers. He was as he'd always been, alone.

Rest was what he needed. Moving into an obscure corner he snapped his fingers, as the worshipers fled. Taking a long lingering look at the mortals a bone deep weariness filled Adam's soul and he produced a couch and sealed all manner of entry so none could enter. Then he slept. Even in sleep his thoughts were troubled.

Eventually Adam woke and looked around shaking the sleep from his body. A sigh escaped him. For weeks he'd had the same dream: that he'd done as he'd set out to do and had killed them all the moment he'd returned to find Eve at death's door. He wiped a hand lazily across his brow as he thought of allowing Eve to send him into the past.

Still, this was a lesson: Don't ever underestimate a woman and never ever underestimate the vampire who was also his wife and a witch to boot. He toyed with the idea of returning to the past and doing things differently, of removing this sin from Eve of judging and executing vampires before she could commit it. But he couldn't; that would be giving up. They were going to remain in their own time and maybe eventually he'd tell her the truth of it all. Maybe then he'd carry out his plans the way he did in his dreams. In real life he'd shown more mercy than he should have. Mistake number two.

Finally Adam glided out of the church, looking in disdain at the mortals daring a glance at him. He watched as they crossed themselves or denied what their eyes told them was true. What he was doing they would think impossible. He couldn't be for real, for they knew for a fact that the devil didn't attend church. He thought back to Eve's words whispered to herself, *that the devil did indeed attend church*. If he hadn't thought he was the devil before... A groan slipped out and Adam stopped gliding and walked as a mortal man out of St. Peter's Square. He walked for miles, coming to rest inside the ruins of the Coliseum to wait for Evan.

***

A wave of anger reached out and grabbed Adam, suffusing him with the heat of his friend's wrath. Adam waved a hand, clearing the ledge of debris. He smiled slightly and beckoned Evan with a finger to sit, amused when he didn't take the invitation.

"What the hell have you done, Adam?"

"Nothing more than what I had to do."

"Had to do? For over two years Sullivan was your wife's lover and now you say you had to kill him. I don't understand that."

"It's not your business to understand." Adam spoke with deadly calm.

"If you had killed him the moment you found out about the affair it would have been understandable but now it's..."

"It's my damn business." A low rumble filled Adam's chest. When it came out, stones fell from the ruins.

"Don't destroy this place any more than has already been done, Adam."

"Are you ordering me now, Evan?"

"I'm asking a favor. Already Rome is in an uproar. The reports are coming fast and furious that an earthquake or vandals hit the Vatican. No one knows what the hell happened, at least not mortals. You sealed the whole damn church so no one could get in. And yet you wonder why you and I cover the same ground. Don't tell me you don't know the meaning of your actions. You tell me that you don't seek absolution and yet the church is always the first place you go when you have done something truly horrible. Think about it, Adam."

"I have thought about it and you're wrong. I went there because I can."

"To find peace."

"Because I can."

"To find redemption."

"Leave me the hell alone."

"You're making more enemies every moment that you breathe. Are you aware of that?"

"I am."

"And Eve, what of her? What the hell happened to make you kill them all? Dr. Meah was your top scientist. You liked him. As for the mortal, it's not as though I give a damn about him, but it's you who said you didn't want to kill them. So tell me why."

"I owe you no explanations."

"Your friends are dwindling, Adam. I daresay I'm your last one."

"I don't require friendship in order to survive."

Evan thought a moment, then smiled and gave Adam a look of pity. "No, you don't but you have it just the same. Unlike you, I find that I do require your friendship to survive. I require you. You're my only family. I would and have killed for you and I will again. I would also die for you and I know without your saying it that you would do so for me. Your behavior will not turn me away. It never does." Evan sighed and sat down in the spot Adam had cleansed. "Why, Adam? I'm only asking."

Taking a long look around the ancient city, a feeling of distress lay heavy on Adam. So much beauty destroyed for no good reason. It was one of the reasons he enjoyed coming here, the sense of loss of an entire civilization he equated with his own personal loss. Evan was right. Adam would and had killed for him and he'd do it again. In truth it was Evan Adam trusted with his life, not Eve. He was wondering why Evan was withholding the bigger question of why he'd not felt the deaths of Meah and Sullivan. But since Evan hadn't asked he wouldn't volunteer the information. He'd play along for now, answer the questions as they were put to him.

With a resigned groan Adam quirked a brow in Evan's direction and began. "I allowed Sullivan to care for Eve while I looked away. A lot of that time was spent with you, I might add."

"Now you'd like to bring me in as an accomplice to the things that you've done." Laughter started then stopped abruptly once Evan understood that Adam truly was not in a joking mood. "I'm sorry for interrupting," he muttered quietly. "Please continue, Adam."

"If you interrupt me again I will not tell you. Are we clear?" There was silence and a stare from Evan. Good, just what Adam wanted, silence.

"In all this time until I returned to her, Eve had never drunk from mortals." His eyelids fluttered and he shook his head in amazement. "She had not fed properly in over two years. Can you believe that? My stubborn witch of a wife refused to feed. When she was mortal I used to call her, Little Healer."

His thoughts took flight, taking long moments to return to the present. "As a healer she was determined to heal herself, to revert from being a vampire back into a mortal." Adam's voice filled with pride. "If anyone could have made the transformation it would have been my wife." He stilled and again reached out mentally for Eve.

"If she didn't feed, how did she survive?" Evan asked.

Adam gave a laugh at the startled look on his friend's face. "I know. I also found it hard to believe. The good Dr. Meah cooked up some poison for my wife."

"Poison? But he was a friend of yours and afraid of you, I might add. Why would he do such a thing? Did he hate her?" Evan jumped from the ledge and began pacing in frustration.

Again Adam laughed. "No, I think the man was in love with her." He glanced at Evan. "You met Eve briefly when I visited you in the past. There is something about her that makes men fall in love with her. They want to protect her, to challenge me for her love. They don't even care about dying." Adam shuddered, remembering Sullivan's last words had been his declaration of love for Eve, his last move to protect her.

Closing his eyes tightly Adam took in a deep breathe then released it. There was a question he'd been meaning to ask his friend. "Evan, did you find yourself with an urge to protect my wife?"

"Quite the opposite. I saw the elusive quality that she has but my urge was to protect you from her, my friend. Even now that is my urge. You've never been this….this…scattered. The fact that she's a witch makes me worry about you more. I will not sit idly by and allow anyone to harm you, not even your beloved Eve."

"Are you aware of what you're saying?" Adam hissed between clenched teeth. "You're threatening my wife."

"Not at all, I'm stating a plain and simple fact. Call it a promise if you will." Evan shrugged and snorted as he glared at Adam. "Just so there is no misunderstanding, I'm saying that I will do what I've always done, everything that is in my power to protect you."

"If you harmed Eve I would kill you."

"Again, I wasn't speaking of simply harming, but eliminating her," Evan replied his voice as cold as ice.

Adam's voice turned even colder than Evan and he said each word slowly. "Were it not for the fact that we are family, that you are my only family, you would be dead already. You should be dead already! You're right about one thing. Loving Eve has made me soft. You owe your life to Eve. You should thank her for each breath you take. From this moment on, you breathe because of my love for her."

"Then by all means, Master Omega, I will give thanks to your wife. Eve, if you can hear my voice I thank you for my very life."

A bolt of electrical energy shot from Adam and hit Evan in the chest. Adam glared at him, then extended his hand to Evan and helped him up. "You're too sarcastic for your own good."

"Agreed. Still, we know where we each stand. Now let's get back to the original topic. I think it would be safer, at least for me," Evan smirked and moved away from Adam. "Am I to understand then that you killed Dr. Meah because he loved Eve?"

"No, because he poisoned her. He helped to make her weak."

"But why?" Evan insisted.

"Because she requested a blood substitute."

"Then it wasn't truly his fault."

"He should have known better than to test out his potions on my wife."

"And the mortal?"

Adam held Evan's gaze. "He was in love with her also. He was a puny, weak mortal that allowed vampires to feed from him freely and in the end he too died trying to save her. Tell me, Evan, what is it about my wife that makes a weak man strong and a strong man weak?"

That Evan didn't answer and Adam was truly grateful. He didn't like the weakness that Eve invoked in him.

"And Sullivan?" Evan asked.

"Sullivan allowed this to take place. He knew Eve needed to feed. He knew she was not doing so. Sullivan and I had an agreement. I shut my eyes to the fact that he was making love to my wife. I shut my mind to the fact that she was falling in love with Sullivan. And I shut my heart to her telling me that she loved me more. I shut my soul to her pleas for me to come for her, to love her as she was." With infinite sadness Adam swallowed and stared into Evan's eyes, holding his gaze. "You've been with me almost since the beginning of this nightmare. Even before we became friends you were there. You know my reasons for not going to my wife. You know my reasons for the thing I am now and you know why I had to make sure Eve can protect herself, Evan. All that I've done has been for her protection. I am what I am because of my need to protect her." Adam swallowed again and severed the telling gaze.

"But..."

"No buts. She should not have given herself to another, not if she truly loved me. How could she? Talk is cheap. With her lips smelling of Sullivan she lied about her love for me. When Sullivan came into the room, her eyes sought him out as she breathed what she thought was to be her last breath. She wanted to look upon Sullivan, not me."

"You killed Sullivan out of a jealous rage? You Adam? You who are so disciplined? From the moment I knew of your existence I have been proud of you and even prouder of your accomplishments. I have been most proud of your unwavering discipline. Now you do something like this because of a woman. You sicken me." Evan bristled, almost standing until Adam's hand pressed firmly against his shoulder, pushing him down. "I have one last question, my friend. Why is it that if you have truly done as you said I did not feel their deaths? Why do I not sense it in you? Why are there places in your mind that are shut to me? And why, Adam, did you leave yourself open to be read by me, but look as though you're surprised. You're aware I probe your mind and you know that I know you lie."

"Remember what you said, Evan. I no longer have any other friends. I would like to keep you for a while longer but if not I can survive without you."

"Threatening me is not the way to do it," Evan snarled, pushing Adam's hand from him. "I'm a hell of a lot stronger than you think, Adam. You don't give me credit for that. But while you've been mooning over one woman for the last thousand years I've been learning a few things. I'm not afraid of you and killing me will not be as easy as it was to do whatever the hell you did to Sullivan. I'm not here to protect your wife. My dying thoughts will not be to sacrifice myself for her. Like you, I'm a survivor and I will survive. You think your wife is still an infant, yet in many ways she's stronger than some who have lived for hundreds of years. I will tell you this as a friend. Should your wife come up against me, I will destroy her."

"And I will destroy everything you hold dear," Adam snapped. "I will find your mortal family and as for your wife, I will drain her of every drop of blood that is in her body. I will do it while I make love to her and she's screaming out my name. Then I will kill her."

"Pray tell, what will I be doing?"

It annoyed Adam that Evan was not remotely angry, that his demeanor remained calm. He was unruffled as Adam generally was. "Do not think our standing will prevent what I have to do. I will make you watch while I make love to your wife and watch while I kill her. Then I will kill you."

"As I said before, I do not fear you. Not only am I your only friend but your only true family. I do not worry about your wrath."

"You are like me more than most," Adam conceded. "But you are not me. Just remember that. And remember you should not push our friendship too far. You are neither my counselor nor my priest. I am not making a confession to you nor do I plan to pray for forgiveness. What I've done is done and will remain so. Eve will do what she needs to and that will be the end of that."

"You think that even if she doesn't want to feed from mortals, she will. Are you really that arrogant? There are a million blood banks across the world. She never has to feed if she doesn't want to, not in that sense anyway."

"But she will. My blood fills her veins. She will require more than blood from blood banks. She will require the link." Then Adam gave a shrug. "But it matters not if she so chooses not to feed as she should. I have achieved what I set out to do. Eve can protect herself should the need arise. She can take what she needs to remain strong, to fight off any attacker. I've seen to that personally."

"And what of you? Are you no longer her protector?"

Adam looked bemused. "Actually at this moment I would say I need protection from Eve." His eyes glittered and he felt the pull from violet to red, stopping it at the remembered look in his wife's gaze.

"What do you think she's going to do next?" Evan asked.

"When last I checked she was open and not thinking."

"Did you link?"

"I attempted."

"And?"

"And there was nothing. Eve didn't push me out nor did she speak. It is as though I'm dead to her and she's dead to me." A chill came over Adam, one that sent a tremor of fear through his immortal soul. "It is done," he whispered.

"What's done, Adam?"

"My sins." Adam stared at Evan. "It is complete, my total transformation into the darkness, the abyss." My need to protect Eve has backfired. Until now she was a product of my creation, a victim if you will. Not anymore. She's no longer blameless, yet the things she have done were done because of me. She's seeking revenge and in doing so she's damming her soul. With my actions concerning Meah and Sullivan I have begun something that I don't know if I have the power to end."

"Eve?" Evan breathed in, then allowed the breath to escape in a soft whistle. "Adam...what are you going to do?"

Adam closed his eyes and disappeared from view without answering Evan. Eve's soul was now up for grabs.

Chapter Sixteen

Weapons of mass destruction were at Eve's disposal, weapons that wreaked carnage on the vampire world. She felt little of what she'd wanted to cling to, what she would forever think of as her own humanity. She felt a bit of it slip away each and every time she made a kill. And each time she did, she whispered Adam's name, knowing that one day it would be the great vampire she faced. The right or wrong of what she was doing had blurred for Eve. She only wished to make the world safe again by killing one vampire at a time. And then one day she'd kill the baddest of the lot.

"Do you hear me, Adam?" she whispered.

"As always, Eve, I hear you," Adam whispered back.

"Good to know," she said, pulling out an atomizer as she walked down the street. *Three vampires together*, she thought. *They don't think anyone knows what they are.* She moved to block their path, saw a slight hesitation, a moment of recognition, and then poof, they were no more. Eve barely allowed their deaths to register.

"This is what you've reduced me to, Adam," she said and continued on her way.

***

"I know you felt it," Adam said softly, turning his gaze on Evan, stopping him before he could say anything. "There's nothing I can do. The deed is done. This Eve is operating without emotion, anger, or pain, just carrying out a calculated plan to kill the unsuspecting."

"Yes. The deed is done, isn't it? There will be no turning back for your Eve now. Tell me something, Adam. Was this what you wanted for her?"

With a derisive snarl Adam moved away from Evan. He paced silently for several minutes, then turned back. "You know damn well that was never my intent."

"You need to stop this."

"Do not return to threatening my wife."

"Why would I?" Evan asked. "We've both stated our cases and the truth of the matter is that we are both true immortal beings. If you don't want to roam this earth friendless for all eternity, I would suggest you stop your wife."

Adam smiled slightly. "It's beginning to look as if I have little choice." He held Evan's gaze. "You're aware that what I told you I would do should you harm Eve was not just a possible scenario. I was serious and I want to make sure you're aware of that."

"I am."

"Then my suggestion to you is to stay out of Eve's sight until the situation is contained."

"Believe me, Adam, I have no desire to go up against the female version of you, one who believes her killings to be not only justified but somehow ordained."

"It's the past, her religious past," Adam said quietly.

"Then remind her that she's no longer mortal. She's a vampire. She's one of us, no better than any of us."

Again Adam felt the stab of pain for the things he'd done. Had his trying to right a wrong only served to make matters worse? Was vengeance not meant for him to dispense? Feeling weary he closed his eyes, connecting with Eve. Just as suddenly as he'd closed them his eyes snapped opened and his gaze locked with Evan's.

"Eve's still pissed?" Evan asked.

"You'd better believe it."

With a disgusted shake of his head, Evan chastised Adam as he'd done many times. "All of this is your fault, Adam. You started the ball rolling with getting rid of Sullivan. You could have told him, 'hands off.' You could have not done the things that you did centuries ago and Sullivan would not have gone looking for your weak link, a woman who could help him destroy you, a woman whom the entire vampire world was aware that you mourned. If you had done none of those things Sullivan would have never met Eve, never fallen in love with her and you would not have been forced to eliminate him from your wife's affections in a jealous rage."

"That wasn't what happened."

"Tell that to someone who doesn't know. Hell, I'm surprised you allowed him to breathe the same air as you for as long as you did."

"It was because of Eve that I allowed it. I acknowledged the wrong I'd done to my wife by turning her, then not wanting her. I soothed my conscience by allowing her to toy with Sullivan for a time. Eve wanted him so he lived and in the end she didn't want him."

Adam sucked in his hurt. "Yet, in the end I sensed she was trying to find a way to forgive him, to continue loving him, to remain with him. He'd done the same thing I'd done yet she didn't hate him."

"That's because he still loved her, Adam. He still wanted her."

"I still love her. I want her."

"But you still haven't shown her that. I've told you a million times to let go of your silly vow and you've refused to listen to me a million times. You should have known if you couldn't show your wife that you truly loved her that someone would. Sullivan could and he did, Adam. I can't believe you would try to lie to me again. You did not get rid of Sullivan for placing Eve in harms' way. Those were her choices; she freely took the experimental blood. She was trying to hang on to her mortality.

"That's natural," Adam insisted, "And it has little to do with me. Eve is…was… extremely religious. It's her background."

"What she's done does not come from any religion or church. It's coming from you, from your veins, blood of your blood. Rather fitting, don't you think?"

"Eve is not my punishment. She's my redemption and my salvation…only she hates me."

"And after all of this you still love her?"

"Of course I love her."

"Then you need to stop her, Adam, before her own soul is beyond redemption and can never be transformed. So far with your blood flowing through her veins she's been lucky. But it's time to make her stop the killings."

"I'm afraid she can't be stopped by my murmuring sweet nothings in her ear. She wants me dead."

"Then maybe you should see if she can accomplish that feat."

"You're absolutely no help. Why I even bother with you is a mystery."

"Not a mystery. I'm the voice of the conscience you abandoned years ago. I'm that nagging little voice deep inside you that keeps telling you that you should do the opposite of what you're doing. You'd lead a much happier life. Mine is the voice that first spoke to you and told you not to take your fool self into the sun or you would die." For the first time in awhile Evan smiled. "Even then you proved me wrong. You didn't die, did you? You're very much alive, yet you're still unhappy."

"What the hell is wrong with everyone? We're vampires, Evan, you, me and yes, damn it, even Eve. That can't be changed. It is what it is."

"Until some vampire puts a stake in her heart and kills her."

"And that vampire would be immediately dead."

"Are you once again giving me a message?"

"Only if there's a need. We're friends, Evan, have been for many centuries, but I will not hesitate to kill you should you harm one hair on Eve's head."

"I do understand that, Adam." Evan smiled, allowing his own fangs to descend. "Hurting your wife is just for you, turning her… well, hell that's your job, getting rid of the only beings she felt safe with and the ones that loved her—." He stopped, shrugging his shoulder. "I guess that's your job also." Evan turned sharply, then glared over his shoulder in Adam's general direction.

"Then I'd say stopping her is your job also. I understand her pain, really I do. But the vampires she destroyed today were innocent of any crimes against her."

"Vampires! That's the key word."

Evan watched as Adam turned slowly, causing the winds to shift direction, stirring the clouds so that they formed a halo around Adam. For a moment Evan just stared in awe. "Maybe you are blessed," he said softly. "Maybe that's why you can do what you do."

"As I was saying," Adam continued, ignoring Evan, "my wife is on a mission to rid the world of monsters, one monster at a time. She doesn't see what she's done as wrong or sinful," he said ruefully.

"You talk in terms of sin, Adam, and yet you say you don't seek absolution. Why don't you admit it? You've been trying to live in two worlds for a long time, that of mortal man and that of Grand Master Vampire, that of a sinner and that of a saint. You're not a priest any longer, Adam, of any order. And it does little good that you rail against God. You shall never be a priest again."

"You think you know me," Adam fumed. "You know nothing at all. Yes, I once railed and it did no good. I've long ago accepted what I am, what my fate is."

"If you've accepted it, why the hell have you tried so hard to ensure the hatred of our kind? Our females vie to get in your bed and all these years you have refused their advances, allowing them to go so far and no farther, knowing that is not our nature. Then there are your other annoying habits, your temper for instance. No one wants to be around you because who knows when you will blow. Of course your most irritating habit is your constantly spouting biblical quotes. Yet you are the greatest offender of them all. You love to say, 'Judge not,' yet you judge mortals and vampires alike and have found us all lacking. You've taken it upon yourself to create the world according to Adam. When a being does not go alone with your dictate, you get rid of him. We are more than friends, Adam. More than brothers, more than family. We are blood and it is because of this that my allegiance to you will remain intact. You have little tolerance for things that displease you and people have come to know how you treat your enemies and your friends."

"Have I not dealt with you as a friend?" Adam thundered.

"That depends. If you call threatening me every time we're together dealing with me as a friend, then yes, you've dealt with me as a friend."

A loud roar came from Adam that carried the weight of all that he'd felt. In many ways Evan was correct. Adam mentally flipped through the centuries of memories. He couldn't remember a time that Evan had not been around, either on the fringes or in groups. It was Adam who'd sought out Evan for companionship. At the time he'd thought, *Why not? He was always around anyway.*

"I have been much less a friend to you than you've been to me, Evan. You're right, my friends are few. I'm sorry I don't keep up with your life as well as I should."

Adam raised a brow. "As your friend I should have known about your mortal wife and your children. I've bored you for centuries with my tales of Eyanna and of late, Eve."

"Perhaps if you'd paid more attention to my life you would not now be at odds with your Eve."

Awareness that Evan was trying to lighten the mood brought on by the harshness of their words was not lost on Adam. He'd do the same. With the threats hanging between them, something was needed to make things right. Adam had no idea what that could be for he'd meant every word. As much as he loved Evan, if Evan harmed Eve, Adam would end his friend's life without hesitation. He would miss him, but he'd still kill him. For a long moment they stared until the tension eased and they both smiled. Then and only then did either of them dare to speak. As usual, it was Evan playing the role of peacemaker between them.

"I think it's time you learned how to treat a wife, Adam. Perhaps if you learn the proper way to handle women your wife will no longer seek to kill you. I'd like you to come to my home and meet my newest family."

Laughter pealed from the back of Adam's throat. Meet his family? That was rich. Evan was a wonder and now he sought to teach Adam something. Well, hell, he didn't have the problems Adam had. He didn't have a wife he didn't want to make love to. He didn't have a wife he'd longed after for a thousand years. He didn't have a wife that he gave up his life to protect.

"It's been awhile since you've been to Amsterdam. I'll bet you didn't even know that I'd secured a home there," Evan reprimanded softly. "Generally, we meet at one of your homes or a place of your choosing."

"Another oversight and another regret. I'll come to your home, Evan, and I'll meet your wife. And I'll see what your mortal wife can tell me about dealing with my vampiric wife who's filled with my blood and my strength, and whose only wish is to see me dead. Yes, Evan, I believe that's all that I need," Adam replied sarcastically

***

It was a wonder Adam wasn't ill what with the way Evan was living in little more than a hovel with his mortal family. There was no need, all of Evan's other homes were lavish beyond belief. They rivaled Adam for opulence. Why had his dearest friend chosen to live in obscurity? For what reason? To think that Evan who had always had scant regard for mortals should even for a time live as one was disheartening. There was no way Adam could abide the pretense that his visit to his friend's home was a normal visit, that his friend with the mortal wife and children was in fact mortal. The entire charade was ludicrous; the way Evan and Dalai moved around the room, ridiculous. A low rumble simmered inside Adam's chest cavity. The woman was nothing to look at, rather plain if truth be told. Adam didn't see any other remarkable qualities that she possessed so he probed her mind.

Nope. Nothing much there. Dalai was thinking about her damn grocery list and wondering if Adam would like the meal. He frowned and turned his attention toward Evan, shrugging his shoulders in question.

"What?" Evan's brow twitched.

The pastel colors of the room were making Adam ill. The frills and tattered linen adorning the dining room table were deplorable. Why it wasn't even real lace. What was the meaning of this? Evan was almost as rich as Adam. "Why do you live in this manner?" Adam intruded uninvited into Evan's mind as his friend was most wont to do to him.

"Because I can."

"But why?"

"I choose to."

"You're just being sarcastic and giving me the same answer as I give you when you question me. But this....the way you're living....this is...this is. This is crazy," Adam said at last. "For all the money that you have, you're living as a peasant.

"I find it best."

"How the hell could you?"

Adam jumped up, fidgeting, pacing the length of the small boxed in space, feeling caged. He'd never be able to live in something this small. He thought of Eve, his precious Eve, who'd thought to remain in that little cave she'd called home rather than move into his home. What was wrong with the world? Was everyone mad?

Evan speared Adam with a glare and Adam paused to take note of Dalai. Her hands were clutched together. She was tense, wondering what was wrong with the visitor.

"I'm sorry, forgive me." Adam turned on his heel and headed toward the woman. "Dalai, I'm not being a very good guest. I'm sorry I've made you nervous. It has nothing to do with you or your hospitality. There are worries on my mind."

"Yes," Evan piped in, a hint of a smile curling his lips. "Adam finds his wife angry with him. In fact she's extremely angry."

"Not divorce?" Dalai asked.

He could not believe she'd asked such a question in a whispery soft voice. *Divorce.* Adam's head tilted first toward Dalai, then toward Evan. "I wish it were that simple," he said quietly, taking the glass of wine that Evan had stepped away to get. He gazed into the glass for a moment before deciding to take a sip. With a small frown he touched the glass and turned the liquid into something more to his liking. He couldn't stomach cheap wine. When he finally sipped, he held the glass toward Evan and smiled, knowing Evan was aware he'd changed the mediocre wine into a much better vintage. He studied Dalai while sipping his wine, trying to decide how best to answer her question. Truthfully was the only way. Adam and Eve were bound together for all eternity.

"Dalai, my wife and I belong together. There will be no divorce." A smirk slid across his face and he laughed, turning his attention to Evan. "You spoke of children. Do I get to meet them?"

Rude, abrasive, perhaps, but Adam had had quite enough talk about Eve and about divorce. The door was closed on that subject and would remain so. He opened his mind to Eve, needing to know that she was safe. Wanted or not he'd have to return home to protect her. Evan was right, it was he who'd put into motion the things that Eve had done. If only he could see a clear path. His eyes closed of their own accord and he whispered, "Father, please."

With a vicious snap Adam opened his eyes. What was he doing? He would find his own answer as always. He would protect his wife.

***

The plunge of the woodened stake as it entered the chest of the unsuspecting vampire and the widening of his eyes made Eve cringe for only a moment. Then she deftly stepped away, knowing what was going to happen would be the same as always. Sulfur cooked the vamps from the inside out. That was her best explanation since she smelled sulfur. Or was it that she kept her weapons soaked in a special potion she'd created. Or perhaps it was the extra insurance of dosing them with holy water before using them. The holy water had worked the first time she'd killed vampires and it seemed to work now.

Ignoring the pity that tried to come, she reminded herself of her task. She had to rid the world of her kind. She was going to take them out, every single one. A shiver traveled up and down her spine. She'd tried while still a mortal to tell someone, anyone, that vampires existed. No one believed her and the ones that did didn't care.

Now it was Eve who didn't care what would happen to her. She wanted to take out as many vamps as she could and most especially the ones that moved about in the daylight hours. Those were the ones most like Adam. The way she looked at it, they were the most dangerous, blending in, working among mortals, having families.

A thought was pulling around the edges of her conscience. *What will happen to the families? What if the vampires she killed were decent?*

Vampires decent! Eve dropped to her knees on the sidewalk. People stared at her as though she were crazy but continued on their way. Clutching her hand to her heart, she closed her eyes and wished herself home. What had she done? She'd had no right.

"Sullivan," she whispered when she found herself home. "It was all my fault. I'm so sorry. I miss you and I miss Dr. Meah." She thought about all the vampires who'd befriended her at the company. *Oh, God, what have I done? I'm so tired of this.*

Her thoughts went to Adam, his telling her he'd prayed and it hadn't helped. Still, she didn't know what else to do so she prayed. It didn't cause her physical pain to call on God. It just wasn't doing any good. Yet, she prayed. "God, help me please." Once again she thought of Adam and yelled out to the cosmos knowing he'd hear.

"Adam, this is your fault. I'm tired of fighting monsters. I'm wrong and I know it but what am I going to do? I'll continue until someone stops me."

Fingering the amber cross she wore around her neck Eve thought to rip it off. It had given her an unfair advantage over those she'd killed. The vamps that walked about in the daylight spotted her as one of them but the cross gave them pause just long enough for her to move in.

As she continued to touch the cross she wanted badly for it to be over, to be able to know her task was done. But it was too late for that. She'd gone too far, done too much.

At any rate it wasn't as though she could just say she was sorry and stop. There was a price on her head. Vampires wanted her dead. She didn't blame them. Funny thing was she'd be glad to oblige them. Only before she died she still felt compelled to take as many of them with her as she could. Awareness of her conflicted contradictions gave Eve pause. *Kill, don't kill. Feel pity and guilt. Feel victorious having taken a step to save mankind.* Her mind whirled with her mixed emotions.

Tears fell as she used her hand to draw a scared circle. Revenge magic, something that should never be used lightly. Her home was impenetrable. The only vampire who'd dare enter would be Adam Omega and how she wished he would. She had something special for him, a potion with his blood, taken from her veins, one she'd sent all the energy that she could muster into. For the first time she'd called on help from other deities in making it. She'd never heard of these deities a few short years before and even if she had, she would have never thought to call on them for help.

Sacrilegious was what Adam called what she did. Why not? Her entire life was sacrilegious. Though every kill took her one step closer to hell Eve had to believe there was some right in what she was doing or she'd go insane. She'd think of Sullivan and cry for what she'd become. Then she'd think of Adam and kill again.

***

A duller existence than Evan's couldn't be had if one wished for it. He'd had no idea of the kind of life his friend was living. Had he known, he would have done everything in his power to put a stop to it. The hairs on his body were tingling. The internal rage was not toward Evan or the hovel he called home. That much Adam was aware of. It was because of this incessant need he appeared to have developed in the past few years to call out to God. There were no answers coming and had not been for over a millennium. He'd thought he'd ridded himself of the habit. *Eve.* Pleading for Eve had become a new habit with him and he didn't much care how she remained safe, just that she would. But the constant praying? That had to stop.

Adam walked the outer edges of St. Peter's Square. Today he didn't feel inclined to go inside and wreak havoc. If there was a reason he felt drawn to the place he would eliminate it. It was becoming increasingly tiresome to be bothered with Evan filling the role of his unasked for counselor.

"Damn you. Go home. Go back to Amsterdam, go to Greece, France. I don't care where you go, just leave me the hell alone. I want to be alone," Adam hissed, whirling around, snarling, allowing his fangs to lower and allowing the blood haze to cloud his vision. He ignored the fact that the sun was blazing high in the sky, that he was terrifying anyone that looked at him. He scanned the people who'd seen him, the ones pretending they hadn't and the ones crossing themselves. He smiled at the shocked looks on their faces as they spotted the crucifix that hung about his neck. A simple enough item but one they didn't think he was entitled to, or able to wear.

Why not?

Adam had asked this question a million times He knew better than most what it represented and he believed in the power more than most. Adam didn't consider himself the abomination that his dear wife and others thought him to be. No, far from it. He growled as Evan finally materialized.

"I thought you were the angel to warn me away. Why are you here?" Adam asked, advancing on his friend. "Why can't you just leave me alone?"

"Because you'll self destruct if I do. And I think your destruction should be much more grand, don't you?"

With a snarl Adam disappeared into vapor but not even then was he safe for he didn't travel alone.

"Leave me the hell alone," Adam roared. "I don't require a baby sitter."

"But you do. I can read your thoughts, Adam. You have not suffered enough. You have not been rejected enough. So, I know what you're going to do. You're going to the new club. You want to force the hands of the vampires, make them hate you even more, have them beg for mercy, have the women look at you with longing and lust, have them…what, Adam? You tell me."

Sadness darkened Adam's features. He had flashes of things long past, being mortal and hearing the confession of the most beautiful woman he'd ever met, finding her heart and spirit to be even more beautiful than her face, their getting married, their making love. He shook his head as he hurried past the memory of her death. A lump lodged in his midsection, a knot of pain at his memories of seeing Eve for the first time, of falling in love with her, taking her, his brutality to her and hers to him, her betrayal, then at last her love. A shudder filled him. What did he want?

He wanted Eve; he wanted to change his past and his future. Adam swallowed, allowing his mind to search out Eve.

"Get the hell out of my mind," Eve screamed out. You're no longer welcome in my thoughts."

Adam ran his tongue along the roof of his mouth and opened up his eyes to stare at Evan.

"I want what I am," Adam said softly, "to be me. Adam Omega, Grand Master Vampire, the one to strike fear in the hearts of mortals and vampires alike." His eyes scanned the land and he tilted his head slowly, feeling the breeze pass though the heavy locs that were now hanging almost to his waist.

"Yes, I am going to the club because no one can do a damn thing about it and I refuse to cower because they don't want me there."

"Then I'll go with you." Evan smiled.

"Your lust?"

"I have needs like most, Adam, needs that my mortal wife cannot satisfy even if she so desired."

"I thought this was what you wanted, a life with a mortal, making love to her. Are you telling me now that it doesn't fulfill your need?"

"Why don't you tell me? Does your making love with mortal women fulfill the need to go all the way, to take the bite, to become one with that person?"

The taste of Eve's blood hit the back of his throat and Adam's flesh enlarged from the memory. "I don't need you to baby sit me." He snapped the words off and vanished into the mist, reappearing inside the club. He laughed as he heard the growls, saw the snarls. *Yes*, this he could handle. He dropped fangs an inch, then another and another. Adam was thoroughly pissed.

With each stride he took, he gauged the room, counting, pretending not to, going up to the bar, staring, then glaring at the barkeep until he passed over the best liquor he had. Adam continued glaring until the barkeep handed over a tray with ice and glasses, then he settled himself at a corner table and poured the liquor.

A loud sigh escaped him as mist swirled around him before settling into the chair opposite him, coalescing into the form of Evan. Adam frowned. "They can smell fear."

"Are you afraid, Adam?"

"No, but you are and it wasn't necessary for you to follow me. Perhaps it's your advancing years that you're unable to either hear or process the information that I give to you. It has to be something because I distinctively remember saying several times before what I'm about to say again. I don't need a baby sitter. How many times do I have to tell you that?"

"Maybe not a babysitter but a friend. No one wants you here. You need someone to watch your flank."

"And you've taken on that chore?"

"Of course, who else would do it for you?"

A bevy of voices started as a whir, then increased in volume. "How timely." Adam took a sip of the liquor, then gave a shrug and a smile toward Evan. "You still have time to leave," he said softly. "This party is for me but if you insist on being my guest, then the reception will undoubtedly be the same for you as for me."

For a moment Adam started to leave in order to keep this last friend safe. It wasn't that Evan was weak but the alliance with him was fast draining his resources. Shawn, a vampire of immense size, snarled and moved closer to where Adam sat.

"Please." Adam closed his eyes for but a moment and prayed before opening them again. "Please, Shawn, I find that I have the need to kill. Killing you, killing all of you, should take the edge off." From his corner vision he saw Evan watching him intently and shrugged. "What? I spoke the truth." Just then Shawn took a step backward and Adam raised his hand and aimed a powerful beam at him, incinerating him on the spot.

"That was unnecessary," another vampire screamed while Adam smiled. Putting one hand on Evan's shoulder to keep him seated, Adam rose lazily, stretching, smiling with lethal intent. The need to kill, to help his wife rid the world of monsters, to make her safe, was his only thought. He advanced on the group. No trickery was needed, no laser. He stepped close to the group of six and murmured, "Say farewell." Then with one swipe of his hand from right to left, making his hand do the work of his sword, he beheaded them all. Only then did he incinerate the bodies. There would be no regeneration for these vampires.

"Why did you do that, Adam?"

The sound of the shrill female voice gave Adam pause. He turned and smiled at Melvina. "I did it because it felt good."

Planting himself in front of her and knowing what the woman was going to attempt, he waggled a finger. "Don't do it. This will be your only warning." The moment the words were out Melvina lunged herself in Adam's general direction, only to be met by the force of a slap across her face that sent her crashing into the corner wall.

"Oh shit," Evan muttered and stood next to Adam.

"Don't," Adam admonished. "This is my fight. I've been away for too long, they've all gotten restless, thinking me weak for finding and turning my wife. That will not do. They think I will no longer kill them. They need to know that I will. I am still in charge."

"I thought your reason was to safeguard your wife."

"That is at the core of what I do. But I have realized that I have neglected to keep them fearful. Now, leave me be, Evan. As I told you the last time, this is child's play. I could do this all day." Adam grinned and walked into the center of the club. Stopping the music he waited for silence, putting a finger to his lips to quiet the vampires.

"I came to have a good time, to have a few drinks, to dance with a few women." He took his time looking at the women in the club, sending them words of lust psychically, laughing as his words took hold and the male vampires became so angered that the whole room was filled with anger. Evan was shaking his head in disgust at Adam's antic but true to his word, Adam could tell that Evan had his flank. There was no need. Adam could and would take care of his own flank. Now he would give the vampires fair warning. The seven he'd killed had taken the edge off; the knot of tension was releasing.

"We don't want you here, Adam. Look at what you've done. In less than ten minutes you've killed seven of us. Leave."

"Make me," Adam said calmly. The smile disappeared from his face and what had merely been child's play before turned into an adult game. "I go where I please when I please, and I leave when I please." He looked at the voluptuous vampire standing next to the challenging vamp. "Your woman?" Adam asked. He saw fear finally settle in the man's eyes. Adam turned his gaze on the female. "Come here," he ordered and lest there be any mistaking what he was doing he added, "of your own volition. I desire you."

"He's lying," Melvina screamed. "He won't make love to our kind, you all know that. He only wants the human… his wife."

Adam dared a glance in Melvina's direction. *Ahhh, so he was wrong. They weren't all yet aware that he'd turned his mortal wife. Interesting. This should work even better than he'd hoped.* He looked again at the blonde vampire in the skintight jumpsuit. He held out his hand but did not smile. "Come to me. Now!" he ordered, still not using mind control. The woman moved toward Adam and her companion stopped her, his hand on her arm.

"Bitch, you will not go to him, not while I'm standing here."

"Then don't stand there," Adam said, glaring in his direction, aiming a beam at him, ending the vampire's existence. He turned back to the blonde. "Are you coming?" he asked.

"Yes," she replied, barely glancing at the pile of ash directly behind her before rushing over to Adam's side.

Adam smiled as the blonde plastered herself to him, touching him, placing kisses from his scrotum to his throat. When she reached his throat Adam put out a hand and stopped her with a cold smile. "No."

"See, what did I tell you?" Melvina yelled for the third time.

Adam turned his head slowly and raised his eyes. Then he lowered his fangs and bit into the woman at his side. He drank his fill before lifting his mouth and wiping away the blood. The blonde merely stared as the orgasm Adam had produced by drinking her blood made her sway. "Adam," she murmured.

Adam smiled, turning his attention to another and beckoning for her. When he was done, he repeated the ritual with seven more females, all the companions of other vampires. The club was so quiet that each vampire's heartbeat could be heard.

"I am sated for now," Adam announced as another female came to him. He snapped his fingers, making a table appear in the center of the dance floor. He walked with all the grace of a predatory animal and sat in one of the chairs, his eyes coming to rest on Evan. "Come," he said softly. He grinned and in a booming voice said, "Please return to your partying. I am quite satisfied for now."

"What the hell just happened, Adam?" Evan asked, his adrenaline spiking. "This was a little much even for you. And please tell me why you drank from the throats of other vampires' women?"

"Don't you know?" Adam chuckled softly. "I thought you knew me so well."

"This made no sense."

"Judge not for you know not what I do." Adam stared at Evan. "I suggest you either look in front of you or leave the table." Adam didn't even bother to stand as the group of angry vampires moved quickly on them.

"Leave," one Adam knew as Andrew said, his face only inches from Adam.

"Have a breath mint." Adam produced one and shoved it into the vamp's mouth a moment before severing his head. In less time than it took for any in the group to say a word, blink or move away, Adam had killed them all. He cracked his jaw. "Aw, now that feels better." He raised a finger in the air for the waitress and ordered drinks. Evan was eyeing him.

"This wasn't random, was it, Adam?"

"Nothing is ever random with me, Evan."

"Can you tell me why?"

Adam smiled. "There is talk of revenge, of killing the person responsible for the slaughter in Chicago."

"So you brought their hatred to yourself hoping that it would stop them from going after Eve."

"No, I killed the monsters for my wife. And I will keep on killing them." He held his hands out and looked at his palms. "My hands are so covered in blood that they can never be clean." He lifted his eyes. "I can take killing monsters, Eve can't. Eventually she will stop being angry and then she will be vulnerable. I intend to make her world monster free.

"With one exception."

Adam smiled. "With one exception." He saw the sudden look of warning in Evan's eyes and turned slightly. "Melvina, what do you want?"

"I want you dead, Adam."

"If that's what you truly want, then I'm sorry to inform you that you'd better take a number." With that Adam grinned and grabbed for her. Holding her in his steel embrace, he trailed lightning fire across her carotid artery, then sank his fangs into her, holding her as she attempted to squirm away, drinking deeply as the squirming turned into lust, then unbridled passion. Adam drank from Melvina until she came and her flush of embarrassment filled her face. She glanced briefly at Evan.

"I think I understand now, Adam. So, that bitch Eve—"

Melvina couldn't finish the sentence because Adam's fingers were crushing her windpipe. "Don't you dare," he snarled. "Don't you dare ever call my wife a bitch again in my presence or out of it. I will hear you and I will kill you, Melvina. That's a promise. I will peel the skin from your bones and I will make you suffer. Do you understand me?" He squeezed tighter. "You may not be able to speak but you can nod your head."

Fear made the vamp's eyes bulge out and she nodded slowly. But Adam did not release her. "You're a friend, Melvina, and I wronged you once," he said, "so you get this one chance to live. Once and only once. Is it clear? Do not think your being a woman will stop me. It will not. Do you understand?" When Melvina gave a frightened nod, Adam released her. "Then go away and be a good girl."

Adam took a sip of his drink.

"Don't you ever worry that they could slip something in there to poison you?" Evan was staring in amazement at Adam.

"I'm a true immortal. They cannot kill me. You're aware of that." But he wasn't so sure they couldn't harm his wife. Then his mind went to Eve and he thought of her potions and how they had affected him. *But the bartender wasn't Eve.*

"You should have killed her," Evan said softly.

"You surprise me, Evan."

"You're killing the monsters so they can't harm your wife. You've just allowed the greatest threat to Eve to escape."

Adam laughed. "Eve has my blood. One on one I think she can take Melvina." He saw his friend wasn't amused. "Seriously, Evan, Melvina will not go after Eve. I put a suggestion into her mind while I drank from her."

"Whatever the suggestion was, it didn't stop her from calling Eve a bitch, now did it?"

Adam glanced toward the corner where Melvina sat rubbing her throat, glaring at him despite his warning. He connected with her and whispered, "Stop that damn glaring at me or I'll kill you this instant." One final glare and Melvina disappeared from the club.

"See," Adam grinned. "All taken care of and I didn't have to kill her."

"This is one time that I think you should have. But like you said, you don't need my counsel. You know best."

Ignoring Evan's sarcastic tone, Adam sighed, then gave a small chuckle. "You're right. I know best."

Chapter Seventeen

Sanctuary Crystals was now a place of refuge for Eve, a place of peace and solitude. The shop had been sealed against evil. Well, most evil, Eve thought as she continued walking around the shop until she spotted a woman staring at her. Eve smiled at her, knowing the woman knew or thought she knew what Eve was. Eve also knew what she was. The woman was a witch. Eve made her way over to where the woman was sitting holding court.

When Eve approached the path parted and the woman picked up her deck of tarot cards without being asked. She shuffled them as Eve sat before her.

"Cut," the woman said to her and Eve did as instructed. Perhaps in the cards she'd find another way. Maybe she could finally think of ending the killings.

The woman dealt ten cards. "The heart of the matter is nine," the reader began. She went through the explanation of each card until she went through the ten cards, giving Eve a look into the things she already knew. No new information was forthcoming.

"So you know what I am?" Eve asked.

"That's a strange question," the witch said. "You didn't say who, but what. Did you make a mistake?"

Eve was aware the woman was fishing. She smiled at her, turning around to see the others watching them. "My question stands."

"In that case, I suppose I'll have to say, I'm not sure."

"Do you have ideas?"

"I do, but in the light of day they make little sense."

"Do you think I'm evil?" Eve couldn't help smiling as she asked the question.

"If you were you would never have been able to enter the shop."

"Do you really believe that?"

"Are you telling me that you would have been able to cross regardless?"

Eve laughed. "We won't know, will we? I don't plan on turning evil. Or let's say I don't plan on becoming any more evil than I am at the moment. I've done evil things and I now wish to find a way to stop."

"What are you?"

Eve turned the question back on the woman after picking up the woman's tarot cards, shuffling them and laying them before the woman. "What are you?" Eve asked with boldness.

"I'm a witch," the woman answered.

"And I'm not," Eve lied. "And even if I were, so what? That should be enough for now."

"The cards say differently. They also say that you're a very powerful psychic. Is that true?"

"I used to be a long time ago and I plan to be again in the future."

The woman's eyes went down and she gazed at the cards. "Do you read the tarot?"

"Yes, I do."

"And you're going to read for me?"

"Yes, Toni Greathouse." Eve smiled in amusement and picked up the first card, turned it over and read, stunning the witch with her accuracy.

"You're very good," Toni said.

"I can be better." Eve smiled and continued with the reading. When she was done, she glanced at the clerk, giving him instructions on delivering the huge crystals. Laughing at their thoughts, she walked out the store and climbed into her Hummer, wondering how long it would be before the store ran out of things that she needed. Even she was aware she came partly to escape into a world where she wasn't totally feared or shunned. But she knew better than to push her visits longer than she should. It wouldn't take much longer for all there to begin to figure out something wasn't right with her. She didn't know if she had the patience to erase the memories of so many mortals the way Adam did. But as Adam had told her, she had to protect herself and if need be she would do what was necessary. It was well past time that Eve called her husband to her.

***

Dark brooding eyes met the glare of brown eyes with flecks of gold. Her anger was palatable as it reached out tentacles, grabbing him with icy fingers. A quiver began in his soul and continued until it spiraled throughout his body. Adam sucked in his breath. Did he regret? Hell yes, he regretted the things he'd done to Eve, the things he'd made her do. *And why then had he done them?* he wondered as the tears, blood red, ran down his cheeks. He'd told himself it had all been in the name of love. Yet he could still not force himself to give her that which she sought. He could end this hellish nightmare for Eve, give her relief. He could kill her and let her go, free her spirit. Adam groaned, wondering what would become of her if he did. Had he done the ultimate? Would she go to hell for the crimes he'd forced her to commit?

"You're aware why I called you to me. Why did you come, Adam?" Eva asked at last.

"It's time for you to stop killing other vampires," he replied.

"And you're here to make me?"

"I made you, so yes, I suppose you're right. I'm here to make you stop."

"I've learned the things you've long wanted me to know. I can protect myself." Eve circled the room, putting some space between her and Adam. "I'm not a baby vampire any longer. I know who and what I am. Call me a witch, Adam. I don't give a damn. Call me a healer, a seer, call me a psychic, none of the titles matter to me."

She smiled, icily, and it made Adam's blood run cold. "Which are you?" he asked.

"I'm all of them and I know very well the life I lived before, the power that I've had. Your old Eyanna, she's dead, Adam. But she did possess power, power that even you're not aware of. She did love you. That much I know."

Feeling Adam's mental probe Eve dropped the gate that guarded her mind, keeping her secret locked firmly inside. "I think I made a mistake in calling you to me."

"Your call was not what brought me. It was time for me to return home."

"Why the hell did you return?"

"You needed me, and as always when you need me I'll come."

"Why would you think I need you?"

"You're alone as I am alone. We need each other, Eve."

"I wouldn't be alone if you had not taken away those that love me."

"That's over now. Can't you let it go, Eve?"

"Did you think I would have forgotten all that you've done? Or that time heals all wounds? I hate you and there is no other emotion I will ever have for you. I hate what you are, what you stole from me, what you made me. And I hate that you took from me the one man that loved me completely. That I hate you for most of all."

"No, that's not true."

Eve's eyes snapped furiously and she advanced on Adam, narrowing her eyes as she moved. "Don't you dare try and tell me my reasons for hating you. You can't possibly know."

"Even now you hate me. I know that," Adam said, going around the room touching his fingers to the crosses that still adorned his home, dipping them in the water in the urns, the holy water, the water he'd blessed. He laughed, the sound hoarse and grating through him. He glanced at the tapestries on the wall. The millions of dollars he'd paid for them as nothing. He'd lived an extravagant life and he would continue to do so.

"Sullivan left you all that he owned. Why did you return here to live?"

"It's my home."

"Still, you didn't have to return here. You were aware that one day I would return. Where do you sleep?"

He watched as a shiver ripped through her body. She wanted to kill him. That much he'd known before he'd even gotten within two cities of her. "You still love me, Eve." He turned swiftly, bracing for the attack he knew was coming. With a banshee cry Eve ripped the ceremonial blade he'd given to her as a gift from her pocket and ran toward him, slicing away at the air, almost connecting with his flesh.

What irony. Adam sighed, moving from her reach. At first he'd thought the blade was unsharpened. As it nicked his flesh, he became aware that wasn't the case. With one snap he slapped the offending weapon away.

"Stop it! That's not going to accomplish a damn thing," Adam bellowed. He watched as Eve bent to retrieve the blade and make another pass at him.

"Stop it," he said again, knocking the knife from her hand. When she went for it a third time and then plunged the knife into his chest, straight into his heart, Adam stared.

Eve was pissing him off big time. "If you do that again I will slap the hell out of you. Do you understand? I have warned you that I do not like being hit. I have told you that if you do not want me to hit you, then you will not hit me." His fingers grabbed the hilt of the blade and he pulled it from his heart, looking with disinterest at his blood that covered the weapon.

"All that you've done to me, Adam, and you now think you shouldn't be hit by me."

"I never struck you, Eve."

"No, you did much worse. You made me your prisoner."

"I'm a damn vampire, Eve. Do you know what the hell that means? I made you mine because you were. I did nothing out of the ordinary."

"How about turning me, Adam? Was that not out of the ordinary?"

"I saved your life."

"And turned me into a vampire."

"The deed is done and has been for years. Stop whining and get over it already. Suck it up and behave like the vampire you now are, not like the vampire slayer you're trying to become."

"Suck it up? Get over it? Whining? I will never get over it. You took something from me you had no right to take, Adam. You took away my free will when you made me into a vampire. Even God doesn't tamper with our free will. And you're not God, Adam."

"I gave you the gift of immortality."

"Vampires are not immortal! You've proven that." Eve held her hands up to her face and peered for a long moment at them. "I've proven that. I will prove it once again when you lay dead at my feet."

"I'm a true immortal. You can't kill me."

"I don't believe it. You've killed hundreds, perhaps thousands of vampires, and so have I. Vampires are not immortal, you're not immortal. Admit it Adam, that's a lie."

"Is it?" Adam asked quietly. "Then let me tell you this. You can not kill me because I am Adam Omega. Now how does that sit with you? I've just proven it to you. The wounds you've inflicted on me are already healed."

"You may well be Adam Omega, Grand Master Vampire, and you might even be immortal. But there is more to it than that you believe it. There has to be. I don't believe it and I'm not going to stop trying to kill you." Before she'd finished speaking, Eve retrieved the knife Adam had carelessly dropped and ran full force into Adam, plunging it even deeper into his heart, twisting the blade, shoving with all her vampiric strength, hammering the hilt of the blade with her fists. All the while tears of frustration and anger washed over her.

Then suddenly she felt pain as Adam pulled the knife out of his flesh and slapped the hell out of her just as he'd promised

His dark hair swayed with his movement as he advanced on her, his fists shaking in fury. When he reached her, he lifted her from the floor, shaking her like a rag doll before tossing her against the wall.

"You want to challenge me, go for it. You're a vampire with my strength and my blood. I will not treat you like a mortal woman. Do you understand?" A roar came from deep within his chest. He'd known it would come to this. Even Yas had known and warned him.

"Do you for one moment believe that I would think you'd give me special consideration?" Eve glared. "I am what I am because of you. You abused me when there was no need. You took from me that which I would have freely given had you only asked. My body was yours, my heart, my love. But you never asked for anything from me. You took. And you think I believe you're holding back your rage because of some ill conceived love you say you have for me. I didn't ask you for favors, so if you think I'm going to beg you to go easy on me, I'm not. One way or another, this ends tonight, Adam. You're going to have to kill me to make me stop because I plan on kicking your ass before I kill you."

"You're not capable of it, my love."

"I'm capable of a lot more than you've given me credit for you, arrogant bastard. Tonight you will die and it will be by my hands."

"One of us might very well die tonight, Eve." Adam shook his head slowly. "Please don't make me hurt you."

"Hurt me? Do you think you can? You've done all that you can do to me."

"I gave you over two years with Sullivan. That was a hell of a lot more than either of you deserved. My wife, my beautiful vampire whore. I should have killed you the moment you had the thought to bed Sullivan."

"But you didn't, did you, you bastard? You waited until I fell in love with him. Then you killed him."

A moan started low in his chest and for the hundredth time Adam knew that his sleight of hand had not been the right decision. He could do nothing now but continue the charade. He'd caused Eve enough grief. Her knowing the truth would only cause her more. With a growl Adam decided to continue the game. "Sullivan was warned and so were you."

"And who, pray tell, made you God? You're nothing but what I said in the beginning. You're a bully, a vampire bully. You came here to chastise me, to tell me I have to stop my killings. Well, guess what? I have. There is only one more that I have to kill and then it will be over. Then I can forget." She rushed toward him but before she could reach him Adam reached out with the power of his mind and slapped her so hard she flew back against the stone fireplace.

"Stop it," Adam railed, his voice raw. "Don't make me hurt you."

Sagging against the wall, she felt the pain of the stones pressing into her flesh. "Hurt me?" she hissed, rising slowly. "I have no feelings left. You can't hurt me." She closed her eyes, feeling the power of Adam Omega flow through her brain. She then sent his power out toward him and smiled as it connected with its intended target. She laughed aloud as Adam sailed over the countertop and landed with a hard thud against the opposite granite wall.

"This isn't how I want it." Using the power of her mind to lift the blade once again, Eve brought it to her and ran for Adam. She wanted to feel his flesh give way beneath the crush of her hand, to be the one to kill him. She wanted him dead and she would prefer to kill him with her bare hands if it were possible. But the blade he'd given her would be a perfect substitute. This time instead of plunging the knife into his heart, she hacked away at his perfectly chiseled body. Blood spurted from several holes, red blood that became a deep velvet color as it hit the floor. Though her movements were swift she saw the look of pained shock in Adam's eyes as she delivered each blow. Then his fury took over and he knocked her across the room, then marched after her, hitting her repeatedly.

"Is this what you want?" he asked. "Is this the monster you've created in your mind? Is this satisfactory? Why the hell do you provoke me?"

"I want you dead."

"Damn it, Eve, without your love I'm already dead."

She shook her head. "No, I want you gone from the face of the earth. I want to know you no longer exist. I want there to be no Adam and Eve. I want it to stop."

"Then I'll oblige."

He raised his hand to strike her. She waited, tensing her body, thinking at least one of them would be gone and there'd be one less evil in the world.

"It stops now. Do you understand?" Adam whispered.

Adam dropped down on his knees beside her and pulled her into his arms. She waited for his bite, for him to drain her. In fact she welcomed it. But what she felt instead of his fangs piercing her skin was his tears, hot and scorching her skin.

"No, damn you." Eve pushed away. No, it wouldn't happen, not this time. "No." She pounded on his back, trying to push him away. "No, Adam."

"I love you. Damn you and damn me. I'm so sorry that this has happened. I take your sins on my head. In all that you've done I give you absolution."

"You can't give me absolution, Adam. You're not a priest any longer."

"Then I give you my love, all my love." He allowed her to continue her pounding of his flesh, blocking out the blows, her hatred, and her shouted curses. "Show me how much you hate me, Eve. Take the plunge." He bared his neck, then saw the fear in her and knew in that instant she was afraid not of his killing her but of what she possibly felt for him still. She didn't want to love him; her hate was safe. Adam understood that to love something as vile as he would make her as bad as him. *Wouldn't it?*

"No," Eve roared as Adam bit into her neck. He felt her shiver, her head rolling on her shoulder as he drank of her blood, pushing past the hatred, the fear, the pain. Finally as the sweetness of her blood filled his mouth, he tasted her love, her sadness and renewed pain.

Eve was still hitting him, not wanting him to know. Yet Adam felt her feelings of invasion. He'd intruded on her most private thoughts. Now new hatred flared in her blood only to be burned off by the passion she had for him, her love winning out. He brought his head from her throat, blood dripping from his incisors.

"Now you," Adam whispered softly into her ear. He tenderly wiped at the tears that were coursing down her cheek.

"No," Eve said as her lips moved toward his throat. "No," she moaned and shivered. Her teeth changed and the fangs appeared. Adam did not push her way. She pierced his skin and he held her to himself, allowing her to drink, to see what he'd seen, to become one with him again, to know he loved her above all else.

This wasn't what she wanted, not this utterly eerie feeling of right, of a millennium of wanting becoming complete. Her memories merged with those of Eyanna's and her love became Eyanna's, their pain the same. Adam, the man who'd given his heart, then his soul, all because of love. It grieved Eve's spirit that he'd endured for so long alone. And it vexed her spirit more that even when she'd surrendered her love to him it had not been enough. It never was and it never would be.

Eve shuddered once, then again. The drinking of blood with the man who owned her soul as well as her next breath was much more than the drinking. It took them each to a different dimension, one of total and pure love, of only rightness. In the drinking they became one again, their bond irretrievably strengthened, never to be broken. Eve was aware of that. Not hate, not even death would kill their love for each other. Adam was as much her prisoner as she was his. As much as she might not wish it to be so, they were true soul mates, two halves, whole, only when they were together.

A moan washed over her as she drank. Terror filled her, for she had no idea how her and the man she couldn't truly live without could ever live together. She tried to hide her emotions from Adam. She did not want him to know just how deeply her love for him went. It would make what she would have to do all the harder. *I have to put a stop to us, I have to.* She sent the refrain throughout her mind and ignored Adam's whispered refrain.

"We can make it work, Eve."

Still, she had to do what had to be done. Only she could do it. Eve trembled in Adam's dark embrace, his midnight tresses falling across her face, her breasts. She felt his passion, his heat, his lust, and then above all she felt his love, never ending, always there. And she felt his grief, his agonizing sorrow at what she had become. He was mourning the loss of her innocence. What had he expected? He'd made her into what she now was. What had he wanted when he demanded that she drink blood? Now she was drinking it, taking her fill, as though she'd never known any other substance.

Desire flamed in her veins stronger than anything she'd ever known. Tamping it down was out of the question. "Adam," she choked on his name. "You've bewitched me."

"No, my love, it's you who've bewitched me."

He shuddered as she once again began to drink from him, taking his power with each sip. And she continued until she was spent, keeping her eyes closed, not wanting to see the disgust that was always reflected in his eyes when he touched her in lust.

"It's not there, Eve."

Her lids fluttered and she opened her eyes slowly. She saw the love glowing from the pit of Adam's soul, saw it reflected back at her in the dark purple haze. Her heart had never felt this way, as though it were being broken and mended in the same instant. How could that be possible?

"Adam, how can you? You hate touching me like this."

"I hate even more not touching you. Besides, you forget who I am. I'm Adam Omega, Grand Master Vampire," he grinned. "I can conquer all, even my own inhibitions. You are not Tarasha."

With that Adam moved over her and entered her, then lowered his head to suckle her breast. "I love you, Eve," he moaned, "you my witchy wife, my Achilles heel, my reason for living. I love you." As he thrust within her, his mind connected with hers and he bathed her in love. When she came, sinking her fangs into him, he accepted it and the bliss that accompanied it. He held her to him until she was done, kissing away her blood tears, knowing why she'd stopped using the potion to make them run clear. Then he moaned and fell on her, sinking his fangs gently into her and taking from her. This time there was no hate, only love and surprise. When they were spent he held her in his arms.

"I have done you a great disservice, wife. I do not know what waits for you or for me if we truly die. I cannot allow you to be tormented should that be true."

Eve thought about the vampires Adam had slain for her and she held him tighter. Through their bonding she'd seen all that had transpired with Adam just as he'd seen all that she'd done. Could it really be over? But what of it? She was Adam's wife. She was a vampire, a vampire killer. She'd made her own share of enemies and she would kill again to preserve her life.

Adam was right once again. Was it truly, judge not lest ye be judged? She'd judged Adam. Now what would her judgment be? Did she still end it as she'd promised herself that she would? She felt Adam rolling her over, then his tongue at the small of her back licking and trailing fire through her veins.

Why couldn't he have done this before? she wondered. If he had the last three and a half years of her life would have been different. Sullivan, she thought briefly of him, would not be dead. She shivered...and poor Dr. Meah...nor Mark, nor the scores of vampires she'd killed and Adam had killed in her defense. If he'd not made her and then rejected her touch, none of it would have happened.

Lust curled in her belly as liquid fire washed over her. Adam's tongue icy hot and so so good tended to her needs, mending her broken spirit. And with each flick of his tongue she was bound more deeply to him.

She'd said he would die without her but it was also true that she would die without him. Shame washed over her as Eve realized that in spite of all that Adam had done she loved him still. He was indelibly carved on her soul. She'd never be rid of him.

A delicious tremble ran the length of her body and she pressed backwards to be even closer to Adam, wincing a little as he entered her. Her back to his front was erotic to say the least. She tilted her head back, knowing that when he came he would want her blood. She'd give it gladly to him now. His large palms covered her breasts, tweaking them until they ached for relief. Her entire body ached for relief but there would be no suckling of breasts. They were not positioned for it. Before the thought had a chance to coalesce she felt Adam, suckling her, his hands trailing her body, between her thighs, covering every inch of her and she moaned in rapture. Only Adam could fill her in this manner. Only Adam had the power to make his breath wash over her in agonizing waves of heat. Her body was singed by his heat and her arousal.

"Adam," Eve screamed out, hearing his chuckle as he bit into her gently, his tongue trailing heat over her carotid artery. He kissed and lapped away, not really taking the plunge but teasing. "Adam," she moaned, pushing herself back even farther, knowing she was Adam's whore, knowing he was chuckling because she'd sworn to never become so desperate for his touch. She would die if she only could. She wanted to feel him drawing on her blood. He slid her body around so that she was looking into his eyes. How they stayed locked in their embrace was a mystery, but they did it.

"Let's do this together, Eve."

There was no need for Adam to ask her twice. She'd longed for this in her heart. Simultaneously they each bit into the flesh of the other. Eve feared her body would have floated away if Adam had not restrained her. Exquisite pleasure beyond anything humanly possible bathed her. She was thrust backward in time, connected to Adam. She was Eyanna, his mortal bride, madly in love with him. And she was Eve.

Adam Omega's vampiric wife.

Chapter Eighteen

Sated. Not hardly but he should be. Adam lay sprawled over Eve's body as his mouth suckled her breast. What a fool he'd been to have denied himself the pleasure of his wife's body. He was a vampire and his going against his nature for over a thousand years surprised even him. Having the taste of Eve's blood on his tongue as he came while being suckled by her, was such an exquisite treat that it caused Adam to damn Tarasha again. Had she not turned him while making the experience one of untold passion, Adam would not have assigned himself a thousand years of blame, guilt for having betrayed his wife in the arms of a vampire, guilt for having derived pleasure from it.

Then there was Sullivan. Adam's senses flamed, knowing of the passion his wife had found in another man's arms. He couldn't help snarling in anger. Immediately Eve's hands worked their magic, soothing him, touching him, reaching between them and finding him ready. Flipping his wife onto her back Adam gazed down at her.

"Never again, Eve, will you lie with another. Do you understand? He didn't wait for a response but merely took her, riding her hard, knowing she could take it, knowing she wanted it and him. Their gazes remained locked and a gentle smile graced Eve's lips. Her words were relayed to his mind, then his heart.

"I am yours and you are mine," she said. "Forever and ever."

Adam raised up then, growling fiercely, bringing Eve with him, wanting more. The soft mattress seemed to be preventing him from going as deeply as he needed to be. He waited only a moment for awareness to dawn in his wife. Then he took the plunge, going into her hard and furiously, lowering his fangs and drinking as he came, feeling Eve's fangs sink into him as well. Lust lifted them from the bed and magic kept them afloat. This woman was his, she'd always been his and as he'd done in the past he'd give his all to protect her. He'd already given his life and his soul. Whatever he had left, whatever would be required, he would continue to protect her. Only one thing would stop that and it was Eve herself. But Adam had no plans to allow that to happen. There could not possibly be anything now that could keep them apart. They'd jumped all the hurdles and had come through the fire. They were whole and would remain so.

"Adam, Adam, Adam."

Adam took Eve's whispered refrain into his heart and gave her back the song of her own name. Eve, Eve, Eve, m*y beautiful, precious wife, my soul.* And he had a thought. Did it take a thousand plus years to have one's prayers answered? For they surely had been answered. Perhaps he'd not been patient enough. Perhaps all he'd needed was a little more faith, a thousand plus years of faith. None of that mattered anymore for he now had what he'd prayed for. He had his wife and he would not lose her again.

As he suckled the sweet honeysuckle taste of Eve's body, Adam was aware that duty would soon pull him from his wife's bed. He had to ensure her safety at all cost. He had to proclaim Eve queen of the vampire world. Trying to keep her safe by keeping her identity hidden from others was no longer an option. All vampires the world over needed to know of her. They needed to know that she existed, that she belonged to him and him alone. He would not tolerate any other vampire thinking to lay claim to her. He would kill for the mere thought. And he would kill a thousand of them if they thought to harm her.

Hearing Eve's moan of pleasure Adam let go of his previous thoughts. There would be time for warning others later. For now he would seek and find his pleasure in his loving of Eve.

***

"Touch her, think of touching her, even think of calling her an inappropriate name and I'll hear." Adam gazed coldly over the group of assembled vampires. He'd sent out an order for them to come to a meeting with him in France. He was doing that which he had to do— putting the fear of Adam Omega into them.

"Eve Omega is my wife, your queen. She's the mistress of the entire vampire world and will be treated as such. Should any have a problem with that, speak your mind now and let's have it over and done with.

"Your wife killed many, Adam."

Good. Adam thought this would go much better with a demonstration. Opening his hand so quickly that none could have seen him, he shot out energy, killing the vampire where he'd stood. "What of my killings? I've killed many more than Eve, and will kill more still. My wife's sins are mine. If you have a problem with anything that she's done, add it to my account and deal with me here and now."

Suddenly reaching with his right hand over his left shoulder, he ripped his unseen sword from the scabbard and beheaded more than a dozen vampires in a blink of an eye. When the assembled group merely stared at him, he said slowly and coldly, "I did tell all of you that I am monitoring your thoughts. I will not allow you to even think of harming my wife. Is that understood?" He looked down, flicked his nails a couple of time and blew out his breath while waiting. It was then he spotted Evan near the fringes of the crowd smiling in curious amusement at him.

"A question, Adam, merely a question." Betram spoke softly, not wanting to incur Adam's wrath. He waited for a permissive nod from Adam before continuing. "Are you here to tell us that our queen is now officially one of us, that she's done with the killings?"

Adam smiled. "Very good, Betram, flattery will get you everywhere. Yes, that's exactly what I'm telling you. Eve Omega, your queen, is one of us and yes, she's done with killing vampires. She's leaving that job to me," he said with a wolfish grin.

"Any more questions?" Adam asked. He waited. When none spoke he waved his hand slowly from side to side. "Then you may now eat, drink and enjoy. Make sure all you come in contact with, all of your underlings, receive my decree. For it will be you I will hold responsible for their actions."

Never had Adam heard such silence. It pleased him and he smiled his acceptance of their acquiescence. Connecting with Evan, Adam beckoned to him.

"So, Adam, you've now proclaimed your Eve queen of the vampire world. I suppose that makes you our king," Evan laughed.

Adam grinned and waited.

"You are some piece of work, Adam."

"I know."

"You're going to need me now more than ever."

"I'm aware of that." His gaze held Evan's. "Do I have your support?"

"Until death, as always. As I've told you a million times, you are my only concern, my only family."

"You have Eve now. She's also your family. When Evan didn't answer him Adam probed. "You still don't trust her, do you?"

"My sole purpose is to look out for you, Adam, to keep you safe from any harm, from any source. I'm not yet convinced that your queen will not harm you given the chance."

"Then you will have to visit us and see for yourself that my wife wishes me no ill. Do not worry about me, my friend. All is well in my kingdom. Just keep an ear and an eye open while I return to the States."

"When do I get to officially meet this new queen?"

"All in good time, my friend. All in good time. For now you might say my wife and I are honeymooning. We've not yet tired of each other. When we do, you will be the first visitor." Adam laughed. "But don't expect an invitation for a long time, maybe a century, for I do not see myself ever tiring of Eve."

"Never say never," Evan laughed. "Besides, Adam, I know you better than you know yourself and I'm sure I will be answering a call from you much sooner than you expect."

Snapping his fingers and making two flutes and a chilled bottle of champagne appear, Adam poured two glasses and drank heartily. When they'd polished off the bottle he gave Evan a look. "I'm needed at home." He grinned as he tuned into the sweet sound of Eve's voice calling out seductively to him. "The time of my desiring my wife has not yet waned so I will take my leave." He grinned. "I'll see you in perhaps a thousand years," he said and took off to make love to the mistress of the vampire world, his wife, his queen, his Eve.

***

It was a time of peace so profound that neither Adam nor Eve had words to describe it so they didn't try. They reveled in it, not worrying about any in the world outside the two of them. When they traveled it was as a couple and for now that was fine. The need to protect Eve drove

Adam. The need to be loved by Adam kept Eve quiet. It was a quick trip to Sanctuary Crystals that eventually drove Eve to leave Adam's side. It was his protesting that he didn't want her out alone that forced her to insist that he not accompany her.

"Adam, you're stifling me. Please, do something else. I hate to tell you I told you so, but if you'd not killed Dr. Meah and Sullivan..." She stopped and shrugged. "Let's say you'd have one as a friend and the other to just go and annoy. But then I'm not one to say I told you so."

She ignored the look in his eyes, the one that said he didn't trust her, that even now in this time of goodwill between the two of them he was keeping secrets from her. For Adam that was to be expected so she didn't probe. It bothered her a fraction of a second that she didn't. She'd known the time when she would have picked at the problem like an itch until out of exasperation Adam would either tell her or roar and they'd fight.

A sigh escaped and Eve was surprised by it. She gazed at Adam, loving the worshipful, adoring look in his eyes. Still, a prickle of awareness tried to niggle its way inside her brain. There was something different about them, about her, but what? She was borrowing trouble, she decided. Better to let it be. She loved Adam and he loved her and that was all that she needed to know.

"Adam, I will not try anything, I promise. I will be safe. I need to get back to living my life, okay?" She kissed him. "I'm going. I don't want you with me. Also, I'm taking your little vamp car, by the way, it's cuter than my Hummer," she said as she made her way out the door.

The entire time Eve was out she expected to see Adam pop in. When she didn't, she breathed a sigh of relief. Nothing could have prepared her for the sight she encountered when she returned home.

She stood watching Adam wielding a sword, his chest bare, his legs clad in black slacks. He was beautifully toned. Not an ounce of fat was to be found anywhere on his body. He turned and walked toward her, a grin on his face. Confidence and sexuality oozed from his pores. She dropped her bags to the floor and walked toward him. As he lowered his blade, she moved to stand in front of him, her hand reaching out to touch his abdomen. Her finger was trailing the stream of sweat toward the waistband when Adam caught her hand.

"We're not alone," Adam murmured. He turned Eve gently by her shoulders and wrapped his arms about her waist holding her close, kissing the side of her neck as he whispered to her. "You were wrong, Eve. I do have a friend. Meet Evan, my only true friend."

"What about me, Adam?" Eve whispered back.

"Evan is the only being that doesn't wish constantly for my death. He's the only one that I firmly believe has my back." He laughed and continued kissing her, trailing butterfly soft kisses the length of Eve's neck.

"Evan, my wife."

Eve was amused. She watched as Evan tipped his sword toward her in greeting. There was something vaguely familiar about him. "Have we met before?" she asked and caught the look that passed between Adam and Evan.

"Never," Evan said, moving smoothly toward her, taking her hand and kissing it, looking into her eyes with a clear gaze.

Hmm, Eve thought as she observed Adam's friend. He was almost as smooth as Adam. But there was something about him that made her dislike him instantly. Perhaps it was because she knew the words Adam spoke were true. Evan was her husband's true friend. Of that she had no doubt. But she sensed a secret Evan was keeping from Adam. She and Evan stared into each other eyes for a long moment as though they were each staring into the other's soul. His cold gaze washed over her. He didn't like her. That knowledge chilled her and she attempted to probe his mind but was shut out. Eve gazed into his eyes again and he smiled. Adam was already aware of Evan's dislike for her. So what could the secret be that he was keeping from Adam? She didn't know but she was determined to find out.

***

If climbing the walls was a literal phrase, then Evan was quite prepared to do just that. He'd answered Adam's call as always, only to find that he was not in danger but merely wanted him to visit, to forge something that would undoubtedly never happen, a friendship between him and Eve.

Three weeks of holiday with Adam and his wife had more than worn on Evan. He missed his friend, missed the wildness in him. This tamed lion was not what he was used to. He'd heard many tales of the fights between the man and wife and had thought on his visit he would be a referee. Only once had he and Adam ventured from the house to party, feed and let off steam. Even then it had not been the same, for Adam's mind had been on his wife.

He could be still about the matter no longer. In disgust Evan laid down his sword. Even with the lack of practice Adam was still the best, his natural grace and skills far superior to any he'd parried with.

"I'm bored with fencing. It's all we've done since my arrival. I wish to speak with you about your marriage." Adam growled as Evan had known he would but it didn't deter him.

"Adam, you're aware I'm going to state my views, so, why don't we both stop pretending that I'm not."

"Go ahead but be careful of the things you say. I'm aware that you're still not overly fond of Eve."

Tapping a finger against his chin, Adam contemplated the three weeks of Evan's visit. "Eve is also not your biggest fan. Did you do something to her when I gave you permission to visit her in the past?"

"Of course not. And that you would even pose such nonsense to me is the reason for my concern. You are not the Adam Omega that I've known from the beginning. We are family, Adam, and that gives me the right to bring this to you."

For a moment Adam stilled and thought to just enter Evan's mind to obtain the information. But he wanted to hear the words spoken by his friend. He had a good idea what it was that had Evan wound so tightly. At least he hoped he did.

"Eve is still young, Adam, yet she still doesn't seem to have a need to feed."

A warning look quickly came into Adam's eyes and he growled. *Evan's question was not what he'd expected.* "When Eve feeds is none of your business," he answered.

"I know what you're doing. You stated you wanted her to know how to feed, how to care for her own needs. Yet, she doesn't feed. You feed and in turn she feeds from you. That is not how it's done, Adam."

"Eve can protect herself. That was all that I wanted. She can feed if she has to."

Adam glared at Even before lifting his sword. Ever so slowly he ran his finger down the sharpened weapon, drawing blood and watching it drip to the floor. He stared at the small puddle of blood before tearing his eyes away to look at Evan.

"As long as I'm around Eve has no need to do anything that she doesn't want to do."

"Unless it's something that you insist on, correct?"

"Leave me be. Isn't it time you returned to your mortal wife? You're getting on my nerves."

"That's because you know I'm about to hit a nerve. This is all very curious, Adam. Do you mind if I'm straight with you?"

"Like you haven't been straight with me for more than eight hundred years? Continue," Adam grunted.

Evan waited a moment and when it was apparent Adam didn't object he continued hesitantly. "From everything you've told me, I have long envisioned your relationship with Eve. I have wished for such passion and devotion that you have. But as for the rest, I have to tell you, the two of you are boring as hell. There is no excitement of the crazed witch trying to kill you, no sparks, no fighting. You have not bellowed once since I've been here. You've not threatened me even.

"And your wife," Evan said in disgust. She behaves more like a mortal than Dalai. She's too happy, too docile. She fawns over you. It's sickening. I don't think you'd get a rise out of her no matter what you did. And don't think that I haven't witnessed you trying. But she merely kisses you and then you get this guilty look on your face that tells me you've once again done something wrong, something you should not have. If I'm wrong and this is really the existence you want, then I will be leaving, for I cannot abide seeing you behave in this manner. This opulence you surround yourself with is much worst than my hovel."

"I didn't say you lived in a hovel."

"You thought it..."

"Sorry."

Evan laughed. "You are not sorry, Adam. You hate the way I live and I hate the way you live. But the way I live is not a thousand year dream. I marry mortals and have families with them out of sheer boredom. I live a modest life with them because it doesn't draw attention. Besides, I have my other homes and I *had* you to bring real excitement into my life, until recently." Evan couldn't prevent the scowl and sarcasm that filled his voice.

"But, Adam, when I'm done with playing house I will move on. I have no real attachment to the mortal families I take, unlike you and Eve. You love her. This I know so tell me why. I've lingered here so long in hopes of seeing it for myself, seeing why my friend has done things so unlike him for the past few years, to see why much more blood stains your hands recently than in the last hundred years. There is a reason and if that reason is truly Eve, then, Adam, I'm sorry to say that from what I've seen here she's not worth the fuss."

Evan raised his own sword as Adam moved toward him. "Please allow me to finish. You were the one who told me not so long ago that it would be a century before you invited me to officially meet your wife. Barely a year has passed. From what I could tell from the stories I've heard from you, about the two of you fighting, it seemed to be your thing but you're…. If I had to live like this and I was finally with my great love and this was all there was, I'd stake myself."

Evan moved backwards away from Adam to prepare for his wrath. What he got was a calm Adam.

"Thanks!" Adam clasped Evan about the shoulder and pulled him into a brotherly hug. "I am most grateful to you. You are the one being I trust; the only one I can count on to be straight with me. Seriously, as many times as you've told me I needed to get help, that I was insane, this has been the only time that I've truly thought I could be."

Pacing around the oak paneled study Adam glanced at the changes Eve had wrought there. Crystal was everywhere and not something that he could tolerate like a bowl or vase, but massive chunks of hewn stone. He growled, flexing his fingers, pacing the room and shooting sparks of energy from the tips of his finger. He stopped and turned to face off with his friend.

"I would never have thought I would be saying these words. I still can't believe I'm about to. For the first few months after I returned to stop Eve, things were great." He shrugged as images of their bloody and brutal fights returned to him. He winced at having struck Eve and he winced again in remorse at the many times he'd done it. Then he swallowed. That was over. There would be no more fighting.

"What's wrong, Adam?"

"I'm just thinking of the many wrongs I've done my wife. Our being together and being happy is probably the worst thing I've done to her." Narrowing his eyes, he held Evan's stare. "I've done some pretty nasty things to Eve. You don't like her because she wanted me dead. Believe me, Evan, she had reasons to wish for that."

"Adam," Evan called gently. "You always start to tell me something then get lost in your misdeeds. I dare say if you didn't commit so many offenses you could carry on a decent conversation. Please take me from when you returned to stop Eve from killing more vampires."

Smiling, Adam welcomed his friend's ability to get him back on track while temporarily assuaging his guilt.

"As I said, it was great in the beginning until a thought entered my head and wouldn't go away. I kept thinking 'something is off; this wasn't us.' It isn't us, Evan. It's not like I like to fight with Eve." He shrugged and laughed. "Maybe I do like fighting with her. But this is different. You're right in your observations. The only time there is real fire in our relationship and we're the way we were…the only time this existence doesn't bother me is when we...."Adam stopped, his eyes closing as he tried to fix what was wrong.

"Yas," Adam whispered then shouted. "That witch put a love spell on us."

Evan laughed but Adam didn't.

"For a vampire who can't be hexed you sure have a lot of witches putting spells on you, Adam. I'd suggest, my friend, that you stop leaving yourself open to witches. What the hell is the point? So what if your wife is a witch? You're the most powerful vampire in the universe. Can't that be enough? Stop trying to dabble in the black arts and maybe witches won't be able to be close enough to you to put spells on you. Can't you for once just be a good little vampire and stop trying to control your wife's gift? Isn't being the most feared vampire enough?"

"No."

"It might just have to be."

Nodding in acknowledgement, Adam gave a wry smile. "There is one thing you're right about, Evan. I will have to stop being a willing victim in witches' spells. Women. Damn. They have always been man's undoing, from the first Adam who allowed a woman to lead him astray. And then there's me. My own Eve has caused me many sleepless nights and yet, I would not want another."

"I take it you will be making another trip to visit Yas."

"You take it right." A long, weary sigh filled Adam and he glanced at Evan. "I can't leave Eve here in the States alone" He sighed again, not wanting to ask but knowing he couldn't leave his wife alone just yet. "Evan—"

"You don't have to ask," Evan interrupted and smiled.

"I know... but I want to make sure she's safe. She wants to live without restrains and so far none have come out against her. It's been nearly a year and my decree so far seems to be working but..."

"But you don't trust that."

"Of course not, not when I'm not here to enforce it. The only time I feel Eve's life is safe is when she's with me. The only one I trust to take care of her in my absence is you."

"Thank you. I do know what that means. You could take her to Greece with you, however."

"And tell her what, that a witch put a love spell on us, that more than likely it's my fault? I'll have to go alone. I have never asked you for a more important favor, Evan. Now more than ever I need you to have my back. I need you to protect my wife with your life if necessary."

"Eve has been the only bone of contention we've had in eight hundred years."

"You threatened to kill her."

"I did not. I said I would not allow her to destroy you. And that if she came up to me to kill me she would not be the victor."

"What's the difference?"

"The difference was that as long as she did nothing to harm you or me, I would do nothing to harm her. Besides, you also threatened to kill my wife and children, and to my face no less."

Adam's eyes narrowed and he glared. "Evan, had another vamp said those things to me we would not have had a shouting match. He would have been dead instantly."

"I'm aware of that."

"I need to know that besides the truth in both of our words that you will be able to put it all aside for now, and do what needs to be done. I'm asking you to be my wife's protector in my absence. What are your feelings about her at this moment?"

"What I do, I do for you. I would never betray you. You asked me to protect your wife and I will do that with my life. I would never break my word to you, Adam."

Rubbing his chin, Adam leaned back into the chair and stretched his legs. "You do see my dilemma in leaving you, the only being I trust to take care of the only woman I love, whom you have no special affinity for, don't you?"

"Your dilemma is not in leaving me here to protect her. For that you know I will do without fail. Your only dilemma is that you have a choice. You can keep Eve under and have Yas remove the spell from you or..."

"Don't remind me. I can have a docile wife, or a wife whose sole purpose has been until recently to see me dead."

Adam shook his head and Evan stared at him.

"Where is your wife, by the way?"

Where she spends most of her free time, at Sanctuary Crystals. Her determination to return to her mortal state is still on her mind."

"And if she does, Adam, what will you do? Will you allow her to live and die as a mortal, knowing that when she does she will have to pay for the blood she now has on her hands."

"When that day comes we will see. But you can not judge Eve. The both of us have more blood on our hands than my wife will ever have." Adam stopped and gave Evan a look. "I will fight my wife's battles from here on in. I will do her killing for her should she require it. No more blood will stain her hands."

"Except maybe yours when she finds out what you've done."

Evan smiled and Adam gave him one in return. "Not even then. My death will not be on Eve's hands. For I will not die."

Chapter Nineteen

Crystal dust covered the opening of Sanctuary Crystals, as usual. Why didn't they just give it up? Their toys had no effect or him nor Eve. Adam stood at the threshold for a moment, wondering what those inside would do if he blew their establishment to smithereens. Grinning, he reprimanded himself. He'd not come to have fun and scare the mortals. He'd come to tell his wife that he had to go away for a day. He walked in the door and walked immediately toward his wife. Eve was seated at a table and a clerk was bringing her items for her inspections.

Memories of previous visits to the store caused Adam to smile. Much had transpired since their first visit to the store. Now, no one questioned Eve. Everything in the store was hers for the asking, no matter who wanted it. It was understood. Adam stood for a moment before her until her eyes raised and her lips curved into her special smile that was just for him. He'd never seen her smile at Sullivan in that manner and that was a good thing.

Options, Adam thought. Yas had once again left him with options. He waited as Eve rose from the chair and came toward him.

"Did you miss me?" she asked of him.

"I always miss you," he replied.

"I get lost in here. I'm not aware of the time."

"Or you're aware and this is the one place where you feel protected without me by your side. No apologies are needed."

Their gazes held. Purple fire and brown flames met, making Adam's heart lurch with longing. Eve moved closer and he drew her to him, kissing her softly, his arms going around her to hold her. He wondered if he'd still receive this greeting when he ordered Yas to remove the spell.

"What's wrong, Adam?" Eve asked quietly.

"We have been bewitched."

"Bewitched? You're kidding me. You told me that no one can put a spell on a vampire, definitely not on one as powerful as you." Eve moved away, remembering how she'd managed to send Adam back in time. She frowned. "The old crone you told me about, she did it? When? I don't feel anything? What did she do?"

"She put a love spell on us."

"Are you certain?"

"Pretty much." Adam smiled and stroked Eve's cheek with the pad of a finger. "Think about it. When was the last time the two of us had a knock down, drag out fight?"

"Are you wanting that?"

With a dismissive shake of his head Adam tilted her chin. "I believe I would behave the same regardless, so maybe I'm not the one affected by Yas's spell. But you are."

"Why, because I love you and I tell you that I do?"

"Exactly."

"What's the spell? Do you remember the words? I can probably reverse it."

He rubbed her chin with his thumb. "I thought of that but I don't really know the words. She spoke in a made up language." Realizing that was how Yas had performed the spell suddenly struck Adam as funny. He couldn't stop the laugh from coming. "She did this deliberately. She wanted to remember me and more than likely wanted to force me to return."

"Is there no woman that's not in love with you? Are you sure she's really old?"

"She's ancient, she's sneaky and— "

"And you like her."

"Yes, I like her but I do not like having your love because of a spell." He sighed. "I'm going to Greece to see her and have her remove the spell. I won't be gone long. I was wondering if you'd mind if Evan remains here in my absence. He's not ready to end his vacation."

"What malarkey," Eve laughed. "Please, Adam. I know why you're leaving Evan behind. I do not need the protection of your friend but if your witch friend put a love spell on us, I want it off. I'm not going to object to Evan staying. But I want to tell you I think you're wrong. I loved you long before you ever met Yas. I love you and I will love you after you return from Greece."

***

Mist turned to matter. Matter became form and the form became Adam. He stood for a moment in Yas's home waiting for her to acknowledge him.

"You're back, Vampire."

"As you intended. Yas, you lied to me. You put a love spell on us. I want it removed. But first I want to know the English translation so I may give it to Eve. I want the words written down. Why did you do it?"

"I wanted you to find peace. I wanted you happy." Her eyes held his. "Were you happy?"

"I was for a time but I knew something was wrong." He hesitated. "I knew it was you and didn't know if I wanted to return and have you remove it. But that is not the way I want the love of my wife, not like that, Yas. There is no joy in having her that way. I am many things and I have done many evils to her, more than I care to recount but this one…. this one I can not do, Yas."

"You do not appear angry."

"I am not angry with you but perhaps with myself. A lot of what happened with Eve is my fault. Perhaps if I'd used a different method we could be where we are on our own. But damn it, Yas, I'm a vampire. I do not have to romance a woman, not even the woman I love. I have taken what I wanted for so long that I know no other way. It is not in my nature."

"You are conflicted."

"Of course I'm conflicted, but not about my request to you."

"Your request or your order?"

"Yas, remove the spell. I have no wish to use threats or force with you. And this meeting I will not erase from your mind. I promise. Now tell me the words you spoke." When she began to speak in her Gaelic fashion Adam smiled and repeated the words in English.

> *Healed are the rifts between them.*
> *Warm is the light that springs across*
> *The gulf that is no more.*

Grinning at Yas's astonishment Adam explained, "I have always had an affinity for languages, even ones made up by witches in a secret code. I only need to hear it spoken a few times and spoken clearly and I can translate it."

"Then you know the words I used were not meant to harm you. I only intended to heal the hurts between you and your Eve so that you might find your way together again."

"There was more, Yas, tell me the rest." Adam watched Yas as she watched him. At first she didn't speak the rest of the spell. Then she sighed in silent resignation and began.

Happiness steals upon the scene,
For love is the word and love is the light.

"Vampire," Yas said stopping again. "Was I wrong? Didn't you have happiness?"

"I had happiness, Yas, stolen happiness."

"What about the love? There is something different about you. I could swear you are more in the light than before. Don't you wish to remain there, Adam? Love can and will do that for you."

"I wish to remain who I am, Yas. Adam Omega, Vampire. Now please stop procrastinating and give me the last lines of the spells."

"Very well but you're going to undo my best and most unselfish work. You are aware that when you gave me access to do this I could have put a spell on you to make you love me. l could have replaced myself with your Eve."

A cocked brow was Adam's response. "No one could replace Eve with or without a spell. That would never have worked. And, Yas, just so you know, I would never have allowed you to have open and complete access to me."

"But…"

"But for a moment when I was with you I purposefully opened a link to Eve. It was only for a moment. I regretted it the moment it was done and I thought perhaps it hadn't worked, that Eve was much too powerful to allow it, that she would know immediately."

In remorse Adam bit his lip and sawed it with his teeth until a bubble of blood dropped on his tongue, making him pause. "I have wronged Eve in more ways than she can possibly know. Even coming here I lied to her. I told her that we were bewitched. I even told this to Evan. You did not bewitch me, Yas. You bewitched my wife and I allowed it."

A smile appeared on Yas's lips. "I'm aware of that, Vampire. I did not live this long not to know that you would not allow me to go deep enough into your psyche to cast a spell on you. You would have been a fool to have done that, especially since you'd allowed your wife access to you and she'd betrayed you." She patted his cheek. "But I understand the difference. You love her. You wanted with all of your heart to trust her, so you put your soul in her hands. I was aware of this. I wanted you to finally have the peace you've sought for more than a thousand years. I do love you, Vampire, and it was not a spell you cast on me." She shrugged. "I wanted you happy and still do."

"The last lines, Yas," Adam spoke quietly.

> *Differences forgotten; unthinking words erased.*
> *Love is the salve that heals all hurts."*

"Now take the spell off Eve, Yas. And tell me how you were able to accomplish it in the first place."

"I told you I went to visit her. I took some of her personal possessions, little objects that she wouldn't miss." She smiled. "Hair, nail clippings, a couple of her smaller crystals. I did not put the spell on the woman that was here in the past but your Eve that you wanted desperately to return to. But the spell would not have worked had you not made love to her. It's the last line of the spell. Love is the salve that heals all hurts. Your love healed her hurts, Vampire. So in essence it was you that put the spell on your wife, not me."

Adam held out his hand and Yas moved across the room to open a drawer and remove a bag. She dropped it into Adam's outstretched hand.

"Will you still leave my memories intact?"

Adam heaved a loud sigh. "I shouldn't, Yas. I'm more aware of that than you know. Leaving you with your memories, leaving you alive, I leave a possible danger to Eve. How can I do that, Yas? How can I possibly return home and leave you alive?"

"I do not worry that you will kill me. Your heart is filled with anguish."

"But I have killed those I loved before. Others I have simply made disappear. I have removed those who would harm Eve so, how can you be so sure that I will not kill you? You're a threat to Eve."

"You know that I love you and will do nothing to betray that love."

"What if someone came to you looking for ways to get to me? Nothing would be sure to cause me more pain than for harm to come to Eve."

"You would die to protect Eve. I will die to protect you."

Adam stared in astonishment at Yas. She was the second being who'd said those words to him. And he believed her as he believed Evan.

"Yas, I can do no more evil to my wife. I am going to give her back the chance to hate me and we will go from there."

"What will you do?"

"The one thing she will find unforgivable, the most sacrilegious. Now, Yas, remove the spell. One last thing. Yas, do you speak the truth? Are these the only belongings you have of Eve's?"

"I would not lie to you about this."

"Then remove the spell."

"Your wife will not be open to me and I'm sure you will not open her up to me. You have the words I used. It was a very simple spell. Give the word to your Eve. She's a powerful witch. She will know how to reverse it."

Yas turned from Adam and stirred some flowers she had in a bowl. "Do you have to leave now?" she asked.

The hope was in her voice and Adam heard it. He'd come prepared for it. To have a mortal having his back was a new thing. Yas was open to him. He'd read her thoughts and found no guile. She'd die for him, of that he was sure. For one who would do so much he could spare a few hours.

"Thank you, Yas. I have a gift for you," he said and moved his hand from the top of her head to the tip of her comfortable shoes. As the wrinkles smoothed and soft young looking skin replaced what had been leathered and aged, Adam smiled at his handiwork then produced a mirror to give her to check it out. "I planned to take you out for dinner and dancing, a real night out on the town. My repayment. Twenty-four hours of youth and beauty," he smiled.

There were not many recent moments that filled Adam with pride but the look on Yas's face as the men in the club he took her to fawned over her made this one of those. Again he thought, this mortal he truly liked.

**

It had been a matter of only hours since Adam had left for Greece. It felt more like the thousand years he'd lived. If she'd thought Adam's hovering was stifling, then Evan was downright suffocating. He was standing like a sentinel as she tried out her potions. Standing too closely, he unnerved her with his stance and his cold look of disdain. Finally Eve could take it no longer. She glared at him, hoping he'd at least glare in return but he did not. He merely cocked his head at her and shook it a little as though to say, why would Adam bother with such as you. The message was loud and clear.

"Okay, Evan, why did you agree to baby-sit me?" For the first time Eve witnessed Evan smiling at her.

"It seems that you and your husband do have some things in common. He also thinks that I baby-sit him." Evan shrugged his shoulder. "So why not you?" He raised a brow, narrowed his eyes and stared straight at Eve. "You have killed many, Eve."

There was no need to pretend otherwise. Despite what Adam might want, he would not pretend what Eve had done was nothing. It was a crime. She'd had no right to judge the vampires she'd killed and less right to mete out punishment.

"Though you don't seem to care particularly about your safety, Adam does," Evan continued. "Adam worries about you. For what he had to do he couldn't take you with him, so he needed to know someone to whom he could entrust with your life was here to care for you. Someone who is feared as he is. I am that someone."

"But you do not like me," Eve stated holding his steady gaze. "I do not like you either. So why would you volunteer to take this job?"

"How do you know I volunteered? How do you know I wasn't drafted? Adam asked and I accepted. And you're right, I do not like you but that is no secret."

"What have I done to make you not like me?"

"What have I done to make you not like me?" Evan countered.

"I asked first," Eve said and moved across the room to sit. "Since we're having this little heart to heart, we may as well get comfortable. Come," she offered. To her amazement Evan followed. "You tell me why you don't like me and I'll do likewise. You first."

"My reasons are obvious. You have done nothing but betray Adam from the moment he met you. If it were up to me, you would be dead. Adam should not have turned you. Now he has to worry about you for longer than he should have. Adam is unlike any I have ever known. He is…he's unique. And I like that. I have known him longer than you can imagine. He never behaved in such an irrational fashion until you surfaced." Evan shrugged again, "Or resurfaced. It depends on one's beliefs. Anyway, you have taken something from Adam that he can not afford to lose. He thinks that you're special, unique, that because you refused to take blood as it was meant to be done it was a feat of great courage and morality. I disagree. I think Adam is the one with great courage and even greater restraint. From the moment he was made he insisted he would never allow any to drink from him. He has also refused the delights that can only be had by the coupling of two dynamic Beings, two vampires. So to me, Eve, you're little more than ordinary. You should feel blessed that Adam loves you above all others."

"You're jealous. You sound as though you're in love with Adam." For the second time a smile graced Evan's lips.

"Eve, you more than anyone are aware that since Adam was made he has not touched vampiric females...that is, until you. His aversion to them is mild compared to his aversion to having a male touch him in an intimate fashion. No, I assure you if what I felt for Adam was lust we would have never become more than friends."

"To my ears you still sound jealous. That makes sense. You were his best friend before I came along."

"I'm still his best friend. You're his woman, but not his best friend. And that might be the real reason I do not like you. Adam's welfare is not your uppermost concern. You put the welfare of mankind before him. I do not."

For a moment Eve was speechless. "And you don't think I should? That's crazy. Of course mankind is more important that I am, than Adam, and you. We have no right to be in this world."

"Reason number two I do not like you."

A moment of silence and Eve asked, "Anything else?"

"Do you really need more reasons? What about you? Why do you dislike me, jealousy perhaps?"

"Try concern. I sense that Adam doesn't know all there is to know about you."

"Adam has known me from the beginning and you not even five years. Yet you think there is something more he should know about me. This is past ridiculous." Evan laughed. "I've told you that Adam and I are family. We are blood."

This was the second time Evan had said he and Adam were blood. Eve's head snapped up. "You and Adam are family? You said blood." For a moment she saw a spark of anger and a hint of fang. She could tell Evan was mentally willing himself to not harm her. But there was something about his mentioning him and Adam being blood that had not been meant for her to catch. Very interesting, something to investigate, Eve thought.

"I was speaking metaphorically," Evan stated.

"Yet there is a secret that you're hiding from Adam."

"Is there now?"

"Yes. Tell me something. I'm curious. I think you're much older than Adam just by the way you behave. How old are you?"

"Why? It does not have anything to do with your reasons for disliking me."

"True, but I'm curious."

"Didn't Adam ever tell you that curiosity killed the cat and could kill Eve?"

"Evan, I thought you were here to protect me, not threaten to kill me."

"You're right, my mistake. In that case it is none of your business how old I am."

"Were you there when Adam was turned?"

"What difference could that make?"

"I'm not sure but the puzzle pieces would fit better if I knew more about you."

"Eve." Evan pulled his sword from his back and played with the blade. "If there were a secret that I'd kept hidden from Adam for more than a thous…" He stopped. "For more than eight hundred years, do you really think you could find it out so easily? You're still an infant, a fledging who does not even feed properly," he ended with disdain.

"But I'm also a witch and I can sense these things."

"Could you sense that you were under a spell?" Evan stared at Eve, refusing to allow her to look away. He gave a noncommittal shrug. "I would think not."

"Touché," Eve said softly. "I think our talk is over." The rest of her thinking she would do alone. "Just so we're clear, Evan, don't you do anything to harm Adam or you'll have me to contend with."

Evan stuck out his hand and laughed. "Mrs. Omega, why don't we call this a truce? As for your warning, please consider it a promise on my part that if you harm him you will have to deal with me. And do remember that you are the only vampire in this room who's ever tried to harm him." Evan snapped his fingers and produced two glasses and a bottle of Visanto.

"To our agreement," he said, offering Eve a smile. "Don't worry, it's safe to drink. I did promise Adam I'd take care of you. Excuse me.

Just in case you decide to take that the wrong way, I'm here to protect you and that means I will not harm you. Drink up."

Evan laughed as he tipped his glass toward his lips, sipping and eyeing Eve warily. When she took his challenge and drank, he laughed and emptied his glass, tipping his head in Eve's direction.

**

Adam waited a moment before materializing. For a nanosecond he hesitated, wondering what changes would be wrought once Eve removed the spell, once she knew the complete truth that he'd left her open for a psychic attack. He sighed. She wasn't going to like it, that was for sure. Then he smiled. Wasn't that the point of going to Yas, to bring Eve back to her normal feisty combative self? One good fight and they could return to the life they were carving out for themselves, only it would be a hell of a lot less boring. He truly didn't want a smiling, obedient wife, no matter how many times he'd wished for just that.

"I'm back," he said, materializing and knowing the announcement wasn't necessary. He stared at Eve standing inside her protective circle. His eyes narrowed. There was fear on her face and the sight of that started his heart racing. He turned toward Evan who was standing only about a foot from Eve. *Too close*, Adam thought, glaring at Evan and moving swiftly toward him. "What did you do to her?" he demanded.

Soft hands and a softer voice that also held a tinge of fear stopped him. "Adam," Eve called to him.

"It's not Evan. Seeing you home, I thought about the love spell your friend put on us, on me. It's what I know had to have happened. There was but one way for this to have happened." She held out her hand.

"Give me my things and the spell." She turned briefly in Evan's direction. "Please leave us, Evan. My husband and I need to talk."

Handing the slip of paper to Eve and the juju bag filled with her personal belongings, Adam waited. He watched as first disbelief then anger filled Eve.

"I will not ask how this happened, Adam, for I know how it happened. I didn't give her access to me so there is only one that could and it's you."

"Yas said it would be a simple matter to reverse the spell."

"She's right but that's not the point. No one should have ever put a spell on me, not even a love spell. That's irresponsible and taking away the free will of another. There are also many unseen consequences. Your

Yas is an unethical witch. She's broken the witches' creed. *If it harms none*. Her spell harmed me. It harmed us. How would she like it if I put a spell on her?"

When Adam attempted to move toward her, Eve pushed him away. "I have always loved you, Adam. To do this was unnecessary. Will I ever be able to trust you? I doubt it," she said and vanished.

"Trust is a double edged sword, my love. Will I ever be able to trust you?" Adam whispered and brought the ceremonial blade from inside his duster pocket. He stared at the object for a long moment, taking it out of the scabbard. The solid, gold tipped blade caught the light and reflected it back. Adam ran a finger over the blade, sharpening it with his powers as he did so, testing it against his flesh. It pierced his finger and drew blood. Placing the finger in his mouth he shook his head slowly. The blade was now lethal. He was satisfied. Sliding the blade back into the solid gold and jewel encrusted scabbard, he was aware of what would come next. He had to enact yet another scene in this little play that he and Eve called life.

It was time he did as he'd told Yas he would do. It was time to test Eve's love. He would do what would incur her wrath more than anything that he could do. He would take her to church, a place he'd not been able to get her to go since turning her. He would take her by force if necessary. He was determined to give her back the ability to hate him if she chose. He wouldn't deny that he was hoping love would win out but when he was done he doubted the possibility. With resignation Adam went in search of Evan, his one friend he'd never lied to. Now he'd told him two lies.

"So how did it go?" Adam walked to stand in front of Evan. "You're both still alive and that's a good thing. Are you and Eve now friends?" Adam asked.

"Not likely but we did have a talk. I will concede that I do believe she loves you."

"That's old news." Adam laughed. "I've always known that."

"I also know that given the chance to restore humanity to a vampire free world she'd take it." Evan narrowed his gaze so there would be no misunderstanding. "She would still kill you if it would free the world."

"Also old news." Adam sighed and shrugged. "I wish it could be different with her but it was the same with Eyanna also. A woman who thought she was evil but with a heart so pure…except in the end…except toward me." He smiled sardonically. "Eyanna's actions are one reason I say judge not. I judged her perfect and in the end she was not."

"We're not talking about Eyanna, Adam. We're talking about Eve, your very much alive and very pissed off wife who just happens to be a vampire. And not any vampire, but a vampire made with your blood." He closed his eyes for a moment and opened them to stare sadly at Adam. "What an astronomically unwise thing for you to have done. And now you bring her a gift, a blade no less. And you sharpen it."

"Do you spy on me, Evan?"

"Does it matter?"

"It matters. I don't want you spying on me."

"As you wish. But if I spy on you as you say, my interests are only for your welfare. The last five years my senses have been on the alert in that area. But no matter. I will do as you ask. If you find yourself in need of my assistance then you know how to reach me. As for your wife, I can't say that I blame her for her rage over what's happened. How are you going to handle that?"

"I have a plan." Evan groaned and Adam laughed. "Seriously, Evan, I have a plan. Eve said I took away her free will by allowing Yas to be able to put a spell on her. I agree. I will give Eve back her free will. I will give her back her ability to hate me."

"You worry me, Adam. You truly do. I have a sense of what you're planning. Leave it. Give Eve a few days to vent her anger. There is no need to go to such limits with her. It will only lead to disaster."

"Stop worrying so about me. Sometimes you take your duties of a friend too far. You behave as though you're my parent." Adam hesitated as Evan blinked rapidly.

"I didn't mean that as an insult. It's just that you worry too much about me. You don't have to. I promise you this is the right thing to do. You will soon be leaving and there are things I must confess to you. I must apologize for lying to you." When Evan smiled Adam saw that he already knew.

"How did you know?" Adam inquired.

"I know you, Adam. I know what you're capable of even if you don't. I know you have friends that you don't call by that name. Sullivan and Dr. Meah are your friends, so I knew the facts concerning them had been blurred, shall we say... As for Yas putting a spell on you, come on, Adam, give me credit."

"Did you know that I unknowingly assisted her?"

"Unknowingly?" Evan laughed. "Let's rephrase that. Did I know that you opened a link for Yas to put a spell on Eve? Of course I knew that. I was just wondering how far you'd take it and how long it would be before you tired of the game. How long would you have continued this if I had not visited you and pointed out the obvious?"

"Having Eve so agreeable," Adam mused. "Believe me, I was slowly reaching my limit. I don't think it would have been much longer before I asked Yas for the spell on my own. But I do thank you for pushing me to do it sooner rather than later. And I thank you for standing in for me and being my wife's protector." Adam shrugged. "I suppose I should offer some sort of apology for what I thought when I first returned and about what almost happened when I came in and saw the fear on my wife's face. I'm glad I didn't have to kill you."

"Of course that can't seriously be looked on as any form of apology. But then I didn't expect one, not from the Adam that I know and admire. Now how about Sullivan and Dr. Meah? Their plight was what caused Eve's elevated hatred, making her seek revenge on all vampires. Are you going to tell her the truth about that?"

"What good would it serve? At least now Eve thinks she had a righteous motive for doing the things she did. If she knew the truth it would not be me she couldn't forgive, but herself. Besides, I tried to tell her, Evan." Adam began to quote scripture and even stopped him.

"Please, Adam, no more quotes, not now."

"But this is the exact moment that a quote would come in. Considering that my quoting scripture offends you I will for once acquiesce to your will and not do it. You should never judge another, Evan. Remember that always. None of us knows what we would do in any given situation. I've tried to tell that to Eve."

"Can it possibly be that there is One that you fear? Do you believe that one day we will all be judged for our deeds?"

Adam swallowed. "I don't want Eve judged now or ever. I have to find a way to prevent that."

"More lies?" Evan asked.

"Yes. More lies," Adam replied.

Chapter Twenty

Walking through the rooms of his home Adam took in a deep breath of oxygen. It was now or never. Weeks of silence were driving him insane, making him wish Evan were still around. Only in bed did he and Eve put their anger aside and take comfort in each other's arms. But not even vampires could spend all of their time making love. Adam had business to attend to, an empire to run. He had to rebuild the lab and reinforce the building against even the vampiric powers of his wife. Reassuring the remaining vamps and the new ones who'd joined in the quest had been a monumental task. When it had been accomplished, Adam felt high on his own powers of persuasion.

He'd have to send new U.S. President a congratulatory card. The power was heady. What a rush. He wondered how the young president dealt with his mortal wife and if she were possibly as obstinate as his vampiric wife. Eve was not making things easy. She spent much of her time doing things to annoy him, working continually on her many potions and speaking to him only if he asked her a question.

Adam growled a second before throwing several of Eve's witchcraft books to the floor and sent an energy bolt toward what Eve called her sacred circle. "You do not need that nonsense," he began. "How many times do I have to tell you that? You can do all of this in your mind."

"But I don't choose to do it in my mind, Adam."

"It's sacrilegious, Eve. How many times do I have to tell you this offends me deeply?"

"It offends me that you would knowingly allow another to put a spell on me. Does that not matter? How many times do I have to tell you that our entire existence is sacrilegious? You bought me several tools, which you also said were sacrilegious so that can't be what this is about, not anymore. You're trying to pick a fight with me. Why?"

"How long are you intending to do this…this…mortal thing of refusing to speak to me?"

"Until I'm ready to do something else."

"You annoy me, Eve, yet not enough. You told me before I went to Yas that you loved me and would love me regardless but now…is this your idea of love?" he asked. Her eyes lit with fire. *Good*, he thought, a true emotion. "Would you like to go back to hating me? I can arrange it. Come, Eve, I have a surprise for you. I will give you back your hatred."

"Adam—"

Before an objection could be voiced Adam whisked Eve away to St Michael's. He waited a moment as she looked around the sanctuary in fear, then shocked disbelief.

"You call what I do sacrilegious?" Eve asked in an angry whisper. "What do you think this is? *Eric.* Eve saw him sitting a few pews away. She ducked her head as Father Keller walked down the aisle.

"I'm leaving," she hissed, attempting to leave and finding herself unable to do anything. Adam was holding her there by force.

"Release me, Adam."

"Use your witchcraft. Do a spell, an incantation. Try it."

"You're aware that I will not do that here. Why are you trying so hard to make me hate you?"

"Because it's what you wish."

"It's not. I don't hate you, Adam. I don't want to hate you. I love you. Don't you understand that? You're the only one I have left to love. Don't take that from me, Adam."

"You've said many times that you love me because you can't help yourself. And as I feared, you love me because there are no others for you to love. Well, guess what? My love for you is not so shallow. I love you enough to allow you to hate me. You should be thanking me for what I'm doing." Adam glanced at her, holding her gaze. "You're not looking very thankful, Eve."

"I'm not thankful, I'm angry. Now for the last time I demand that you release me, Adam."

"No, Eve, you're aware of how much I enjoy being here. We'll stay."

"Don't make me stay here. If it's fighting you want, then we can do that. We can have the mother of all fights, but this… Adam, this is wrong on so many levels I can't even begin to tell you. I promise my not speaking to you will be over and done with. I'll stop trying to behave as though I'm still mortal. Just name what it is you want. Let's go home and talk. Let's leave this place."

People were beginning to turn toward them, as she'd known would happen. Finally Eric turned and looked at her, glaring at her, and shame washed through her. Adam. Damn him, she thought.

"Why would you want to make me hate you?" Eve asked, taking the conversation into Adam's mind.

"I want to give you what you need. You need to hate me and I need to give you the means. I am giving you back your free will."

"Adam, this is crazy. Think about what you're saying. You're saying you want to give me back my free will, yet you're making me a prisoner here in this sanctuary. If I had free will, you and I are both aware that I would leave. Please, Adam. I want to go home. Let's leave."

"We will stay here, Eve," Adam insisted, reaching for a bible, touching his hand to the bound leather and sighing in remembrance. He sang with the choir, with the parishioners and then he stood and sang along, his voice crisp, clear and hauntingly beautiful. Blood tears ran down his check. He ignored them and the mortals in the church. He was closed to everyone except the one sitting besides him. He was releasing Eve from any hold he had on her. If any residual effect of Yas's spell remained, this would take care of it. This oh so public display of who they were. He'd taken the last link she wanted to hold on to, the last thought that made her believe she could be killed by ordinary mortal means and yanked it from her.

The mortals were filled with fear. Not wanting to believe what they were seeing, they remained rooted in place. Father Keller was staring at him, crossing himself, his mouth hanging loose. In this place Adam had done many things but never had he done this. Never had he so blatantly announced his true nature.

When the service was over, Adam went to the fount at the back, blessed the water, and dipped his hand in the holy water, wondering as he always did why Father Keller, a non-catholic, kept such trappings. He crossed himself, looked toward Eve, then dipped his hand in again.

"It is done," he whispered as he glided toward Eve, gathering her in his arms and whisking her away. When they were home he deposited her inside her sacred circle and looked at her sadly. "It is done," he said yet again.

***

Dropping on the floor inside the circle, Eve's eyes brimmed over with tears and she sat there while Adam traced one tear along the path from her eye. And as it dripped from her chin he rubbed the liquid between his fingers.

"I'm glad you're back to using the potion."

Adam opened his arms and Eve hesitated for only a split second, then stood and allowed Adam to carry her to their bed. The things he'd done had not been necessary but then again maybe they were. She loved him and would always love him as long as either of them lived. Their love was sick, twisted and filled with pain for both of them. It needed to end. Adam Omega was an addiction of hers.

Perhaps if Eve had only her own love to contend with she could have possibly broken away. But there was a much stronger pull. It was the love of a woman who'd lived more than a thousand years ago, a woman who'd given her life to the man she loved. A woman who'd tried to protect Adam with her birthright. Eve knew that as well as she knew that neither Eyanna's love nor hers for Adam could ever be broken.

Her hands twisted in the deep purple silk sheets as heat poured over her. Adam's breath bathed her in heat, his amethyst gaze staying on her, the low growl in his throat claiming her. He touched a finger to the base of her spine causing lust to invade her nether regions and travel her spine.

"Adam," she moaned. Somewhere deep inside of her she felt the ending to them. Her hips arched toward him wanting to feel his heaviness inside her, wanting the rightness of the two of them. How could she possible think of their ending when Adam was looking at her with such, tenderness?

His gaze shimmered over her and lust blazed anew. Searing heat arced between them. The potency of their remembered couplings skittered through her. It was as though time had tattooed this man onto her very soul. She belonged to him and he belonged to her. He entered her, taking her to heights of pleasure that no mortal could ever reach. And when he took her blood she felt the slide into another realm and succumbed. She trembled beneath him.

Adam had that power over her whether he was whispering her name or touching her in what could be viewed as an innocent gesture.

Nothing was innocent about Eve's loving or her lust for Adam. Shivers of carnal delight played over her spine. Thinking was abandoned. When Adam was done he offered his throat freely to her and she took his blood seeing all that they were and had ever been. Somewhere they'd lost their way. Eve was the one that had to bring them peace. This…what they had, wasn't it. Her legs wrapped around Adam and she cried out as they came. "I love you, Adam." Then once again hot tears fast and furious fell from her eyes. There had to be a way out of this mess.

"And I love you, Eve. I always have and always will. I have wronged you in many ways my love. I do not have to bond mentally with you to know your thoughts. You want us to end. Nothing will ever end us, Eve, not even death. You should be aware of that now."

The look in Eve's brown eyes as she looked at him nearly did him in. There was so much pain in the depths. Wrapping his arms even more firmly around her he allowed the shudder of sorrow to invade his soul. He felt her pain to his very core. If his love for Eve could stop her future actions it would be an easy thing. He knew of her plans. But nothing had been easy for them since they'd first met. Somewhere deep inside of his wife was the steadfast need to save him. He'd long given up the dream of salvation. He'd accepted his life, he was comfortable with who he was. Hell, he'd had a lot of practice being Adam Omega, vampire, more than he'd had been Adam Omega, mortal.

Yet another shiver claimed him and he swallowed his despair. He would love Eve now as though it would be the last time. With that realization he began running his hands over her body imprinting her softness on the tips of his fingers. If only he were wrong about what he thought. But he seldom was.

"Open your eyes, Eve," Adam commanded softly. "I want you to look at me and remember this time."

"I will remember every caress, Adam. There's no need to worry about that."

Eve's answer stilled Adam's movements for a moment. He stared into her eyes. There was something amiss in her answer, something that pointed to the fact that he'd accurately read her thoughts from her eyes, her touching of his body, her loving him as though each caress would be the last. Adam wanted 'no last' with Eve. He wanted only the next and the one after that. If there were a way to stop what would happen he would. But there wasn't. There was no need for his repetitive thoughts. He belonged to this woman, his heart, mind, body and soul. There would be no preventing the breaking of his heart yet again, the decision had been made.

Unable to withstand the knowledge that shone from Eve's eyes Adam's gaze slid downward. The heat from Eve's body coupled with his. His strength was fortified with the flick of Eve's tongue along his carotid artery. He shivered in anticipation then paused to control his need. This loving of Eve would be done with intense slowness. He would savor every touch, every sigh, every moan. He'd do as she was doing; behave as though this would be the last time he would make love to her.

"Adam, why are you looking at me like that…like….stop, okay."

"I can't stop looking at you in the manner that I am, Eve. You are the heart of my heart, my reason for being. If I could right the wrongs I've done to you I would."

He kissed her roughly stopping his words and hers. "No more talking," he sent the words telepathically to Eve. "Let me love you as I will."

Eve shivered and Adam became aware that the mind melding had spilled many secrets. Biting her tongue gently he trembled as her blood hit the back of his throat. It was but a morsel, he thought as he moved to suckle her drawing blood as he bit into her. Every part of her had a distinct taste and he was of a mind to taste every part of her. There would be no satisfaction until that was done. Blood dripped from his fangs as he rose above her. Pressing his palms against her cheeks he studied her.

"You are mine, Eve. When heaven and earth cease to exist you will still be mine." The he took her as he'd wanted to do for the past thousand years he'd been without her. He became her, in her body and filling her mind. He roared repeatedly trying to vanquish the onslaught of pain.

"You are mine," Adam repeated again and rode Eve's body as though he was being chased. When she screamed his name in pleasure he slammed into her heat with vampiric need. As she dug her long painted nails into his flesh, he realized the same need controlled his wife. Releasing his seed, giving her everything that he had, Adam sighed in satisfaction not believing the intensity of their combined orgasm that appeared not to abate. When at last the shivers of Eve's body had subsided Adam pulled her to him as he rolled to his back. He wrapped his body so tightly around Eve that she couldn't move. He had no plans for her to move. He needed sleep and he needed her besides him.

***

Her limbs ached from the marathon lovemaking she'd indulged in with her husband. But the pain in her body was nothing compared to the ache in her heart. Eve loved Adam beyond all reason. There was nothing he could do to stop that love, she knew that now. She would and had killed for him. And he'd done the same for her. What would become of them should they remain together for eternity? What would become of the world and the mortals in it if their love went unchecked? Who would pay for crimes real or imagined against either of them? Could she take that chance?

A shiver of hatred traveled over her body but this time the hatred was not for Adam. This time it was for herself. She'd betrayed three others who'd loved her, Sullivan, Dr. Meah and Mark, and she'd gone as easily into Adam's arms as any willing innocent, someone who knew not of the things he'd done and the things he was capable of. That was not her. She'd known full well and still she loved him. No wonder he called her a whore. She was much too easy where he was concerned. She had to do something about it.

Eve turned to watch Adam as he slept. She touched her hand to his body, relishing the texture of his skin, the hard muscles that contained so much power. She played with his fingers, his magic fingers that brought her so much joy. Sadness encapsulated her and she wondered what other things she'd do left to live as long as Adam had. If she were allowed to die she would. But Adam would never allow that and the thought of the many sins she would undoubtedly commit overwhelmed her.

Eve was extremely aware that the only way she could find peace, to die herself, was if her husband were not alive to prevent her death. For a moment Eve thought of Evan. She had no doubt he'd come quickly and do the deed, kill her if she killed Adam. They'd each promised and she had no doubt that he'd carry out his promise. But she wouldn't give him a chance. She'd follow Adam into death by her own hands.

My poor husband, she thought as her fingers trailed over his flowing raven hair. *I have been to hell and back since I met you and you, my love, have lived in hell.*

Kisses, she had to kiss him, so she did, tasting the sheen of perspiration, moving down his chest, kissing him until she'd tasted every inch of his beautiful body and still he slept. Pain struck her. Adam slept because he trusted her finally, trusted in her love. He had no idea of the thoughts she was having as she lay beside him adoring his body, trying to grab every ounce of his essence and pour it into her soul. Someone should warn Adam of her thoughts. Someone should tell him that he'd just brought the devil into his bed and didn't know it. Adam Omega could not be allowed to get away with the things he'd done. He needed to pay for his crimes, all of them. *I can not be allowed to get away with my crimes. I must pay also.*

There was just one little thing. Would she be able to sleep in his arms and make love to him and plot his demise for a second time? Yes, she thought as she burrowed against him. And then she would be no more. Her gaze fell on the amber ring on Adam's finger and once more she had flashbacks, not enough to hang on to but enough to let her know that the ring was significant.

"Eyanna." Eve murmured the name in her head. "Help me please, our husband has gone astray. You tried to save him and so did I. I don't think it can be done. Help me to end this. Adam has to—"

"Did you call me, Eve?"

Sweat beaded instantly on her forehead and a sliver of fear entered her heart. Eve was so startled by Adam's arm sliding around her, that he'd heard her thoughts. She'd not thought to close her mind against him. But still, she should have felt the intrusion.

"Eve, what's wrong?"

"Nothing," she answered, knowing her voice held the tinge of deceit.

Adam sat up and looked down on her. "Ah, I see you're still trying to find a way to end my life." He sighed. "You weren't calling me, were you? You were calling Eyanna. You want her to help you. You think there is some secret thing that she knows. Eve, Eve…after all that we just shared, still you plot against me."

You would hesitate to kill your wife, Vampire. She will not hesitate to kill you. Yas's words pained him. Adam would have bet a year of living that would not be the case. But he could see now it would be a bet he would lose.

"I want to know Eyanna," Eve persisted.

"You do."

"No. I want you to take me back to the time you were married. I want to know her. I want to know her feelings, her thoughts, and her deeds."

"Admit it, Eve. What you want to know is what secret protection Eyanna imparted to me. You forget during the early days of our marriage I could not enter her mind at will. I didn't know her thoughts. So, if you're thinking I can show you her secrets, you're wrong."

"There has to be something, Adam, something that has made you invincible for so long. I am weak where you're concerned. You look at me and I tremble in lust. You whisper my name and I'm yours. You touch me and all else is forgotten. I've done great evils and you've done more. The two of us can allow this to end. I don't want to live forever and I know you will not allow me to die if you're here to stop it. There is but one way for me to go in peace."

Adam stared at his wife for a long moment in disbelief. "Are you thinking I can help you find a way to end my life?"

"Adam…"

A roar ripped through him and he clasped Eve's face between his hands. "Then do what you must, Eve. Do it and do it quickly." Adam opened his mind, ignoring the anguish that filled him. He held on to Eve. "Search, Eve, for whatever information I have that can help you to destroy me."

He saw the same things that Eve saw, the glimpses of Eyanna, her begging him to wear the amber ring that had been on his third finger left hand for over a thousand years. He saw her saying it was an amulet, that it would protect him. He felt a jerk and released Eve.

"So you think you have the answer," Adam snarled.

"It's the ring." Eve gasped in surprise, reaching out to touch the glowing amber but looking instead at Adam as he moved the ring away. So the great Grand Master Vampire thought he was invincible, did he? I should have known Eyanna did something to protect you. It's because of her, because of her love for you that you have survived." She started to laugh. "You're no different than the rest of us, Adam. All this time, all of these years, the one thing you found to be the most sacrilegious has been the one thing that has prevented you from being defeated. It was my birthright, Adam, it was witchcraft." She continued to laugh as Adam moved from her. The rage in him causing sparks of electricity to shoot out in all direction.

"You're wrong," Adam shouted. "There is no such amulet. I control my destiny, Eve, I always have."

"You can be killed, my love." Eve ignored his frowning face. "Think about it, Adam. You were turned when you took off the ring. If you don't believe me, take off the ring now. Give me a chance to test my theory."

"Would you still have me dead, Eve?"

She didn't answer and once again the words of the ancient witch came to him. Would he actually kill Eve? Was this all his doing? "Options," Adam whispered, looking at her and speaking softly.

"What?"

"I have options, Eve. Do you?"

"Take the damn ring off, Adam. I gave it to you. Now I want it back."

"Eyanna gave it to me."

"And I'm Eyanna. I demand you give back my gift."

Over a thousand years of pain, ongoing hopes, unanswered prayers flitted past him like so many grains of sand that he couldn't hold onto. This too seemed to be of those times. He would not blame himself for the outcome. He'd made a few mistakes, sure. So what? But his judgment of himself would not be rendered either by himself or any man. Adam held Eve's gaze. "Are you sure this is what you want?"

"It is," Eve answered. "You and I should be no more."

"Then let's do it right," Adam said, going for the blade he'd given Eve as a gift. "You, my love, are my Judas Iscariot."

"No, I am your wife and as sacrilegious as you'll think this is, I would be your savior if I could."

"*Luke 17:3 Take heed. If thy brother trespass against thee, rebuke him; and if he repent forgive him;* I have repented, Eve."

"Just give me the damn ring, Adam."

"Eve."

Adam sighed and released the pain. "Do you think the actions you seek to take are just and righteous, that you have a throne from which to judge me? It is yourself you seek to punish. You love me and you love the thought of my making love to you. You feel guilty about Sullivan and you wonder why and how you could have professed to love him yet come alive in my arms, think of nothing other than the fact that you're home with me, that you want to forever remain so, to have me burrowed to the hilt inside of you. You know that as well as I."

"Adam, stop it."

"Leviticus 19:15-17 "*Ye shall do no unrighteousness in judgment: Thou shalt not hate thy bother in thine heart: thou shalt in any wise rebuke they neighbor, and not suffer sin upon him.*' To wish my death is wrong, to kill me is a sin, Eve."

"You talk far too much, Adam, and quoting scriptures will not save either of us."

"The ring does not belong to you, Eve. It is mine and I will never give it back to you."

"You're afraid I'm right, aren't you? You truly are a coward. You put your faith in a ring. Why don't you do as you always say, believe in the power of your mind, Adam. Give me the ring and stand there while I ram the blade through your heart, your blade that you gave to me, Adam, and let's see if you can die. If you're not a coward you'll give me the ring and allow me to end this. You will not retaliate."

"You foolish woman. All this time and you know not yet who I am."

"I know very well who you are. You're Adam Omega, Grand Master Vampire. You are my love, my soul and my heart. And you are my damnation. I don't want to end this out of any hatred for you, Adam, but end it because I love you. You are my weakness and I fear what the two of us might do should we continue. We've already accumulated a mountain of sins."

"*He that rejecteth Me, and receiveth not My words, hath one that judgeth him: the word that I have spoken, the same shall judge him in the last day.*" John 12:48' I will be your judge, Eve, to that you can have no doubt."

The time for trying to make Eve listen to reason was past. She was too stubborn. Adam sighed as he remembered once again Yas's words. *You will be forced to kill her or she will kill you. She will not hesitate to kill you, vampire.*

Though his heart was heavy and Eve's words bore out Yas's warning, Adam did not believe it. Eve loved him. He was her Achilles heel. She would not be able to go through with it.

He studied her for a moment; saw the distress that covered her face and the pain that filled her voice. There was no anger. Anger he could understand. There had been anger earlier when he'd first returned and she'd attacked him. Now there was cold resolution, logic. As if she'd come to a long awaited decision. He stared at her. There was love. He took in a breath and held if for a moment before exhaling it.

And what if I'm wrong? His heart was heavy. Adam stared hard at Eve, wanting to shake her until her teeth rattled. The fool. Of course he would not allow her to die. Was she totally insane? Then again, if she were, so was he. He'd given her back her free will, her choices and this was what she'd chosen to do, end his life and hers. He'd read her mind, knew her thoughts. As he'd told her he had another avenue.

Sleight of hand.

He had options.

Eve did not.

"Adam, give me the ring." Eve was now pleading with him. "I've had enough of this life. Give me the ring. If you truly love me you will give this to me, to us."

The clink of metal hitting the stone fireplace in their bedroom, the anger in Adam's eyes told Eve what she wanted to know. Her husband was defenseless without Eyanna's protection. He could die. Adam held out his gift to her. She looked down at the blade for a moment, then back at him.

"What I do I do for us. I love you, Adam, and always will, even through death." He didn't answer, just stared at her. She reached out her hand to touch him, caressing his face, moving her hand down his chest toward his groin. A shudder passed through him and she kissed his lips softly and moved away, backing up until she was on the other side of the room. Eve held Adam's gaze for a long moment before closing her eyes and running with her vampiric speed and strength. She ran straight toward him, opening up her eyes finally for one last look

In true Adam Omega fashion Eve noted, Adam didn't move. He didn't even flinch. She heard the swoosh as the blade pierced his body, saw the blood on the blade and watched as the blood dripped to the floor. She saw the look in Adam's eyes change from anger to disbelief and finally to sadness. She stood motionless as he fell to the ground. He made a movement with his lips so Eve kneeled beside him to hear his words.

"So you have judged me and found me guilty. I have tried to warn you, Eve, judge not lest ye be judged. And now it has happed. I have judged you and found you likewise guilty."

Caressing Adam's face, Eve placed kisses on his lips, his eyelid, at the base of his throat. "But the difference is, Adam, you are no longer in a position to carry out my execution. You can never do anything again to me that I don't want. You can no longer prevent me from ending this existence."

"Never say never, Eve. After all, I am Adam Omega." He smiled, then coughed up blood. "Grand Master Vampire," he finished.

Eve stared at him, her gaze locked with his. She felt sadness as the beautiful purple of his eyes mesmerized her then became clouded and his eyes closed.

"You were Adam Omega, Grand Master Vampire, my love. You are no more. And I will no more be Eve Omega, your queen, mistress of the vampire world." Sorrow filled the marrow of her spirit. Then she heard a voice.

"Now comes the judgment."

Author's Information:

F. D. Davis also known as Dyanne Davis is an award winning author. F. D. Davis lives in a Chicago suburb with her husband Bill, and their son Bill Jr. An avid reader her love of the written word turned into a desire to write. She retired from nursing a decade ago to pursue her lifelong dream.

F.D. Davis has been a presenter of numerous workshops. She has a local cable show in her hometown to give writing tips to aspiring writers.

When not writing you can find F.D. with a book in her hands, her greatest passion next to spending time with her husband Bill and son Bill Jr. Whenever possible she loves getting together with friends and family

A member of Romance writers of American she served in many capacities for her local chapter, Windy City, including two terms as president.

F.D. loves to hear from her readers. You can reach her at FDDavis9@aol.com. You can reach Adam at adamomegavampire@aol.com
You can write to both at,
 P.O. Box 1218 Bolingbrook IL. 60440

Acknowledgements:

As always I give thanks to the creator. I thank you for giving me so many signs during this venture that what I was attempting was the right decision for me.

To Parker Publishing, thank you for your understanding of the things I needed to do, for myself, for being the one to bring Adam Omega to the readers for me with IN The Beginning and IN BLOOD WE TRUST.

To Sidney Rickman, what can I say about you that I haven't said a dozen times already? You're the best. I would not have even attempted to do this had you not been the editor.

To A.M Wells, Congratulations on your first publication. I wish you much success. Thanks for 'THE SMOKING HOT' cover.

Once again to all the readers who wrote to tell me how much you loved the series, you kept me going during this process to bring this new episode to you. I hope you enjoy it. Write me and let me know what you think. davisdyanne@aol.com or snail mail. P.O. Box 1218 Bolingbrook IL. 60440.

And bringing up the rear, the most important two people in my world. Bill, my love, my hero, my romance story comes to life, you are loved by me and you still have my heart. It's hard to believe that in a few months we will have been married forty years. Wow!! And you still do it for me. To our son Bill Jr. You continue to make me proud. As always you have my love.

Dear Readers,
Mr. Omega has requested that I extend an invitation to you for the chance
to have your letter included in the next volume of his misadventures. You
can send your letters to, adamomegavampire@aol.com. Below is the
winning fan letter. Please check out Mr. Omega's advice column.
http://adamomegavampire.blogspot.com/

Dear Adam,
　　When first you appeared floating above me in the wee hours of
darkness while I slumbered in my bed, I thought you'd come at last to
claim me as one of your own, the walking undead. Though, my mind
screamed that I should fear you, my body quivered with anticipation of
the possibility of just being so near you.
　　That first Sunday morning when you boldly walked into His house
and stood in front of His alter before the congregation, confounding us
all with your knowledge of His Word. Though the elders could clearly
see you, your benevolent offerings closed their eyes and allowed you in
time and time again. What else did you expect, Adam, already you knew
their human nature when tried would fail the test.
　　Then one by one you easily seduced my spiritual sisters. Leading
each astray from the light, undercover of night. Once you'd taken your
fill, they were returned to the flock, their light now shown to be dimmer,
and minds erased of all memory of their blissful fall from grace.
　　It would be inevitable that it be my head you next decide to turn.
And you did prey upon me with your piercing hypnotic amethyst gaze.
Suspicious that I was not the first, nor by far the last, still I fell like all
the rest. Of my own free will I went into your embrace. I allowed myself
to become yet another vessel from which you drank, giving you the
sustenance that sustains your very existence.
　　Real or imagined, Adam, with you I have been reborn. My life was a
dull lonely existence of conformity to the rules of human kind. Tonight I
wait for you to come and take me to paradise one last time. Before you
leave I have but one request that when my life is at its end, you will
come to me once again and give back that which now you must take. For
if I am to be judged and condemned then let me enter the eternal furnace
with a smile on my lips.

Respectfully yours,
A. M. Wells

www.ingramcontent.com/pod-product-compliance
Lightning Source LLC
Chambersburg PA
CBHW020748250626
47155CB00003B/975